LAST STAND

THE BLACK MAGE BOOK 4

D0166644

RACHEL E. CARTER

Last Stand (The Black Mage Book 4)

Copyright © 2016 Rachel E. Carter

ISBN: 1-946155-03-9

ISBN-13: 978-1-946155-03-0

Publisher's Note: This is a work of fiction. Names, characters, places, and incidents are a product of the author's imagination. Locales and public names are sometimes used for atmospheric purposes. Any resemblance to actual people, living or dead, or to businesses, companies, events, institutions, or locales is completely coincidental.

Cover Design by Deranged Doctor Designs
Edited by Hot Tree Editing

To Craig,

Because you're so much more than a memory.

You were the goodness inside that most of us push aside as we grow older, the kind of light we don't deserve, the kind of hero we only read about in books. You saw beauty and joy in everything, and you were first to believe in the best of us.

The world never deserved you, but you deserved the world.

You once told me you couldn't bear the idea of cremation because you needed a place to cherish the memories of those you loved, that you didn't want their memories to fade over time. Your parents built you a beautiful headstone, and this book is my plaque for you. This dedication is my way to make your memory eternal, a way to tell the world exactly what kind of person they lost.

I've been waiting nine years to write your name. Craig LeAron Cagley Short. This book is for you, because if anyone ever deserved a happily ever after, it was you.

May the world someday be the kind of place that deserves you.

RIP Craig LeAron Cagley Short (1987-2007)

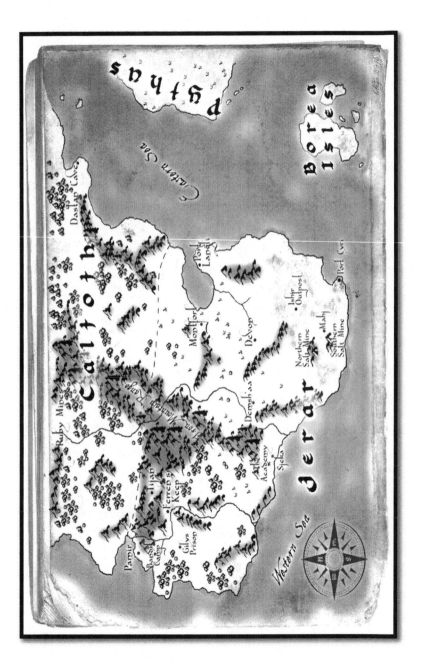

ONE

IT WAS SUPPOSED to be the best day of my life.

The noise was deafening. Cheers, clapping and thunderous applause, even hysterical weeping came from Jerar's most privileged families as they shared in a moment that they believed would save them all from the Caltothians' tyrannous plague.

If only they knew it was all a lie.

I forced my lips into a shaky smile, my heart fluttering like a thousand wings against my throat.

The prince's eyes met mine across the small podium we were standing on. For a moment, that was all I needed to hold on, and I was able to exhale. The corner of his eyes crinkled as he took in the expression on my face. I'm sure he imagined it was due to the hematite crown the priest had just placed upon my head.

Darren had no reason to question my fear.

The prince reached out to pull me forward by the nook of my arm, slowly, until there was no space left to cross. His eyes held mine as his other hand took my trembling chin and tilted it up.

My skin burned under the pads of his callused fingers. I

didn't have a choice. I caught fire every time.

His breath was warm as he leaned in so that his lips brushed my ear. "And now to kiss my beautiful bride."

Darren's mouth found mine, tasting of hot cinnamon and cloves, and for a moment... for a moment, I forgot. And the girl let herself melt into her prince's embrace; she kissed him back, letting that elation rise up in her chest, her cheeks flushing crimson as he dipped her low and proceeded to kiss her so thoroughly, a second applause rang out from the crowd.

And she was happy. In this beautiful, perfect moment, she was soaring.

The girl had her happily ever after. She had the boy she loved, and it was all she would ever need.

Hundreds of petals rained down from above.

"Long live the Crown!"

And the moment their voices rang out, that girl disappeared. Elation was met with shame. Guilt. Self-hate and flagellation. Shards of glass twisted in my gut, and I jerked back from the kiss, nearly stumbling down the steps in shame.

I couldn't pretend. Not when I knew our future was a tangle of lies, and that he would never look at me the same when he discovered the truth.

"Careful, dear sister..." Icy fingers wrapped around my wrist. They were all that kept me from plummeting into the crowd below.

It took everything I had not to react, to remain silent and still when every part of me was writhing in a storm cloud of red. It was *him*.

The king of Jerar. The young boy whose tragedy had made him the worst man of all.

My hands trembled and the white-hot rage boiled, threatening to sputter out. In another second, I wouldn't be able to stop—

"Ryiah?" Darren's voice caught me just in time.

The king of Jerar let out a laugh as he handed me back. I was still shaking, my pulse thundering in my ears. "A bit of shock. She just became a princess of Jerar, brother. What else would you expect?"

I barely felt Darren's hand slip around my waist as he helped me down the final step. "I know it's a bit much," he whispered. His words called me back, twisting and weaving their way across the chains that had taken hold of my lungs. "I'm sorry."

I wanted to tell him I was too, but my tongue was too heavy to lift.

All I could see was my little brother's lifeless body sprawled out against the marble tile and the look on Alex's face when I told him Derrick was dead.

The priest's loud declaration brought me back to the present: "And now to present the Crown Prince and Princess of Jerar. Together, for the first time, as husband and wife."

I made myself breathe. And swallow. And then I made myself move, one foot, then the other, as the prince and I traversed the great hall.

It was supposed to be a beautiful fairy tale.

But there would be no happily ever after.

* * *

As the Crown's carriage paraded down the streets of

Devon, I did my best to mirror Darren and Blayne's gestures with my own. Courtier smiles and nods to all. It was an acknowledgment and a promise. I saw it in the hundreds of eager faces shoved into every alley and shop, waving hands and throwing seeds and chanting blessings at every corner we passed. Their hope was contagious. Even the ones hiding behind their dirty windowpanes, I could see it shining there too, past tight lines of worry and fear. It was a great beacon driving them to look and stare.

They believed the Crown would save them all.

I couldn't consider them fools. I had shared the same dream just hours before.

And now your life will never be the same.

Darren caught my frown and squeezed my hand, mistaking the reason for my discontent. "I'm sure your parents would be here if they could."

I glanced down to where his fingers interlocked with mine and swallowed. I needed to say something. The longer I remained silent, the more his worry would grow.

I wet my lips and cleared my throat. "It would have been too painful." It didn't matter that it was their only daughter's wedding—and to a crown prince of Jerar. After Derrick's death, they refused to set foot in the capital ever again—not after their youngest had been strung up from the palace rafters, branded a traitor to the world.

My parents might not have blamed me with their words, but I'd seen it in their eyes. Their child was gone, and I should've found a way to save him.

They weren't wrong.

But how was I to know? Not even Derrick had guessed

how far the Crown's treachery had gone.

I'd been so busy defending the boy I loved that I'd forgotten to look to his brother. And why would I? Blayne had played his part well, so well that after years of cruelty, he had still managed to convince me there was something of the boy he used to be. I had believed him to be somewhat good. A man whose horrible past had hardened his edges, but still left him capable of kindness. Benevolence. Regret. Better than his tyrant of a father.

That had been my biggest mistake of all. The two children might have been raised in darkness, but only one was capable of light.

As I adjusted my seat, the yellow silk ruffles of my dress shifted, and I prayed Darren didn't notice the small splotches of red staining their base—my blood from just an hour before.

"We can visit them on our way, if you'd like."

I swallowed, my mouth as dry as sand. "That would be nice." As soon as the weeklong celebrations were over, the two of us would be tasked with hunting the rebels. I wasn't surprised by Darren's decision to go north; he'd been discussing it for weeks.

Marius, the former Black Mage, had already scoured the south during the last ten years of his reign. It had made sense at the time. All the attacks and sabotage had taken place in Jerar's southernmost towns—primarily the Red Desert, Port Cyri, and the salt mines in Mahj, wherever a shipment was due. Why wouldn't the rebels have been stationed nearby?

Unfortunately, the new Black Mage had other theories as to why the rebels had never been found—theories that would eventually lead to Ferren's Keep and my brother and friends.

To the rebels.

Panic squeezed my lungs as I took a shaky breath.

It was up to me to lead Darren astray. I knew full well this act would cost me my prince in the end.

It was the only way. I had seen the bond between brothers. Even now, the two beautiful boys cracked jokes during our procession across the city, neither quite aware that the girl beside them was bleeding out from the inside, screaming for help.

Gods, I had lived out my own choice just two months before. Given the choice between Derrick and what was right... I had chosen my brother, not that it had mattered in the end. I had acted too late, and that was still before I had realized the nefarious ploy of the king, before I had realized Derrick had been telling the truth all along.

Back then I had believed my little brother to be a traitor to the Crown. I had known full well that, should he escape with the information he had stolen, hundreds of lives would be the debt to pay, possibly—*definitely*—more. And yet I had been willing to risk them in the end, anything to save my brother from a horrible fate at the gallows, and I knew Darren would do the same.

It wouldn't be my husband's fault if he made the same mistake for Blayne. Darren's father had groomed the second-born son as his brother's protector through years of abuse, and when one spent so many years protecting someone they deemed a victim, it became impossible to see them any other way. Even after everything Blayne had done—assaulting my best friend and tormenting me all throughout the apprenticeship when he thought I was just some pitiful lowborn that had caught his brother's eye—I had still pitied the heir.

Besides, there were some choices one should never have to make, and I never wanted to give Darren that choice. I didn't want to let him choose wrong. I didn't care how selfish that made me. If he went to his brother first, if he gave Blayne a chance to explain, the evil king would have the whole world up in flames before Darren had a chance to recoup his mistake. Two of the country's most powerful mages were nothing against a king's army. Everything would burn and shatter, and every one of the rebels would be put to death at the crack of dawn.

Not me, of course. Blayne was too shrewd, too calculating. He disliked me from the start, and yet he had made me a part of his plans. As sick and twisted as the king was, he cared for his brother and wanted his support. Until Blayne could turn Darren against me, the king would have me rotting in a cell. And once he'd succeeded, *then* he'd take my life.

And then the king would go to war—a pointless, costly war that his father had been staging for countless years, all part of an elaborate scheme to portray Jerar as the victim and Caltoth as the aggressor. The other two countries in our nation's Great Compromise would break with King Horrace, and Jerar would become the country with the biggest army, and the wealthiest.

No, I couldn't tell Darren, not until I had undisputable proof and the other countries' support. Because right now, all I had was the ranting of a madwoman.

Darren had never seen the little girl in the stands of the Candidacy. He wouldn't be able to piece together her face with the noblewoman and her daughter we'd stolen away in a mission to Caltoth so many years before. The blackmail of Lord Tyrus and the murders during the Victors' Ceremony were all parts of the same ploy to frame King Horrace and win the support of two skeptical nations.

Darren would only see a lowborn who had never liked his family, a girl who had lost her youngest brother and was desperate to clear his name.

And even if he saw past all of that, I couldn't risk the chance he'd choose wrong.

I had chosen wrong just two months before. What was to stop Darren from doing the same? There were too many lives at risk. This was bigger than the both of us. This was the world.

And if he never forgave me for my breach of trust… well, that was my cross to bear.

An invisible hand squeezed my chest. I knew I was making the right choice, but it felt *wrong*. Two hours into our new marriage and already I was plotting to betray my husband.

"The two of you should make an effort to question the villagers while you are in Demsh'aa." Blayne leaned back in his seat with a lazy smirk. He had been listening in on our conversation.

I flinched as the king's gaze caught on mine.

"My apologies, Ryiah, but I doubt you sought to question them during your last visit… you had more pressing affairs at the time."

Like breaking my family's heart? Telling them their youngest was dead? Watching Alex scream that he's never coming back? My best friend following after my brother, knowing both could die for the rebels' cause? Nails dug into my palms, and it was with the greatest effort that I unclenched my fists.

A second too late, I realized I had still been holding onto Darren's hand. The prince's startled gaze fell to mine, but when it did, it was sad.

His thumb pressed against my palm and he shot his brother a scowl.

"That's enough, Blayne."

"Your wife isn't a fool. Her brother was a traitor and put our whole kingdom at risk. Surely she doesn't fault me for considering her village a possible base for rebel activity. Do you, Ryiah? After all, we've never investigated the towns of the north."

Play the part. That's the only way you can honor Derrick's sacrifice now. Show your hand, and this plan will be over before it has begun. "No." I made myself meet the king's gaze head on. I made myself breathe. "Of course not."

Blayne smirked. "See? Even she understands."

"It doesn't mean we have to talk about it." Darren's voice was low and imploring. "Please, not tonight, brother."

The young king's eyes slid from Darren to me, and he heaved an impatient sigh. "One day you must tell me what makes this one so much more special than the rest."

You'll know the moment my blade is at your throat. I made myself scoff outwardly; Blayne would expect as much. I wasn't known to back down from a challenge. Holding on to silence would only garner suspicion. "Don't worry, by the end of the year, I'm sure you'll find out."

"Ah," the king played along, enjoying our little game, "preparing something big?"

At least I didn't have to lie. "Saving a kingdom from corruption."

"After the rebels?" Blayne's brow shot up. "And here I thought you would want to take on the villainous king himself."

My heart stopped beating and my body drew cold, the color draining from my face.

"King Horrace is mine." Darren's voice was hard as he cut in. "When the time comes—after everything he has destroyed—he is *mine*."

The air whooshed out from my lungs. *Of course.* The Caltothian king. The man Blayne and his father had convincingly portrayed as the enemy.

For a moment, I had thought Blayne knew.

"Not if I get to him first." I blurted the challenge as fast as I could. *Good, Ryiah, keep pretending. Keep smiling.*

"Horrace should be afraid." The young king brushed himself off, standing as the carriage came to a halt. We'd finished our procession through Devon, and it was time for the ceremonial feast in the palace. "I've got the two most bloodthirsty mages in the realm." It was impossible to miss his pride. "The war will be over before it's begun."

It will. But not for the reasons you think.

I followed the king with my eyes. With his back turned, he was saying something to a guard as he descended the steps. For the barest second, I entertained the notion of what it would be like to end this here and now, to strike down the king of Jerar in cold blood and let the pieces fall where they may.

It wasn't my responsibility to make sure everything worked out in the end. Blayne was a villain. For all the innocent lives he and his father had stolen, did it really matter whether he lived or died? If I got rid of him, I would be doing the world a favor, and someone else could figure out how to put it back together.

But something stopped me. *Guilt.* And it wasn't necessarily tied to the boy whose heart I would break.

I had always wanted to be a hero. It was what had driven me to the life of a warrior in the first place. I had chosen Combat because it was the most notorious faction of all. Again and again, I'd taken the hard road because it was the most celebrated.

After last year and my terrible case of jealousy leading up to the Candidacy, I'd been able to recognize that drive for what it really was: ambition. Sure, I'd wanted to save people, but I'd also dreamed of the status that came with it— something to distance myself from the others, something to make a name for myself... A glorious Ryiah on the battlefield, slaying villains and receiving recognition from the king and his people for a job well done.

Combat mages were ambitious and vain, after all, and if they weren't, they never reached far. So silly girl that I was, I had chosen to chase after a lifetime of prestige. And over the years, my eyes had opened to the realities of that choice.

All of those soldiers in the forest of Caltoth.... That wasn't Blayne's doing. That was mine.

My hand gripped the side of the carriage rail, and all at once, my body was too hot and too cold. I felt faint and my vision was dancing in front of my eyes.

That was me.

It didn't matter that I had been under Mage Mira's orders during the mission. I had killed men fighting for the right cause, all because I had believed in a lie. Those deaths were on me. It was my magic that had ended the men's lives.

And how many others would suffer under the same choice? All because they had wanted to be a soldier, a knight, or a mage of Jerar?

I couldn't just walk away. I had blood on my hands. I owed this to them—to all of the others who didn't know what their villainous king was capable of—to stop this before they were tainted as well.

During my ascension, I had made a pledge to Jerar to defend those in need.

I needed to be a real hero, not just the easy one.

Killing Blayne wasn't enough; I needed to stop the war. There was no guarantee Pythus would pull out if Blayne was dead, no guarantee the truth would come to light without proof. I needed to stop others from making the wrong choice, because it was the only way to right my own wrongs.

The gods had to be laughing up above: *You want to redeem yourself? To be a true hero, not just the one you dreamed up? Here's your chance, but there's a catch: to do so, you'll have to betray the one you love and spare the brother that killed your own.*

Destiny was cruel, and it was breaking me, piece by piece.

"Ryiah?"

Startled from the churning sickness in my gut, I saw Darren waiting by the door. His gaze was soft, free of arrogance or challenge, the countenance of someone happy and in love.

How I wished that could be me.

"Are you ready, love?"

I followed the prince outside the carriage and through the palace gates.

I had wanted to be the hero.

I just hadn't known the price.

* * *

The ceremonial feast was spent toasting our marriage and the prosperity of our nation. I sat at the head table beside my new husband and his brother, who sat at the end in his father's towering chair. A row of advisors were to our left. I spent those three hours forcing myself to swallow small bites of venison, my appetite long forgotten.

Darren's gaze kept falling on me as the evening wore on. His hand slid underneath the table to grip my knee, and he leaned in close. "Please eat, Ryiah. I don't like seeing you like this."

I forced myself to spear a bit of cabbage and chew, painfully aware of his concern. I needed to appear well. "I'm fine."

The prince's face grew grim. "Ryiah, you aren't—"

A loud voice echoed across the chatter, cutting off the rest of Darren's reply.

"Six weeks!" It was one of the Crown's advisors, a hefty man with expensive, but threadbare, Borean silks. He had grown more boisterous with each helping of ale. "Then forty

Pythian warships set sail for Jerar. Would that I were a knight, so I could gut those Caltothian traitors myself."

Six weeks, I swallowed, the previous moment's brevity forgotten.

Darren seemed to be thinking the same thing. "How long do you think it will take them to reach our shore?"

The man preened under the crown prince's stare, some of the words slurring as he spoke. "A month, Your Highness. Not a day before."

Another advisor, a severe woman with a sharp jaw and jutting lips, set down her glass with an exaggerated scoff. "Two weeks, Cletus. You of all people should know. You are in charge of overseeing the Crown's trade, are you not?" Her lips curved into a sneer. "Or have you been spending all of your time at dice?"

The man's face turned mottled and red in embarrassment. He gasped, stuttering, "How d-dare—"

"Is that true, Cletus?" The question came from my end of the table, and it was deceptively calm. The man had captured the attention of his king, and not in a good way.

Cletus sank in his seat, the legs of his chair scraping against the marble tile. "Perhaps, sire. I don't have my charts here to advise me—"

"And yet I pay you well enough to have them memorized." The young king's voice had gone flat. Gone was the celebration, and in its place was disgust. "Hestia is right. I have no use for wastrels in my court. Guards, see that this man is escorted off the premises immediately."

"Blayne." Darren's murmur was only low enough for me to hear. "Is that really necessary? The man has had a lot to drink. You could question him when he is sober."

The king's angry gaze slid to his brother, and then he turned back to the advisor, his words growing cold. "We are to go to war in two months' time. Your loose calculations could cost my men's lives. Show your face in my court again and I will not be so kind."

"Yes, sire." The man didn't hesitate. He was out of his chair and staggering out of the hall in an instant, with labored breaths and ruddy cheeks as he shoved past servants, musicians, and wandering courtiers unaware of his transgression.

"I'm sorry, brother," Blayne said, once the volume of the room had returned once more, "but that needed to be done for the good of Jerar."

Darren didn't dispute his claim.

And that is why I never suspected a thing. Who could fault a king for actions that would save his subject's lives? If he were cruel, it was because the alternative would reap a greater loss.

Only the truth could bring his deception to light—The fact that his actions weren't necessary. The Caltothians were a peaceful people, and it was only by King Lucius's greed and scheming that the rest of the kingdom and neighboring countries believed any different.

I shoved my plate away.

If I hadn't had the stomach for the evening's meal, hearing the other advisors now praise their new king's dedication to Jerar was enough to make me sick. It wasn't their fault. They didn't know... or maybe they did? I had to wonder if Lucius had shared his plan with anyone besides his eldest? If Blayne had shared it with anyone besides the head mage of his regiment, Mira? The latter's knowledge was probable, given her quick promotion following King Lucius's murder—but were there others?

And then a new thought occurred to me: of all the king's advisors, how many knew?

The room started to spin and I slumped back against the frame of my chair. *What if they all knew?*

"Ryiah?"

I had managed a ceremony, a two-hour procession through the streets of Devon, and a three-hour feast. I had withstood more than any person should ever tolerate in a known murderer's presence. I needed to get away, if only for a couple of minutes.

I needed space away from everyone and everything. It was all becoming too much.

I turned to Darren and wove my fingers in with his. "I'm feeling a bit overwhelmed." It wasn't a lie, at least. "Do you think your brother would mind if I slipped away?"

The prince's gaze never wavered from my face. "I'll make your excuses. If Blayne takes issue with my new wife's absence, he can answer to me."

There was a tightening in my throat, and I made myself look away before I fell to my knees and spilled all my secrets out of shame. I didn't deserve Darren in moments like this. A mumbled "thank you" was all I managed before I quietly left the table, the king busy in conversation with a visiting lord.

I wandered the halls, not bothering to admire the palace decor with its vibrant tapestries and gold-plated pillars. I'd seen enough of it in the months after the Candidacy. Everywhere I looked, sconces lit the way. I only wanted shadows. Even my dress was one bright flare of incriminating light with its cream yellow skirts and a gold and orange beaded bodice. The dress was the most beautiful thing I'd ever worn—or seen, for that matter—but the color was a constant reminder of just hours before and the revelation that came with it.

Ten minutes later, I found myself at the entrance of my chamber, which had been transformed over the course of an evening into a sitting room by the servants.

Gone were my oaken trunks and the beautiful cherry wood bed against the wall. Now there was a private table and cushioned benches to share with my husband. The only thing that had remained the same was the small adjoining room with its tub and chamber pot.

I wasn't sure how long I stood there, staring. It was just one more thing that would never be the same.

With my barest casting, the flickering candlelight ceased, and I was ensconced in darkness. I reached around, not bothering to turn, and shut the door behind. My knuckles remained locked on the handle, holding it in place as my chest rose and fell, the mask crumbling away.

I held onto that door as time passed. Ten minutes, an hour? I lost count in the tears that followed. I was choking on air, and it made no difference. There was no such thing as time. A couple minutes here and there wouldn't make up for everything I knew. They wouldn't make up for the weight of the world or the crimes I intended to commit for the good of the many, but at the expense of a few.

I didn't know how I was going to find the proof my brother had missed. I didn't know if I could convince the rebels I had joined their cause when I was a part of the Crown. Even my twin didn't trust me. And Pythus and the Borea Isles? How was I ever going to convince them to go against the New Alliance, the treaty Blayne had managed to secure following his father's death and my marriage to his brother? How was a young woman supposed to convince a king and an emperor of two neighboring countries to betray a pact they had struck up with her country? Even if I came bearing proof, would they listen?

I should have drunk the wine, I realized. I'd never had a taste for it, but at least it would have numbed all these feelings. All this fear. It would have been something to push it all away, even for a little while. I had thought I would feel better in the freeing cover of darkness, but in some ways, the release only made it worse.

Perhaps the sensation would get better with time. But I didn't have time. Hours were slipping by, and if what the advisors were saying was true, then we had six weeks until the Caltothians set their ships for sail and eight before their barges arrived on our shore. Our armies would march on Caltoth not long after.

The old me wanted to revert to the broken shade after Derrick's death, that girl who had been a wandering ghost, resigning herself to despair and going about her days in a haze.

It was so much easier to be broken than strong.

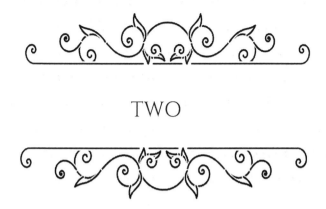

TWO

HE FOUND ME later that night, huddled against the wall of my old chamber, clutching my knees.

His magic sent off light to the sconces, and the next thing I knew, he was kneeling in front of me, his mouth opening and closing in a silent succession of words. His hands pressed into my shoulders, shaking me, but when I tried to explain, nothing would come out.

I must have been crying, because his thumb brushed my cheek, and when he pulled it away, there was a look of confusion.

When I saw the tears, I realized that today, already, I had managed to fail. Darren was never supposed to see me cry.

"I wasn't supposed to see you cry?" The words were spoken inches from my face, and I realized he was repeating what I must have said aloud.

"I'm sorry," I whispered.

"Ryiah, why are you apologizing?"

"Because…" My voice caught. It would be so easy to tell him the truth.

"Because you are still in mourning?" Darren swallowed,

the lump in his throat rising. "Ryiah, Derrick might have been a traitor, but he was also your brother. Gods, if it had been Blayne…"

He was trying to help, but he had only made it worse. I tried my best to wipe my eyes, but the prince caught my hand in his.

"Please," he whispered, "don't hide from me, not like this. I know with today, not having your family here and what happened to Derrick… Ryiah, I don't want you to go through this alone."

He was so good, and his only fault was loving his brother—a crime I had committed just the same.

I made myself nod as the prince helped me to my feet.

"My brother wants us to return to the ball." Darren's garnet eyes met my own as we entered the hall. "But I think he can handle a night of formalities without the crown prince and princess, just this once."

A warm wave of relief crashed over me until I saw the prince's hand still along the handle of the adjacent chamber.

A couple months before and this moment would have been everything. It would have been the two of us and every tangled feeling that had been brewing between us for years.

But now? Now, as he unlocked the door and tugged me inside, the warmth of his fingers heating my own, the only thing I could think was that this was one more betrayal I could never return from. One beautiful memory Darren would grow to hate, and as much as the girl wanted the boy, I didn't want this.

I hated myself for what I was about to do, but I would never be able to face myself if I didn't.

"Darren, I..." I froze in my tracks. "I can't do this. I know what the c-court expects..." My voice was hoarse and my eyes locked on the floor. Shame was crippling me out from the inside. "B-but I can't."

"Tonight I want to hold my wife in my arms." The prince's voice was quiet. "Nothing more."

My heart was breaking. I wanted to say something, anything to explain. "I'm—"

"If you say you are sorry one more time, you will break my heart, love." Darren took my hand and pulled me in front of the mirror—the same one from my chambers earlier before the ceremony, a beautiful thing gilded with pearls. The lighting of our chamber dimmed from his casting as he stood gripping my waist from behind. Garnet shown against the shadows reflected in the glass. It was smoldering. "You have me here, a man and a prince. You have the Black Mage at your feet."

My stomach hollowed at his words.

He lifted one of my hands and pressed his lips against my palm, watching me in the mirror. "You have me as your husband."

Darren's hands rose to the stays containing my dress. Slowly, the laces trailed to the floor. The bodice came next. And as my pulse hammered against my throat, yellow silk glided down my skin to reveal a thin chemise and little else.

I felt his lips press against the hollow of my throat, and his fingers undid the fastenings in my hair. "The first night I touch you," he said, "it will be because you are so captivated you can want for nothing else."

My breath hitched, warmth pooling low in my belly.

"You have me." Darren's eyes held mine against the backdrop of darkness and light. "You always will."

His fingers released my hair so that locks of scarlet framed my face, illuminating the girl with pale gray-blue eyes and white cotton clinging to her frame. I looked soft, lonely, and innocent with the barest stain of pink against my cheeks.

It was all a lie. Wetness formed at the corners of my eyes.

"Until then, I wait." The prince stepped around me, blocking the mirror to stare down into my face. What I saw took my breath away. I let him lead me forward and onto the canopied bed, scattering petals. He enveloped me in his arms, and I rested my head against his shoulder.

It felt so good—the rising and falling of his chest, the way the scent of clove and pine lingered against his skin. I could still smell warm cinnamon on his breath.

I knew it was wrong to enjoy being so close to the boy whose heart I would break. But I was selfish. He was beautiful, and I was weak.

I had already denied myself so much, and the other part of me knew I couldn't pull away—not without arousing suspicion.

That part of me delighted in any part of Darren she could get.

…All of me did.

And so for that first night as husband and wife, the prince held me close. I gripped him back, telling myself this wasn't wrong—it was necessary.

The girl clung to the boy so she could chase away her dark. He was light, and she was fading. She was drowning, and she just couldn't stop.

She was about to enter a world of shadows, and as she drifted off to sleep, she listened to the beating of his heart.

Somehow, she told herself, she would find a way to make all of this right.

* * *

The next day, I was expected to join the Crown in a daylong set of festivities. But when I awoke, Darren had already convinced his brother to grant me yet another reprieve. I knew the king's benevolence wouldn't last. I couldn't avoid the court forever, so I pushed all self-hate aside and locked myself in my previous chambers, writing out lists only to burn them in the room's hearth minutes later.

Again and again, I continued to write out possible plans. Plans to search and raid the palace from every square tile of marble to the lookout tower at its highest turret—any place my brother might have missed. Plans to hide my talks with the rebels when I reached Ferren's Keep with the Black Mage in charge of its investigation, and plans to secretly correspond with the kingdom of Pythus with no one the wiser.

In truth, I wanted to throw all of this planning to the wind. Plans took up precious minutes, hours that I didn't have. But if I didn't plan, I was afraid I would lose the momentum I had and find myself spiraling into a depression like the day before, or worse, be caught like my brother and tossed in the dungeons before I had a chance to explain.

I needed reason and caution—two sentiments that were hard to embrace when my emotions were spiraling all around me, begging for action. Decision. Change.

I needed to be strong. With so much weight on my shoulders, I couldn't afford a mistake, especially not now when I had just become a member of the Crown.

Now a princess of Jerar, I had access to things that even a mage at the top of my class didn't have. First-rank Combat employed by the King's Regiment, second only to Darren, didn't grant me a part in the Crown meetings, but becoming a princess did. Only members of the Crown, the Crown's Army commander, and the Three Colored Robes, the reigning Council of Magic, had access to those.

The important thing was, up until now, I had never been present in those dealings, and since Darren was in charge of the Combat mages' movements in the battle to come, I;d been missing out on a great deal. Those meetings were where they planned a war, down to the strategy of every city's regiment.

Now that I was part of the Crown, I had a chance to influence those plans in person. I would also have knowledge the rebels could never obtain any other way. Asking Darren a constant string of questions, even as his wife and comrade, would draw too much attention, but listening in on Crown talks would not.

I need to convince them to have a meeting, I realized, *before Darren and I depart for Ferren's Keep next week*. It could be my only chance to pass along information to the rebels, and I needed to get all that I could now.

As much as it bothered me, searching the palace would have to wait. I stood, scattering papers as I put on an evening cloak. The castle's temperature had dropped rapidly from the day before, and I was wearing yet another dress out of tradition for the week's custom. Winter was rapidly approaching, and in a couple of weeks, we would have our first snow.

The palace air already felt like frost.

If Ella were here, she would be cursing up a storm. She hated the cold.

My jaw clenched. I missed my best friend.

And right now, she was alongside my twin in the rebel base, surrounded by people Darren was in charge of discovering.

Argh! I slammed the door of my chamber behind me. I couldn't think about Ella or Alex or Ian or any of them.

I needed to focus on *now*. The one thing I could control, and that was the Council meeting.

* * *

"Absolutely not."

"Mira," Darren's warning growl silenced the head mage of the King's Regiment in an instant, though it did nothing to keep her frothing glower from me.

I wasn't a cruel person, and more so than ever, I had to keep my hostility a secret, but Mira and I had never seen eye to eye. She was the one person I was allowed to openly hate.

We had a history, one of which the Crown was well aware of.

I shoved my shoulder past, throwing a bit of magic into my thrust, so that her back slammed against the wall with a loud thwack. The crunch of her chainmail against stone was satisfying.

That was for Derrick, you murderous hag.

I pretended to be oblivious to her snarl as I entered the

Crown Chamber. Blayne, Commander Audric, and the other two Colored Robes were already present.

I heard Mira's angry draw of breath and shut the door in her face.

It made me secretly pleased to note that she was right, I *was* a traitor, but not even Blayne believed her, all because she had been too vocal of her distrust early on.

To be fair, she had hated me from the start, ever since I disobeyed her orders during a mission to Caltoth during Darren's and my apprenticeship. That hate had only multiplied since she had taken up residency in court and persecuted my brother.

I couldn't wait until the day I exposed Blayne and his loyal right-hand for the villains they were.

Darren's voice was low in my ear. "Was that really necessary?"

I feigned indifference with a shrug. Inside, I squelched unrepentant rage. It felt like I was sawing away at some part of my soul, bit by bit, small flares of pain sparking along my chest.

I took my seat at the left of the long rectangular table. Karina and Yves, the Colored Robes for Restoration and Alchemy, were already seated across. I sat with the king and the leader of the Crown's Army, Eve's father. Commander Audric controlled the largest regiment in Jerar; it housed over ten thousand men, though a couple hundred were always on continuous patrol while the rest awaited orders at a base just miles outside of the capital. Unlike the city regiments, the Crown's Army answered to Jerar as a whole.

"So," Blayne took the opportunity to speak, leaning back

against his chair, looking every bit his father's son, "why such a pressing meeting during a week of festivities. Surely, Darren, your wife can't be so terrible in bed that you ache for war instead?"

My whole face burned, not just at the implication—which was terrible in its own right, but made worse because I had actually pushed Darren aside—but that the rest of room and his brother had been witness as well.

"You will leave my wife out of this."

Blayne's surprised gaze shifted from his brother to me, and a crude smile crossed his face as he caught my expression. His shrewd observation missed nothing. "Interesting."

"Enough." Darren's curt command gave away none of the emotion beneath. "We have more pressing matters at hand."

The young king gave a flick of his wrist. "So I hear, and yet you still haven't revealed why the meeting was called."

"It was for me. I made him call it." I made myself break the uncomfortable pause. Best to put my anger to use. "I can't stomach the thought of a week gone by playing the princess in love."

Again, I caught the hushed intake of breath. The others thought it a slight to Darren, but it wasn't. "Not when the rebels are loose, not while we are on the brink of war with a Caltothian king that could strike any day. Blayne, I'm blind to the state of this country, and as a part of the Crown, I deserve—no, I *need*—to know where we lie. I can't sleep knowing that we put Jerar at risk just to give the crown prince and I a week of festivities. Your gift is too much."

I caught the nod from the villain and knew I had won his

approval. Nothing I had said had been a lie, even the fervor in which I used to tell it. Blayne had no reason to suspect anything amiss.

The Pythian ambassador had been the one who told me I was a terrible liar. I hadn't grown up spinning lies like the rest of the highborn court. And so, I had found a way to spin my truth, never mind that the king's interpretation was different than my own.

"I applaud your earnest appeal, Ryiah." Blayne folded his arms. "But I must say it's unwarranted. Commander Audric and the Council have seen to our strategy firsthand. There is nothing left unaccounted for." His face hardened. "I believe this meeting was called for in error. Darren, perhaps reveal the reason behind your request before calling us to meet at such a late hour in the future."

"Please." My tone grew strained. "I can't just remain in the dark. There must be some way I can help—"

"Ryiah," Blayne's reply was curt, "you are neither a commander of my army nor the Black Mage. You are allowed to listen in on our future meetings as a courtesy to your new position in the Crown, but that is *all*."

My face fell. No, I needed information to bring to the rebels. This was ending before it had even had a chance to begin.

I tried to appeal to the one thing out of Blayne's control, the loose end in his plot. "But the rebels are still out there—"

"Rest easy, lass," the gruff commander spoke up at my left, turning in his chair. "No one blames you for your brother's actions. My Eve was first to sing your praise, before." His face contorted painfully.

There was an abrupt silence, and then Darren's hand shot out to grasp the older man across the table. I had almost forgotten that the man had trained Darren during his youth, and his daughter alongside.

There was a look exchanged between the two, something deep, and I quickly averted my gaze.

But not before I noted the flare of envy in the king's eyes. It was gone as fast as it appeared.

Darren cleared his throat a second later. "Blayne, Ryiah is right. We should discuss the rebels."

"And we can, *after* the week is over." The king's words were sharp. "This time isn't just for you, it's for our subjects. They need something to inspire hope before we go to war."

Once again, Blayne played the gracious sovereign. I caught Karina and Yves nodding along, never the wiser.

"Then send your brother to start the investigation now." The commander had taken up his prince's cause. "Darren grew up a warrior, Your Highness. Sitting and waiting is never something we do well."

"I already sent out five units to our north." Blayne sounded irritable. "That's over sixty of your men patrolling the countryside, Audric. We are hardly sitting and waiting."

Darren's response was to laugh. "They aren't me, brother. You can hardly expect the same level of competence."

I saw my opening. "And how can you trust their reports?" A king whose legacy was steeped with lies would have trouble trusting anyone, especially with rebels abroad. "What is their strategy for scouting the villages? What sorts of tests must they run?"

Tell me your plans, I added silently, *so I can stop them.*

"I don't trust the others' reports," Darren added. "Someone has not been doing their job, brother. I find it highly suspicious that we haven't received one bit of information in all these years. Wherever the rebels are hiding, they have the townsfolk protecting them. Until I question the keep's men myself, you cannot rule out the northern base. Their soldiers come from all over the north. One of them has to know something. You should send Ryiah and me now, never mind the celebrations."

What? No! My nails dug into the table's edge. This wasn't where this conversation needed to go. I needed more information, not to leave sooner.

"You can keep the celebrations going, if you'd like," Darren continued. "And Audric can continue sending his scouts, but you can't afford to waste this opportunity."

Karina cleared her throat. "I agree."

"As do I." Yves was nodding right along. "The Council is in favor of the Black Mage's proposal. We cannot afford to wait."

Commander Audric was in favor as well.

"If it is in everyone's interest," Blayne scowled, "then we will go ahead with this new plan. Ryiah, it appears you got your wish."

I gave a weak smile, cursing my luck. The meeting had the worst outcome I could have planned.

"I'll have Mira see to it that your guard is ready by sunup." Blayne was first to withdraw from his chair, the others rising as well. The king gripped Darren's shoulder in passing. "Don't be a hero, brother. I want you to return in one piece."

Darren gripped his brother in similar fashion, neither comfortable with an embrace. His expression was dark. "You know I will never leave you to rule this kingdom alone."

Blayne's voice lowered as we entered the hall. "I don't care if you risk the others, but don't risk yourself. This isn't that blasted apprenticeship—"

"Gods, you sound like our father." Darren ground his teeth. "I know what I'm doing, brother."

The king growled in frustration and lowered his gaze to me. "You will keep him safe, Ryiah. The two of you are the only ones I trust."

Besides the ones keeping your nefarious secrets, I thought, *like Mira.*

"I don't care what he tells you. Do *not* leave his side." Blayne snatched my arm. "Those rebels would jump at the chance to destroy this kingdom, and they would sooner slit a prince's throat than listen to reason. I need someone on guard when my brother is not—"

"Blayne." Darren tried to interrupt. "I can—"

"Promise me!" Blayne's nails dug into my wrist. For a moment, I saw that boy he used to be, the boy that cared for his brother and no one else.

It was the only thing that saved him from a blade across his throat, that dark, twisted love between brothers that I couldn't break.

At least we could agree about Darren. I had no intention of leaving the prince alone with the rebels, even less now that I had so little to offer.

What had Darren said to me that first year at the

Academy? *"You are possibly the one good thing about this place."* Gods, how the tables had turned. The dark prince had turned into a thing of innocence, and I was the corrupting shade. But I would protect him, and I told the king as much, fervently, my eyes glowing in the flickering hall.

"What a touching moment." Darren raised a brow. "Out of concern for me, the most powerful mage in the whole kingdom."

"Don't think anything of it." The king gave his brother a look. "I just don't want to go through the trouble of replacing you."

"I wouldn't want to replace me, either."

Blayne just shook his head and walked away.

Something tugged at my chest; I could still see the grin on the corner of Darren's mouth. It was the same one touching the king's.

"It doesn't have to make sense. They fight and they yell, but in the end, they are brothers." It was clear as day how much Blayne would break Darren's heart in the end; we both would.

As soon as the king had disappeared from the premises with Mira alongside, the crown prince pulled me into a darkened alcove and tilted my chin. "You can try to protect me all you'd like," he teased, "but I will protect you until the day I die."

I knew I was doing the right thing, *but just then*, I felt like the villain. I sucked in a sharp breath to keep the hysteria at bay, and then I walked away.

I told myself I was the hero. Even if he would never

understand.

THREE

WE SET FORTH at dawn.

Mira assigned us ten of the King's Regiment for each member of the Crown, twenty in all. Five Combat mages each, two healers, two alchemists, and a total of six knights—our personal guard, Henry and Paige included.

Our trek was fast and efficient. Winter had yet to reach the midplains of Jerar, but it was cold enough that travel was less common for most. It helped that our procession was dressed as a standard patrol for the Crown's Army. No one expected anything different, and so those that did traverse the King's Road didn't come to see a crown prince and princess in its ranks.

Most of the first three days were spent passing rust-colored foliage and barren fields. The fall harvest had come and gone, and many of the country's youth were attempting their first year of study in one of the kingdom's war schools, the rest sticking close to home, taking on the extra chores for a family trade.

We stuck to camping, not wanting to draw extra attention in any of the local inns. For the most part, the days were long, but I would have gladly suffered a constant sun to avoid the night and the jesting of our more brazen comrades. After all, Darren and I were husband and wife. The jokes that passed were innocent, but the silence that remained long after when Darren and I retired to our tent was not.

Silence and the momentary flicker of pain. Darren tried hard not to show it, and I tried hard to pretend I was blind. Even when he held me, as he had since that first night of the wedding, I felt a growing divide. Not grief, which would surely thaw, but guilt. It built with each moment that passed.

My nights were spent endlessly tossing and turning. *If this is us now...* But I couldn't bear to think of the future. I just prayed to the gods it was worth it.

By the fifth day west, we had reached Demsh'aa, nestled at the base of the Iron Mountain Range.

Darren and the rest set to questioning the villagers, leaving me standing at the doorway of my parents' apothecary. Paige stood guard further back, giving me privacy. I wasn't worried about Darren's safety, the village—contrary to Blayne's belief—contained no rebels whatsoever. Derrick had made it clear Ferren's Keep was their only base. The rebels hiding out down south were nomadic, never remaining in the same town long.

I watched an older woman explain something to a young girl at the front. She had the beautiful blonde hair and keen blue eyes of my brothers. *Brother.* Her lips were pressed and hard.

A man at her right with curly locks and a crooked nose helped another young apprentice with a potion for one of their waiting clients. The shop was packed full with waiting customers. The flimsy boarding had been reinforced and painted over, and new brocade curtains covered the windows. It was easily the most profitable building in the whole square. The coin Alex and I had been sending home during the apprenticeship had been put to good use.

As I watched my parents, it felt as if a palm were pressing down on my chest. Their demeanor had changed since that last visit. They had dark shadows under their eyes, and they were slow to smile.

You did this. I made myself take a little step forward and another, until I was at the front. I waited for them to notice.

My mother was first. For just a moment, there was light in her eyes, and then it died. She reached out for her husband, and then my father turned and spotted me as well. They left the shop to the girls and walked me back to their house across the way. It, too, had undergone many changes.

For a moment, there was a stilted, uncomfortable air as the three of us entered the building in silence, and then my mother made a small choking noise, pulling me into her embrace. Her arms went around my shoulders and her face pressed against my hair. My father's feet shuffled across the room, and then the pressure tightened until I was listening to their hitched intakes of breath, a wordless moment fraught with emotion as the familiar scent of woodsy pine and cloves enveloped me whole.

"I wish you had been there," I finally croaked.

"I'm sure you made a beautiful bride." My father's voice shook as he brushed my hair along the back of my head.

My mother was sobbing. "The capital where Derrick..."

I clenched my eyes, blinking back the tears at the mention

of his name. I knew why they had refused to visit, but it didn't make the pain any less.

I wasn't sure how long the three of us stood there in the entry. The first hour was spent in silence with locked limbs, white knuckles, and glassy eyes.

These were the two that had raised me. Their presence begged for the past, for when I was just a little girl crying to my parents instead of an adult who so easily made mistakes. When I was just Ryiah, not a mage, and certainly not tied up with the Crown, in love with the brother of an evil king. I wanted them to tell me this was all just a dream, that I could make the nightmare vanish, that we could turn down the hall and see my youngest brother laughing in the corner with an impish smile.

But I couldn't.

And yet, for the first time in the last two months, I didn't have to be so alone. My parents needed to be prepared for what was to come in case I failed. I had no doubt the first people the king would seek out were my family.

It was much later into the evening, as wax dripped from candles long forgotten, that I finished telling my parents everything that had changed. It was much different than my visit before. Their hearts had already been hardened to loss, their youngest was dead, and their second son had joined a rebel cause. Hearing that their only daughter intended to betray the Crown, that she intended to break up the New Alliance and help the rebels all the while under the Black Mage's nose? I suppose they had come to expect that the gods were not in our family's favor.

"Oh, Ryiah." My mom's hand shot out to grasp my own.

"You don't have to be the one to do this."

My response was devoid of feeling. "Don't I?"

She looked away, biting her lip. My father said nothing.

They knew it even if they didn't want to admit it. I was the only one, and wishing that I wasn't the girl stuck with this destiny wouldn't change a thing.

"We will do exactly as you say." My father had finally spoken. "We'll have one of the apprentices keep an eye on the roads and keep a bag of necessities hidden away. The moment we hear of anything unusual, we'll leave."

"Where will you go?"

My mother cleared her throat. "South. I have a cousin who lives just outside of Port Ishir. We'll tell her we're looking to start up a second apothecary closer to sea and give a change of names. You and Alex have certainly given us enough coin to open a second shop, and the girls can run our first in Demsh'aa. No one will be the wiser."

A bit of relief worked itself into my chest. Their plan could work.

"You need to be careful, Ryiah." My father pushed a lock of hair to the side of my face. "This Blayne..." His eyes darkened as his fist curled in his lap. "He isn't the type to overlook things. If you make even one mistake—"

"I won't." My shoulders tensed. "You and Mom won't lose another child."

"And your husband?" My mother's gaze locked on my own. She knew how much he meant; she could see it in my eyes. She was afraid of the thing *I* would lose. She was afraid for me.

I thought of what the Pythian ambassador said on the

night we met: *"You've found yourself a happily ever after in a time when there are none."* If only I had realized the truth before. "Justice has a price." I looked my mother in the eyes. "He is mine."

* * *

We arrived at our destination a week later. Frost coated the grass, making a crunching noise as our party approached the base of the great keep fortress. It was as towering as it was dark, a menacing stone beacon like the mountain itself, built directly into a portion of the Iron Range. Hidden away behind it was a small town accessible only by passage within; it housed the country's most talented blacksmiths that supplied the king's regiment.

Ian's parents were two of them.

I now wondered how many weapons they had hidden away amongst their own, unnoticed, while fulfilling the Crown's orders for steel. I wondered how long their son had known about his parents' cause, and my view of the apprenticeship took on a whole new light.

All those times Ian had tried to strike up a friendship with the unfriendly Darren, perhaps it hadn't been quite so innocent as I thought. Would he have been quite so enthusiastic to spend time alongside me if I hadn't been the girl who caught the prince's eye? Everyone had seen the way Darren talked to the lowborn girl, shunning the rest of our year.

My stomach churned. Gods, every one of us was tainted. All of us shades of gray. This world of innocence was a lie.

Our group declared itself at the base of a raised walkway. The sentries spent a moment checking our seals before they recognized their guests. We were waved forward, and the first of two iron gates raised. By the time we passed our second set of sentries, a hostler was ready for our steeds while the twenty-two of us disembarked and stood, rubbing our arms underneath layers of wool. The keep's entry with its stone tunnels was even colder than the outside.

We were told to wait.

Commander Nyx arrived ten minutes later, the air of surprise touching her mouth, but a sharp distrust lingered in her steel eyes. Her gaze locked on me, and I wondered how much Alex had told her since arriving several weeks before. Did she suspect I was here to turn over the rebels to my husband?

I kept my eyes level, willing the commander to silence until I had a chance to explain. The woman had to know the keep could easily overtake our party if we were here to arrest. Darren and I might have more power than most, but the keep was comprised of two thousand members, and they had the backing of several northern townships that kept the rebels' cause.

"To what do I owe this unexpected visit, Your Highness?" Nyx's tone betrayed none of her emotion; if anything, it showed more warmth than I had ever experienced during my stay in her regiment just one year before.

Darren frowned at the openness of her request. The prince wasn't fool enough to discuss his mission in an open tunnel. Who knew what others might be within hearing. The many floors of storage were just beyond. Some of the crates and barrels were large enough to hide a man. Darren's sharp gaze flit over the shadowy crevices at the entry of the keep's central passage.

"Can we speak somewhere private?"

Her gaze narrowed. I could tell she was unwilling to find herself alone with the Black Mage. Not without knowing my relation in the matter. Not without knowing whether or not I'd told him the truth. Because if he knew, it would mean certain death.

Still, if Nyx voiced her reluctance, it would put the commander at the top of his list.

"Of course. My personal chambers would be best."

We followed the commander down the passage and through the storerooms. The lowest level of the keep was also the coldest, its air made chilly by stone walls, untouched by insulating tapestries to keep away the frost.

After passing through a locked set of reinforced doors with another set of guards waiting nearby, we reached the commander's personal chambers. She produced a ring of keys and paused, her hand on the door's lock.

"I trust that you don't need your guards to partake?"

She sought to limit potential witnesses.

Darren was quick to agree, but I was not. I did not trust the crown prince of the realm alone with the leader of the rebels. I'd never been privy to the secrets of the keep—who knew if there was a secret collection of mages and knights that she had already readied, waiting just beyond the commander's walls to accost a threat before it became more?

"I will join you both."

Darren gave me a raised brow, no doubt recalling his brother's orders and thinking himself capable of meeting the commander alone, but he didn't question my decision aloud.

Nyx looked anything but pleased.

"Very well. If you both would follow me."

Paige let out an angry huff as we passed. She wasn't pleased about being left behind; Henry at least trusted me to see to the prince. Paige did not trust anyone but herself.

She was the wisest of all.

The rest of our unit resigned to wait.

Commander Nyx turned the key and led the two of us into a large barren chamber. The draft wasn't much better here than the hall beyond. Its furnishings were bare, save for a thick rug and the seating area on the left that included a long, rectangular slab of a table and twenty chairs.

One for each head knight in her squads, I assumed, to meet in private and discuss strategy before addressing the whole of her regiment in the open.

My eyes immediately studied the chamber for any hint of rebel activity, but it was far too plain to be incriminating.

I wondered if Nyx had one of her men do a quick sweep while we were in the hall. How many documents were being burned while the crown prince and princess were occupied? By the time Darren took up his investigation, there wouldn't be a scrap of paper indicating their cause.

Darren didn't miss a beat. "King Blayne has sent me to check on our northern post. The Crown recently discovered a rebel who was a former soldier of your regiment. I would like the keep's full cooperation while I lead this investigation. I trust you can keep your own men in line." He had used a similar train of speech for the lord overseeing Demsh'aa during our visit. The only difference was that man was a fool and had almost fallen over his round belly thanking a prince of the realm—he had seemed to forget his prince was also the Black Mage—for overseeing his town for that "rebel rubbish."

"Of course." The commander pressed her lips into a tight smile. "I will assist in any way that I can. May I ask who the rebel was?"

She was going to make him say it.

I swallowed back a mouth full of bile as I answered instead. "Derrick." Darren didn't know about Jacob and the other rebels who had been involved in my brother's escape. They had never been identified, even the ones who died. All had been too careful to bear incriminating insignia or paperwork on their person.

The commander feigned a sharp intake of breath. "Your brother, Your Highness?"

"My little brother." *That you recruited and brainwashed into service to further your cause.* I stared her down, letting the woman silently ponder how much I knew. I wanted her to sweat. I may have taken up her cause, but that didn't make her blameless. Commander Nyx had used Derrick to use me, and I couldn't help but think how even the so-called heroes had blood on their hands.

Every hero was a villain in the end. War was corrupting us all.

"We have already investigated his parents' village." Darren's voice seemed to echo across the room.

My eyes flitted back to my husband.

"Ferren's Keep was the next logical choice. Even if the rebels reside elsewhere, there is a good chance someone here knows how they were able to recruit. Her brother never served south, so it is highly probable that at least some of the rebels or their contacts reside north."

"A very apt conclusion." Nyx was nodding along, her shoulders relaxed, not one tense muscle in her stance. No wonder she had managed to keep her role so long without suspicion.

Then again, she was a highborn like her brother, the young advisor who'd overheard King Lucius's plans so many years ago. And if there was one thing the Pythian duke had taught me, it was that every highborn could lie.

Ironic, really, that the leader of the rebels was a highborn that only recruited lowborns.

A short break of silence followed.

"I need a list of each unit's men," Darren said, "with their years of service. I need the names of the cities they transferred from, as well as any personal notes you or your guard find peculiar to their service. My team and I will start interrogating the first squad at dawn. Bring us the one Derrick was a part of first."

"He received a promotion to Sir Maxon's squad before he resigned from our keep. Maxon is returning from a patrol along the border. His men should be back in a week and a half."

The prince shifted from one foot to the next. "Then bring us Derrick's first. Perhaps someone there will have noticed a change before his promotion."

"Certainly. We have a dungeon in the back of the keep, do you require such methods in your interrogation?"

Darren's eyes went dark, and a bit of ice burrowed into my lungs. "I would prefer to question them before it comes to other... methods."

But he would, if necessary. Darren had confessed that to me during our trip. He would do anything to protect his country, and if he had to hurt a man, or many, he would.

I had tossed and turned every night since.

I needed to make sure it didn't come to that. If it did—it wouldn't. This was why I was here. To lead the Black Mage astray. To keep the rebels safe.

To keep Darren safe from their blood on his hands.

"Then I will have them report outside the cell at first light. No other squads will be present. Is there anything else?" The commander's eyes were on the prince, but I knew the question was for me.

"Private accommodations. And I want a row of cots for the rest of our unit just outside it. We will use our own guards." My tone came out harsh and abrupt. It was reminiscent of Paige, and for the first time, I realized exactly how hard my friend's station must have been, guarding a girl who believed she was capable of her own defense. There were people one inevitably let down their caution for, and they were the reason guards were needed.

I told myself I would make it a point to apologize the first chance I got.

Darren wasn't safe, not until I had a chance to talk to Nyx and the others alone. I'd never felt so tense or alert in my life.

Lowborn modesties aside, I would sooner have the keep presume me demanding than allow Darren to sleep in a barrack full of armed men. Let them think I was the snooty princess from before. Blayne's orders had given me all the leniency I needed. With Darren, my goal and the king of Jerar's were one and the same.

I would play whatever role it took.

"King's orders." My smile was strained. "You understand."

Darren was giving me an odd look; I didn't sound like myself. I knew he would remark on it later, but for now, I kept my gaze locked on the commander.

"I'll see that the two of you are given the chamber across the hall." Nyx crossed the room to rummage through her drawers and produced a single brass key. "We reserve it for just this sort of affair. I would never want a prince of Jerar sleeping among the rest."

I almost snorted, recalling just the opposite sort of reaction a year before. She had been most pleased that I had chosen to take up with the rest of the regiment's women in the barracks, much to Paige's outspoken disapproval.

The commander saw us back to the hall without incident. "I'll have my men bring out cots for the rest of your lot."

And here was my opportunity. "Thank you, Commander." I grasped the woman's wrist as she retreated, slipping a thin roll of parchment just under her sleeve. It was a move I'd practiced in the mirror that first night we arrived in Demsh'aa. It took all of three hours to perfect just the right twist of the wrist and shifting of my cloak.

The commander stiffened in shock but recovered far too quickly to voice her surprise aloud.

I'd composed the letter that same night. My mother had sewn it into my cloak with a bit of thread, and I'd worn the smelly thing ever since, refusing to take it off even for a moment. The last thing I'd wanted was for Darren or the others to find a mysterious letter hidden away in the paneling of my sleeve.

"Darren and I appreciate your cooperation in this matter," I said hastily, taking a step back to stand beside the prince. "We hope not to take up too much of your regiment's time."

The woman smiled. This time there was a confidence that she hadn't carried just a couple of seconds before. Nyx was an intelligent woman; she knew the paper held some purpose I could not speak aloud.

"I am more than happy to cooperate. I, too, have this country's best interests at heart."

* * *

Fifty minutes later, I made an excuse to Darren and the others that I needed to bathe despite the extremely late hour of our arrival. The stench of my cloak was enough to discourage any protest on the parts of our guards. Darren had been immersed in his scrolls, reviewing everything the Crown knew about the rebels in preparation for the interrogation that following morning.

Paige, of course, accompanied me. Luckily, however, we'd spent over a year at the keep and she had come to consider bathing trips a simple task.

I feigned a quick search of the bathhouse.

"There's no one inside. I'll be as quick as I can."

My guard nodded along absentmindedly, her gaze locked on the dark corridor beyond. Rebels were far more likely to be stalking a princess in the halls, not hiding out in the unheated waters of an unoccupied bathhouse an hour past midnight. She trusted my inspection without question.

When I entered the building, Nyx was waiting in the shadows on the opposite dais. I knew she would come; the commander had far too much at risk not to.

The first thing I did was cast out a listening "wall." It wasn't foolproof, just a thick, stagnant wall of condensed air, but I wasn't planning to shout.

I didn't bother with the candles. If Paige took it upon herself to check on me later, I wanted the inside to be as indiscernible as possible.

"Your Highness—"

I held up a hand, stopping her. "Derrick told me everything."

"Everything?"

"Before he was caught, my brother confessed the truth about this keep—the truth about you, the truth about the old king and Caltoth, all of it. At the time, I didn't believe him…" I paused and looked her straight in the eyes. It was hard to see them in the dark, but I thought she looked scared. I wondered what she thought of me. "Every word out of his mouth sounded like something you had constructed to recruit naïve rebels."

"I swear, every word was the truth!"

"I know that now." My words were bitter and low. "But I didn't then. I didn't because you never gave me the chance. You used my new position to fund your regiment, you had one of my best friends return just to test my loyalty to the keep, you sent my own brother to abuse my ties to the Crown, you made me lie to my *husband*—" my lips started to tremble, but I made myself carry on, "—but never once did you *ask*."

"Ryiah." Nyx's whisper was apologetic.

"You can understand why I doubted your cause." The rage rose and boiled in the center of my chest. It was back, and however misdirected, I couldn't keep from relaying it to her in an angry hiss. "I lost him, Commander! I lost my own brother because you never gave me the chance to understand. I lost him because I was overwhelmed and blind and I couldn't see the truth until it was too late."

"King Lucius was a tyrant." Nyx stood a little straighter, arms folding across her chest. "I couldn't risk the chance you'd run to the Crown and destroy all those years of planning. There was too much at stake. Derrick was never supposed to tell you. That was never a part of the plan—"

"But he did." I clenched and unclenched my fists, trying to send the anger away before things got too heated. It would be too easy to yell, to raise my voice and forget why I was here. "I just didn't believe him."

"I am sorry for your loss." The woman paused; she seemed to have difficulty speaking. "He was a great soldier, one of the brightest I've seen."

"He was."

"Derrick reminded me of Raphael." One of the dead lords who had tried to poison Lucius. "He kept begging me to recruit you against the others' advice, telling me I was making a mistake." She paused. "I suppose he was right after all."

For a moment, neither of us spoke.

Then she asked, "What changed? If you didn't believe him while he was…?" She averted her gaze.

"Alive?" I took a deep breath and braced myself against

the wall. This was it. What I was about to say now, I could never take it back. But if I didn't, we would go to war. And so I told her, leaving nothing out, sharing every detail from my mission during the apprenticeship to the girl in the Candidacy stands, and especially the king.

When I was done, the commander was silent. She kept parting her lips and then swallowing, unwilling or unable to speak. When she finally cleared her throat, her words were hoarse. "I thought the worst of it was over... I-I'll admit, a small part of me considered that Lucius had passed down his secret to his sons, but I thought it was Pythus."

The rebels thought King Joren had orchestrated the murders the night of the Victors' Ceremony in Montfort.

"Darren is innocent." I needed her to understand what I was about to say. "All of this, it was Blayne."

"And yet it is the Black Mage who is investigating our keep."

"Because his brother asked him to!" My whisper came out a defensive shout, and I made myself lower it. "Darren risked his life to save your soldiers that day of our apprenticeship. If he had known the attack was planned, he wouldn't—"

"Perhaps Darren wanted to look the hero." She was unconvinced.

My nails dug into my palm. "He lost his best friend that day, the daughter of Commander Audric, Eve. He would never sacrifice her."

"Perhaps—"

"Perhaps nothing!" I took a menacing step forward. "I watched the prince cry for the apprentices who died during the attacks in Mahj, the attacks *you* initiated."

"Salt is a precious commodity. Cutting off the Crown's primary resource would have forced Lucius to cut back his army—"

"I watched Darren sacrifice, again and again, for his country. He is nothing like his brother, *nothing*."

Nyx wore a frown plastered to her mouth, but said nothing. She had spent over twenty years nursing a distrust of the Crown. She didn't know Darren the way I did. The commander might not have been there in Mahj the day the rebels tried to kill the prince, but it was her cause that had been willing to sacrifice the boy I loved.

I needed her to understand that could not be the case.

"I will help you," I said softly. "I will finish what my brother could not. I will find the proof we need and convince the Pythians not to honor the New Alliance. But I need your assurance Darren will be safe from the others. What we are planning, however it plays out, Darren will not be charged with his family's crimes."

"He is a prince of the realm. When the Crown's secrets are exposed, no one will trust him on the throne. Even if I were to believe you, that Darren is innocent, you can see that the others will not. They will never trust a prince of tainted lineage to lead."

"He doesn't need a crown." I had already made up my mind. "When this is over, you can put someone else on the throne, but Darren is free."

"Any acts he commits under his brother's orders—"

"He will not be accountable." My words came out a growl. "Darren is not responsible for whatever the king requests of his Black Mage."

"He is hunting rebels." Her voice was hard. "You expect my men to stand by as—"

"I expect you to tell them whatever it takes. If anyone harms a hair on his head, I will turn this entire regiment over to the king."

"You would sentence thousands to die?"

"*You* would sentence thousands to die. If you cannot control your men, it would be their blood on your hands, not mine." I was bluffing, but she couldn't read my expression in the dark. "You will not be able to stop this war without me. You need me."

"All for *him*?"

"All for Jerar." I folded my arms. "But I will not let Darren be the cost."

Nyx was silent. I knew she would say yes; she had no other choice. She couldn't afford to walk away.

"Very well." The woman drew in a resigned breath, and then another. "I will report everything you have told me to my men and send word to the Caltothian king. Horrace needs to know about this new development. How can we assist?"

"Darren believes the rebels reside north and that the southern attacks were feigned to lead the Crown astray." My tone was flat. "I need you to give him a reason to believe he is wrong. The longer we remain at the keep, the less time I have to search the palace and the higher the chance the whole keep is exposed."

"You want me to stir up activity in the south?"

I shook my head. "Blayne has Marius and several patrols combing the Red Desert as we speak. No one would be safe.

I want you to have one of your own put on a good show here. Make Darren believe he has discovered one of the rebels. Have the man claim he was paid to recruit for a leader in the south, and that there are rebels hiding among the palace staff, biding their time, waiting for their chance to murder their king."

"I would be sentencing this man to certain death."

I took a shaky breath. "Darren will not kill the rebel, not right away, not if he believes he has information that can help him identify the ones in the palace. Have the man bargain with his life, claiming that without him it will be too late for Blayne."

"And then?"

"I will find a way to help him escape." My mind was already made up.

"A rebel escape under the Black Mage and twenty of his closest guards? That's an impossible feat."

"Just prepare the man." I folded my arms resolutely. "Make sure he knows the hideouts your people keep in the Iron Range. And whatever you do, do not send him south. That's where Darren will look."

"How much time do I have?"

"At least a week. Darren would be suspicious if he came across a rebel too easily."

"And after you return to the palace?"

"You ready your men, and you wait."

"I have one of our own stationed in Devon." The commander paused and her tone grew somber. "She was the one who was able to inform us the day your brother was caught. We didn't have enough time for a rescue. The only group we had on standby were not enough…" She cleared her throat quietly. "Saba will keep watch over the palace. Should you need to reach us, visit the lower city blacksmith. I will send word you are working with us. Any communication can be sent through her. The palace envoys are watched."

The two of us continued to talk strategy.

"Everything depends on Pythus." The commander's brow was furrowed. "I could send word to Horrace to contact King Joren himself, but their countries' ties were severed after the New Alliance. Do you have a plan?"

I bit the inside of my cheek. "No, and the Pythians are set to arrive in six weeks."

"I would not trust a letter. Not even an envoy. You need to approach their ambassador in person. Duke Cassius will be traveling to oversee the warships?"

I was certain.

"Good." Her response was terse. "And whether or not you find proof, you need to convince him to turn. That will be your only opportunity to stop the alliance. After, it will be too late."

She wasn't saying anything I didn't already know, but that didn't stop the sinking feeling in the pit of my stomach, the anxious fear squeezing at my lungs and choking me out from the inside.

"The Pythians might not be swayed by justice." Nyx said this as an afterthought. "Promise them whatever it takes. Give them a reason to pick us. Even in their greed, they have never sought to stage wars on their own people. Any rule is better than that of a corrupt king."

I nodded.

"The Pythians might not be enough." The commander placed a firm hand on my shoulder. "The Crown's Army is twice the size of their own. Even with the rebels and Caltoth standing united, we still may lose."

I was silent. I didn't want to think of an outcome in which we lost... what the world would be like if we did.

"Your twin and his wife arrived at my keep a couple months back." The commander sounded apologetic. "They made it very clear they wanted a part in my cause. I have them as part of Sir Maxon's squad. Would you like me to send word before they arrive?"

"Yes." My voice caught and I shook my head, shaking away the sudden emotion at the mention of my brother and best friend and the last time we had crossed paths. "Tell them everything," I croaked. "I can't keep sneaking away to meet like this. It will raise too much suspicion. I had to risk tonight because... because I was afraid of—"

"Of what we might attempt with a prince in our keep." Nyx didn't bother to shy away from the truth. "I understand. And you wouldn't be wrong."

"It will give them some time to prepare. For Alex to... to understand."

"It will be hard for everyone."

"It already is."

I disrobed and stepped into the shadowy pool. My teeth were chattering from the cold, but I needed to wash. Paige was waiting just beyond the door.

The commander watched me. "It will only get worse, Ryiah. No matter how hard it gets, you must not tell the prince the truth."

I started to lather my arms with soap, forcing myself to concentrate on the task at hand. I didn't want to think about Darren now. Nothing would change. I wouldn't tell him and I would hate myself every second of it.

To do otherwise would be to put the others at risk. I trusted Darren with my life, but he also loved his brother. I couldn't trust him not to give Blayne a chance to explain. And it was that chance I feared. Because a king had too much power in a chance.

Maybe I was making a mistake, but the stakes were too great if I wasn't.

"I know you think the worst of me," Nyx added, "because I was—*am*—willing to sacrifice those you love, but what you do not understand is that we will not be able to save everyone. For a cause such as this, no one will come away clean." Her voice lowered. "Least of all us."

Commander Nyx had made hard decisions all her life. She'd spent years building up a rebel army as she watched a tyrant of a king stage false battles the people didn't need. I wondered how many people she had lost along the way. What had she been like before all of this? After she'd lost her brother, did she have anything left to feel? All these years of biding her time, waiting, knowing there was an evil plaguing the lands but she couldn't yet strike.

For the first time, I pitied her. I only had to see this through to the end; she'd had *years*.

The next ten minutes passed in silence, and then, as I finished and stepped out of the cold, I brushed the hair back out of my eyes.

"Commander?"

"Yes?"

"I'm sorry you lost your brother."

Her intake of breath was soft. "I am sorry you lost yours."

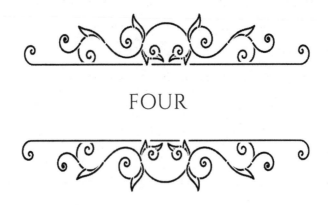

FOUR

A COUPLE OF hours later, I awoke to find the prince sitting at the edge of the cot, his hands folded above his head as he stared straight ahead. He was already dressed in a formal leather jerkin and a thick wool cloak, heavy boots at his feet.

"Darren?" My voice cracked as I sat up in bed, clutching my thin chemise to my chest. My breath fogged up the air—I had forgotten how cold the keep's winters could get.

The sun wasn't even peeking through the window bars. Our room seemed to be the only one facing the outside of the keep, and I could see the darkness still pooling across the barren landscape, the keep's flaming torches lining its fortified walls.

"I can't sleep." He still hadn't raised his head. "I keep trying, but all I can think about is Caine. What will happen if I find a rebel today? Gods, Ryiah, what can they possibly think to gain? A nation in ruins so the Caltothians can tear us apart? How could anyone wish for that?"

There was a pang in my chest, and I swallowed it down. I couldn't confess. Telling Darren the truth would only relieve my own guilt.

And what I felt, what I wanted for him, none of that mattered. The country did. The people did.

But I didn't.

I swallowed, my mouth full of sand as I spoke. "Some things will never make sense."

Darren sighed and lifted his head. "I'm going to the training courts. I can't just sit here waiting."

I was standing, pulling on a pair of breeches and a tunic. "I'll join you."

"Ryiah." His eyes found mine, and I could see how fatigued the prince really was. He must not have slept at all. "You don't have to do this. What my brother said—"

"This isn't about an order from my king." In another second, I was pulling on a pair of woolen breeches and a quilted jacket of my own. I was failing him in so many ways, but the gods themselves would have to keep me from Darren's side when he needed me most. "This is about me keeping an eye on the Black Mage to make sure he hasn't gone soft."

"Soft?" A small smile tugged at the corner of Darren's mouth. "Are you planning on a rematch?"

I remembered that terrible ache of jealousy, back when I had lost the Candidacy, back when my worst problem had been envy. Now I had to wonder if I had won the robe instead, how things would have changed.

I might have missed the signs. I might have been leading a war against my brother and friends, instead of my husband.

"When the war is over—" I swallowed back the knowledge I'd never get the chance, "—we'll duel."

"No one has ever challenged one of the Colored Robes

during their twenty-year reign." Darren's words were laced with humor. "Some might say it's against Council rules. The Candidacy exists for a reason, Ryiah."

In twenty years, will you forgive my betrayal? I made myself smile and feign ease instead. "An heir to the Crown is a mage. What happened to the Council's Treaty?"

Darren's grin spread. "Some rules were meant to be broken."

"In that case..." I raised a brow.

The prince gave an unexpected laugh. "Very well. When this war is over, you'll get your chance, love. You win and I'll hand you the robe myself."

When this war is over, will you still care?

* * *

Two hours later, we left the practice court, our guards trailing sluggishly behind. I wasn't sure who had trained harder, the Black Mage or me. Our faces were flushed and we were dripping sweat from a battle against opponents no one else could see. Pain was preferable to the shadowy recesses of our minds.

We were one and the same.

Fifteen minutes of winding, spiraling passages and we were at the narrow hall that led up to the keep's prison. Just as Commander Nyx promised, a hundred men stood nervously in line, waiting for the Black Mage and his team. The hall could barely fit five men shoulder to shoulder. The twenty-two of us had to make our way to the end of the hall, one by one, waiting for soldiers to move aside as we passed. Paige scowled at every face along the way.

The walls were looming, almost cavernous. The passage

lacked any natural light. We were in an offshoot of one of the keep's many floors, and the air was a bit musty but clean. This was nothing like the rot and festering odors of the palace dungeon. The cells to the prison were just beyond a pair of heavyset doors barred by steel.

I had always wondered why the commander sent local criminals to the jail in Gilys instead of her dungeon at the keep, but that was before I had found out she was recruiting them to her cause. No one had ever been going to jail.

I stumbled, choking on air as a familiar set of hazel-green eyes caught on mine in passing. And then another. And another.

And then I was face to face with Sir Gavin at the front.

Derrick's former regiment preceding his promotion had been mine. How could I have forgotten? Ian, Lief, Ruth, Sir Gavin, the soldiers that hated me, as well as a few of the disgruntled knights, I had seen them all many, *many* times before.

I had to swallow down the panic and focus on the torches flickering above their heads. I could do this. I could feign indifference. This was my first test.

"I am sure all of you are wondering why we are here." Darren cleared his throat loudly as he addressed the squad before us. "Why Nyx summoned you to meet with me under such discreet orders. I'm not going to bother with formalities. It has come to the Crown's attention that the rebels might reside north instead of the south like we formerly thought. The king has sent a team to help me identify potential traitors in your keep or information that might lead to their capture. I will be interrogating each one of your comrades over the next couple of days, and I have no intention of leaving until my men and I've met with each and every one of you."

There was a hushed collective of breath. I dared myself to look. Not a one appeared upset or suspicious. Even Ian had wide eyes and a perfectly timed "oh" framing his mouth. It was almost convincing.

Then again, most were probably oblivious to the truth. Sir Gavin's squad sought to test potential recruits' loyalty to the Crown. There were only a select few who knew the truth in the starter squad. The rest were promoted to one of the higher squads, like my brother and Ella.

Darren carried on as the rest of our guards examined the crowd.

There was no point in trying to hide our purpose. Darren was wise to see how an investigation would carry rumors to the other squads. In truth, his speech was more than a little convincing.

The prince carried just the right degree of emotion as he touched on our upcoming war and the lives we had lost in past rebel attacks. There was a hint of a plea as he beseeched them to turn over any information they had while promising not to charge any man or woman brave enough to come forward.

And finally, the threat: should someone with information fail to come forward, the Black Mage would embrace less favorable methods of interrogation.

When Darren was finished, our guards split in two. All but the prince and I remained outside to keep an eye on the crowd.

I followed Darren into the dungeon. The information Nyx had promised was stacked neatly in a pile on a slab of stone that could only remotely resemble a desk.

"You spent close to a year in this keep." The prince's voice was much softer now that it was just the two of us inside. "If you notice anything—"

"I'll speak up." My stomach seemed to curl in on itself, and I forced myself to state the obvious aloud. It was better to warn him now. "Sir Gavin was my squad's leader. I know this group well."

Darren ran a hand through his hair and then cast his eyes warily toward the door. "That means Ian is out there, isn't he?"

I bit my lip, wondering how he would react.

"It doesn't matter." Darren shook his head, the decision already made. "I'm not here to settle old feuds… Perhaps his infatuation will help for once." His gaze fell on the scrolls at the desk, and he began to sift through them and their list of names. "Ian might be willing to spy on his comrades if he believes he is doing it for you."

"I can try but…" I grimaced. "Whatever Andy said at the Victor's Ceremony, Darren, she was wrong. Ian didn't come to the keep because of feelings for me." The best lie always started with a bit of truth. "He's very loyal to the Crown. I know he would be more than happy to help." *And point you in the wrong direction.*

The prince's mouth tugged in an uncertain line, but he didn't voice his doubts aloud. Instead, Darren twisted the door's knob, waiting as two of our guards brought the first man forward.

Sir Gavin entered the prison chamber.

And so our investigations began.

* * *

The first two hours were the longest. A squad leader was the person most likely to take note of his men, and Darren pressed every bit of that advantage. Fortunately, from his line of questioning—like his shared confidence with Commander Nyx—I could see that Darren didn't entertain any suspicion of the leader. Most of that time was spent learning about the squad itself.

Sir Gavin presented all of his answers with ease, and why wouldn't he? As head recruiter, the man had spend a good many years lying to most of his squad. He hadn't "noticed any suspicious activity" and he was "very concerned with the possibility of rebels in the keep." He was even so bold as to redirect Darren's attention to me. With a serious gleam he noted, "Your wife was a part of my squad. Were any of my own rebels, they would have pressed that advantage, no?"

Darren frowned. "If the rebels stationed recruiters in the keep, perhaps one or two working alone, they might have considered an attack too revealing."

The commander blinked, startled that the prince wasn't so easily swayed.

Even though I didn't want him to discover the truth, I swelled with a bit of pride. My husband was nobody's fool.

"It is possible, I suppose." Sir Gavin paused. "What do you think, Ryiah? Did you notice anything suspicious?"

"I believe my questions are for you, not my wife." Darren sounded just the slightest bit irritable. "Any concerns Ryiah had would have been reported long ago."

"True." The squad leader was back to nodding right along. The remainder of his time was spent detailing the last five years of his unit's patrols and detailing the behaviors of the names and backgrounds Darren had picked out of the pile. By the time they were finished, both Gavin and Darren were on a first-name basis.

The knight was shaking the prince's hand as he left, promising to report anything unusual in the days to come.

As soon as the knight had exited the dungeon, Darren turned to me. "What do you think?"

"About Sir Gavin?"

"About his men. Do you think he could have missed something because he is too close to his squad?"

Like you are to me? "Gavin is a good leader. I answered to Lief, but Sir Gavin was very aware of all of our squad's goings-on, even the mages. I think he would have noticed if something was awry."

Darren nodded absentmindedly. "I feel the same. A shame we still have to question all of his men. Twenty squads is going to make for exhausting work."

"You would always wonder if you didn't." I walked toward the door as Darren returned to his pile of papers, sorting through the names. "Who would you like me to call next?"

The prince frowned at his scrolls and then sighed. "I don't suppose it matters much, does it? I'll see them all eventually. Send Ian in. The sooner we question him, the sooner I don't have to think about him waiting outside that door."

Might as well get it over with. I opened the door and called out Ian's name, watching as Paige and Henry escorted my friend.

The brawny mage stepped forward, and I ducked my head, avoiding Ian's gaze as he stepped past to come face to face with his former adversary.

For a moment, there was no sound. A quill could have dropped to the floor, and it would have made more noise than the two young men in front of me. I shut the chamber door, and the thud of heavy wood slamming against stone was enough to break the silence.

"Your Highness."

Darren raised a brow. "After all these years, you finally use the title."

Ian managed a slight grin. "'Darren,' it is."

"I would say it's good to see you," the prince's lip twitched, "but we both know that would be a lie."

"And I would never want you to lie." Ian folded his arms and leaned against the wall, his grin widening. "Let me guess, you think I'm a rebel?"

"Hardly." The prince gave the mage a smirk. "Ian the villain? That would make my job too easy."

I coughed uncomfortably. "Darren and I are only doing this to see if you noticed anything suspicious among the men."

Ian glanced at me, and his eyes spoke the questions he dared not voice aloud. "I haven't, and you know I grew up here. The keep's men are hardly the kind to betray the Crown—that's the southerners, no?"

"We think the rebels reside north." I made myself look him directly in the eyes, conveying a silent message as I did. *Don't give anything away.* "We aren't certain, but the southern attacks could be a trick. Perhaps the rebels' base is somewhere along the border, and they are recruiting from the keep."

"I find it hard to believe a single one hides among us." His eyes were asking questions in return. *How much does Darren suspect? Do you understand what risks you are taking in bringing him here? The risks you are putting everyone through?* And perhaps the hardest to ask: *Do you forgive me for your brother and the lies?*

"I find it hard to believe they wouldn't try." Darren's voice was incredulous, and I watched Ian cringe. The prince was so, *so* close. He, like the rest of the king's board of advisors, only believed the rebels to be two hundred at most. Nowhere near the size of the keep, give or take a hundred permanently stationed south.

"If that were the case, we would have identified them years ago." Ian gave the prince an easy smile, his ease returning to the banter from before now that he was no longer staring at my face. "We've got the best. Our men could spot a traitor a mile away."

"Then you wouldn't mind helping us."

The mage straightened. "Of course."

"Keep an eye on your squad, and the others if you get a chance." I cleared my throat a bit too loudly as the silence in the room grew. "We were hoping you could report any oddities while we're here. Anyone acting strange now that the keep is under investigation."

"We could use an extra pair of eyes to keep watch from the inside. Someone loyal to the Crown that's not in a position of command. And while *I* don't find your infatuation with my wife particularly charming, I know I can trust you to keep her requests."

"*Infatuation?*" Ian's eyes were wide.

I shot Darren a glare and then looked at the older boy. "He didn't mean anything."

"I know why you took up station at the keep." Darren narrowed his gaze on the rebel. "Don't do me the disservice of a lie, Ian. I'm not that gullible, and you aren't that thick-headed."

"*Darren!*"

"I'm not—"

"I always thought you were the better man, but it appears it was just an act." The prince didn't look upset, just amused. "Not that I blame you. I would have done the same." His laugh was dry. "And I did. Regardless, I trust your love for my wife outweighs your hatred of me, in this assignment at least."

The incredulous—and confused—expression on the mage's face would have been laughable in any other situation. When Ian finally looked back at the prince and me, he was fighting to keep a contrite expression as he said solemnly, "I would be happy to help."

"Good. Then our time here is done. Let's not share in more of this awkward moment than we have to." The prince stretched his arm out to the door, his motion unmistakable.

Ian rolled his shoulders and shot me a look that said *we have some things to discuss*.

I shook my head ever so slightly. If my plan was to work, he would have to rely on Nyx. I couldn't afford to explain myself; Ian would just have to trust I knew what I was doing.

Darren would question any time I spent alone with my former... friend.

The rest of the day was spent in quick succession. Darren had the names of those he had most reason to suspect, and if someone didn't draw his attention, he preferred not to drag out their interrogation. Occasionally, I would fixate on a minuscule detail and lure Darren's attention away from the oddities of others. It didn't always work, but Darren wasn't suspicious. He believed I was like him, overly cautious rather than ignorant.

We went through half of Sir Gavin's squad the first day alone. By the time we finally arrived at the dining hall for our last meal, we were dragging our feet and rubbing the creases of our eyes just to stay alert. Interrogation brought a different sort of fatigue than our training and patrols.

I hardly paid attention to the stares the rest of the room was shooting us. The five units that were on reprieve for the next week had made it a point to sit as far away from the Black Mage as possible. Even Ian was avoiding our table when we finally took our seats, but that was expected.

I kept my head down, not wanting to meet any curious eyes.

Darren covered my hand with his. "Is it hard to be back, Ryiah? When your brother..." He paused. "When Derrick sent me a letter petitioning a position in the palace, he said you had a falling out with your squad before you left. He felt responsible."

I was too afraid my expression would somehow give away the truth. It was harder to lie when I felt the unspoken questions filling every corner of the room, pressing in against my skin. Stifling and hot, the lies were as dense as syrup and just as thick. So many half-truths were dancing across my tongue, and I didn't want to lie. Not again.

"It wasn't their fault." I gave the prince a weak smile. "I was distant. The others didn't like it."

"They were a bunch of outspoken vagrants." Paige's drawl came from my left. She was sawing into her roast with a vengeance. "You were better than the lot of them, my lady, and they promoted Ray instead."

Darren cocked his head to the side. "You never said a word."

"There was nothing to say." I silently cursed Paige for bringing it up. And the worst part was I found it endearing that she cared enough to still be angry on my behalf—even if it was drawing the prince's attention to things best left alone. "They knew I would leave the keep at the end of my year. Ray intended to remain. It made sense that they would give the position to someone who would stay."

Paige snorted skeptically. "You didn't believe that last year."

Because I knew Ian should have been promoted before Ray if that were the case. I just shook my head and forced a laugh. "I've had a year to reflect."

"I still think they are idiots." My guard speared a potato with rosemary and lifted it to the air, swinging it violently as she declared, "You proved yourself during the Candidacy. Mark my words, they are regretting it now."

Darren gave her a curious look. "I had no idea you were so sympathetic, Paige."

"I'm not. I just don't like fools."

The corner of his lip turned up. "Fair enough."

Thankfully, the conversation took another turn as some of the guards began to exchange stories of my knight when she was a squire. I was grateful for the change in topic. Paige was far too observant for her own good. It wouldn't do for her to renew Darren's suspicions when we were halfway through Gavin's men. I couldn't let him suspect they were hiding something.

Not for the first time, I wondered where my guard's loyalties would lie. But, like Darren, I knew I couldn't put her devotion to the test. I was trapped lying to the two people I was closest to, and it was eating me alive.

I could only hope Nyx had a clever plan for her rebel "reveal." It would take a lot to fool the most intelligent warriors I knew.

* * *

The next day came and went. We made our way through the rest of Sir Gavin's squad. I hadn't expected the interrogations to last so long. After all, most of the men and women were innocent.

The second squad, on the other hand, was not. After the first three men and the head lady knight, it was clear Jinna's squad had a dramatically different air than the first. Nyx might have warned her people, but most were not used to hiding their allegiance after so many years in service. They weren't tasked to recruit with lies and a smile on their face. It worried me.

Luckily, Darren and the rest of our guards believed the growing tension a natural progression. "Nothing out of the norm," one of our knights had noted, "when one believes a traitor is in their midst."

It hadn't occurred to my party that the "traitor" was most of the keep.

Whenever we passed the men in the halls, they watched us with the wariness of the hunted. They were like a flock of tense birds.

Or coiled snakes ready to strike.

The sixth morning my worst fear came to pass.

"Neither of you noticed when a pack of thieves snuck in through the back of your camp and stole fifty pounds of medical supplies?" Darren's voice boomed across the dank dungeon walls.

Across the cell were two cowering soldiers. Sweat was pooling across the man's forehead and the other had trembling hands she shoved into the pits of her arms.

I already knew the truth. The rebels were building an army, and clever Nyx had found a way to make the Crown indirectly pay for it. All those years of missing supplies and armor—I had a strong feeling there were secret storerooms in the keep hoarding the very supplies in question.

I stood against the wall, watching my husband pace back and forth in front of the two guilty rebels, running his hand along his jaw as he glowered at them both. I knew Darren hadn't wanted to find a rebel. I knew he wanted his suspicion to be wrong.

"It was dusk, Your Highness."

"T-thought it was the horses acting up," the second stuttered.

"Your squad has suffered more losses in the last year than the others combined. *Three of those losses were suffered during your patrol!* Each time your reports explain those circumstances away, but you know what I think?" The prince took a menacing step forward, his eyes flashing crimson in the shadowy cells.

Which one did Nyx choose? I watched the young woman swallow, the lump in her throat rising and falling as the prince scrutinized them both. Both of Nyx's picks were doing a terrible job; were I in Darren's shoes, I wouldn't fail to suspect them both.

"I think the both of you are the worst soldiers in the land, or—" His move was so sudden. A flash of the Black Mage's hand and the two were slammed against the wall, clutching their throats against an invisible hand that held them in place, their brawny legs struggling in vain to reach the ground. I heard the panicked squeal of leather and metal as each fought their hold. "Or you are both cowards and liars and part of the rebel cause."

My heart jumped to my throat, the panic beating against my skin like quickening drums. I knew Nyx had instructed her rebel to put up a fight prior to confession, but it wasn't making this easier to watch.

This is the price of your lie, a part of me nagged. *Had you chosen to tell the prince the truth, none of this would come to pass.* I dug my nails into my arms and stilled, telling myself that the rebels knew what they were doing. They could brave Darren's attack—the Black Mage would never kill without a confession.

But why did there have to be a second rebel? I wasn't prepared to watch Darren hurt two.

The prince was too focused on scaring his prisoners to

notice my sharp intake of breath.

I couldn't watch Darren turn into his brother; I had to do something.

You think stopping him will solve anything? You hold your ground and let them give the prince a good show.

But that made Darren the villain.

I shoved my way forward, channeling my panic into fury as I grasped Darren's wrist. "Allow me?" My voice didn't waver at all, and for that I was grateful.

The Black Mage's casting faltered as Darren's gaze flitted to mine and then back to the two soldiers struggling for air. "Are you sure?" His question was rough, but I had seen the flare in his eyes. "I thought after your brother you wouldn't want—"

"You watch their reactions as I lead." I willed my words to steel and refused to look away, even as I heard the older knight and his retching gasps. "I'll give you a confession."

"Very well." The prince dropped his casting as the two crumbled to the floor.

I took a menacing step toward the prisoners. "The Black Mage won't hesitate to kill you both." I could feel Darren's eyes at my back; I prayed he didn't approach. "And neither will I."

"You t-two have…" The older man gasped for air as he crouched over the ground, kneeling. "…t-the wrong idea! It w-was an h-honest—"

"Don't lie to the Crown!" I grasped the collar of the soldier's tunic, dragging his ear to my mouth. *"Which one of you did Nyx send?"* My whispered words were followed with a heavy blow to his face. My fist stung from the impact.

The man screamed as blood spewed from his nose. It was the easiest bone to break. It was also the easiest to heal, or so Alex had always said. I prayed he was right.

"Let him be!" the woman cried.

"S'not us!" He choked.

Did Nyx really want them to put on a show? I had hoped the man would "betray" his comrade or confess. How long would we have to carry this out until Nyx's "traitor" confessed. How far would I be forced to go?

"Ryiah," Darren began.

"No!" I raised my hand to stop the prince from leaving his post. It needed to be me. I wasn't going to let their blood be on his hands.

"You can confess now," I warned my audience, "and stand a chance to live. But choose to wait it out, and I will not be so kind."

"We confess to nothing!" the woman shrieked. "Because we are not rebels!"

Nyx must have wanted more interrogation first. I swallowed bile back down. It was one thing to attack a perceived enemy on the battlefield; it was another to attack someone on the same side.

Magic shot out of my palm. Fire transformed into a whip of red that lashed across the woman's shoulder. The soldier howled and her skin bubbled as my fire ate away at flesh and singed cloth. The stink of burning flesh crowded the cell as I maintained the flames' hold.

With trembling fingers, I held onto the casting for another five seconds before letting go. "Still keeping to your lies?" I shouted to cover my shame. "And *you*!" I pointed my finger at the other man. "You want to watch your comrade die? You want to join her? I've got a whole batch of castings I've been waiting to use on your kind!"

The woman clutched her arm, shrieking her innocence as the male continued to protest their innocence. *Fools.* I ground my teeth and sent out my next casting: bolts of ice that buried into exposed flesh only to melt away and leave dripping wounds behind.

Still nothing.

Howls of agony filled the room as I grabbed a dagger out of my hilt and proceeded to stalk forward with rage. I didn't have to fake it—my fury at inflicting pain was enough.

I held the blade against the man's neck, letting its sharpened edge nick his skin. "Who did Nyx send?" I whispered.

The soldier looked at me with such hate I lost my breath. "I hope you rot in the darkest parts of the Realm of the Dead, choking on your own filth."

Don't just stand there. Darren will notice. "Confess!" I screamed.

He glowered at me, his eyes red and livid. "NOT US. NOT US. *NOT US!*"

I stumbled back.

Not us. His words... It wasn't an act.

The soldiers weren't the rebels Nyx had sent. Darren must have spotted an error in their documentation that Nyx's men had failed to catch before turning in their reports that first day we arrived. They were rebels, but not the right ones. *Not us.* Neither was the rebel Nyx had intended, the one with a story prepared, the one that knew what to say and when to break. The one that could lie, and lie *well*.

These two were in danger every moment they were here. If I didn't find a way to get them out, they might say the wrong thing. They couldn't confess. If they did, all of our plans would be ruined, and their stammering lies might lead Darren in a different direction than the one Nyx and I hoped. It could lead straight toward the keep, instead of away.

"Ryiah, do you need me to take over?" Darren had come forward at some point while I stood, hands limp at my sides. Horror flooded my chest.

What have I done?

"I don't think you're right." The words fell from my lips, barely more than a murmur.

The prince turned me around, pulling me away from the two bloodied soldiers. He kept his eyes locked on the two beyond as we moved to the other side of the room.

"Love," he said, "we've barely begun. I didn't expect them to confess this fast."

"No." My stomach churned with the realization of what we had started. I had let Darren... I had let me... A shiver ran straight down the base of my spine as a wash of ice flooded my veins. I had to stop this *now*. My grip on the prince's arm tightened. "Darren, we are wrong."

"How can you know?" His expression was sympathetic, but hard. His muscles tightened beneath my fingers, preparing to take over my task.

"I-I..." How could I even explain? I hadn't served on their squad. I couldn't shift the blame to Nyx's rebel because I didn't even know who she had prepared or if they were even in this squad.

"Ryiah, this is too hard for you. After Derrick, I can understand why it might be difficult to perform. We can get another guard to swap places with you, take a break from the interrogation before it gets worse."

Where is Nyx? How was she going to fix this? Did she even know? Darren had shown up that morning for the squad's interrogation without a word of what he had planned. No one had known, not even me, until he called these two inside and shown them the reports in his hand.

"It's not too hard. Just give me a moment—"

"Ryiah." Darren's tone had taken an edge. "You aren't ready for this. Go outside and get one of the other Combat mages to take your place."

"I'm staying." I didn't have a choice. I folded my arms against my chest. "Perhaps we should try questioning them one at a time." Anything to spread out the interrogation.

"These prisoners are trained soldiers. They have been hardened to pain. But no one is unbreakable."

"What about a hallucinogen?" I begged. It could buy us precious hours.

"I need them conscious. And with hallucinogens, I have no proof the Alchemy mage is not a part of the rebels' cause. Right now I only trust our own."

The prince pried my hand free as he started toward the two huddled soldiers. They were far from broken, but they had come into an interrogation expecting nothing more than a quick release.

I could only thank the gods they hadn't tried to fight back.

Darren pulled a dagger from a thin sheath at his waist. I had to think of something fast.

The papers! "Wait!"

The back of his neck twitched. "What is it, Ryiah?"

"The report! Let's discuss it with their squad leader and Nyx. They might be telling the truth or perhaps they can shed more light. If they find the activity suspicious, we can proceed—"

"I find it suspicious." Darren was irritated and had yet to turn back around. "Believe me, Ryiah, I spent hours studying those reports each night while you slept."

Even though I knew he didn't mean it, I still experienced a punch to the gut. A prince of the realm shouldn't be so restless each night that he studies scrolls to fall asleep.

Yet another way I had failed my husband.

But I couldn't fail him in this. I couldn't let him look back on this day later and hate himself. He could hate me all he wants after the truth was revealed.

"Please." I willed my voice to break, tears to well in the corner of my eyes. I was calling on every ounce of desperation and will. "Please, Darren, can we just check? I could never forgive myself if—"

"As you wish!" The prince's anger cut me off as he turned on his heel and stormed to the door, calling on two of our own to hold the soldiers until we returned.

"Are you coming, Ryiah?" he barked.

I scrambled after the prince, avoiding Paige's gaping stare as we entered the hall.

Darren began shouting summons for their leader and Nyx. The tension radiating from his shoulders could have cut the air like a knife; I felt the sting of it just racing to catch up.

I swallowed as I followed him through the winding

passages of the keep. I had just undermined the crown prince's control. He was the Black Mage, and I had just made him look weak in front of potential enemies of the Crown.

As soon as we were alone, Darren spoke without looking back. "Don't ever do that again."

He would never understand; he couldn't.

In minutes, we caught up with Sir Bolton and Commander Nyx. Both looked shaken, though they were doing their best to appear calm. Abrupt orders to meet in a situation like ours... The commander's eyes were wide as she addressed the prince.

"What is it, Your Highness? My men said it was urgent."

"We identified two of Bolton's men I believe to be rebels. We have them inside the cells for interrogation. They have yet to confess, but we thought it best to seek you out before continuing to much *crueler* methods." Darren managed to state the last line as if it were reasonable, instead of a direct insult of his skill.

"Dear gods, who are they?" Bolton interrupted. "Which of my men and how long—"

The commander's boot caught the man's shin before he could say anything else. Luckily, Darren was too busy producing the scrolls in hand.

Nyx kept a neutral face. "What is the report?"

"Three incidents of stolen supplies in the last year." Darren's voice was flat. "All with the same patrol. You can't tell me that is coincidence."

"I would be hard-pressed to doubt your theory, Your Highness." The commander cleared her throat as she continued to look over the papers. "However, I believe we are at fault... Sir Bolton, have a look and tell me if you see the same."

"Yes, ma'am." The lead knight took over the scrolls and feigned understanding. "Yes, yes, Commander, I believe you are correct."

"Do explain." Darren's tone had an impatient edge.

"The supplies were stolen, as reported, but the two soldiers in question are blameless." Nyx bowed her head. "The truth of the matter is I asked Mendel to omit the details of the report to spare Bolton's squad—and myself—the embarrassment. I feared the king might come to question my command if he saw them."

The prince's eyes narrowed to slits. "Why would the Crown be upset?"

"When you know what it is to lead, Your Highness, you view every loss as a reflection on yourself. An irrational fear, I suppose, but one I am guilty of all the same. I feared the Crown would see the circumstances—a sleeping draught—as a result of my negligence. One incident might have been forgivable, but three..."

Darren scowled. "A sleeping draught?"

"Bandits, perhaps they were rebels, drugged our supplies. When Mendel was writing up the report, Bolton thought it best to make the guards appear negligent and I agreed."

The knight expanded on Nyx's lie. "We didn't realize what was happening at first. Like you, I blamed my men and took away their privilege of drink... But after a second occurrence, I started to suspect something else. They hadn't touched ale in months, and still they had slept through a theft on duty." The knight adjusted his belt. "The two went a month without pay. But the third time it happened, one of the other guards had taken ill and foregone his evening meal. He noticed the unusual slumber—too early for most, it was barely dusk—of our *entire* squad during a run to the latrine, and while he was too late to prevent that final theft, a healer was able to confirm his suspicions. We've taken on a taster ever since, and the theft has stopped. I assure you, we will never be caught unawares again."

"Your men never mentioned this in questioning. They led me to believe it was their own negligence."

"Bolton's squad was given orders to never say a word."

Darren's jaw clenched. "Your orders to *spare your keep of embarrassment* almost cost two of your soldiers' lives. You didn't think to mention this little detail before you submitted your reports? Are there any other *omissions* you failed to mention before I consider another innocent man's life?"

"No, Your Highness." Nyx exhaled. "None that I am aware of."

"Good," the prince barked, "because this is not a good reflection on your command. Should it happen again, I will have no choice but to recommend a replacement."

Nyx hung her head as the knight shuffled his feet guiltily. I drew in a sharp breath, praying Nyx didn't miss anything more in her reports. If the Crown recommended someone else for command, their whole operation would be at risk.

"I understand."

Darren turned heel and stormed out the passage behind us.

I started after him.

"Ryiah." A rough hand caught my wrist.

I paused to look the commander in the eye.

"Thank you."

I tried to keep my anger at bay. "I can't do that again."

"I know." Her lips pressed into a thin line. "Two more days. I have the traitor on Sir Maxon's squad. We gave him time to prepare for interrogation. I thought it best for the rebel to be a man of Derrick's final squad, it'd be the easiest conclusion to draw."

"Who is it?"

"A young knight named Tallus. Recruited to the keep a year before last."

"How will I convince Darren?" I dug my heel into the dusty stone tile. "What proof can he offer?"

"Tallus will have an incriminating letter hidden in his personal cot. It will be up to you to lead the interrogation."

I started to turn and then paused, glancing back. "You will need two healers for the soldiers in that cell."

Nyx took a deep breath. "Yes, I will see to them right away... I'm so sorry."

"Not as sorry as them." I retreated back into the hall. *Not as sorry as me.*

FIVE

THE REST OF that day passed with the subtlety of a storm. Sir Bolton's squad was furious. After two healers carried out the two soldiers, squinty eyes and hard jaws promised a hate that would remain long after we were gone.

Our interrogations were filled with stony silence and little else. By the end of our second day, the exhaustion was palpable to all.

I wondered if any of the rebels believed Nyx's faith in my word. Either way, the grasp of peace was tenuous at best.

After that second night, Darren was quick to call a meeting with the rest of our own. "The distrust has shifted toward me. Keep your eyes open and your sword at hand at all times. I want everyone patrolling in pairs." His laugh was cold. "Until we discover the rebels, the men of the keep will continue to blame us for what transgressed with those soldiers. I'd love to direct them to their errant commander... But they prefer to fixate on their prince."

I reached out to Darren, but he jerked away from my hand. He didn't say anything in front of our audience, but his whole body was tense. The prince might blame Nyx, but he was still angry with me.

I shouldn't have questioned him in his role. *You didn't have a choice.* I bit my lip until I tasted blood. Everything was becoming a mess of lies, and with every passing hour, the temptation to confess was growing worse. The only thing that bought my silence was the knowledge that the true rebel would be arriving that next morning and that we would be able to leave this terrible masquerade as soon as he was caught.

"Did I tell you Alex and Ella joined the keep?" I was determined to break the uncomfortable silence that night as we lay down for bed. Darren had taken the last night to pacing like a caged lion, unwilling to look at me except for infrequent glances torn between exhaustion, gratitude, and frustration. I suspected a part of him was relieved I had called off his orders, but the stubborn bit of pride refused to admit it. He was proud to a fault.

"Oh." That was the length of his response.

"They joined after Derrick was caught. Alex wanted to find the rebel that recruited him. Like you, he suspected north. They are a part of Maxon's squad." The lie would go a long way to explain their presence. "I wish he wasn't here. I don't like him putting himself at risk for revenge."

"Well," the prince paused, "your brother might have more merit than I thought."

"I'm sorry I questioned your orders." My voice sunk to a whisper. "I only—"

"I don't want to talk about it, Ryiah."

"Why not?" I couldn't help myself. "You can't keep doing this. You have to let me in. If you are mad, then yell, but don't you dare shut me out." I was such a hypocrite, it was amazing the gods hadn't struck me down themselves, but I couldn't bear to watch Darren suffer alone.

The prince advanced on me, eyes flashing. "The Black Mage is not infallible. *Is that what you want to hear?"*

"Darren—"

"Imagine the worst mistake a person can make," he hissed. "Two lives, Ryiah. Two soldiers because I was so sure of myself. Do you have any idea what that kind of responsibility is like?" His bark of laughter was grating against my ears. *"Do you realize what I could have done?"*

I did, but he couldn't know the truth of Dastan Cove. Those three Caltothian warriors were my burden alone. I was carrying that guilt with every breath I took. I wanted to tell the broken prince it got easier if you screamed into the silence, but I still saw their ashen faces next to my brother every night I dreamt. There was no such thing as peace. "It wasn't your fault." *You were right to suspect those men. We tricked you.* The guilt was a festering plague in my chest. "Nyx was trying to do what she thought was best for her men—misguided, yes, but she truly thought a change in leadership, with the approaching war, would be a mistake."

"Had we time, I'd disown her of the position myself." The prince's fist found the wall, and I watched as he pulled it away, dripping blood. "As it stands, I believe her men would riot if I tried."

You wouldn't be wrong.

"Their loyalty is strange." He stared at the chamber door. "If I didn't know better, I'd suspect there was more to this keep than it seems."

I forced out a laugh. "Besides their united hatred of the Caltothians raiding their border?"

His brow furrowed. "I suppose—"

"I served at the keep for close to a year, and don't forget our apprenticeship." I stole a nearby tunic peeking out of a drawer, wrapping it around the prince's bloodied hand. This time he didn't jerk away. "The northerners look down on the south because of what they had to suffer. They can't understand your role. They don't know what it means to carry the weight of a country."

"And you do?" The words were softer, barely more than a murmur.

"I know what it means to be in love with someone who does." I pulled Darren toward the bed, promising myself I would pull back once that spark was gone, once those suspicions stopped dancing below the surface in those garnet eyes like tidal crashes of crimson in a darkening sea.

Two hands gripped my waist so hard it ached. I hadn't finished wrapping Darren's bandage; there was probably blood on the sheets, but I didn't care.

"I don't deserve you, Ryiah."

"You aren't the only one with darkness." I pressed my palm to the prince's chest. "I'm still fighting mine." *More than you can ever know.*

Understanding and shame lit up his garnet stare. He was remembering Derrick.

"I'd rather hear your angry words than watch you hide in pain." I touched the prince's face, tracing his jaw with my fingers, memorizing the strong lines that made up the man I love. "Nothing you could ever do would turn me away."

Darren caught my hand with his own, rough calluses enfolding my fingers in his. We were two warriors fighting for what we believed in and suffering our faults in silence. "Promise me the same."

Too late. I nodded, not trusting myself to speak, refusing to speak the betrayal aloud. I let the dark prince pull me into the crook of his arms, and as he fell asleep—for the first night in days—I spent the hours counting cracks in the walls and the lies drowning my heart.

* * *

My eyes were locked on the tree line ahead. I just barely made out a growing cloud of silver on the heady orange horizon. Chainmail glittered against the morning sun and crystalline white of snow. Winter had come early this year.

As the squad drew closer, my stomach twisted and turned. Would Alex look at me the same as before? Would I see the hate that had shattered my heart?

It turns out, I needn't have bothered.

"Ryiah!" My twin dismounted and ran the last twenty or so yards. Ice crunched under his heavy boots as he shoved past the rest of his squad.

I stood there, numb, as he pulled me into a giant embrace, crushing me against his chest. Alex smelled like iron and sweat—so different from before. When he released me a moment later, his gaze was earnest. I couldn't find a hint of that festering rage from before.

I knew it was all for the prince. Nyx had already sent envoys to warn Maxon's squad. But that didn't stop his smile from warming my chest.

"Ry! Ooompf!" A second set of arms locked around the

pair of us both. That reassuring voice had supported me every year of the apprenticeship. It was the voice of reason, one that promised not to take itself too seriously so long as I did the same. It was one of the best sounds in the world.

Ella's arms were draped in heavy furs. How could I have forgotten her distaste of the cold? Her black curls brushed my face as she leaned in close, enveloping us both. "I missed you—*we* missed you. So much."

I didn't bother to reply. I just stood there, holding on to that moment. I didn't want to let go. Letting go would mean it had passed, and I wasn't ready to give it up to the rest of the world.

"Ella. Alex." Darren was standing just behind us when we finally pulled away. I blinked back hasty tears, and for a second I could have sworn my twin did the same. "We missed you at our wedding."

Alex brushed his dirty palms on his shirt. "After what happened... I couldn't possibly return."

"She explained your reasons."

Alex shot me a look.

"You wanted to find the rebel who recruited Derrick," I said quickly.

Darren continued. "I can't say I wouldn't have done the same, were it Blayne."

"Your Highness," Sir Maxon, the leader of Derrick's former squad, stepped forward to introduce himself. "I understand you're investigating our keep for rebels. Nyx sent envoys prior to our arrival. May I offer up my own squad at your convenience?"

"And here I was just about to ask."

The man clasped the prince on the shoulder. "Think my men can grab a quick bite in the dining hall first? We rode most of the night."

"I'll join you." The prince followed the knight, and the rest of us trailed behind.

And so began the first hour of the end of our stay.

* * *

Make it look good. Make it real. Convince Darren. Try not to think about the blood. Tallus knows his role. Don't think about the pain you inflict. Think of how many his confession will save.

I backhanded the knight before using my other hand to pull him up by the collar of his shirt, rattling him against the bars. "Confess! Your comrades claim they saw you go off with Derrick alone. The innkeeper claims not to recognize your face. You were never playing cards. You were converting my brother and stealing supplies."

I raised my hand again, telling myself flesh was better than the blade.

"Ryiah!" Darren caught my fist, dragging me away from our chained prisoner. "What are you doing?"

"He's a rebel!" I was shrieking loud enough that our audience outside the chamber could hear. "Just look at him! This is the man that took my brother and made him one of *them*! Took him in with his lies and his status as a knight!" It hadn't been hard to steer the investigation and then take over when Tallus started to stammer over his words. It was surprisingly easy, the words flowed from my mouth like a script. A small part of me admitted this was the way I had longed to confront Nyx the day I arrived.

Make it as emotional as possible and he'll miss the lies beneath.

"He's a rebel!" My lungs expanded and contracted with the heavy intake of air. "I know it, Darren. Just *listen* to him. *Look* at him!"

"You don't want to make the same mistake as me." Darren locked his arms around me. "Love, I'm going to take over now."

"Don't you dare set him free!" I clutched Darren's arm.

"I promise this man will not leave the cell until I am thoroughly convinced—"

"Check his clothes. Check his belongings and his cot. Check his saddlebags! There has to be some proof. There has to be something to show!"

Darren's grip tightened on my wrist. "You have my promise, Ryiah, but I need you to wait. Do you think you can do this?"

I growled my reply. "If it is him, I want to be the one to wield the blade. For Derrick." I needed his promise now, before the truth was discovered. I needed to spare the prince this tainted act from his conscience.

"Is that what you really want?"

"It's the only thing I ask."

The prince nodded and then knocked on the prison door, summoning one of our men from the other side. "Check Tallus's belongings. Don't leave a boot unturned."

"Right away, Your Highness."

The prince closed the door and returned his gaze to Ferren's Keep's "only" rebel. "I hope for your sake my wife is wrong."

The knight lifted a bloodied chin, a red bruise already starting to swell across his right eye. "You won't find anything." The words were resolute and full of spite. "You are making a mistake."

Thirty minutes later, a knock sounded at the door.

"Your Highness, sewn into his pillow was a list. Your wife's brother is one of the names."

The prince turned to me. "Ryiah, I believe it is your turn."

In my hand, I produced a blade.

* * *

Tallus confessed after a long night in the cell. It was one I'd never get back.

"There are no rebels in the capital!" Darren paced the dungeon. "All of them were caught during the attack."

"That's only what they wish you to think." The man laughed, his whole body shaking violently against the corner of his cell as blood and saliva dripped down his face like a madman.

"Then tell me why they lie in wait. Tell me why they haven't made a move."

"They've been waiting for the Black Mage to leave," Tallus spat, "so the king is unprotected."

Darren charged the cell, and I snatched his arm before he could strangle the knight with his bare hands. "*You lie!* We have guards, hundreds—"

"Everyone knows the prince is hunting rebels north, even my leader in the south." Tallus broke into a vicious grin. His whole mouth was crimson. "They know the king is unprotected. All it will take is one—"

The knight broke into a cry as Darren's casting sent him

sprawling against the prison wall.

"Darren!" I jerked the boy around so he was forced to look me in the eyes, instead of at the man he was attempting to kill.

"He's talking about Blayne." Darren's eyes were wild and his nails were cutting into my arms. His pulse was beating wildly against his throat. "Ryiah, I—"

"We can't kill him. He can help identify the rebels in Devon." I took control of the situation, trying not to think of the man who had willingly suffered to help me perform this terrible lie. "We will send envoys right away. Your brother will be fine. Have Mira double the King's Regiment and call Marius back from the south."

I waited, feeling the grating pressure on my arms slacken. Then I addressed the prisoner. "You will reveal these rebels in exchange for your life."

The man said nothing, his chest rising and falling as he fought back the pain of his latest blow.

"We will grant you a king's pardon."

"Never!" Darren tugged away, fighting my grip, but I refused to budge.

"This man will never betray his own without it." My eyes were locked on his. "It may not be what you want, but surely one man's life for the king's safety is worth the price of revenge."

"Fine." The prince bit out the word and crooked his neck to glare at Tallus over my shoulder. "We grant you this, *traitor*, but if you fail to comply, you will be strung from the palace rafters like your brethren."

It took every bit of resolve I had not to react to Darren's

threat. It was impossible not to remember Derrick.

"Yes." The knight took a retching breath and forced his words into a command of his own. "But I will not say a word until the document is signed."

Darren said nothing. Instead, he marched to the other side of the room and began shoving reports into a file. I had a feeling he wouldn't sleep at all that night—he'd be studying those papers, searching for anything missed.

In a way, our reactions were one and the same. The things I did tonight, they would haunt my sleep for years to come.

When my twin finally arrived as part of the healers to clean up the mess, we could finally leave. Darren wasted no time in taking off.

Paige remained behind with me. I prepared for the look of outrage when Alex took in the scene before us—a beaten knight and the sister with his blood coating her fists.

Even Paige had to flinch and look away.

But all I saw was grief when Alex's gaze met my own. And pity. He didn't say anything as Paige stood nearby, supervising the healing. We needed the rebel "fit to travel but nothing more." My twin's expression was far better than I deserved.

I wondered what he would say now that he could see the price of my choice, the price of *all* of our choices in siding with the rebel cause.

I waited until Nyx knocked on the door, conferring the results of that night's interrogation and distracting Paige for the moment I needed. "I am..." My breath hitched and I couldn't speak.

The knight shifted against my brother's casting, and his

fingers touched my wrist. I started against the movement, and my eyes shot to Tallus's face.

"D-don't b-be s-sorry." The words were crumbled and bare. "S-save u-us a-all."

My brother placed his hand on top of Tallus's and my own. "You aren't alone." His gaze conveyed everything he was too afraid to speak aloud.

I swallowed, my throat raw. My eyes stung from fighting so many tears. When did I become the villain of my own tale? Why should anyone place so much faith in a girl as flawed as me?

"I promise." Could I honor that vow? Or would it—and all our dreams—go up in smoke the moment the lies fell away?

SIX

"IT SHOULDN'T BE you." Ella's beautiful face was splotchy and stained. *"It shouldn't be you, Ry."*

Darren and the rest of our guards were waiting by the horses while I said my good-byes. Alex stood next to his wife, clenching and unclenching his fists. He refused to say anything. He just gripped me tightly, his heart beating heavily against my own. Now that the rebel was healed enough to make the two-week trek to the palace, the Black Mage's procession would be on its way.

I knew Alex regretted how fast things had come to an end and that he wanted to say more, do more—*make amends*. We'd shared two meals since Sir Maxon's squad arrived, a bit of venison stew and then cold porridge the following morning, but there had been no opportunity to slip away. Not after Tallus. And now I was leaving. If looks could convey a word, then there was a story writing itself.

Some foolhardy part of me had hoped, upon hearing Darren's plan for the keep weeks back at the palace, that I'd have the entire stay with my twin and his wife. But fate had a mind of its own.

So many tiny details were at play, and I knew it would be

selfish to prolong a visit when the Pythian ships were closer to reaching our shores with every day that passed.

No, now I needed to focus on Tallus's escape.

* * *

Freezing rain turned the entire mountain to slush. Snow melted away, leaving behind dark puddles and patches of ice. Mud splattered against our horses' hooves, a splish-splash as the procession crawled up and down steep switchbacks on an ever-winding trail buried knee-deep in pine.

I couldn't ask for better circumstances if I tried.

Storm clouds continued to roll across the cold winterscape, turning day into night and night into black. Thunder rolled in the background like the gods' angry roar.

A couple more hours and we were forced to dismount and carry on by foot. Even war steeds weren't immune to lightning, much less pelting hail and a slippery slope that grew worse with each step we took.

Eventually we were forced to make camp, several hours ahead of schedule, to wait out the worst of the storm. The King's Road was adjacent to a meandering stream, one that had turned into a coursing river within the span of a day. It was a good source to wash in during the summer, but the current now was strong enough to overtake a man.

The group of us sat huddled around a hissing fire—it only held against sleet thanks to an alchemy potion that kept wood dry.

"Here." Paige handed me an empty mug so she could pour steaming cider from a hot kettle nearby.

"Thanks." I shot the knight a grateful smile before

blowing on the steam and curling my fingers around its heat. The rest of our group was busy in conversation and Paige was never one for talk. Right this moment, neither was I. I was counting down the minutes, waiting for the moment my plan took effect.

"Do you think I should offer some to *him*?" The girl's lips curled as her gaze slipped to Tallus, bound and gagged at the edge of our camp. "That filth that calls himself a knight."

I flinched and made myself look away, focusing on Hadley, one of the mages who was preparing our dinner of dried herbs and hare stew. "He's cold like the rest of us."

"Humph."

"It might prove useful if the prisoner doesn't freeze. We need him alive."

My guard grumbled as she poured another cup, cursing as she dripped hot liquid on her wrist, and walked over to Tallus with barely restrained disgust.

The only thing that spared Tallus of the fists of our party was the information he carried.

Two more hours, three at most. I made myself get up and join Hadley at the fire.

"Let me take over. I cooked plenty of meals for camp during the apprenticeship. You deserve a break."

The Combat mage gave me a small smile. "It's no bother. Cooking gives me something to do with my hands, and I'm never cold here."

"Paige has a kettle of hot cider there." I pointed to the second fire. "And truly," I lowered my voice to convey my request, "I need a distraction. Thinking about that rebel after my brother…"

"Say no more." The woman laid her rough hand on my shoulder and squeezed. "I will make myself scarce. Call on me if you need help."

"I will." I gave her an appreciative nod as the mage left me to fix the meal on my own.

No one noticed minutes later when the contents of two waxen green bottles slipped into the rabbit stew. They were from Nyx's inventory at the keep. Certainly no one cared that the prisoner was refusing to eat.

"Did you do something different?" Darren poked at his bowl, his nose wrinkled in distaste.

I shrugged. "I followed the same recipe as Hadley. Why?"

"It tastes…" Paige frowned as she dug into her own and took a big swallow, making a face as she chewed. "Strange."

"Strange can be good."

"Not as my dinner." Darren attempted another spoon, cringing as he swallowed. "Something must have been rotten. Or some mice got into the packs."

"If I get sick," Paige looked me in the eye, "the gods won't be able to spare you my wrath."

"I ate it too."

"Where is your bowl?" Darren stared at my hands folded in my empty lap. "Ryiah, even if you don't like your own cooking, you need to keep up your strength."

"I already ate." Lie. "And I didn't taste anything strange."

"Ryiah, this stew is terrible!" one of the Combat mages started to laugh. "What did you do?"

Another followed. "I wouldn't feed this to the palace hounds."

"Leave her alone," Hadley was the only one to speak up

in my defense.

"Gods, I would take the slops those mutts are given over this."

"See?" Darren's lips twitched in a smile. "We aren't the only ones."

I drew myself up, feigning upset. "I tried to do something nice. Remind me not to offer again!"

"Don't bristle at us." Paige rolled her eyes. "We were only teasing."

"Ryiah," Darren began, "we didn't mean—"

"All I wanted was a distraction!" I raised my voice into hysterics, hating this ploy but knowing I needed to act it out all the same. "Three days I've been forced to pretend the traitor who recruited my brother isn't standing three yards away, set to live for a crime my brother never could!"

Before Darren or Paige could say a word, I stomped over to the other side of camp, splattering mud against my heavy cloak and entering the royal tent. I waited for my husband to follow me inside.

Sure enough, Darren appeared moments later, rainwater dripping from his hair and lashes.

"I'm sorry." The prince's eyes sought my face; they were filled with shame. "I didn't stop to think what this might be like for you. You've been so...." The prince took a step closer and cursed as his boot caught on the bottom of the tent's flap. "Sstrong through all of thisss." Darren made a face as he tried the words again, only to slur once more. "I f-forgotttt—"

The prince slumped forward, and I caught him in my arms.

I slowly transferred Darren to the ground and wrapped him in heavy furs.

Don't. Don't you dare think about what you've just done to the boy you claim to love.

The sleeping draught had hit just in time. The Black Mage was fast asleep, and when he awoke, his last memory would be my barely restrained outrage over the rebel's life. The whole camp would remember that rage. I would never be a suspect in Tallus's escape.

I brushed away Darren's choppy bangs and pressed my lips to his forehead. "I'm sorry." They were the words I could never say to him before, and it felt so good to say them now. "I'm sorry for everything."

* * *

I waited until the murmur of voices died down and there was only the patter of rain. Then I tiptoed back into the center of our camp, taking care to duck around trees just in case someone was still awake.

No one was.

Twenty knights and mages were sprawled across the camp's floor. Twenty of the Crown's best unaware of the true traitor in their midst.

I ran forward to adjust Hadley so that she could breathe easier from her position on the ground. I felt guilty while thinking of my comrades—my friends—left out in the pouring rain to freeze, but I couldn't draw suspicion by dragging them all under cover. Paige and Henry were clustered together on the ground, drawn swords scattered close by. *They caught on faster than the rest.*

I made one final scan of the scene before hurrying over to

Tallus.

"Thank the g-gods." The man's breath was coming out in white puffs of air, his limbs shaking from the cold. Someone had taken his blanket away after I'd left, probably because of my scene. I bit back a groan. *The price of my speech.*

"Here." I slashed at his bonds with a cooking knife before tossing it to the ground. I couldn't let anyone think he'd gotten free through magic.

"We need some of my blood on those ropes," the knight croaked. "No one will believe I escaped that easily."

"I'm not letting you take any more injuries." I grabbed the knife, but Tallus snatched it away, his reflexes surprisingly fast.

His expression was sad. "It has to be me. You can't awake with new injuries. They would know something was wrong."

I ground my teeth and looked away as the knight let out a low grunt while cutting into his palm and then pressing it against the rope's end. *You know he's right. You need to focus on what comes next.*

"You have two hours, three if we're lucky."

"Only three?"

"The stew diluted the potion's effects, but it was too risky to drug the ale. Most only took a bite or two at most." I flushed in the dark. "It wasn't a pleasant aftertaste."

The knight studied the range behind us. "Nyx stocked a hideout for me a day's ride north from here. Enough supplies for a month."

"We need to get out of here now. Don't worry about covering your trail. I'll do it on my way back." I tossed the knight some bandages from my saddle pack. "Wrap your hands."

Tallus opened his mouth, his question already on my mind—

I cut Paige's mare loose and watched her flee south. My guard would kill me if she ever found out.

"We're going on foot." Tallus needed as many distractions as two hours could buy. "When they try to decide which path you took, Darren will assume you've fled south to the rebel base after he tracks those prints."

The prince wouldn't want to waste time combing the forest when his brother's life was at stake. He would send others later after he was back with the king, but by then Tallus would be long gone north.

The knight swallowed heavily. "Thank you, princess."

"I'm one of you first." *Darren would never have made me his wife if he knew.*

I gripped the knight's waist as we started forward, using my other hand to cast a light. A day in the prison and three days of travel with old injuries hadn't helped, even prepared as Tallus was.

"Tallus..." I cleared my throat and squinted up through the pouring rain at the man who had braved so much for his cause. We had walked an hour together, and as much as it pained me, I had to turn around. Any more time would jeopardize our cause.

The knight didn't regard me with disdain, but I wouldn't have blamed him if he did. After all, I subjected him to that night in the dungeon. "Your sacrifice won't be for nothing. I promise."

"Derrick was—" Tallus's voice cracked, "—a great friend

of mine. I volunteered for this role."

I never knew. I opened and shut my mouth, finding no words.

"It is an honor to help the sister he cherished so much."

Breathe. My hand shot to my throat and the leather cord hanging just beneath my cloak.

Tallus didn't leave time for a reply. The knight had already turned back, a limping shadow against a mountain of black.

I shut my eyes and took a deep, steadying breath. But it didn't work.

All I could see was Derrick. My little brother, the bravest of us all. And I had left him to suffer alone.

I saw his angry face yelling at me in the palace cell.

And then I saw the final night. Jacob thrusting Derrick before me, crippled and hopeless, waiting for his older sister to take his life. Waiting for me to betray him.

I slumped to my knees.

Tallus's words entered my heart. *The sister he cherished so much.*

Salty tears mixed in with icy sleet as the howling wind took control of my hair, whipping locks of scarlet against wind-chapped lips and a breaking heart. I reached up to clutch my brother's ring through my cloak, holding on to the copper circlet like it was Derrick's hand instead.

I won't let you down again.

* * *

An hour later, I sprinted into camp, soaked to the bone. Raw magic danced out scattering the last foliage on the ground.I prayed that what my casting would be enough to mask Tallus's trail.

It was another reason I had chosen night. It was harder to track.

In minutes, I was sliding into the tent, discarding my cloak, and drying my hair before feigning sleep beside the prince.

Ten minutes later, the first person awoke.

"Darren! Ryiah!"

The prince stirred once, and then his head fell back to the side.

"Your Highness!"

Darren shot up at the same time as me. His head crashed into my chin. I fell back, tasting blood as the prince placed a hand to his head, wincing. "Paige? What is it?"

"The rebel escaped—"

"What?"

"He—"

Darren staggered out of the tent, shoving his feet into boots and shouting for the rest of our men before she could finish. "Henry! Markus! Landon!"

"Paige?" I groggily blinked my eyes and attempted to stand, falling back as if I were much weaker than the rest. "D-did you say the rebel es-escaped?"

"Must have slipped an elixir in our meal."

"M-my stew?" I groaned and reached for her shoulder. "The s-storm! The supplies were w-with Hadley."

"She was also in charge of transporting the rebel."

"The s-storm must have made it easy f-for him to slip it in t-the food."

"I don't know how he got it. We searched him thoroughly

before we left." The knight helped me up, her back tense. "The whole camp was out for hours after you left."

My heart caught in my lungs. "L-left?"

Paige raised a brow. "When you stormed off to your tent. The prince went after you, and then everyone started dropping at once. Do you remember anything at all?"

I shook my head, feigning ignorance. "I remember Darren a-and then he fell and I... I guess I must have drifted off too."

The two of us started toward the camp, Paige half-carrying me as I got back "control" of my limbs.

"I m-must have eaten too much."

Paige snorted. "At least now we know it wasn't your bad cooking."

"Hmmm."

"I'm sorry, my lady." Her serious tone returned as she addressed me directly. "Earlier I was out of place. I know how much this must upset you now that the rebel is loose."

I waved the knight's apology away, quickening our pace toward the others. Darren had already gathered everyone else by the horses; their voices grew loud as we approached.

Ten minutes later, we were pouring over a map of the territory.

As I had hoped, they had discovered the missing mare and drawn their own conclusions.

"We don't have time to debate the context of his escape!" Darren's voice rose above the storm, stunning the rest of our unit to silence. "Gods only know how many hours we lost already!"

"You think he'll try for the king?" One of the mages

folded his arms. "In that condition, he's hardly a threat, and we already sent out an envoy—"

"He has *my* horse and he's headed south!" Paige snapped. "If the rebel has any sense, he'll warn his comrades in the palace and take up in the desert with the rest of his traitorous kind."

"The rebels have managed to stay hidden for years. This man was our *one* chance." Darren fisted the map, the whites of his knuckles visible under the others' light. "I am not going to waste our time prowling the mountains in the middle of the night. That traitor is headed south."

I ducked my head as the others nodded along. I couldn't believe our luck. If Darren insisted no one remain behind, Tallus would have better odds than we hoped.

"Ryiah and I will return to the palace immediately with our guards."

"But the king's orders—"

"The Black Mage and his second-in-command are more than capable of taking care of themselves, contrary to my brother's opinion." Darren glowered at the knight who had spoken. "The rest of you are to scout every inch of the south. The minute I arrive in the capital, I will have more of the Crown's Army dispatched to help find that traitor while I investigate the palace. I'm not going to sacrifice our search for my 'protection.'" Ember flared in the crown prince's eyes. "If Blayne has a problem with it, he can take it up with me. You have ten minutes to pack up your gear and split into three parties."

"That thief stole my horse!" Paige stomped around our site, throwing her saddlebags against the ground ten minutes later. "That no good, piece of—"

In ordinary circumstances, I might have laughed. "You can ride with me."

"If I must." The knight grumbled as we finished loading my roan with supplies. "But no talking. We are hunting a rebel, my lady, not building a friendship."

"I would never dream of it." I yawned—this time from real fatigue—and swung up into the saddle, reaching for Paige.

My guard was too busy staring at a dark stain on the top of my boots.

The rebel's blood. I had been standing too close when he cut himself for the rope.

My heart pounded violently against my chest.

"When did you injure yourself, my lady?"

"Oh, that?" I laughed uncomfortably. "Must have cut myself when I..." When I did what? Paige was always nearby. "You know what? I think that might have been from the rabbits caught for the stew."

"So not old, then."

Was it just me, or did she sound suspicious? "Well, old as this evening."

Paige continued to stare at my boot.

"My lady and Paige." Henry's call rang out over the din of orders. "We are ready to head out."

Grateful for the interruption, I turned to Paige with a nervous grin. *Don't see my fear.* "Time to return to the palace."

The guard didn't say anything else as she helped herself into the saddle.

SEVEN

IT ONLY TOOK us eight days to reach the capital.

It took all of one breath to watch Darren race across the throne room to his brother. That twisting in my chest was a rising suffocation, and it was all I could do to stand there next to Paige pretending I was glad to see Blayne was still alive and well. I didn't want to see that young, proud king relaxing in his gilded chair with a healthy glow and that lying courtier's smile plastered to his face. I didn't like to see the way Darren's face lit up when he took in the same.

Seven nights of riding on and on, trading mounts at each inn we passed, only remaining long enough for a meal and an hour's sleep—two at most.

All because the Black Mage feared for his brother.

I tasted bile and made myself swallow. I should have been ecstatic—Tallus was safe, the keep's rebels were undiscovered, and, with our good time, I had an extra week to search the palace while Darren and the others inspected the Crown's guard. After all, every second counted now that the Pythians had officially set sail, and I only had three weeks before they would reach our shores.

"Ryiah…"

I glanced up to find Blayne beckoning me forward with the crook of a finger.

I approached and the king gave me a lazy smile, leaning back against his throne. "Well, you look a lot more like your usual self, sister dear. I must say the dresses never felt sincere."

I will never be your sister. My nails stabbed into my palms, and for a moment, I couldn't move, save for the rise and fall of my chest.

"Ryiah isn't a lady of court, brother. She's a war mage."

Darren's voice brought me back to the present. *Breathe.* Over a month away from the enemy and I'd forgotten what it felt like. If I didn't get control of my emotions, someone would notice—any of the guards or Mira who stood scrutinizing my appearance with a scowl. *Good to see you, too.* I looked up through sopping locks and pressed my lips into a shaken smile, listening to the drip, drip as slush collected on the tile beneath my boots. *Breathe.*

Now speak.

"Funny." My voice sounded strange even to my own ears, hoarse and too high. "I was going to say the same about you. Sitting on a throne while your brother and I protect the kingdom. Anything more would be off-putting."

Speaking such words at his father would have resulted in the guillotine, but Blayne was evil wrapped in grace. Verbal spars were nothing he couldn't handle.

"How I have missed your humor." The new king narrowed his gaze, fingers tapping loudly against his armrest. "And yet my brother informs me that the rebel escaped. Right under your watch."

"He drugged our supplies—"

"Used in the meal *you* were cooking," Mira interrupted callously. "How convenient."

"Go ahead and say it. *I dare you!*" I started forward, but Paige jerked me back with a sharp tug on the wrist that stung.

I fought her grip, but the knight held me in restraint. "Don't bait her," she hissed.

Little did they know it was all for show.

I wrestled in the knight's grip for a moment longer, playing up the part while Darren bristled in my defense.

"Ryiah is the last person who would help a rebel escape, Mira. I had to tear her off the man during interrogations. Believe me, my wife would have liked nothing better than to slit the rebel's throat who recruited her brother to their cause."

"Who's to know he didn't recruit the whole family? Or did everyone forget the year Ryiah served at the keep alongside *both*?"

"I never met the man!" I spat. "He wasn't even on my squad!"

"Once again, a convenience!" the woman barked. "You are so full of excuses, and I, for one, am tired—"

"Enough."

The room fell to silence as Blayne shot up in his chair, his heavy cloak snapping against the legs of his chair. His expression had shot from amusement to distaste in the blink of an eye. Now his lips were thin and his words were cold.

"I am done listening to this never-ending spat. Mira, Ryiah has more than proven her loyalty to the Crown."

"But—"

"Not another word on the subject, not unless you wish to be replaced."

Mira's face darkened and her eyes sparked in outrage. When she looked at me, it was enough to peel flesh.

Why must you continue to bait her? I ground my teeth together. Mira was the chink in my armor, and I needed to hold my tongue. Blayne's reprimand would only make her obsession worse.

"And, Ryiah—"

My gaze went to the young king.

"I am tired of finding you in the middle of these investigations. Do us both a favor and make sure there is not another." Blayne heaved an irritated sigh. "Darren, what is being done about this runaway criminal? I assume you returned to keep watch over my court."

"I have the rest of our patrol combing the countryside. I'd like to dispatch some of Audric's men and send an envoy to Marius as well. Believe me"—Darren's tone was ominous—"that rebel's freedom will not last."

"Whatever it takes." Blayne's drawl was hard to miss. "After all this effort, I'd hate to find an angry band of vigilantes when we are already engaged in war."

"The rebel was injured, barely fit for travel, and he made his escape during the middle of winter." I made my scoff mocking. "The traitor is more likely to die from black frost than anything else."

"The true threat is here in the palace." Darren studied his brother's regiment with a frown. "What are the rest of you doing to root out the traitors?"

Mira balked. "We had a thorough investigation of the entire staff after your envoy arrived. I've seen to every one of them myself. Your rebel must have been lying."

"Or perhaps you aren't doing your job, *mage*." Darren's retort was biting. "This is your king's life at stake. And you have already proven that your loyalty to the Crown doesn't amount to much. Or did you forget you were so willing to sacrifice a prince of Jerar in Dastan's Cove?"

"I…" Mira paled and I saw her eyes dart to Blayne and then jump to the floor. *I knew it!* "T-that wasn't my call, Y-Your Highness."

The king cleared his throat, and I knew it wasn't my imagination when Blayne's expression turned a bit *too* confused as he addressed the accusation. "What is this?"

"Port Langli's regiment was deployed during my apprenticeship. *Mira* was more than ready to leave Ryiah and me behind under the guise that her mission was more important." Darren frowned. "Father couldn't even recall the prisoner when I asked him about it a year later."

My gaze was locked on the king. Three of us knew the truth, and I wondered if Blayne would betray his loyal guard to appease his brother's suspicion.

Blayne tapped against his wrist, his fingers increasingly erratic.

Oh villainous king, how will you free yourself from this lie? I sucked in a breath, waiting.

"I overheard Lucius's orders. Mira is innocent."

"What?"

Blayne folded his arms and stood a bit straighter. "Father wanted that Caltothian wench at all costs, brother. Even if it meant your life."

"Y-you heard him?" Darren had gone as pale as ash. My fingers shot to his, and he jerked back, away from his brother and the room.

"Father wanted you to take part in the mission. Who do you think suggested the contest for a Combat apprentice in the first place?" Blayne's explanation was heartless. "You always were the best. He didn't want anything to happen, but if it did..."

"A prince's life is grounds for war." The words fell from the Black Mage's lips without emotion, hollow and hoarse. "They were on orders to leave you behind."

"Why?" Darren's voice broke. "Why would he—"

"Caltoth is merciless. You know that. Father was willing to sacrifice whatever it took." The king plunged his lie like a dagger to the heart, twisting and turning until all that was left were his brother's shattered remains. "You might have been the favorite, Darren, but a second-born son doesn't amount to much. You were more valuable as a tool of war."

Darren's eyes fell shut as his breathing stilled. I saw that broken prince on the cliff. I saw the boy ready to slip away, running from a monster I couldn't fight. I stood there watching Blayne, hating him so much and wondering how I could just stand there as the traitorous wife, biding my time when there was someone laced with so much poison he was destroying the very air we breathed.

Even though Blayne was lying about the king's orders, his explanation rang true. Everything the king said was the justification *he* had used to secure his own reign. Blayne might love his brother, but he was willing to sacrifice him for the cause.

And yet here I was, willing to do—in some ways—exactly the same.

I wondered if the attack during our time at the keep had been a coincidence after all.

What kind of person was willing to sacrifice the one person they loved?

I am not Blayne. My hands locked to fists. Blayne was much more than his abusive father. His motive was still war, greed, and control.

My motive was everyone else.

I couldn't give in now. This wasn't about my guilty conscience or the villain in the room or the boy who would shatter when it all came to light.

To be the hero, I had to be the villain… I wondered if, at some point, the tyrant before me had considered himself the same.

I wanted an answer.

I wanted the gods to reach out and tell me the path to take. I wanted them to tell me why it had to be me, him, and his brother. I wanted to know why this was our story instead of another's.

I prayed to the gods that night.

They never answered.

* * *

Over breakfast the next morning, Darren was granted permission to question the palace staff. Blayne made it clear he viewed the practice a waste of his Black Mage's time, but he'd relented all the same.

The catch, of course, was that Mira would take part in his

discourse and lead the supposed investigation. "Since she already interrogated all of our staff, she will be invaluable in your search."

I suspected the gesture was in large part due to other secrets the king didn't want to come to light by questioning the servants who were involved in his nefarious dealings. They hid bits and pieces of information that could point out inconsistencies in his tales and might lead the Black Mage to question the past, which was just what I needed to collect.

Meanwhile, I'd been granted a temporary elevation in the palace regiment, serving Mira's role until she and the prince were done with their false hunt.

I couldn't have asked for better fortune if I tried. Mira was busy trailing Darren across the palace, and that left me free to roam the remainder, relatively unwatched. If anyone asked, I was checking up on the rest of the guard, the same as Mira was known to do when she was leading the role. Blayne even gave me an approving nod on the third night when he asked what I thought of the palace patrols.

I made it a point to praise the changes in place, insisting there was no way a rebel could ever breach their new defense. That part was true. The regiment had taken on stricter measures and the men were held to a higher standard after Derrick. Shifts were shorter. Previous patrols containing one guard had been replaced with two. More mages had been transferred in from the Crown's Army.

Now there were just as many Combat mages as knights. Soldiers previously serving the courtyard guard had been transferred out so that mages could take their place. Not one of the new recruits had less than ten years serving major ports or cities across Jerar.

Every single member of the palace's reformed regiment was the best of their year.

All of the changes would have made any commander proud. The castle was a fortified stronghold. I hadn't paid attention after the incident with Derrick, but I noticed now. Darren and Mira had been busy while I was holed up in mourning, and I was struck by how fortunate the rebels were that I had come across the truth after all. The castle would be impossible to access now.

Not without an all-out war. And though the rebels' number was far greater than the rest of the country believed, it still wasn't enough. We had three thousand or so north, thanks to the keep and some of the soldiers serving bordering villages, and a couple hundred hidden among the main outposts of the south. Even with the backing of six thousand from the Caltothian army, our number was still a far cry from the twenty thousand of the Crown's Army, the fifteen hundred of the King's Regiment, and all the major city regiments. The rebels were mostly made up of lowborn soldiers, which meant they were severely lacking in mages and knights, something the Crown was not.

I just need to find proof. But every stone I turned came up clean. As that first week drew to a close, the panic set in. There were six more days before we set forth to Langli to greet the Pythian warships, and I needed something of value. I needed to find it *now*. Nyx's words played over and over as the hours ticked by: *"The Pythians might not be swayed by justice. Promise them whatever it takes."*

What could I promise that Blayne could not? The only

thing I had to offer was evidence of his deceit, and the chance of finding such proof was growing slim.

That wasn't my only concern.

At any moment, Darren's investigations would draw to a close and Mira's shrewd gaze would fall back to me. Then I'd be stuck guarding the Council chambers with another where any deviation would be reported back to the one person who would jump at the chance to try me for the same crimes as my brother.

My careful searches grew increasingly frantic. I stopped caring which explanation to offer when someone asked. I was the head mage of the regiment for the time being, and I was ready to abuse that power for all it was worth. I'd inspected every surface lining the Crown and Council chambers, every scroll tucked into place, every cushion left unturned, every nook and cranny in most of the castle storerooms.

By the tenth day, I had breached most chambers, save the king's quarters and the palace barracks, the latter of which was never empty enough to escape notice, and the former required an explanation I could not offer.

I continued to circle back to the Crown hall at the end of each long day. A part of me had known it would always come back to this, that anything I needed would be in the king's quarters. I doubted Blayne was fool enough to hide incriminating evidence among his men.

"Neither of their highnesses have returned."

I didn't flinch as I looked to Conrad, one of the four guards standing at attention in front of the very wing I needed to inspect. There was no chance I could enter the wrong chamber unnoticed. If it were just the old man, perhaps, but all four guards were Mira's hand-selected recruits. Knowing her, she had probably told them to pay *extra* attention to "the sister of the rebel," princess or not.

"Thank you. I wasn't sure if they had." There was no point in pretending I needed my shared chamber with the prince.

"Mira was looking for you." The head guard scratched at his beard, his expression kinder than the others. I suspected he took pity on the lowborn girl who was the subject of the head mage's wrath. We'd been on friendly terms before Mira had taken up her role in the palace. "She said to tell you their investigations are over and you are to report to the Council hall for your regular post starting at dawn."

Inside, my chest withered away at the news. My time was up. Ten days and I had nothing to show for the effort. I was a master at plans and a failure at action.

"Tell her I will be thrilled to put my talents to use guarding an empty room."

One of the others chuckled, quickly muffling their snort with a cough.

"The prince is in the practice courts with the king."

"*With* the king?" I was sure I had misheard.

"His majesty might not share his brother's propensity for magic, but I say he isn't the worst I've ever seen with a sword."

"He trains?"

"Not as often as the regiment, mind you, but he does join on occasion." The man brushed absently at his tunic. "He took it up after the prince left for the Academy. My own boys would rather quarrel than spend an hour in one another's company, but that is not these brothers' case."

I wished it was. I wasn't thrilled to hear Blayne could fence, even less so that he had taken it up to impress Darren. The more time those two spent together, the stronger the bond... and it would be that much harder to convince Darren his brother was a heartless dictator when the time came.

"How—" There was acid on my tongue; I made myself swallow. "—touching."

"Are you planning on joining them?" One of the guards looked on eagerly. "Our shift is almost up. It's not often one gets to see the whole of the Crown duel."

If you stick around long enough, you might get the chance. I shook my head, wisely choosing to not speak that last thought aloud.

"Very well, Your Highness." The older knight gave me a parting nod.

I started to walk past, only to pause in afterthought. My stomach twisted. "Conrad?"

"Yes?" The guard gave me a surprised cough; I could tell he hadn't expected me to remember his name from before.

"No 'highness.' It's just Ryiah, please."

"Very well, your—that is to say—Ryiah."

"Thank you."

I turned a key to my chamber lock, twisting it so hard it hurt.

I was a mage and a girl, and that was all I would ever be. Anything else was a lie.

* * *

"Don't drop that shield. It should be an extension of your

arm, my lady."

I glowered at my guard as we switched positions. We'd been dueling like this for an hour. Originally it had been my idea—a way to distract from the last week and a half of fruitless searching in the palace—but now I was regretting it. Paige was more critical than any of my training masters when we practiced.

I wanted a quick victory, but Paige was determined to make me work for it.

I'd neglected my training for most of a month, and it showed a bit too well when matched against a knight without magic.

"You can't be mortal." My teeth gritted against the effort to hold the shield level with my chest. "These weigh at least double the regiment standard."

"Crown issue or not—" Paige met my sword, side-stepping with impossible ease. "—that's no excuse to neglect your training."

"I'm not." I lunged forward again with a thrust of the sword.

The knight parried my cut. There was the loud clang of metal on metal, and we drew apart. "You are. You do half the strengthening routines you should."

"Not all of us are built with the arms of a bloody mule." I exhaled, darting left. "And I'll have you know, I do the best I—"

"She's too used to employing her magic in the lift." Darren's voice rang outside the barracks' outdoor arena; his chuckle grew louder on approach. There was the shift of worn leather against snow and then his voice rang out from the stands with a laugh. "Sorry, love."

"Traitors." I scowled at my guard and husband as they exchanged smirks. "The both of you."

I needed a victory, and instead, I was getting a lesson in humility. Frustration sang out beneath burning veins. *I needed this.*

Paige and I circled one another for the hundredth time that afternoon, and I could feel every inch of magic throbbing just underneath my skin. I ignored it the best I could; they were right, of course. I had grown too complacent in my training, relying on magic more and more to make up for variances in strength.

Ever since the Candidacy, I had fallen behind. First from jealousy, then in mourning, and most lately from a lack of caring. Darren was the Black Mage, and I was just the girl trailing behind. What did it matter whether I continued to be second best?

All that hard work and where had it gotten me?

Deep down, there was a truth plaguing my heart, but I was not about to face it now. Instead, I threw myself into the duel. I shut out emotion and breathed the adrenaline, feeling the surge of blood and heat as my aching muscles warmed to the familiar drill at hand.

Paige was an excellent swordswoman, but I hadn't spent the whole of my training on casting alone. There was a reason mages were considered elite warriors, even without their magic. Years of training had given me a reason to brush past the pain, to push myself where others might have quit.

Five more minutes passed.

And then finally I caught a break.

Our swords shattered on impact, shards of metal in a flurry of silver as the two of us ducked and tumbled to the ground. I didn't have a moment to recover; it was Paige's brawny arms against mine. The two of us locked in a hold that only one could win.

The snow was icy cold, biting into my skin even with the tunic and vest. Everything was slippery and wet.

My limbs quivered, I could feel that familiar quake in my arms. Another minute and I would give under the strength of her weight. I was helpless and I hated it. I was so sick of losing.

"Surrender?"

For a moment, I stopped seeing my friend. I saw Blayne's hands pinning me in place. A cruel smile played across pale lips as he tilted my head, forcing me to watch as Derrick and his friend limped down the dark castle hall.

Mira appears, throwing her head back as she laughs. A flare of white lights up the room.

I writhe against the king's grip and my foot catches against a small catch in the tile. I throw my weight, everything I have, and roll hard. My right shoulder roars in protest and a white-hot pain tears up along my arm.

Suddenly the pain stops and the weight ceases.

Blayne slams against the marble. His head hits the floor with a crack, lolling to the side. A small trickle of scarlet puddles just underneath, staining the marble as I stare.

"Ryiah!" Two hands jerked me back. The biting pain returned as I fell into something wet and numbingly cold.

My vision blurred and I blinked rapidly, watching as the king dematerialized and my guard took his place. I wasn't in the palace hall; I was outside in the barracks' arena. I was sprawled back in the snow as Darren knelt in front of Paige, calling for help as blood seeped beneath her amber braid. Her eyes were shut and her chest was rapidly rising and falling beneath her vest.

"Paige..." My tongue was so heavy, the words faltered and fell. "I-is she g-going t-to—"

I blinked and a pair of healers were suddenly beside the prince, carefully using their hands to trace the knight's injuries. Their magic sparked a gentle green, slipping just under the skin as she groaned.

Darren took a step back and found his way to me. Dark hair fell across his face, making his eyes unreadable. "She'll be fine. Ryiah, you have to be more careful."

Even as the Restoration mages worked their magic, my eyes remained glued to the russet snow just beneath Paige's head. It was growing darker as I stared.

I couldn't believe what I had almost done. What I could have done, had Darren not pulled me away.

"I-I didn't m-mean..." I tried to sit up and a sharp pain flared, sending me back against the icy snow.

"You dislocated your shoulder." Darren's hand caught my wrist before I could try to move again. "You need to wait for a healer." The prince's voice lowered to almost a whisper. "What happened, Ryiah? One moment you were fine, and the next..." His breath rattled. "It was like you were a different person."

I could never tell the truth. "I wanted to win."

Darren made a frustrated sound through his teeth.

Better the prince thought me reckless than a girl driven by hate. I had stopped seeing my friend in that duel. All my helpless rage had channeled a manifestation of his brother instead. I'd been willing to kill.

I *would* have killed, had he not stopped me.

A palm pressed against the small of my back and my tongue rammed against my teeth. It was as if someone had taken a chain and twisted it around my ribs, squeezing until I couldn't breathe. Vaguely, I heard the prince thanking the healer as their casting began to knit itself under my skin.

"Your eyes—" Darren started and then stopped. I knew exactly what he was unable to say. Three months of carrying this horrible truth. It was a festering poison inside. It was making me helpless and angry and guilty and desperate.

It was making me a different person.

* * *

That night I found myself in the kennels.

Paige was recovering, taking the rest of the day to rest in the infirmary. I'd tried to apologize earlier, but she wouldn't have it.

"Why are you sorry?" she'd demanded. *"I didn't take that hit as I should. You're a warrior not a healer, stop coddling me."* She'd thrown me out with a stiff reprimand to stop "feeling sorry" for myself.

How could I tell her it wouldn't have mattered, that I wouldn't have stopped? That everyone needed to stop trusting me. I was a liar, and I was weak, and apparently all it would take was one moment of feeling helpless for me to hurt someone I cared about without a second thought.

I greeted the palace hounds, not caring as wafts of fur and slobber speckled my cloak. Wolf was at the front of their pack, caked in mud and skinny garden weeds, barking happily as I knelt to the ground.

Sitting there, surrounded by such simple joy, I could almost pretend I was somewhere else. I didn't have to hide my emotions here. I could sulk and be miserable and the world wouldn't know. It didn't matter that I had slipped up and let my rage get the best of me, that I had almost killed one of my friends in the span of a breath. The hounds didn't care that I was tainted and lying to the world. All they cared was that I was here, feeding them scraps from the kitchen and scratching their coarse heads.

A couple of years ago, I'd feared them. Ha. I would give most anything to go back. My fears were so much greater now.

"What should I do?"

Wolf let out a yip, thumping his tail against the dirt. I choked, coughing up more dust as he rose.

"Should I keep searching the palace? I'm bound to get caught. Now that Mira has me on guard duty and she's back in charge—"

A sharp bark made me pause. One of the others was demanding my attention, its ears cocked to the side.

"You are right, of course." I scratched under the corner of the hound's head and chuckled, almost madly. "Silly me, I need to give this all up and become a dog."

Ten days had come and gone, and what did I have to show for it? The Pythian ambassador would laugh in my face.

Wolf whimpered, pawing at my wrist. I stopped petting

the hound to focus on the shaggy mutt. Darren's childhood had so many bad memories, but I still remembered the day he introduced me to his dog. The mutt's steady eyes met my own, so much like his master's that day years ago: *happy.*

That's when the answer finally came. I couldn't believe it had taken me so long.

I'm wasting my time.

Nyx had reminded me as much at the keep. The Pythians were ruthless. They didn't care about right and wrong; they didn't care about anything except *winning.*

I had spent all this time searching for evidence that might not exist. Would a king as ruthless as Blayne really be fool enough to leave proof of his crimes lying around for the taking? Even well-hidden proof in his chambers? Even proof that might not easily be identified as such? Proof that no one but someone like me, someone already aware of his plans, could comprehend?

The answer was a resounding no.

You know why you keep looking for evidence.

It wasn't for the Pythians. They wanted power. I'd known the moment Nyx had said it: *"Any rule is better than that of a corrupt king."* Jerar would be better under King Joren's rule than our own. The Pythians might be greedy, but they wouldn't stage a war or turn on their people.

I'd known all along what to offer.

These last eleven days, this investigation, it had all been for *him.*

Foolish girl. I had thought if I just searched hard enough I could find it, that one thing that would make my claims irrefutable, something that Darren could never contest. It couldn't be just anything to put so many lives at stake, but I had still assumed it existed.

Even now, I still want to tell him the truth. Tears pooled at the corners of my eyes. I hated myself for being so weak; I thought that by now this guilt would be over. I knew the rules, but a part of me just wouldn't let go.

I suspected that was the same part that had stayed in love with the prince even after his 'betrayal' during the apprenticeship. That part was not subject to reason. She chose Darren over everything. The problem was she believed in happily ever afters, and the truth was much more bitter. She couldn't pick the boy in this story, and she couldn't pick herself.

She had to pick the rest of the world, because she was the only one who could.

I hated that girl. I wanted to be selfish.

Wolf nudged at my knee, and I wrapped my arms around his neck. I didn't know how or why, but I suspected he knew everything.

I wondered if he thought I was making a big mistake. Because right now, I couldn't disagree.

"What would you do?" I whispered.

Wolf whined softly, resting his head in my palms; it was the only reassurance he could offer.

EIGHT

I WASN'T NERVOUS. I should have been, all things considered. Duke Cassius and the Pythians were a scrupulous bunch. I had no idea where I would approach them, or how I would phrase the treasonous words that would start a war, or what they would say in return. I didn't know anything. But instead of restless nights in the dark recesses of my mind, our week-long trek to Port Langli was a vacation.

"Someone looks a bit too chipper this morning." Paige eyed me over her morning tea, her scrutiny narrowing as she fixated on my appearance. "Henry, look at her. Something is wrong with Lady Ryiah."

"What is it?"

"She won't stop smiling."

"So?"

"So this one doesn't smile before noon." The knight made a face. "Or have you forgotten which charge we drag out of bed each morning. Remember that one time? She almost singed off your brow with that casting."

To be fair, they had thought collapsing a tent with me

inside was an appropriate measure. I yawned loudly at Paige's observance. "Maybe I'm just having a good day. Did you ever think of that?"

"Maybe you finally cracked under the pressure."

"You would like that, wouldn't you," I countered. "I'd be much more compliant."

"My beautiful wife? Compliant?" Darren scoffed from the tree where our horses were tethered. It was his turn to see to our charges. "That will be the day."

I rolled my eyes at all three of my companions. "Are we done commenting on my mood? I believe we have some Pythians to greet."

Universal groans met with my declaration.

"I don't know who I care to see most," the prince said dryly, "Priscilla, her father, or Duke Cassius."

The three of us finished up the rest of our breakfast in silence. A couple of minutes later and we were on the road, salty sea air and grassy plains providing a nice change of pace. *Ella would love this a lot more than the keep*, I thought absently. She hated the cold more than anyone I knew. Perhaps when things were over, Alex could take her somewhere along the coast. Winter was a lot kinder by the sea.

As the sun finally set, we reached the cobblestone streets of Jerar's most famous port. It was also run by the wealthiest man in the country, save the king himself, Baron Langli. It was a beautiful town. Months of my apprenticeship had been spent walking the beach—when I wasn't sleeping off exhaustion in the barracks.

Torches lined the paved road to my nemesis's old home.

The castle might have been smaller than the palace in Devon, but it was certainly no less intimidating.

From a comfortable bluff just outside the city limits, white sandstone piled high into the sky, spiraling golden turrets at its peaks. I could see the baron's proud sigil, a white stag against a flag of indigo, flapping from a high window to the left. Where the palace was cold and the Academy rough, this castle was beauty and grace.

I'd seen the baron's home from a distance, of course, but never this close. The barracks were at the opposite end of the city.

Real comprehension of what Darren had given up weighed down on me as I studied the Langli legacy. *Pick the girl you love, or the girl whose wealth could save hundreds...* That guilt only deepened as guards in indigo ushered us forward, taking our mounts and bringing us inside.

Inside was only worse. Thousands upon thousands of abalone shells had been pressed into the walls, their rich inner hues catching light streaming in through the windows so that the entire hall caught fire with the sun. Blue and green and amethyst washed over the entire room like the sea.

"Your Highness, you always were one for impeccable timing." A slim man with hawk-like angles and severe white locks strode across the hall. He was dressed in expensive cloth that draped loosely off his frame. His stature spoke of grace, and his skin was faultless, just like his castle.

"You remember well, Alain." Darren afforded the man a strained smile.

I took in the others—a boy, slightly younger than myself,

whose sulky countenance brought back years of unbridled hate, and an impossibly beautiful girl who I had spent so many years trying to understand.

Neither of us were anxious to exchange greetings.

The baron continued effortlessly. "You remember my family, of course. My daughter, Priscilla, and my nephew, Merrick, who assures me he has had the pleasure as well." There was a pause as his voice tightened, just the slightest change in his tone. It wasn't hard to guess the reason. "I take it this one is your... wife."

"Have the Pythians already arrived?" Darren was doing his best to avoid the growing tension in the room.

"Only an hour before yourself." Baron Langli appeared to have recovered from the unexpected silence. "Duke Cassius and his party took the chambers to the east. After two weeks at sea, they intended to refresh before anything else."

"Shall we take the chambers in the west?"

"You remember our home well."

"Why wouldn't he?" Priscilla's eyes flashed. "He wasn't here all that long ago, taking dinners during the apprenticeship while he courted that one behind my back."

"Priscilla." Her father's tone bespoke a warning.

"She's right." Darren spoke softly to my right, his face paling just the slightest; I tried not to read anything into it. "I believe I can see to my wife and guards without an escort. Thank you for having us."

The girl's eyes narrowed as she folded her arms in a defensive stance. "We didn't have a choice."

"Priscilla!" the baron choked out, his face growing red with rage. "Enough!"

"Your favorite prince doesn't care." The girl didn't wait for her father's reply; she was already sauntering out of the hall, laughing madly. "It's a little late to worry about impressing the Crown, Father. If he wants to wage war on our family, he'll have to get through the Caltothians first."

From Merrick's smirk, I suspected this wasn't the first time they had fought.

"If you'll please excuse her." The elegant lord sounded irritable as he addressed the prince. "You should understand the transition hasn't been easy. She has a bit of a temper."

"No apologies needed."

"When the four of you have settled in, the Pythians will be ready to meet."

"Certainly."

As we followed Darren's lead down the winding corridor, I couldn't keep from grinning.

Priscilla. Like her or hate her, that girl knew how to leave an impression.

* * *

Much later that evening, I sat at a long rustic table overlooking the bluff. From my seat, I took in the dark sea below and the Pythians' ships, just small blotches of ink against the rolling current. *Forty ships and a hundred men each.* I picked at my meal and tried to concentrate on the conversation at hand. I needed to speak up. I watched the duke, all bulk and corn yellow braids, slip me suspicious glances over the lulls; he expected the old Ryiah, the one that declared wars.

I couldn't declare anything with the coil of knots in my stomach now.

If you only knew what I intend to tell you tonight.

I listened as Darren continued on with the Crown's plans, noting the formations Commander Audric had for the Crown's Army and where the king wanted the Pythian ships. Baron Langli remained silent for most of the meal. He was apparently a man of leisure and the context was below his concern. Merrick tried to interject from time to time, but he was usually met with sharp barks of laughter from Cassius's men. The Pythian had brought five of his best warriors to serve as his retinue, and they were just as sharp as the duke.

By the time the meal was over, I had lost what little appetite I had. The mounting pressure was causing panic to press in on my skull, and that little scrap of paper buried in the sleeve of my tunic was burning a hole against my skin. I kept wiping my sweaty palms against my breeches as discreetly as I could, but after the fifth time, I caught Paige staring at me with a raised brow.

Blast that woman for being so keen at observation.

I gave her a weak smile, and she pointed to my brow. I lifted my fingers and found it clammy and moist. I cringed and started to reach for a linen. Paige tossed me her own.

"Thanks," I mumbled.

"We are all afraid."

My gaze darted to the others, but they were all too engaged to hear us. The only one who wasn't was Priscilla, and she was too busy drowning in her third glass of wine to notice.

"Even you?"

Her laugh was bitter. "Every breath I take."

"I can never tell."

"My mask is better than most." The knight stared at me long and hard, and I grew uncomfortable under her stare. There was something she wasn't saying. *Did she suspect?*

Two more flasks of wine were passed around the table, and I seized my opportunity, taking a page from my old nemesis herself. Desperate times called for desperate measures... or senseless measures or whatever they loved to say.

I downed a goblet of wine with gusto, waited ten more minutes, and then stood, letting my balance waiver as I picked my way across the room. Paige shot up to follow. *Loyal to a fault.*

"My lady—"

"And there she is, the second most formidable mage of Jerar." Cassius chuckled as I approached the head of the table. "Here to assure I stick to my promise?"

"Or we will s-sset our fieldsss on f-fire..." I pretended to slur, feigning a stumble as my fingers caught on the ambassador's cloak. A slip of paper fell into his lap and I laughed awkwardly as the man's shrewd gaze shot to my hand. *He knows.* "S-sorry!"

Paige collected me by the arms and Darren cleared his throat uncomfortably. "I apologize, your grace. It's been quite a long day for some of us."

"Has it?" The man's sharp gaze returned to me.

Darren turned to Paige. "Can you...?"

"Certainly." My guard nodded and began to lead me away. I feigned an oblivious smile as we exited the hall.

Thank the gods for wine.

"You disappointed me."

I looked up at Paige, blinking slowly.

"I didn't want to be assigned to you. You were reckless and stubborn, and you never thought before you spoke. I wanted to be in the palace serving the king, and instead I was revisiting my youth, camping out in the forest with a princess-in-training." The knight paused. "But then you kept sticking your neck out for others, and I realized you were different. You didn't let that title change you. That day I found you outside the barracks, you wanted so badly to save us all. You wanted to find a way to beat the duke at his own game, and you refused to give up. You won the Pythians to our side and came in second during your Candidacy. You fought the Caltothians and tried to save Princess Wrendolyn during the attack. You never gave up on anything, you were brave..."

Guilt flared, and I swallowed painfully. *You can't tell her. You can't.*

"You have always been one to conquer your fears, but since your brother's death, you've become a walking shade." Her breath hitched. "I keep hoping you'll turn it all around, given enough time, but—" She sighed. "—it's like you've given up, Ryiah."

I remained silent, not trusting my tongue to work properly if I spoke.

Paige helped me to my chamber and then paused at the door. "You've lost yourself, and I know it's not my place to say it, but don't be the girl I thought you were. Be the one that changed my mind."

How can I tell her I still am?

* * *

I waited until the prince had stopped tossing and his breathing had slowed, deep slumber taking over as his chest rose and fell.

Then I tiptoed down the hall, darting past moon-streaked dips of light, slipping around dark columns and pools of darkness until I reached the eastern wing.

"Nicely done." Duke Cassius stepped out from the shadows, clapping slowly in mock applause. "For a moment, I almost believed you had changed, that the little girl had lost her fire."

I folded my arms across my chest.

"I wonder," the man continued, "what could be so important that we meet in the middle of the night away from your beloved prince and the others. One might almost think you've turned a traitor to Jerar."

"I have a proposal."

The Pythian ambassador leaned against a column with interest. "Continue."

"Have your brother withdraw from the New Alliance and take up with King Horrace of Caltoth instead. Unite with the secret collective of rebels in Jerar and help me dethrone our king." My pulse was hammering against my throat. "In exchange, we will submit to Pythian rule. Your brother will have two kingdoms instead of one."

Silence followed. All I could hear was the lull of the ocean far below. My hands were trembling; I squeezed them tighter against my ribs.

The towering man might as well have been stone; I couldn't even hear his intake of breath.

Then: "Do you care to explain?"

I wet my lips. "Would it matter?"

"It wouldn't. A Pythian is driven by ambition, not heart." He paused and I could almost hear Cassius mulling over the unspoken questions in his head, trying to make sense of my proposal. "Still, we are alone, and I'm a curious man. Something tells me it would take a great deal for someone like you to change course. Just one year ago, you were willing to die for the Crown."

"A lot has changed."

The duke watched me expectantly, waiting.

And so I told him. I told him everything about Lucius's deception and how his eldest had continued to uphold his legacy of murder and lies even after his death. I hesitated to explain the rebels, but there was no point in withholding information now. I was laying everything on the line. If Cassius chose to betray me, it would be too late to make a difference. I needed to give this everything I had; it was the only chance I would get.

When I was finished, the man stroked his broad chin, thick fingers deliberate and slow. "And what of the king and his Black Mage? You ask that I spare their lives—two young men the people will rally behind when it comes down to blood or a Pythian on the throne."

"We imprison them both." It hurt to swallow. "Blayne can rot in the cells, but once Darren..." I was struggling to speak. "Once he comes around, he won't consider the throne."

"You expect a boy born to the Crown to give up his legacy?"

"Darren's legacy isn't to be king! His father raised him t-to…" I trailed off as I saw the duke's expression.

"To protect his brother at all costs? He's the most formidable mage in the land."

"You can keep Darren in the prisons until you see fit." I spat the words, hating myself, hating that this was my only choice. "And once he is convinced, you can kill the king." I was the most heartless thing in the room, but after losing Derrick, I found myself numb to the words. "But I won't help unless you promise to spare them both at the start."

"And if I refuse?"

"Then you will never see a Pythian on the throne."

"And what about you? Where do you see yourself in this bright future you paint?"

"A mage in service to the Pythian king."

"Not the title of queen? Come now, you've thought this far ahead. You expect me to believe you want nothing in return? A tying of two nations is common enough, and you are already a princess."

"No!" I glowered in the dark.

"Ah." His tone was knowing. "Your husband. You think he will forgive you of your crimes."

"Even if he doesn't"—my voice was hard—"I will not take part in the throne. There are plenty of highborn girls who could take my stead."

"Well—" The man paused. "—I can certainly admit I didn't see this turn of events."

"Does that mean you'll join our cause?"

Cassius's gaze flickered in the dark. "You offer me the world. But how can I see through to my prize?"

I faltered, my breath trapped in my lungs.

"Pythus has no responsibility to Jerar after my niece lost her life. She was the only thing that bound us to the New Alliance."

"But you *were* going to honor it—"

"We only kept to the treaty because Blayne offered us the winning side, not because of loyalty or a false sense of guilt."

"So what are you—"

"My dear," the duke cut me off again, "you offer me the crown, but this prize is useless if we lose to a country with the greatest odds. You are far too intelligent not to see this through."

I swallowed.

"Tell me," he said, "how you are going to change the odds. Tell me how we will be victors at the end of your great plan."

"I…" My heart was slamming against my ribs and I felt faint. I hadn't expected resistance. I was offering him more than Blayne ever would. It had never occurred to me the Pythian would refuse. "We would have better odds. The same number of men and the element of surprise." Three thousand from the north, six thousand Caltothian warriors if King Horrace's number was correct, and the four thousand warriors from Duke Cassius.

"Surprise is not enough. You are asking for a takeover on your own soil. Jerar has the greatest army and your warriors are twice the caliber of our own." The man cracked his hands together. "Pythians are bred for trade and the sea. Caltoth enjoys its beauty and chases after precious gems. Boreans are concerned with the scholarly arts; they can barely wield a sword."

My stomach sank with every word he spoke.

"You need to offer me assurances." The duke sighed, and it was hard to tell in the shadows, but I suspected he was disappointed. "I would love to take you up on your proposal, Ryiah. You offer me far more than that boy king ever could."

"Then help us," I pleaded. "I'll do anything—"

"I told you not to beg." The man's reprimand was softer than his words. "A Pythian plays to win. If it were just me, for my niece, I'd see your cause to the end. I know you tried to save her that night of the attacks. Wren was never meant for a world like this..." His tone grew coarse. "But it's my brother's nation, and I can't place them at risk because of personal sentiment."

"Tell me how." I was desperate. "What will it take to win?"

The duke tapped his fingers against his wrist in thought. A minute later he spoke. "If all that you tell me is true, the north is comprised of rebels. That leaves the central plains and the southern desert. How much does that leave us?"

"Around fourteen thousand." It was the same as the north. Give or take a couple thousand if Blayne called on the smaller city regiments.

"How many in the desert alone?"

"Four thousand? It's Ishir Outpost and some of the trading ports."

"That certainly helps our odds. But the Crown's Army is still too big. And it's the best of your best."

"It doesn't always reside in the capital." I thought fast.

"Commander Audric's regiment travels wherever the kingdom needs more help. The Crown doesn't dispatch the whole, but—"

"I would suggest my warships as a distraction," the man said dryly, "but I doubt that would hold their attention when rebels and Caltothian soldiers start making a stampede for the palace."

"If we had time—"

"It's not enough of a guarantee. I need assurance."

I was at a loss for words. For a moment... for a moment, I had thought he would help us.

"I tell you what." The duke cleared his throat. "I am not ready to play my cards, not just yet. You've impressed me in the past. I'm going to give you that opportunity again."

My eyes started to water, but I fought back the tears. The last thing I needed was for the ambassador to see me cry.

"We have two days of rest before we break for war. The prince claims the Crown's Army is amassing in the capital for a march north as we speak."

I nodded along, everything he said I already knew.

"Your king waited this long for Pythian ships. Who is to say he can't wait a bit longer?"

"How?"

"I will insist on speaking with the young king in person." Duke Cassius leaned forward. "I will insist Horrace offered better terms and that we need to renegotiate our alliance. Blayne will be furious, but he will eventually meet my demands. I will buy you two months from today, and not an hour longer."

My knees were wobbly as I thanked him, grateful the

shadows helped shield the desperation from my face.

"That's two months to bring me a solution to our problem." His warning was clear. "I need an assurance that we can win and I will not risk my kinsmen for your cause. If you fail, I won't hesitate to reveal your secret. Pythus needs to be on the winning side."

"I understand." The words came out a rush. "Thank you for—"

"Don't thank me yet." The man stepped away from the column, his expression dark. "I am almost certain you will fail."

NINE

"WE PLAYED OUR hand too fast!"

Wood splintered on impact, bits of furniture splaying across the chamber. I watched as Darren threw another chair, half-drunk in rage. The ambassador had made his announcement that morning. The prince hadn't taken it well.

"Darren—"

"Don't." His eyes flashed garnet. "Don't you dare tell me to be calm when that gods' forsaken *villain* is out there toying with us all like a fat cat and his mice, showing us ships only to call for more talk after all that we've done!"

"I wasn't." I reached out to place a hand on his shoulder, ignoring the surge of guilt as I watched. "I am with you."

"What kind of man," he seethed, "does something like this?"

The kind that wants to win. I bit down on my tongue. At least Darren's bad news came in the morning.

Mine had come the night before. This was supposed to have been *it*. The final instrumental act to solve all of our problems—an alliance that would convince Blayne to surrender and give me time to talk Darren around to the truth.

I should have known I had strung too much of my hope on *this*. Now I was supposed to pray the "opportunity" paid off. And the irony was, had Darren's and my roles been reversed, I was sure the prince would have found a way to solve it. Darren had always been better in strategy and command. It wasn't my fault. Lowborns and mages weren't raised to be leaders of men; princes preparing to be knights and the head of the Crown's Army were.

By the time we had finished seeing to our things, the Langli home was a dark place to be. Duke Cassius had already seen to his men and set up his leaders during his absence.

Baron Langli was aghast at the number to feed. Like Darren, he'd expected the ships to be gone within the span of a week, attacking the Caltothian coast per the original alliance's terms. "You expect me to run supplies to four thousand men?"

"You'll do it," Darren snapped, "and you'll do it without question." If he had to escort the ambassador to an angry king, he added, the baron could hold his complaints.

"Wait, Ryiah!"

I had just exited my chamber, supplies in hand, when Priscilla shoved me back, ignoring an outraged Paige as she cornered me inside.

"I will break down this door," Paige roared, "if you do not unhand my lady this instant!"

"Give me a moment of your time, Ryiah," the girl seethed. The door banged mercilessly behind us. *Bam, bam, bam!* "If any part of you respects me at all, if you can find it in your heart for even a second, give me two minutes."

"Ten, nine—" The guard cursed loudly. "Gods blast it, one!"

"Paige... wait!"

The pounding stopped, and I looked to Priscilla expectantly, my arms braced against my chest.

"I want you to take me with you."

I snorted. "Very funny."

"I'm serious."

"No, you are not."

"Yes—" her eyes grew squinty, "—I am. Do not question me, you insolent lowborn."

"That's *princess* to you."

"It would have been me." Her lips pursed. "And then I would have been free. But no, I graciously stepped aside so you could swoop in and enjoy my place."

"You didn't step aside." I shot her a look. "You fought me every step of the way."

"See?" Priscilla pressed closer. "You aren't as innocent as you think."

I rolled my eyes. "Did you forget the vat of pig's blood our first year? Or when you hog-tied me to a tree during our orientation in Combat? Or—"

"You survived." Her expression grew bored. "I don't care about our past, Ryiah. I want out of here. Now. Darren promised me a place in the Crown's Army when we were married." My insides squirmed. "And he's going to honor it."

"You're not married." My tone was cold. "He does not have to honor it."

"My father won't let me leave, Ryiah, not after I lost the

engagement." Her words were clipped. "He is convinced the only way to save our house embarrassment is to marry me off to the highest bidder." Her voice soured. "At least with Darren I was promised time in a regiment. And as distasteful as that marriage might have been, I knew what I was getting. Not some ugly, old lord who would lock me away."

I cringed inwardly, but outside I was not ready to relent.

"I told Father that, if I was such a blight, he should let me bring honor through our city regiment. You know what he said? He told me that role went to Merrick."

Don't do it. Don't you dare feel pity for *Priscilla.*

But... was I really blameless? It wasn't Darren she had fought so hard to keep; it was the freedom that would have come with his crown. If I had known then... Perhaps...

"Don't you get it?" Priscilla thrust her face into mine. "I've always wanted to be you—well, the *old* you. You might have looked and smelled the part of a sheep herder—"

"I did not."

"—But at least you were doing what you wanted." Her lashes fluttered shut. "Not all highborn girls like your Ella had a choice. Most families *claim* that we can do anything like our brothers and cousins, but the truth is, the older ones, the traditionalists like my father, they only ignore the convent if it helps us secure the right match."

Priscilla opened her eyes and her tone was morose. "My father had me take up the sword the day he realized Blayne was marrying for alliance. The irony was that, for the first time, I felt free."

Gods, no. I clenched my jaw. *You* are *feeling pity for Priscilla.* The girl who went out of her way to torment me during our first year at the Academy, and most of the apprenticeship. *She was trying to secure a role.* She was cruel. *Yes, at times, but so was Darren and you forgave him for that.* He believed in me. *So did she, or did you forget who bet on you during the Candidacy?*

If Priscilla joined the regiment, she would be my enemy.

I looked the girl square in the eye. "You really want this?"

"I wasn't at the top of my class to impress your prince." She snorted. "My father didn't care if I passed the first year trials. When he sent me off to that school, he was already in talks with Lucius for our engagement. I made the apprenticeship because I *enjoyed* it. Fighting and magic, they were the only parts of my life I enjoyed."

And there she went, taking away the last of my defense. I couldn't deny her now. "Darren will issue a mandate that you join the Crown's Army, and we will escort you to the capital. From there you know your way to the base camp."

The girl stepped back with a self-satisfied smirk and unlocked the door. "You are making the right decision."

I nodded absently as Paige marched in with a scowl.

"We leave at noon," I called out after the raven-haired beauty. "You have two hours to gather your things!"

Priscilla didn't bother to look back. "My servants already readied my things in the stables."

She knew I would say yes.

* * *

The day we returned to the capital, all chaos broke loose. To say the king was unreceptive to Duke Cassius's negotiations was an understatement.

Priscilla, true to her word—and Darren's old promise—

was on her way to the Crown's Army camp. I couldn't help but envy her freedom. She could blissfully go about her service while I was trapped searching for a solution to the Pythian ambassador's riddle. Somehow, the highborn had ended up with the fate *I* wanted, and the lowborn had ended up in a web of courtly politics and deceit. If only she knew, I suspected she'd laugh in my face.

Now, instead of searching the palace for proof, I was searching for answers. It was easier to avoid suspicion. I wasn't snooping around in places I wasn't supposed to be, but it might as well have been the same. I had no mind for large-scale maneuvers.

Thanks to Cassius's demands, all waking hours were spent in negotiations, not strategy, so I had little hope of coming across an answer in the war chambers. Asking for a solution straight out, *how does one hold off the Crown's Army*, would draw too many questions. And the last thing I needed was for Mira to call me a rebel. Questions like that were hard to explain, no matter how creative the answer.

One of the things I could do, however, was take a trip to the city blacksmith with a long letter tucked into the extra padding of my boot.

Paige escorted me in the streets, of course, but she'd had enough dealings with Saba to wander the front of the shop, admiring the newest armor and weapons-in-progress, rather than study the wordless communication between her charge and the rebels' capital spy.

I knew Nyx wouldn't be pleased with the newest developments, but it was a far better outcome than Cassius's flat-out refusal. The commander would keep King Horrace and the rebels apprised. We had hope, and she, more than anyone else, would be the most likely candidate to find a solution the ambassador would accept. Knights were strategists, and Nyx was elite. If she couldn't find an answer... I didn't want to think of the outcome.

Three weeks later, I received an early summons from the blacksmith: my new *blade* was ready. An envoy had ridden tirelessly in light of the commander's response.

I emptied the sheath in the solitude of my own chamber. Nyx had given me five different solutions, each more complex than the last.

Warmth surged through my lungs. This was it. After one month of wracking my brain, scanning countless scrolls on war and walking the palace in a daze, Nyx had delivered something I could use. We would have the Pythians' vote.

"This is certainly something," the ambassador said later that night, *"but it's not enough."*

The commander of the second-largest regiment in Jerar had failed to produce an acceptable response.

"You still have a month," he added. *"That's better than none."*

I took another trip to the blacksmith, and then entered the indoor training court alone. My entire vision was red.

Spraaaaat.

My third casting hit the barrier and a horrible screech followed, mimicking nails against glass, rough and unnatural. The entire thing began to quiver.

Streaks of white splintered across the barrier like a web.

It wasn't enough.

I was tired of holding back.

I called on my magic again and again.

For a moment, I was a goddess, bursting with power, shattering the world around me with the flick of a hand. It felt good, I realized, to be free of those mortal troubles.

My palm itched and I ran the dagger along the length of it, watching as crimson drops pooled beneath my boots.

I didn't need anything. I didn't want for anything. I was overflowing with raw magic. It was spilling from me like a fountain; a hungry inferno was building inside my chest.

My seventh casting broke the glass. Shards of silver sung across the air.

My globe's casting kept me safe, but I still heard the small tinkle as thousands of tiny daggers hit the surface only to fall harmlessly away.

I waited until the last of the slivers had fallen, and then I released my shield, watching as violet dissipated to black.

I was tired of being a pawn.

Behind me, the room suddenly burned orange. Someone had lit a sconce.

"Care if I join you?"

Darren's boots crushed the glass as he left the stands to take a place on my right. His eyes were bloodshot like my own, his entire face drawn with lines of fatigue and his fists so strained they were white.

The Black Mage was dressed in formal attire hardly suitable for combat; I was wearing a dress.

The two of us took our places across from one another, the masters' drills echoing like a relentless tide in the dark. Today wasn't the time for a duel; today was time for something more.

I gave a small flick of my wrist and shadows grew, the flames behind us dimming to a small, crystalline blue. Then it was just our outline in the dark.

I drew my breath; Darren exhaled softly across the way.

And the drill began. A sharp whistle sounded as metal found its way to our hands, bringing a biting sting as blood dripped down below.

A casting hovered just beyond each of us, an invisible opponent that knew our instinct like no one else ever could.

A curved sickle sword for me; two hand axes for the prince.

That first winter solstice at the Academy, that day Darren had trained me as my own opponent, it was back with a vengeance. We were battling rage and fighting enemies we couldn't name. Pain casting against one's self, it was the ultimate test.

Our cuts rang out like a storm.

Even in the haze, I identified the different attacks by the ring of each blade. Hard and fast, pull and swipe, hook and hack. Recover. Offense. The exchange was as deadly as they came.

I twisted and turned, a complicated pattern of steps.

Then I cut.

Again. And again.

We continued this way for a long time. Two mages battling demons in silence, just the loud clang of metal on metal and the sharp intake of breath whenever we missed.

When I shifted, our eyes met across the way.

Darren's chest heaved with the effort to fight. The tension in his shoulders rippled across each arm as he swiped and parried two enemy axes hovering just beyond. He jumped and spun, but no matter how he danced, his casting continued to lead an impenetrable assault. I could see it in the tension of his muscles, the way he spun and ducked, the sweat lingering on his chest.

The prince finally spoke. "The ambassador refused our newest offer." It wasn't hard to understand his reason for the drill.

Suddenly I was back to hours before, watching as the duke laughed in my face. *"It's not good enough,"* Cassius had said. Why, after everything, was nothing I did ever enough?

I can't save the kingdom from ruin. My blade parried the second phantom sword; the impact rattled my bones.

I couldn't save my own brother. The vibration was so hard I could taste hot, coppery blood.

And finally, as I ducked to the side, a winning slash of my own. *All I have to offer are lies to the one I love.*

My casting ceased and the weapons dissipated into thin air. I stood there, dizzy and furious, my head spinning from the loss of blood.

A moment later, the Black Mage joined me. Darren was breathing so hard that I could see the hematite stone rising and falling with his chest.

"You've gotten better."

But not good enough. I stood there, lips pressed firmly closed, refusing to speak. Too afraid of myself. Too afraid of this rage and what it could lead me to say.

"Here." Darren tore off the sleeve of his jacket, using the coarse brocade to wrap the steady trickle of blood along my wrist and palm. He was so careful and meticulous. I watched his pulse beating out the hollow of his throat.

And then, when he was done, standing there with his eyes locked on my own, I stopped caring about everyone but myself. I reached out and snatched the prince's wrist, the words tumbling from my mouth. "We should run away."

Darren's hand froze midair.

"You and me." The words were unbidden, and they spoke to the coward I was. "We could leave this whole place behind."

"Ryiah…" Darren swallowed hard. "Do you have any idea what you are asking?"

My nails dug into his arm. I knew I was hurting him, but I was too afraid to let go. "You told me you never wanted this life. This is your chance. You can be someone else. We can find a ship and let the others sort everything out."

"I will not leave my brother to fight this war alone." His reprimand was harsh. "We are war mages, Ryiah. We have a duty to Jerar."

"What about a duty to *us*?" Tears were slipping down my face, and I didn't even care. "Don't you want to grow old together? To start a family? What will happen if—"

"Ryiah." Darren drew a sharp intake of breath. "I know you lost your brother and you are afraid of losing others, but running away won't solve anything. We have to stay and fight."

"But—"

"The ambassador will come around. And even if he doesn't, I promise you, I won't let us lose." The prince's tone drew soft and his bloody fingers raised my chin so that his eyes met my own. "Love, I'm not leaving you."

Yes, you will. I swallowed my choking sob, reality breaking through to my plea. Hysteria and sheer desperation had taken over my control.

Gods, the fairy tales never talked about heroes who chose wrong. I was so lost in self-pity and greed, I had been willing to run away with the prince, even if it meant the villain won. Even if I forsook everyone else.

Darren would never turn on his own. Yet, here I was, ready to give up on the rebels, my family and friends, all because the going got hard, all because I wanted it to be us in the end.

Darren didn't deserve the likes of me. The others didn't deserve to rest their fate on the shoulders of a girl so weak.

When I fell asleep that night, it was with the realization that I hated myself.

* * *

The next morning, I awoke to find the prince sitting on our bed, dressed for a day outdoors instead of another endless battle in the Crown chamber with Duke Cassius and the king.

Darren gave me a half smile as I pushed off against the mattress, staring at him in wide-eyed confusion.

"I have a surprise for you."

A part of me rebelled; I didn't deserve anything after the words I had spoken the day before. If I were him, I wouldn't want to be in the same room with a coward like me.

Darren noted the hesitation on my face. "The two of us are going to be driven mad by these negotiations. Yesterday made it clear we both need to get away from this place. I can't promise you forever." His smile faltered and a flare of regret shone in his eyes. "But for the day, it's a start."

I took a hitching breath and shook my head. I didn't want a day alone with the prince; I needed to distance myself in any way that I could. I needed to simmer in my own shame and spend the day in the library, chasing down more manuscripts on war and preparing for Cassius's refusal.

"You don't have a choice." Darren tugged me to my feet. "The staff are under orders to keep you out. Mira was especially delighted to hear it."

My lip twitched. "Where are we going?"

"You'll see." Darren was already walking toward the chamber door. "And wear that dress, the yellow one."

"From the wedding?"

"Ten minutes, love." Darren turned, a wicked glint to his eyes. "Then we leave, in whatever state of undress that might be."

Later, we were tearing through the forest, gnarled branches making a mess of my skirts.

"Really?" I felt Darren's choke of laughter against my back; it wasn't unpleasant. "You could have told me to wear something else."

"I'm a prince." Darren hopped from the saddle, pulling me down and smirking at my disarray. The dress had ripped almost scandalously high at the waist and my hair had broken free of its tie, leaving scarlet locks windblown and compiled in an endless horror of knots. It would take my ladies-in-waiting at least three hours to untangle the worst. "I get what I want."

"And that is…?"

"You." Darren snatched my hand and began to tug me along the trail. Our horses were tethered next to a stream, left to their own devices while we continued the rest of our trek on foot. We were somewhere southeast of the capital, three hours on a small, untraveled road I had never heard of in my entire time at court.

"What is this place?"

"So many questions." The teasing lilt of his voice was unmistakable. "It's a wonder I didn't have you bound and gagged the whole ride here."

"You know, you could just tell me." I couldn't keep from smiling. I tried not to, but I was failing. "Darren!" I shrieked his name as he dragged me through some overhanging brush, more branches tearing at my dress. "Darren, stop!"

"We are almost there."

"I should light you on fire," I grumbled.

"You tried." He was trying hard not to laugh. "Many, *many* times, love."

The two of us cut through a dense cluster of foliage and came to a clearing.

My heart caught in my throat.

In front of us was a small meadow, hardly enough to constitute a field. It was little more than a hill of green, perhaps twenty yards across. The stream we had been following pooled near its base, and just above, a small waterfall rushed through a pair of twin boulders.

Sunlight rained down through a break in the trees, thin shards of gold between empty branches and pine.

It looked like a scene from a storybook with the soft gray clouds and a misting of amber, the gentle murmur of water cascading down rock, and the soft chirp of birds setting out to build spring nests.

My pulse was hammering against my ribs; I had to swallow before I could breathe.

Darren cleared his throat, one hand outstretched. Dark bangs fell across his eyes as he grinned. "May I have this dance, love?"

It was the moment from our apprenticeship all over again. I was the fool that wanted to say yes, and he was the boy I couldn't refuse.

His fingers brushed mine, and I forgot to say no.

You fool. You are going to ruin everything.

I let the prince lead me to the center of the clearing, silk rustling against the dewy grass.

Darren took his place across from me, one hand falling to my waist as the other held my hand.

I set my frozen palm against his shoulder, and he took a step forward.

I wasn't sure how long the two of us moved. It started off slow. I was all too aware of the hammering of my heart and the way his eyes locked on mine. I heard the soft splatter of mud as Darren quietly led us across the marsh, the quiet buzz of insects greeting the sky. It wasn't supposed to be romantic. I wasn't supposed to feel like my heart was shattering from just one dance.

"What is this place?" I rasped.

"Somewhere away from everything else."

I swallowed and let the prince turn me, trying not to *feel*. These emotions were a current dragging me away, a tide I couldn't break.

For a moment, I couldn't move.

"Ryiah…"

Darren's thumb brushed my wrist. I felt myself starting to break. It scared me how easy it would be to fall under his spell.

"Love—" the words were so gentle, "—please look at me."

"I can't." My voice broke, and I knew Darren could see the tears staining my cheeks. There was no way he could miss the shaking in my bones.

He tilted my chin. "Why not?"

"Because…" I couldn't remember the reason, not when Darren was looking at me like *that,* not when I was looking at him like he was the only thing that mattered in this world.

Darren's lips brushed my hair. "It's just a dance, love."

It wasn't and he knew it. Darren was trying to save the broken girl in his arms. He was trying to save me, and I was fighting him with every last gasp of air.

"I want to dance with my wife." His words were so quiet. I could feel myself slipping. Down. Down. *Down.* "Is that so much to ask?"

Was it? Was it really? Before he cursed my name and branded me a traitor? The girl that betrayed a prince?

"It is."

My confession cut like a knife. Darren jerked away, hurt flaring in his eyes. "You are destroying us." His hands fisted at his sides. "And I don't even understand why."

That pain was my undoing. It broke the control I fought so hard to keep.

I didn't want to hurt the boy. I loved him more than life

itself.

I grabbed Darren's shoulders and slammed my mouth to his, every bit of emotion snapping under that bridge.

I needed him, and I was tired of pretending I didn't.

Darren's chest rose and fell rapidly against my own. For a moment, he didn't move. Then his hands slid up my back, my throat, framing my jaw, capturing me and crushing me against his lips, drawing me in and stealing my soul.

I could have spent the rest of my life letting him kiss me like that, but I didn't want soft and slow.

I didn't care about the consequences. Not anymore.

I implored the prince to move, shoving him back, my tongue dancing across his, his mouth slanting in surrender against my own.

Darren let out a growl, and I gasped as he jerked me forward, choking on air.

He kissed me like he wanted to cherish me and break me in the same breath. His kiss was furious. Unapologetic. Punishing. It spoke of too many nights left alone. It spoke of everything he was holding back.

And then our roles reversed.

I pressed my mouth to his neck and he shuddered. It did things to my senses; my nails dug into his shoulders as I did it again.

I wanted to make him lose control.

Darren's fingers were on my waist as his teeth grazed my neck.

Gods.

My head lolled back and I could hardly breathe. I had no idea one person could feel so much.

The two of us were stumbling across the meadow, tearing at bits of cloth, his hot hands branding my skin.

Darren picked me up and my legs wrapped around his waist. He slammed me against the base of a tree. I forgot the pain as he held me in place, his arms pinning my own high above my head.

Darren pulled back just enough to look me in the eyes.

"Tell me to stop, love," he whispered.

I didn't tell him to stop. I couldn't.

I needed this. I wanted him.

I was tired of fighting myself.

I pulled Darren to me and pressed my lips to his, giving him the answer he needed.

And then Darren's hands were making quick work of my bodice, orange beads splaying across the forest, while I clawed at his shirt.

Darren kissed me so deeply I forgot my own name. The last of my bodice slipped away and his fingers rode up my ribs to the swell of my breasts. My sharp intake of breath caught me by surprise.

For a moment that was enough. Then he dipped his head, his lips leaving a trail of liquid fire against my skin. I couldn't breathe. I was quite sure I was rasping his name like a prayer, again and again.

I felt Darren's smile through the indentation of his lips.

Then he dropped one hand. Darren cupped my knee and raised my leg, bringing me closer than before. There was an ache in the pit of my stomach, and all I knew was I needed more.

I was dying, and I didn't know why.

My fingers raked across his arms, shoulders, and chest following the dips and hollows of muscle and bone. I tried to hold back. I tried to memorize the planes of his body, but it was impossible not to move. Not when all of my senses were screaming; my world was wrapped in cinnamon and cloves. I needed to touch every inch of him, and it wasn't enough.

Darren's mouth found the base of my throat, and I cried out as his hand slipped down, and then *up*.

Time stopped. The pit in my stomach was no longer a lonely ember, it was an inferno and Darren's eyes were heavily lidded flames.

He slowly slid me down the base of the tree, going down to his knees. And then all I saw were stars.

I was dining with the gods, gasping on air.

After, Darren rose up, cupping my face in his hands and kissing me hard. A long, desperate kiss that promised me everything and the world.

And then he drew me to the ground.

I tugged his body over mine, fumbling with the drawstrings at his waist, desperation and need taking ahold of my limbs.

His eyes met mine, and it was just the two of us.

"I love you, Ryiah." He whispered the words only once and I was lost.

Lost and in love. In lust. Over my head. Over my mind, body, and soul.

For hours the two of us ceased to be Ryiah and Darren. The Black Mage and the traitor who would cause so much grief to come.

We were the boy and the girl.

We were a fairy tale. We were dancing in the forest.

We were everything and nothing, and it was the one thing we both needed to be.

TEN

WE DIDN'T RETURN until the sun rose the next morning. I watched it with his arms around me, the two of us standing at the base of the rushing falls, and that moment was perfect. Perfect like all the ones that came before.

A pale light settled over the stream like a slow drawn breath, turning the dark river into a rippling tide of crystalline white. I could have stood on the bank forever. The set in Darren's shoulders spoke the same.

We spent an hour hiking through the forest. Not once did he release my hand. I held my breath, refusing to let anything spoil this day for as long as I could.

We rode back to the palace in silence. Our guards waited with heavy scowls, but the reprimands never came. No one said a word. Blayne smirked, and Cassius raised a brow, but the rest of the court was blissfully silent.

No one remarked on our state of undress. I could not have looked worse if I tried.

Even the prince, he was sporting bruises and patches of dirt along his arms and legs, his shirt missing buttons and stained brown from the mud.

Darren dismounted, swinging me from the saddle, only to

walk me right back into our chamber without another word.

He grabbed my waist with a grin and slammed the door shut behind us.

And then it began again.

When the prince finally left, I was breathless and sore. Dirt and bits of grass smeared the sheets. I felt my cheeks heating as I recalled the way my name had tasted in his mouth.

The way he had shouted it the night before.

The way I had cried out his.

I couldn't wait for it to happen again.

I washed up and spent several hours combing the knots out of my hair, preferring to bathe without my ladies-in-waiting. I wasn't ready for their questions to follow. When I finally left the chamber, I was floating, for once my mind blissfully silent.

"Well, someone sure is glowing." Paige lounged outside the chamber with a cheeky smile.

My fingers flew to my face, and I knew I was blushing. I gave the knight an embarrassed grin, choosing silence instead of words.

"No chatter either. That prince must be good with his hands, or is it his—"

"Paige!" I cut my guard off with a squeal.

She was doubling over in laughter.

"That is not a nice joke."

"I bet he was good."

"Say another word…" I warned.

"Just tell me…" She held up her hands, proclaiming innocence. "Tell me you are happier than the day you left."

She knew me too well. Then again, she was the one to help Darren find me a healer after that terrible night in the indoor training courts.

I bit down on my cheek, hard.

I wasn't going to think about that. If I thought about past events, my happy bubble would break, and I'd be back to avoiding the prince. I wasn't ready to give up Darren just yet. I had one month. Nyx would send another letter; this time she would give us the solution we needed, and then Duke Cassius would take up the rebels' side.

Then, and only then, would I give up the prince.

I just needed to stop worrying about things I couldn't control. If I didn't find the answer in a pile of scrolls—and I hardly believed I would—there was nothing else I could do. It was time to rely on others, and Nyx was a strategist. She would be the hero to our tale; I had already performed my role.

Now it was time to bask in a world of sunshine and give up the shadows that followed me around.

"You know," Paige snickered, "Mira is convinced you have it in for her role."

The two of us turned the corridor, continuing our route to the kitchens. My stomach was a ravaging beast, and I knew Benny would have the answer I needed. "Why does she think that?" Not that I didn't love the head mage fretting over me. She made my life a misery; I enjoyed reciprocating the same.

"She told everyone all you ever do is camp out in the library to study. She thinks you are looking for a way to impress the king." The knight snorted loudly. "She tried complaining to Blayne, and he told her off, saying you were looking for a way to win over Cassius. That you are one of his best assets, and if she continues to vex him, he may promote you instead."

One of his best assets? A way to win over Cassius? The irony was so thick I could cut it with a knife. I gave Paige a broad smile. "If I get a promotion, that's just a bonus. I will settle for demoting her just to watch the fall."

"You do seem to be in a much better state of mind." My knight gripped my shoulder in a rare show of feeling. "I am glad you were able to get away."

A flicker of guilt flared deep in my gut, but I ignored it. I was not going back to that place. "The Pythians will fight for Jerar." *Just not the Jerar you think.* "I'm going to make sure of it."

"If anyone can find a way to convince the duke, it's you." A bit of gum flashed with her teeth. "I only hope I'm there to see the look on Mira's face when you do."

"Here, here." I almost laughed just thinking of the moment the Pythians turned on the villainous king and the mage responsible for Derrick's death. It would be a day unlike any other.

* * *

Another week passed, and the Crown was falling apart. Citizens had gathered outside the palace gate, demanding their king. They wanted to know why the alliance had fallen through, why we weren't marching on Caltoth right away.

Darren was forced to summon Audric and some of his men from the Crown's Army camp to keep the crowds from getting worse; Mira had doubled the number of mages inside the gates.

The people of Devon were growing restless. Cassius, as promised, had continued to stall negotiations with ridiculous demands. Whenever Blayne seemed ready to commit, the Pythian upped his request. The advisors had begun to catch on and warned their king to refuse, and things had become tense. The duke still had three weeks in our term; he delighted in the stakes. Either way, his brother would have better terms than before.

I continued to prowl the library while the others watched. Thanks to the king's prediction, half the palace was hanging their hopes on me. I wasn't even expected to take part in guard duty. I found a new mound of books waiting each time I arrived in the study; Paige had even begun to read the texts aloud to me in the training courts.

The glass barrier had yet to be replaced; my guard's voice carried easily across the platform as I drilled.

I studied the scrolls, doing my best to understand monotonous formations long into the night. I still had another two weeks before Nyx's reply, three if it took her more than a day, or the envoy caught on a delay. Now that the commander knew what Cassius expected, she would craft a much better response.

Two fingers drew the parchment from my hands as warm lips pressed against my neck. I didn't bother to turn; his heat clung to me like a second skin, a warm envelope of cloves.

"It's time to come to bed."

I looked up from a stack of papers, wondering if the crown prince was right. The bell had long since tolled midnight; I suspected an hour or two ago.

I wanted to join Darren, but with each day that passed, I grew a little less amorous with my plan and a little more worried Nyx would fail.

"Or I can stay here." The prince's smirk grew devious. "If that's what you prefer."

"Darren..." My protest was useless. The Black Mage was restless like me, trying to channel all his fear and doubt into something he could manage. He was turning to the one person he thought he could trust.

"Tell me, Ryiah," Darren said, "have you ever wondered what it would be like in the room that started it all?"

A smile tugged at the corner of my mouth. "The palace library isn't the Academy's."

"Oh, but it's better." Heat flared in his eyes, twin coals against a sea of endless black. "We have more tables. And *chairs*."

Hours later the two of us fell into bed, breathless and flushed. It was only then I noticed the new charm hanging from his neck next to the hematite stone.

"What is this?" My finger curled around the object, and I started. Brass and heavy, not a charm. Almost like a—

"It's a key."

I tried not to sound too curious. "You didn't have this before."

"Blayne." Darren shut his eyes with a groan. "He wants me to keep it on me at all times. Doesn't trust... the ambassador... dragging out the negotiations."

"Why? What is it for?"

The prince didn't reply; he was already drifting off to sleep.

"Darren?"

For a second, I lay there weighing my odds. Then I shook the prince's shoulders, unable to keep the question to myself, not when I was standing on the precipice of something new. Not when something told me this key was important. Not when Blayne had suddenly placed it in safekeeping. It could be the answer I needed.

The prince blinked several times before registering my face. "Love?"

"I was just thinking..." I bit down on my lip and then forced myself to finish. "This key, what does it do? Don't you think I should know in case something happens?"

Darren reached out to catch my tapping fingers with his own—I hadn't even realized I was doing it.

"It unlocks the Crown's best kept secret." His lips curved up as his eyelids fluttered shut.

"Best kept secret?" Why was I just hearing of this now?

"Perhaps you were too distracted." He was smiling to himself. "You were always staring at me during Commander Ama's lessons."

"Perhaps I was imagining the best way to rid myself of an arrogant prince."

"Well, I'm not going to tell you now—" Darren yawned, "—since you think I'm so arrogant."

And so he drifted to sleep as I tossed and turned. *Commander Ama? The desert?*

What did she even talk about? Chariots and sickle swords and the best way to breach a defense. Hardly a secret to the thousands of regiment warriors.

Think, Ryiah, think.

I knew there was something important I was missing. Darren wouldn't have made that comment unless he believed I already knew the answer.

Crown's best kept secret? So the commander of Ishir Outpost knew, and clearly the original members of the Crown: Lucius and Blayne and Darren.

Maybe he doesn't expect me to know the secret, maybe that's what this is about.

I ground my teeth. That didn't make the puzzle any easier, and I was sick of puzzles. Cassius already had me wringing my own neck trying to find a solution for his.

Would it be so terrible for the gods to give me an answer once in a while?

I imagined them laughing down from above. *Foolish mortal*, they were probably saying, *you saw the key. We've already given you more luck than you deserve. If you can't pick up the pieces from here, well, then you're undeserving of our help.*

Evil, omnipotent dictators with too much time on their hands.

I told myself the answer would come in the morning.

It didn't.

* * *

"Paige…" I paused in my late afternoon drill, looking over at the knight on my right. She had the day off from her own duties, and she had still chosen to join me at the practice courts after my stint in the library. She should've been prowling the streets of Devon, bartering for that new chainmail she'd been eyeing for weeks, but she seemed to have given up for the moment.

No one wanted to go into the city now.

"Yes?"

"When you were a squire, did you train with four regiments same as the apprentice mages?"

"The best years of my life." Her response wasn't very enthusiastic; she was too busy concentrating on a lift.

I watched her muscles expand and contract, more than a little envious at the definition in her arms. She could give most men a run for their gold.

"Were one of those regiments a part of Ishir?"

"They were." The knight set down her weights and proceeded to stretch. "Why?"

"Commander Ama spent a great deal of time going over strategy. I'm trying to remember if there was anything important I should remember from her talks?"

The guard squinted at me as she switched arms. "This has to do with that duke, doesn't it? You are going to think up some miraculous way to convince him to join our cause? Again."

There was no harm in letting her think I was worried about Cassius—even if it wasn't for the same reason as everyone else. I nodded.

"Well, to start, it was the desert." She made a face. "I never got the appeal of miles and miles of sand."

"And that's important because...?"

"Whoever serves in that regiment is mad."

"Very helpful."

She grinned. "You are welcome."

"Anything else?"

"That desert is the best defense Jerar has. It's just a shame we don't have the same in the north."

"How so?" My logic was failing me. "Ferren's Keep is the largest city regiment we have."

"You are forgetting the Red Gate. If anyone tried to invade the capital from the south, they would be limited to the pass." Paige knelt to the ground to begin her next exercise. "If we had the same wall in our north, we wouldn't need the Pythians to win a war... We'd just line up our army at the gate, waiting for the enemy to enter, one by one."

The northern border was a forest, that strategy would never work... but the south was a desert bordered by red bluffs. The only way through was the Red Gate.

And suddenly everything Paige was saying made sense.

She hadn't given me the answer I needed, but she'd given me something much better.

Cassius had asked for a way to hold off the Crown's Army.

What if his ships staged an attack on one of the southern desert ports?

What if Blayne sent half his army south to save Jerar's most precious commodity? Salt was the main source of Jerar's economy—hadn't the rebels taught me that during that year of the apprenticeship?

And then the rebels and Caltothian forces could storm the capital and send some of their men to barricade the Red Gate. The Crown's Army might have more men, but by blocking the pass, we would have the upper hand.

We'd have enough time to place a Pythian on the throne. I could find a way to distract Darren while the others imprisoned the king. The Black Mage would never see betrayal coming from his own wife. There would be minimal bloodshed, and we'd win a war that never had time to start.

I had found the solution to Cassius's riddle.

"You are right, Paige." I kept my face impassive, fighting hard to keep the elation from reaching my lips. "It's a shame we don't have the same in our north." I started to gather my things.

"You are leaving? Now?" Paige lifted a brow. "You usually train for three hours. It's barely been one."

"I'm going to see if I can dig up any more information in the library." I needed to get to Cassius. Now, while everyone else was occupied. It was almost time for dinner; the ambassador always insisted on taking a stroll around the gardens before. It was the best time to meet—there were too many eyes in the palace itself. If I timed it right, I could still reach him before he returned to his rooms.

"We spend so much time trying to appease these Pythians." She looked angry. "I don't trust that duke at all. We should just go to war without them. For all we know, they'll turn again and demand something else."

She wasn't wrong.

* * *

I found Duke Cassius just in time. We met behind the stables, and I tried not to think back to my last meeting here, when it had been Derrick instead. I wished my brother could see me now. I wished he could see I was a part of his cause.

"I wasn't expecting to meet again so soon."

"I have the answer you want."

"I'm eager to hear it." The man folded his arms. "Let's hope this one is better than the last."

"The Red Gate. It's the only passage in or out of the desert to our south. If your men attack the ports with enough force, Blayne will dispatch the Crown's Army to help. All we need is to get them through the gate, and then we can barricade the army in. The mountains, they aren't like the ones in our north. They're impassable—"

"An interesting theory, but already you have neglected one of your country's most notable features."

"What?" My skin was starting to heat, and my pulse rose. "What is wrong with this plan? You haven't even let me finish!"

"The Red Tunnels, my dear. Or did you forget that your king has countless tunnels hidden away at the base of that infamous range?"

"I…" How could I be so stupid? It was how they named everything. The Red Desert. The Red Gate. The Red Tunnels. "I forgot."

"Yes, well, a Pythian doesn't forget his enemy's best hand. Your boy king's father made sure every one of us knew those were there. Just in case we ever considered raiding his south."

I couldn't bear to listen to the rest of the duke's response. Frustration was a crushing blow, and it was building with every second that passed. I thought this time would be different. The last time we spoke, I'd been so built-up with rage I had shattered what should have been—according to all measurable accounts—an unbreakable glass. The indoor training courts had been treated with the best potions an Alchemy mage could brew.

Then I had tried to convince the prince to run away with

me so I could leave everyone else behind.

"…Of course, our traders heard about them long before your Lucius ever started spreading the word. Some secret, when we had spies at all the ports…"

What would I do if Nyx didn't find an answer? If—

"Three more weeks." Cassius placed a meaty palm on my shoulder. "I want to help you, I do, but my hands are tied."

"We could still win. Darren is the king's best defense, and he will be blindsided. We could—"

"What did I say about begging, Ryiah?" The man released me with a sharp look. "This meeting is done."

"Wait!"

He turned and looked me up and down. "Well?"

Say something. Anything. "Darren has a key." I took a deep breath. "It's new. His brother asked him to start wearing it because he didn't trust your claims. Blayne is beginning to get suspicious."

"Nothing you are telling me is helping your cause."

"Darren said the key was a part of the Crown's best kept secret."

"And what is this secret?" The man continued to stare, unimpressed. "How is it going to help us?"

"I…" I didn't—

Secret. Secret. Best. Kept. Secret.

That's when it finally hit me. All of Commander Ama's lectures. The desert. Red everything. And the irony was the duke had brought on the answer himself.

The apprentices had spent all summer discussing those tunnels; their mysterious location had even become a butt of a joke amongst the mages. Several had even gone so far as to speculate the untimely death of Ishir's previous commander, a man who had taken ill only three years into his reign.

No one knows their location. Not the barons or lords, not even the regiment, only the current commander and the Crown.

Darren had believed I knew the answer because it was obvious—gods, even Cassius had spoken the secret aloud.

Secret.

The Crown's best kept secret.

"It leads to a map to the Red Tunnels. The Crown's best kept secret."

The duke's expression immediately changed. "Why didn't you—"

"I didn't know what it was." My heart was beating so fast I was afraid it would burst. "But as we were talking... I-I'm certain! The desert commander always said that only she and the Crown knew their location. Everyone who dug the tunnels died long ago, and the commander has scouts patrolling the border to make sure no one knows where they are."

"Surely the scouts know?"

"No, they are only assigned a territory to patrol. The tunnels could be anywhere between. Their location was only to be revealed if we went to war. So if we knew in advance—"

"We could use barricades like the Red Gate."

"And the Crown's Army would never expect it."

"The passages are small. We wouldn't need a lot of men to hold them off. We just need to know where they are."

"Well, well." Duke Cassius ran a hand down his yellow

beard. "I do believe you've found an acceptable solution to our problem… But we are still missing one thing. The map."

"I have three weeks." Nothing would stop me from saving us all. We had a plan. Darren had the key. We had time. "I'll get you that map."

"Do you know where to look?"

I didn't, but I knew who to ask.

* * *

"Crown's 'best kept secret?'" I scoffed as the prince and I returned to our chamber much later that night. "More like the most obvious. A map of the Red Tunnels?"

Darren grinned wolfishly. "And yet it still took you a day."

"Well, I am a part of the Crown." I picked at the sleeves of my underdress, trying to frame my next question just right. "Shouldn't I have the privilege of knowing where it is? What if something happens?"

"What?" A smirk was making its way across his lips. "No trust in your husband?"

"You aren't infallible." I kept my voice light. "Even the Black Mage has his limits."

Darren leaned against the wall, taking me in at a leisurely pace. "Do I, love?"

My whole body flushed. I hadn't meant *that*.

"Or shall I show you?" He braced a hand against the back of my head, forcing me back. "Which one of us has the most *potential*?"

That last word was deadly.

Had it suddenly turned to summer, or was it just me? "If I win—" I swallowed, trying to remember how to breathe.

How did Darren have this effect on me every time? Still? After all these years? "—you tell me where the map is."

"Planning on turning a traitor?"

If only you knew.

"You know me so well." I gave the prince a sultry smile. "I'm going to be a Pythian Queen."

The corner of his lip twitched. "A shame King Joren is only seventy years young."

"What are a couple of years when I can have all that wealth to myself?"

"If I had known you were this enthusiastic over Crown secrets, I would have given them freely a long time ago."

"Oh?"

"Still"—his garnet eyes flashed—"it's a shame you will lose."

"We'll s-see about that." My response was breathless and rushed. Darren had me pressed against the door; a part of my mind was already gone, especially when he used his hands.

"If I win—" The prince gave me a crooked smile. "—what are you going to do for me?"

I looked up at him through my lashes. I was trying to remember why it was so important to win, but my senses were failing. "I'm sure you can think of something."

Darren's expression was devious. "Yes, I most certainly can."

* * *

I won. It was the first time I had ever beaten the prince at anything.

To be fair, he had fallen asleep during a deliberately slow massage, but as far as I was concerned, it still counted.

"You cheated."

"If you hadn't enjoyed it, you wouldn't have fallen asleep."

Darren gave me a scowl. "I'll remember this the next time we place a wager."

"My prize?"

"Persistent to the end." He leaned back on his arms with a groan. "Very well. Go on and marry your Pythian King. The map is behind the Throne Room tapestry."

I sucked in a sharp breath. *Thank the gods he didn't say his brother's chamber.* It would have been just like the gods to place the map in the one place I could never breach.

Darren mistook my silence for fear. "It's the best location, love. The first place anyone would search is the king's quarters, or the war chambers."

Ha, I thought weakly.

"But the Throne Room? It's brilliant. Hundreds of people can be in that room at any time and not suspect a thing." The prince chuckled. "The only ones who can enter unattended are the Crown."

I waited until he fell asleep. It wasn't long; we were both so exhausted it could have just as easily been me.

Then I carefully, *very* carefully unclasped the chain around Darren's neck.

For a moment, I just sat there, listening to the stammering of my pulse. Four months of plotting and searching and the crippling fear that this would all fall apart and now I finally had an answer.

The key was in my hand.

The whole of the palace was asleep... well, except the

guards. But the only one I was truly concerned with was busy guarding the ambassador's hall. Mira might not like me, but she distrusted the duke more.

I didn't need to wait.

It was time to act.

* * *

"Your Highness? Why are you up at such an early hour?"

I gave the pair of guards the same explanation I had given the last. It was amazing how easy they took a crown princess's word.

"The prince, he..." I clutched my cloak tighter in a show of modesty. I had deliberately left my hair tangled and willed myself to blush. "He worked up a bit of an appetite. I was hoping to get us something from the kitchens."

"Ahhh." There was a round of elbows and grins. "To be young again, eh?"

They continued to reminisce as I passed, never noticing when I ducked down the west corridor instead of the east.

And finally I was in front of the Throne Room doors.

Of the two guards standing duty, one was a knight I'd served with several times before, and the other, an easygoing Combat mage that hero-worshipped the prince.

I offered up some feeble excuse, pretending I had left something behind, and then I just strolled right into the room. My great betrayal of the Crown, and neither batted an eye.

The hall was beautiful. As I made my way across, little rays of sun were beginning to shoot across the chamber, the stained glass windows casting an ethereal glow along the marble and stone. I would have loved to watch, but every second that passed was another second before the rest of the palace awoke. In another ten minutes, the tower bells would toll for dawn.

I hurried across the rest of the room. The only sound was the hushed patter of my slippers and my own shallow breath.

All this plotting and worrying... I lifted a corner of the heavy tapestry, trying not to stare at the hand-woven crown with golden prongs and black hematite stones—the crest of the family I was betraying. I didn't need to think about that now.

I tore my eyes away and shoved my second hand under the rug, feeling around with my fingers for a variance in the wall. My nails cut across granite, the rough stone an unpleasant sensation against the pads of my thumbs. I didn't care. I ran my hand faster across the surface, glee taking over as my fingers caught against an uneven edge protruding slightly further than the rest.

I traced a rectangular outline of brick and then ducked under the tapestry, using both hands to tug the panel away from the rest of the wall.

For a moment, the brick held. And then, with the last contraction of my arms, it gave. A small plume of dust sprayed my arms and neck as I stared into a small crevice no bigger than a fist.

Inside that hole was an even smaller box with a lock. Nothing special, just a small gray box.

And I had the key.

With trembling fingers, I unlocked the box. It was a moment so simple and so important, that when it finally happened, it was hard to believe it was real.

A weathered scroll, wrapped in a simple slip of silk.

I snatched the map and shut the box, tucking it back into the crevice and then the brick. I stepped out from behind the tapestry, clutching the one thing that would save the world.

See Derrick? I'm going to save us. Look at me now.

I unfurled the map and sucked in a sharp breath. It was everything I knew it would be. A map bordering the central plains and the Red Mountains, small black squares dotting the range. All of the measurements precise, a number next to each, starting with the Red Gate.

The *Red Tunnels* and the key to winning our war.

I rolled the scroll back up with the key, sticking both into the empty sheath at my thigh.

The doors behind me were thrown open; a clap like thunder sounded as they hit the wall. The whole room quaked in response.

I dropped my skirts and my skin plummeted to ice.

"Well, well," a familiar voice drawled, nasal and sharp, "what have we got here?"

I whirled around.

Mira blocked the entry with the king at her side. The two guards who'd let me in stood at their back, and there was a handful more behind them.

"Why don't you tell us what you took?"

My gaze flitted from the mage to Blayne, and I swallowed, trying to ignore the frantic pounding in my chest. They couldn't know. They couldn't *possibly* know.

"I-I don't know what you are talking about." My fingers were clammy and blood rushed to my head.

"Oh, but you do." The head of Blayne's regiment took a

step forward, cackling. "I just didn't think you would be foolish enough to reveal your hand so soon."

"I didn't take anything!" I did my best to look annoyed, folding my arms and lifting my chin in defiance. "You are mad. You've always hated me—"

"And that's what they all thought." Mira's eyes gleamed in the early morning sun. "They all thought I was wrong. Didn't they, your majesty?"

My glance shot to Blayne.

"Please explain yourself, Ryiah." The young king wasn't looking at me like a friend.

"I only came here to look for a bracelet." I let indignation and confusion sweep my tone. "I don't know what she is implying."

"At dawn?" The head mage snorted. "She's lying to you, Blayne. I told you all along."

"If you have nothing to hide," he said coldly, "you'll submit to a search."

"Gladly!" I spat the word with as much indignation as I could, but my heart was racing.

Mira charged forward and tore off my cloak, thrusting her hand in every possible inch. Then she screeched and threw it to the floor.

"See?" My voice was shaky as I clutched my nightdress to my chest. "I don't have whatever it is y-you are looking for."

"I'm not done." The mage snatched my wrist and called on two of her guards.

"This is indecent!" I struggled against their grip. "You can't do this!"

There was a hushed collective of silence. Then: "Search

her."

The woman took a menacing step forward, and the guards tightened their hold.

"Let me go!" My magic bubbled to the surface like an overflowing fountain, fighting, *cresting* to break. "Let me go!"

"Get your hands off my wife!"

Darren. I stopped breathing as my husband shoved his way past the guards and spun on his brother. "What is this?"

"I summoned you here because there is something you need to see. Something to do with your wife."

The prince laughed. He threw back his head and laughed, the sound echoing around the hall like a chorus. "Not this again."

"I didn't want to believe it either."

"Because it's not true!" I fought Mira's grip. "She's lying!"

Darren's gaze returned to my guard and his hands balled into fists. "I'll give you two seconds to step away from my wife," he growled, "before I slit your throats."

I was released; I took a sharp, staggering breath. *Breathe. Control. You can still find a way out of this.*

The prince cut across the room, and I took a hitching breath.

"Darren—"

"Ryiah." He shook his head vehemently and pulled me into his arms. "You don't have to explain."

"She's had it in for me forever." I clung to his shoulders, hating myself. "You know what she's like!"

"I do." Darren turned back to his brother. His whole body

radiated rage. "This has gone on long enough, Blayne. Derobe that woman and toss her in the dungeons. I am done having Mira slander my wife."

"Brother—"

"No!" Darren's voice rose to a shout. "Do you have any idea what Ryiah has been through? Imagine if Derrick had been me, Blayne. This is unacceptable."

"Brother." The king's cool eyes flashed. "Do you know whose idea it was to give you the key to the Red Tunnels?"

I felt the prince stiffen.

No.

"It was Mira's." Blayne paused as the truth sunk in. "Do you recognize this room?"

Darren's pulse hammered against my own. And then it stopped.

"I don't suppose you told her there was a map."

"You gave me the key," Darren's throat was thick with emotion, "to test Ryiah."

And I thought it was a gift from the gods. Fool that I was.

"Your wife's been sniffing around the palace for months," Mira snarled. "No one believed me, but then your rebel escaped and the Pythian ambassador stalled..." Her eyes gleamed. "Two coincidences. Ones a husband could easily overlook."

"Even you admitted something was wrong." Blayne's gaze locked on his brother. "I didn't want to believe Mira, but what other choice did I have?"

The prince's grip tightened almost painfully. "Ryiah would never betray us."

"There was never a key for the map, brother." The king

was shaking his head. "That isn't even the true map. It's in my chamber."

It was a trap. All along.

"Search her." Blayne's order was clipped. "Continue what Mira started, and by all means, if she's innocent, I'll behead Mira myself."

Mira let out an indignant gasp. I was too numb to do anything but stand. I felt like I was outside of my body, watching this horrible scene take place from afar, knowing I would lose.

Darren didn't make a move.

"Brother," Blayne's voice had taken an edge, "why do you think Joren sent forty warships only to renegotiate terms after the two of you arrived in Langli?"

There was only silence, and I held my breath. I couldn't run and I couldn't cast, not with all of the guards and Darren watching... I couldn't. I knew I should, but I *couldn't*.

"I've offered him everything our father couldn't." The king's gaze slid to me. "Joren must have received a better offer from the rebels. The one thing I could never offer. A Pythian in my place."

I felt it the moment Darren recalled our conversation. The jokes about Pythus. *A Pythian Queen.* Innocent, but now... Darren's shoulders tensed. His pulse stalled and then his grip fell away.

The prince took a staggering step back, and then his whole body changed.

Darren swallowed. His eyes were wide. "Tell me they are wrong, Ryiah."

And so I lied. I looked the love of my life in the eyes, and

I lied.

Darren took a hesitant step forward, and then another. His palm reached out to mine, and I took it. A lump rose and fell in his throat.

"I believe you."

"Brother?" Blayne's bark shook the room. "What are you doing? Search her!"

"I don't need to." The prince's lips pressed against my brow, and I relaxed. Darren was choosing *me*. This was over. Mira would lose. I could breathe. I could think. I could—

His second hand dipped and found the sheath at my thigh.

I tried to move, to catch his wrist as it caught on the scroll and key dangling from its silken cord.

"Always prepared, love?"

Darren's eyes found mine, and what I saw... it tore me apart.

I saw us. And I saw the moment we died.

"The problem," the Black Mage declared bitterly, "is that I don't trust myself."

ELEVEN

I HAD WATCHED my own brother suffer, wasting away in these cells. It was only fitting, I supposed, that I would join him in the end.

Had I believed him at the time, Derrick might have escaped.

I might have been able to make a difference.

I might have been able to save us all.

"It pains me beyond measure to see you wasting away in this cell."

"Does it?" I looked up through the bars. The tyrant was taking me in, an ugly scowl framing his mouth. Blayne wanted to know how I could betray the Crown.

And I wanted to know how he could betray his own country.

"Ryiah." The king was curt. "You know it could be worse."

I didn't reply. The both of us knew the only reason it wasn't was because of his brother. I was the inconvenience blemishing Blayne's immaculate plans. He wanted to know what I knew.

"You were given more status than any female in this

land."

Silence.

"Is that it?" The king took a step closer. "You want more? Did King Joren promise to make you a Pythian queen? Or was it something else?"

I took a small breath. The smell of urine and blood was, if possible, less potent than before. But then again, there hadn't been a prisoner in the dungeon since Derrick died.

He didn't die.

Derrick was murdered.

The stench might be less prevalent, but the crime was still there.

I lifted my head and looked the tyrant in the eye. "You want an answer?" I spat the words in his face. "Bring him back."

Blayne's smile twisted. "Your little brother or mine?"

My fingers scraped at stone.

Blayne watched my face, missing nothing. He knew the only reason he wasn't dead was the long line of Combat mages behind him. With Mira at its head.

Darren had watched them take me away. I hadn't even had a moment to explain before the guards charged, knocking me to the floor and binding my hands and legs. I'd choked, gasping for air, trying to call out to him as they dragged me away.

I hadn't fought. I should have—I would have lost—but I couldn't. Not until I had a chance to explain.

"You know," he said, "I think you broke my little brother's heart."

I'd seen it. That moment Darren found the map. I'd taken

that broken boy on the cliffs and walked away.

"The both of us are too intelligent to pretend we don't already know your role." Blayne cleared his throat expectantly. "You are a rebel."

I didn't bother to deny it; there was no point.

"A lowborn Combat mage, who's half-drunk on power and ready to avenge her little brother's death." His tone was dry. "I'm surprised I didn't see it sooner."

Silence.

"The problem," he said, "is that you love my brother. So whatever he might claim, I don't believe Pythus promised you a crown. I don't believe you would take it."

My whole body stiffened.

"Were my brother a different sort of man, I'd expect you were trying to make him king." Blayne's bark of laughter hurt my ears. "Seeing the look on his face in the Throne Room, I hardly believe that's the case."

There was a sobering pause. "So what was it, Ryiah? What convinced you to betray the man you love? Was it revenge, or was there something else?"

I met the king's stare.

"You still care." His snort was incredulous. "That's why you want him here. To explain yourself." Blayne paused. "You give me a satisfactory answer, and I will bring Darren back in."

"Give us five minutes alone."

The king broke out into a smile. I wrapped my arms around my chest, trying to ignore the sudden chill.

"Ryiah, Ryiah." Blayne said my name with a sigh. "You tell me your reasons, you tell me where the others are, you tell me every silly little plan… and I *might* let you live."

"So kill me then." I was taking a risk, but if Blayne remembered my brother—and I knew that he did—he would know Derrick hadn't admitted to a thing. He'd been willing to die, planned on it.

Blayne's eyes flashed in the dark. There was no true light in the dungeons, just a couple of rusting sconces and dripping wax. But I could still see the growing flush on his neck, the way his fists clenched at his sides.

There was another moment of silence. Then: "Mira!" Blayne snarled the words. "Go fetch my brother!"

"But—"

"Tell him he doesn't have a choice!"

There was a rush of movement and the slam of a door.

The king turned back to me. "I know what you are planning."

I held my breath.

"Your little brother tried to do the same thing with my men. He thought he could somehow convert them to your little rebel cause, but look behind me." The king held out his hand, and my eyes inevitably shot to the mages at his back. "They weren't fools, and Darren isn't either. You try something like that and, well…" Blayne's expression turned cruel. "…he might just do me the favor of taking your life. He didn't for your brother, of course, but with you, he might take exception. I certainly would."

Don't let him get to you.

The next ten minutes were the longest of my life.

When the angry voices finally raised outside the hall, I instantly rose to my feet.

There was a terrible screech as two bars of metal slid into place, and then the door swung open, revealing a beaming Mira, the two guards from the outside, and Darren.

The prince didn't even look at me; he just marched straight to his brother.

"I'm not doing this." His voice was flat. "You have overstepped—"

"Brother." The king's reply was clipped. "This is not about your wounded little heart. You don't even have to talk to her. You just need to stand there and look pretty so she'll cooperate."

My whole body trembled as Darren's gaze landed on me, his eyes indifferent and cold.

"She's going to tell us everything," the king said.

"Is she?" Darren's reply was like a mouthful of glass. He was talking to his brother, but he was looking at me.

I told myself nothing could hurt me, but his eyes were tearing holes in my lungs.

The prince took another step forward, advancing on my cell. He stood just yards away when he snarled, "The traitor is going to give us a *reason* why we shouldn't hang her from the rafters like her brother?"

The traitor.

It was a blow I had never expected. Not from him. Not so sudden, not before I had a chance to explain. My resistance was crumbling, and for the first time, I realized there was a chance he might never believe me—ever.

I had known it was there, but up until this moment, the part of me that kept clinging to hope, it was breaking.

But another part was bracing to fight.

"Your brother isn't who you think he is!" I grabbed the bars to close the distance between us, but Darren had already taken a step back, his head shaking, while the king broke into a throaty laugh. "Blayne's lying about everything!"

"Oh, Ryiah." The king was smirking. "You are making this too easy."

"Darren, look at me!"

The Black Mage clenched his jaw as he turned. "My brother isn't who I think he is?" His fists were balled. "What about my wife?"

"Listen to me!" My fingers clutched the bars so hard I could feel the rusted metal cutting into my palms. "Just listen to me! Blayne and your father staged the whole war." Blayne stopped laughing, and my voice rose. I knew what was coming next. Up until that moment, the king hadn't realized what I knew. "They've been doing it for years——"

Blayne's order cut me off as ten castings hit the air.

By instinct, I threw up a magicked shield, but it wasn't enough.

Not when I was trapped in a cell and up against the best of the king's men.

My globe splintered, and my back hit the wall with a crunch. The air rushed my lungs. For a moment, I couldn't see or hear anything. There was so much pain I couldn't even breathe.

And then there was a shout and everything stopped.

I slumped to the floor. All I could hear was blood pounding in my ears as pain enveloped my chest.

"Brother, you have three seconds to get that thing out of my face."

My eyelids fluttered open.

Darren had Blayne pinned against the entry, a blade to his throat. The entire regiment of mages was surrounding his back, ready to strike.

Something stirred in my chest, something besides the agony that was eating me alive. It made me want to move; my shaking palms tried the floor and I rose to my knees.

Darren's weapon disappeared and he staggered back, looking at his own hands like they'd betrayed him.

"I-I don't..." The prince looked from his brother to me, and for a moment, his expression faltered. I saw pain and anger and something like grief.

Then his gaze hardened and he looked away.

The king put a hand on his brother's shoulder. "Don't worry," he said, "I won't kill her just yet."

Darren said nothing.

No. I struggled to my feet.

"Now, Ryiah," the young king said, "this was your chance, but it appears you don't want to cooperate—"

"No." Darren's command was flat. "We are going to let her explain."

Blayne ground his teeth. "I thought we just—"

"She will *talk*." The prince wouldn't look at me, but I didn't care. He was going to let me explain. He was going to listen. "I want to hear her out." His voice was hoarse. "Even if it's all lies."

"She's a rebel and a traitor. How could you possibly—"

"Because I loved her!" Darren's shout reverberated across the chamber; a different kind of pain wedged itself into my heart. The prince was shaking and his eyes were

rimmed in red. *"She's my wife, Blayne!"*

"Very well." The king turned his cold eyes on me, and I saw a promise of what was to come the moment Darren left the room. "Let us hear her lies. It makes no difference one way or the other."

I was still trying to stand. My hands kept slipping on the bars as I struggled to my feet. I hadn't hoped for much, but somehow hearing Darren's plea was worse. *Tell him.*

"C-Caltoth has never been our enemy." I drew a staggering breath as the prince fixated his attention on something behind my head. *Look at me.* "Darren, everything was staged. For years. Your father coveted Horrace's wealth. He knew he would never win a war without the Pythians' and Boreans' support."

"So all of those attacks on our border," Darren drawled, "they were just a big misunderstanding?"

"Yes—I mean, no!" I caught the disbelieving look on his face. "Those men were Caltothian mercenaries your father bought. That attack in Ferren's Keep our fourth year of the apprenticeship? It was a ploy to secure the other countries' aid."

"What an imagination you have."

My plea turned desperate. I knew I sounded mad. I hadn't believed Derrick when he explained it to me before. "Remember that mission in Dastan Cove, Darren? Mira wasn't under your father's orders. It was your brother's—"

"You filthy, little liar!"

"Mira," the king's reprimand was sharp, "we all know Ryiah is lying. No need to intrude."

Now Blayne was pretending to be gracious so his brother

disregarded my words.

"We were sent to kidnap a mother and child, remember?" My voice was rising. "Did you ever wonder why?"

The prince drew a rattling breath.

"I saw the girl in the Candidacy stands, Darren! Your brother was using her to blackmail the Caltothian ambassador. Lord Tyrus was the father. It explains why he was willing to betray his own country—"

Darren was turning away.

"—I know how it sounds, but it's the truth. Blayne killed your father, not the Caltothians!"

"I've heard enough." His sigh was barely audible.

"Darren, please!" I clung to both bars. My heart was right there in his hands. *"Listen to me!"*

The Black Mage spun back around and charged my cell, eyes blazing.

"You want me to listen to you?" he roared. "If that were the case, you would have said something before, Ryiah! Not these lies now after you were caught!"

"I couldn't!" Tears stung my eyes. "I wanted to, but I couldn't risk the chance you wouldn't believe me."

"I don't." His response was apathetic. "I don't believe a single word you've ever said to me."

"You know me." I reached out to touch his wrist, and he jerked back out of my reach, garnet flaring in response. "Darren," I whispered, "please. I was trying to help—"

"Like seducing me for a map?"

He didn't believe me. "No, that wasn't—"

"Tell me, love," his question was bitter, "why every word out of your mouth is such a beautiful lie?"

No. No. *No—*

"I wonder," he added, "if you ever actually loved me."

"I did, Darren. I *do!*" I couldn't even see; tears blinded my vision and I shook so hard it rattled the bars.

I heard him walking away.

"If it helps—" Blayne cleared his throat. "—I do believe she loved you once."

The footsteps stalled and Darren drew a sharp intake of breath.

"D-don't go!" My cry was hoarse. *"D-Darren, p-please!"*

"The problem is that the rebels took away that girl you knew." The king's voice was sickly sweet. "She's been hearing so many lies, she's begun to believe them herself."

"Darren!" I was hammering the bars, screaming his name. *"Darren!"*

"I'm done here." The prince strode toward the door, shoving a guard out of the way that wasn't moving fast enough.

"I understand." Blayne was nodding along. "Mira will handle the rest."

My tongue was so heavy, I could barely speak. *"D-Darren—"*

The Black Mage's hand faltered on the knob, and he turned, eyes blazing.

"I don't know who you are," he snarled, "but you aren't the girl I love. That person is gone." Darren spat the last line as he slammed the door shut. "You are just a stranger with her face."

* * *

The second Darren was gone from the room, the king turned to the rest of his regiment.

"See to it that the rebel is in no condition to cast. I would like to see her when you are done, before the interrogation begins."

He couldn't confront me in front of an entire squad, so he was going to make sure I was too weak to fight back alone.

My hands tightened against the bars.

"Don't you worry." Mira cracked her knuckles against her chest. "I will take care of this lowborn scum."

Blayne looked down his nose. "Just make sure she can talk."

* * *

She couldn't break me.

She and the faceless others broke most of the bones in my body.

But she couldn't break *me*.

I was lying in a pool of my own blood, and I couldn't even lift my head.

Vaguely, I heard a rumble of voices across the chamber, but it hurt too much to listen. It hurt too much to breathe.

I wasn't sure how long I was down. It hurt too much to think.

Everything was on fire. If someone cut right into my flesh, I wouldn't have felt a thing. There were parts... parts that felt wrong. I knew if I opened my eyes, I would see which, but the effort was too much.

Everything was too much.

If there was any magic left, I could never reach it now. I had lost most of it when they began.

I had promised myself I wouldn't fight back, that I would hold onto my magic until the very end, so that I would have something to use when the interrogations actually began... but somewhere after the first hour, my will snapped, and I couldn't hold on.

Every time I cast, twenty regiment mages shattered whatever defense I built. I might have been able to take on five of their most powerful on even ground, but I was trapped in a cage and these were hand-selected warriors from the King's Regiment. Blayne had picked the best of the best, and I was just a doll they tore apart.

Knives ripped across flesh. Boots and fists pounded against bone.

Someone held my head underwater as I thrashed. My nails clawed the tub and I choked, ice splitting my lungs... Eventually the pain stopped, and for a moment there was peace... Until someone dragged me up by the back of my skull.

And then they inflicted something worse.

In the end, it hadn't mattered. I was the victim. Their victim. Some bruised and beaten shade of a girl crippled on the dungeon floor.

How much time had passed? I couldn't be certain. I lost count when someone took an iron to my skin, this time branding a sigil of the Crown to my wrist. They pressed it so hard and so deep I could still smell the burning flesh.

They said those of us that could pain cast had a higher tolerance than the rest. That we were used to holding onto sanity under conditions where others would break.

They never prepared me for this.

I couldn't even open my eyes.

They couldn't break me, but parts of me wished they would. That it was over.

But it had only just begun.

Someone jerked my hair back and my head slammed against the bars of my cell. Someone was saying something, shaking me, and then an iron fist collided with my cheek. They wanted me to look at them.

"Open your eyes, you filth!"

Another blow to the ribs, and then another terrible crack as something snapped.

I opened my eyes, as much as it hurt. I wasn't sure I could survive another blow.

"There she is. Doesn't look much like a pretty little mage princess now, does she?"

I recognized the voice before Mira's face came into focus. My vision was stained with red.

"No. Certainly not."

A second face came into view and I recoiled, every part of me raging against the movement as my back hit the wall.

A fresh wave of pain tore up my spine, and I couldn't control the small whimper that fell from my lips.

"You kept your word…" Blayne looked down at me with a smirk. "I believe her mouth is the only thing you didn't break. She can't cast?"

The woman clucked her tongue. "All depleted. Every last drop. It will take her days to recover her stamina."

"And you sent the others away?"

"Yes. Would you like me to wait outside the door?"

"No." The king's eyes were locked on my face. "I don't

trust this one. I'd rather you stay."

Blayne knelt so that our eyes were level through the bars. The head mage went to stand by the wall, ready to strike at her tyrant's first command.

It hurt to take a breath; I couldn't even lift my arms.

"So, Ryiah."

Every part of me stilled.

"I thought I was a good actor, but you…" Blayne clucked his tongue against his teeth. "…you caught me by surprise."

My pulse hammered against my throat, the air growing thick.

"I hated you at first. Watching my brother fight so damn hard for a lowborn when he never fought that hard for me…" Something like jealousy flashed across the young king's face. "But after the Pythians, I recognized your worth. You came in second during the Candidacy. You risked your life during the attack on my father… You were exactly what I needed. No one would question a king with the two most powerful mages at his side." His tone abruptly soured. "Was it your brother? Was that when everything changed?

"I think it was." Blayne didn't bother to wait for a reply. "It's the only explanation. But I still wonder, those things that you said. They were new. Even Derrick failed to mention the Caltothian girl and my role… which leads me to believe you discovered the truth after he was gone."

My mouth felt like sand; I couldn't swallow.

"What really interests me is what you were planning." Blayne rose to his feet and began to circle the room. "You went after the map. It was just a test, something I knew a rebel couldn't resist, but now I'm curious what you were going to do with it. Were the rebels preparing to take over the desert? Was that what you promised Cassius? A bit more land?"

The king stopped pacing. "The Pythians are predictable, of course. Always ruthless, seeking a better deal." Blayne let out a bark of laughter. "Won't Cassius be surprised when you disappear."

My hand twitched.

"Oh, yes." Blayne missed nothing. "Your *illness*. I thought it best that the court *not* know of their princess's traitorous crime. In time, I'll reveal it to the world, but for now I thought it best to sit and wait. I wouldn't want any of your rebel friends staging an escape, *again*."

I refused to reply. I refused to give him any sort of response.

"I suppose you could tell me everything now." The king gave me a knowing smirk. "But something tells me your answers won't come without a fight. They haven't broken you yet."

"You will never break me." The words burned my throat. "I'll die first."

The young tyrant laughed. He laughed and laughed as he unlocked the cell door and grabbed my face, jerking it up so I was forced to meet his eyes.

"Such a stubborn little girl," he hissed. "You've got spirit. Much more than that friend of yours. What was her name? *Ella?*"

I spat in his face.

Blayne didn't flinch. He just held onto my chin, his fingernails biting into my skin, digging new rivulets of hot, coppery blood. "I'll enjoy watching you die." His eyes were manic. "Just like your brother."

I would have given anything for my muscles to obey, but I couldn't summon the strength to fight.

The king laughed and rose, dragging me up by the collar as I cried out in pain. Everything was red, and I couldn't even raise my arm as he sent a fist flying toward my face.

I stumbled back against my cell.

Everything went black.

TWELVE

THE NEXT DAY, I learned why the rebels chose to take their own lives before the Crown's Army dragged them away to interrogations. I learned why giving up everything was better than clinging to hope.

I learned what Derrick had withstood while I'd thrown tantrums inside the palace begging his surrender instead.

I learned what it meant to bleed.

I lived with nightmares in mortal flesh.

They had me wasting away on hallucinogens, watching over and over as everything and everyone I knew died. They submitted me to devices I didn't even know the Crown possessed.

"N-never." It was the last word before I was flooded with darkness. Again.

Those brief moments when everything ceased to be... I yearned for them more than anything. But I think Mira knew that.

My world was a flood of pain.

I knew nothing else.

I was drowning, and I just wanted it to stop. I finally

understood the release of death.

My lips were cracked. All I could taste was my own blood. The little water they gave me was stale and warm, and the bread was covered in mold.

The room stank of pungent flesh and acidic buckets of waste. I felt each old wound reopen when I shifted in my manacles or slept. My shift was worn to rags.

There were parts of my body that couldn't react. Parts of me that were numb. Parts that ached and burned and sent needles down my spine when I turned.

I couldn't hear anything. The world was a jumble of noise, sharp and soft, colliding with my thundering pulse; they had to shout into my face for me to hear.

When it got too bad, they called a healer.

Only so they could begin anew.

Questions, silence, and pain.

Over and over, minutes and hours melded together, and I lost all sense of time.

There was some sort of commotion when I awoke. I couldn't see it. My eyelids refused to cooperate.

But suddenly I could hear. A healer must have come while I was fading in and out.

"She's refusing to cooperate."

"We should just kill her now."

Blayne and Mira were somewhere inside.

"No."

My lungs stopped. I knew that voice. I knew it so well, and somehow I had almost forgotten it in the hours that passed.

"Darren—"

"She's my wife, Blayne!"

"Brother." The king's voice lowered sympathetically. "Why do you want her alive? Look at her. She betrayed you. She betrayed all of us."

Silence.

"If you want her for *other things,* there are plenty of ladies in court who would be more than happy to warm your bed."

"That's. Not. It."

"Don't you dare tell me you still have feelings for the traitor."

"I don't feel anything." The prince's snarl echoed across the cell.

"Then that settles it." An order: "Mira."

Someone jerked at my chains and pulled me up off the floor. My eyelids fluttered as Mira shoved me up against the wall, one hand holding my throat as a conjured blade rose in her fist.

Did I scream? Her blade pressed into my neck and something wet slid down my shoulders as every inch of me shuddered and burned.

"If you don't feel anything," the king said loudly, "let Mira finish the job for both of us. Let's put the traitor behind us once and for all."

Silence. Again. Not that I truly noticed with a blade cutting into my neck. A dull, throbbing pain exploded just above my chest. *Is this what it feels like to die?* I wondered. *Like your pulse is being taken right out of your throat? Like someone—*

"Give me a week."

"Darren—"

"I'll interrogate her. *Please*, if she doesn't give us the answers—" There was a pause, "—I'll execute her myself."

The blade left my throat; I wished it hadn't.

Up until that moment, I'd forgotten the boy with the garnet eyes.

But hearing him... I felt everything.

* * *

The next time I opened my eyes, I could take a breath without shattering my lungs. Slowly, cautiously, I extended my arm, first one, then the other when the pain didn't make me cry out. My legs came next.

With effort, but not so much that it brought me to tears as before, I drew myself to my knees. My arms trembled and a burning sensation ignited in my limbs, but eventually I was able to stand, pulling myself up with the bars.

When I could finally breathe, I dared myself to look.

There was a silhouette in the shadows watching me.

"I had a healer see to the worst of your wounds," it said. "If you try anything, I'll make them worse than before." The Black Mage took a step from the darkness so that I could see his face amidst the flickering flames. "*Much* worse."

I swallowed, taking a heavy lungful of air.

"You will not speak." His order stole the words from my lips. "Unless it is in direct reply to a question."

I folded my arms and instantly regretted it. There was an ache in the side of my ribs.

"Where are the rebels?"

I stared out at the prince, wondering what he expected me to say.

"Don't make me do this, Ryiah." Darren's warning was

flat. "Don't make me interrogate you like Mira."

I didn't speak a word; it wasn't a question.

"One more chance," he said. "You have one more chance to tell me where they are."

"They aren't the enemy—"

I never got to finish the rest of my sentence. Darren's magic slammed into me like a hammer, or it would have, had I not expected it just in time.

My shield redirected the brunt of his casting to my left.

Bits of stone crumbled to the floor.

Darren looked out at me without the barest hint of surprise. He probably had expected as much, given the healing.

"*Who* are the rebels?"

"Your brother is a liar—"

This time he tried a pair of daggers.

My magic wasn't fast enough, but somehow it didn't matter. Instead of hitting me, the blades shuddered and fell. On their own.

He cursed.

My gaze lifted to the prince. "Darren—"

This time his dagger hit its mark. I bit my cheek to keep from crying out as a sharp blade embedded itself in my shoulder. My pain casting came a second later, and the dagger fell away.

I tore at the hem of my dress. It was little more than a bloodstained rag, but I needed something to quell the flow. I didn't have enough magic to keep a casting in place.

It didn't escape my notice that Darren waited for me to finish.

"We will do this again, and again. I'll break every bone in your body. Is that what you want?"

"No."

His eyes were fathomless. "Then answer me with the truth instead of a lie."

I opened my mouth and shut it as a different kind of pain worked its way up my chest. *Speak.* "I am."

The Black Mage stood there all the way across the room, his arms locked at his sides. His chest was moving, but other than that, there was no sign of life.

Then he turned around and banged on the door, calling for the pair of guards just beyond.

"Put her in the chair."

No.

My eyes shot to the iron chair in the center of the room. I'd forgotten about it until now. Mira preferred hands and blades. Or branding irons. Or drowning. Or nightshade.

"The P-Prisoner's Chair, Your Highness?"

"That's what I said, isn't it?"

The two mages hurried forward, unlocking my cell and then my manacles. I didn't fight. I let them drag me forward by the pits of my arms. I stumbled along, looking at Darren the entire time.

When they finally stood me in front of the chair, I was forced to take a good look at the infamous device. Dark stains of old blood and rust coated the rows and rows of iron spikes lining its surface, from the headrest right down to the legs. There were straps everywhere to keep the prisoner from struggling during interrogation.

I noted the small clasps where they could pull the straps

tighter.

"Place her in it."

My eyes shot to his. Darren wouldn't even look at me.

The guards turned me to face the front of the room.

I didn't fight.

I should have.

But I knew why Darren had ordered the others to bring me there instead of himself. I knew why he had chosen the chair over his magic.

I knew why his fists were locked at his sides.

The men shoved me roughly into the device, and a thousand different kinds of pain ripped across my skin. I choked back a scream. It was all I could do not to writhe and claw at the iron-laden arms. In seconds, my nightdress— what little was not already stained in blood—turned a deep, dark red. Blood trickled down my legs and wrists and then pooled on the floor. Air expanded in my lungs. I was holding my breath just to keep from sinking lower in the chair.

The guards pinned me against the spikes, strapping me in place.

The more I squirmed, the more blood, the more *pain.* An involuntary flinch sent my whole body into panic. I was gasping at forty seconds, and the sharp exhale made things worse. My back jerked against the chair.

The two mages shoved me back harder than necessary and my eyes watered. I wasn't sure how much longer I could hold back a scream.

"This can stop if you tell me where they are."

"The rebels"—I was trying not to breathe, not to move, not even my chest—"aren't the enemy."

I couldn't see Darren now that I was strapped in. He was somewhere at my right. But I imagined the cold fury matched his voice. "Pull her straps tighter."

The guards started forward.

"Why don't you do it yourself?"

For a moment, nobody moved.

Drip, drip.

A rush of steps and then the guards were staggering back, the crown prince bare inches from my face.

I will not break.

"You think I won't?" he snarled.

"If I'm g-going to be int-terrogated by the B-Black M-Mage..." Everything was raw and the pain was getting worse. So. Much. Worse. "I w-would expect h-him to do his own w-work."

"Very well." His laugh was cruel and unfeeling. "If that's what you want."

Darren's fist caught the side of my jaw.

Iron needles raked the side of my face, and for a moment, I couldn't do anything but scream.

The betrayal was worse.

Salty tears mixed in with blood, and when I was finally brave enough to pull away—hoarse gasps pouring from my lungs—I was on fire.

I hadn't really thought he could.

He'd been standing so far away. He'd distanced himself. He'd called on others...

But I needed to reach him. If he felt *anything*.

I opened my eyes.

"You are g-going to h-have to do b-better than t-that."

Darren raised his arm again.

I held still, watching him, blood rushing down the side of my face.

"D-do it." Tears stung my eyes. "H-hit me a-again. Just like your f-father."

Something in his expression faltered, and then it was gone. Darren's fist collapsed to his side. The prince took a step back; he was no longer looking at my face.

"That's enough for today."

"Your Highness?"

"Remove the prisoner from her chair and take her back to her cell!"

My breath caught in my lungs. "D-Darren—"

"She will most likely bleed to death anyway." His hard eyes met my own, and anything I thought I'd seen, it was gone. "I'll be back tomorrow. If she's still alive."

* * *

A couple hours later, there was a familiar squeal of metal sliding into place. The prison door was thrust open for the second time that day.

My shackles were gone.

I was too weak to look up. There was so much pain that I couldn't risk the movement to crawl to my knees and check.

It was probably the same meal as the last. Rotting meat they wouldn't give the hounds.

I raised my head, just the slightest, when I heard the bars click into place. A hand dropped a rough sack and nondescript bottle just beyond my reach.

I stared.

"It's a salve."

My head jerked up, and I saw one of Mira's hand-selected mages staring down at me, his brows knit together in a frown.

"A s-salve?" My lips cracked as I spoke.

"To treat your wounds." The man's face drew tighter. "He said for you to apply it yourself."

"H-he?"

I was too late; the mage was already walking away.

I stared at both items, unwilling to react. It was only after the mage exited the room that I finally pulled myself forward, ignoring the sudden wave of agony, to examine the items up close.

It took me five minutes to crawl the space of my cell.

The brown sack, I realized, was a woolen blanket. Nothing pleasant, very coarse, but thick and heavy to tackle the endless cold. If I wrapped it tightly, it might even sever the flow of my cuts.

Inside the bottle was a dirty gray substance.

I tested it with the tip of my finger. It was cold to the touch and smooth, like mucus. It wasn't unlike the salves my brother used in the infirmary.

With less trepidation than before, I applied a small bead to the corner of my face.

At first my eyes stung and all I could do was hiss, but a second later, the pain subsided, and a cool, dulling sensation replaced the terrible ache from before.

I hastily dabbed some more along the deeper cuts on my thighs and arms. It stung something terrible and my vision spun. My stomach roared, and I was forced to heave up the little contents I had in my stomach.

But minutes later, the blood started to clot. The raging ache became a dull throb.

The salve was an alchemist's potion. A very costly one.

Darren?

My mind raced, but in the end, I couldn't be bothered. There was too much pain, too much of me to heal, and if it was him… I didn't know what to think.

With unsteady patience, I applied the salve to the rest of my body. In time, as the deeper parts began to heal, I was able to reach more. It took me most of the night, or what I thought was the night—I wasn't sure—but in the end, I had treated everything.

The worst of my pain was gone.

After which I was finally able to relieve myself. I was dehydrated and sharp hunger pains chased my gut, worse now that I had lost what little I had managed to keep down the first two days of interrogation, but for the first time, I was grateful for deprivation instead of abundance. I had managed so far to keep to the buckets—their foul odor of which I was now more than accustomed—but I was afraid it was only a matter of time before I couldn't. My brother hadn't in the end.

That last day, he had been huddled in a pool of his own filth, too weak to move.

Eventually, with the rough blanket wrapped tightly around my chest, I was able to settle into some kind of rest. But even that was disturbed. I couldn't stop chasing the memory of Derrick and what his life must have been like in those final days. The days I could finally share.

Heavy knots pulled at my lungs. It wasn't the kind of pain

I could put out with a salve. It wasn't the kind of pain I could escape.

My little brother had been so alone. Mira and the others had done things, the same terrible things they did to me now. My heart twisted into a hundred jagged pieces to know I had been inside these palace walls when they happened. That I hadn't been able to save him, even in the end.

My hand jerked to my neck, to the leather cord and Derrick's ring, the only part of him I had left. It was slippery with blood, but the copper circlet was still there, still heavy in my palm.

This was the reason I could never give up.

Derrick had faced his final moments a hero. They hadn't broken him, even when they broke everything else.

Whatever fear was plaguing me, it was nothing compared to the horrible knowledge that I would never be able to say good-bye to my parents, to Alex and Ella...

I couldn't let the villain win.

Even if that meant dying a traitor at the hands of his brother.

* * *

Darren arrived the next day without the two guards at his side. He came alone.

"Good, you used it."

It *was* him.

I blinked and pulled myself up on my knees. It wasn't as easy as it should have been, but compared to the first three days, I was thriving.

So was hope, as much as I resented its presence. Sending me that salve meant nothing. The prince was a war mage, like me. He knew the best way to extract a confession. Build a prisoner up and then break them back down. It was one of the first things they taught us during the apprenticeship.

Or maybe he—

He promised to kill you in a week.

The first thing I noticed was his right hand.

"What happened?"

Darren's jaw clenched, but he said nothing.

There was a crude wrap around his wrist. It didn't hide the swelling knuckles beneath or the darkening bruise. He'd broken all five of his fingers. They *still* looked broken.

Why didn't he go to a healer?

"If you are done staring at me," the prince said loudly, "it's time for us to talk."

"I wouldn't call interrogation a talk."

His eyes flashed crimson rage. "So eager to reach the end?"

"Wouldn't you be?"

Darren ground his teeth and approached the cell.

He's angry today, I realized. He had emotion—hate-filled emotion—but it was something.

He felt *something.*

I studied his eyes. They weren't just livid; they were bloodshot with dark creases... and was it just me, or did his face look leaner than before? His clothes were wrinkled and old. He didn't look anything like the Darren I remembered.

That Darren was always in control.

"I've changed my mind." Darren shoved a key into the cell lock, throwing open the door. "I don't want you to *talk.*" He spat the last word as he advanced, every part of him bristling with rage. "You are going to *listen*."

I scrambled to stand. "Darren—"

He slammed me against the wall, both hands pinning my arms as he locked me in place. I thought he shuddered from the impact to his hand, but I couldn't be sure.

He lowered his mouth to my ear.

"I used to think you were beautiful," he whispered, "and now I think you are the ugliest thing in this place."

A reply clawed its way up my throat, but I couldn't speak, not with the anger flaring in his eyes.

"You tricked me." His breath was hot on my skin. "I was a prince and a prodigy, and you were nothing. Just a lowborn. Just a little girl. Nothing special." His next remark was seething in hate. "And despite *everything*, I fell in love."

I held my breath as he touched the side of my face.

"Gods, I thought you were too good for *me*." The prince's laugh was bitter. "I was a wolf warning the lamb to stay away when that little lamb was preparing to stab me in the back."

I flinched, my eyes jerking to his. "It's not what you think. I didn't want—"

"You still look so innocent." He shook his head. "Even as you lie to me."

"I'm not lying!"

His eyes locked on my own, and for a moment, neither of us moved.

"You said you were looking for proof." His mouth was a hard line. "Tell me, did you find it?"

I didn't bother to say anything; Darren already knew the answer.

"So you never found proof." His fingers dug into my shoulders until it hurt. *Was he hurting himself, too?* "And you still expect me to believe my brother is a traitor. Not the girl who lied and stole a map." His hands shook with his rising words. *"A map she was going to sell to Pythus to betray her country and everything we ever stood for."*

The worst part was, everything he said was true.

"I know how it looks." I was trembling. "I stole that key and I was going to use the map to help the rebels, but Darren, Blayne is not who you think he is—"

The prince released me in disgust, taking a step back.

"He and Lucius staged everything! Caltoth has never been the enemy, the rebels—"

"You never could accept your brother's death, so you made him the hero instead."

"It's not denial—"

"I helped Derrick escape," Darren growled, "for you. Even knowing he was a gods' forsaken rebel, I betrayed my own brother for *you.*"

I reached out for his wrist. "Darren, please—"

The prince caught my hand with a look of disgust.

"You are going to die a traitor, is that what you want, Ryiah?"

"If that's what it takes."

His whole face was mottled and red. "You would rather die than give them up!"

"You expect me to give up the people that are fighting to save Jerar?" I pushed back. "Why don't you give up your brother! He's the real traitor."

"I expect you to give up a lot of misguided fools."

Darren's fingers were clenched around my wrist. "For *me*."

I faltered. *What?*

"Give. Me." Darren's eyes burned like coals. "A reason. To. Let. You. Live."

I couldn't speak. I couldn't even blink. He was standing there in front of me, his breath coming out in quick, shallow pants.

In another second, I knew Darren would turn and run.

I ran first. I slammed the cell shut, pressing the door to my back so that he couldn't leave. It was the two of us inside a cage of rusting bars. To leave, he'd have to fight me, and something told me the Black Mage wasn't prepared. Not today.

"Move away from the door."

"No." I braced myself, folding my arms. Even if he hurt me, and he probably would, I was going to make him do it here. Now.

Darren snarled. "You think I won't kill the traitor in my way?"

I held my breath.

The prince advanced on me like prey.

Stay still.

His fingers were inches away, a dagger at my chest as he leaned in close.

I looked up and met his angry gaze. The sharp sting of metal pressed against my ribs. The pain was nothing to what he and the others had done earlier that week; he would have to inflict a whole lot more, and we both knew it.

I held the prince's stare as he increased the pressure, the two of us locked in some unspeakable match.

"You really are prepared to die." His eyes narrowed to slits. "You would do it right here, wouldn't you? Right now?"

"Yes." It was hard to swallow.

"For them."

"For Jerar."

Something in his composure shattered. The blade vanished.

"Did you even love me at all, Ryiah? Or was it all some sort of twisted game for you?"

"I—"

"No, *don't*." Darren's laugh was mad. "You are going to die in five days. It doesn't matter either way."

I caught his neck with my hand. He flinched violently, but I held on.

"I've always loved you."

He took a slow, hitching breath.

"I never stopped, Darren." My fingers tightened as desperation seeped its way back into my throat. *Please.* "I love you, still."

I felt him shudder, and for a moment, for a moment I thought I broke through.

Then he wrenched my arm away and shoved me aside.

I was too startled to move.

Darren slammed the cell shut and shoved the key into the lock, grinding it violently as he twisted.

"Darren—"

"You really are the greatest liar I've ever met." His voice was like ice. "I almost believed you, again."

"I'm not lying!" I grabbed the bars, screaming,

"Darren!"

He didn't reply; he was already walking away.

* * *

The next morning, Darren didn't return.

But Mira and her legion of Combat mages did. It was only fitting. The Black Mage had given up. I had a whole new nightmare that was chasing my waking hours, making it impossible to rest.

Never mind the physical torment.

A day later there was a loud, jarring screech; someone had opened the prison door.

I opened my eyes and took a deep, retching breath, praying whatever Mira did would be quick.

But it wasn't Mira I found.

Darren.

I thought he wasn't going to return.

The prince didn't say a word.

He didn't look at me once. He didn't speak. He didn't do anything.

I stared at him across the room.

An hour later he left.

The next day no one came at all.

THIRTEEN

"YOU CAN'T MAKE the choice to die."

Everything ached, but his voice was enough to jolt me awake.

I opened my eyes; Darren was inside my cell, leaning against the back of the bars, watching me. He looked better than before; someone must have forced him to bathe. He had more color in his face too. I wasn't sure if I should be happy or sad.

It was the day before my beheading, and the boy I loved was doing well.

"You are my wife," the prince repeated, "and you chose the Crown. You chose us. You can't take that back."

"Darren..." My throat was raw and it hurt to speak. "...you know... where I stand." I hadn't expected to see him again, and now that I had, I didn't know what to say. From the expression he wore, I knew today would be the worst session of all. Somehow his resilience cut worse than anger or silence or visits from Mira.

I didn't want to hurt him any more than I already had.

Darren knelt before me and took a rattling breath. I couldn't react even if I wanted to; the others still had me bound and chained from the evening before.

"Perhaps your life is not reason enough."

I looked up at him, my heart caught in my throat.

"Perhaps I need to remind you the penalty for the rebel's family instead."

No.

"Yes." He watched the horror trigger on my face; his expression remained unreadable. "Your parents. Alex and his wife, Ella. Your friend Ian... You might be ready to sacrifice yourself, but are you ready to sacrifice them?"

I struggled uselessly against the chains, ignoring the searing pain from injuries not yet healed.

"Darren, they aren't rebels!" Three were, but he didn't know *that. "You can't punish them for my crimes!"*

His eyes were garnet stars in a sea of black. "I would. If that's what it took."

I was still struggling. "But I won't give you the answers either way!"

"Then you sentence them to die."

No. No. This wasn't Darren; he wouldn't do this.

"It's your choice, Ryiah." Darren pulled away.

"But it's *yours*!" I was straining against the manacles. "Darren—"

"No." His words were like thunder. *"You* are responsible for their fate. Not me. You could save them, Ryiah. All it would cost is the rebels." He ran a fist up along his neck. "You think we won't find them? That I don't think there is something suspicious about the keep and that rebel's escape? That I'm not questioning every single word you ever said?"

"Darren." I pulled myself to my knees as far as my

shackles would allow. My voice broke. "I-I can't."

The prince held still, unmoving. Then: "You can, but you won't."

My pulse hammered wildly against my throat. "But they aren't rebels!"

"It doesn't matter, not to me." His laugh was cold and unfeeling. "It should to you."

I didn't answer. I wanted to, but I couldn't betray everyone who had given their lives to this cause.

Even if I wanted to.

Something must have shown in my eyes, because the next thing I knew, Darren was shaking my shoulders, shouting into my face.

"I just told you that I would spare your family. And you still choose the rebels!"

"Darren—"

"Gods, you would betray *everyone*, wouldn't you?" His eyes bore into mine, angry and crazed. "How did they convert you to their cause? *What did they promise you?*"

"I already t-told you everything." Heat was rising to my face. "You just refuse to listen."

"Power, *was that it?*" Darren's fingers dug into my skin. "The crown prince isn't good enough? You want to rule the country yourself?"

"I never wanted to be *queen!*" I spat the words in his face. "It has nothing to do with power and everything to do with the *truth!*"

"Truth?" He was yelling right back. "Really, Ryiah? You want to talk about the truth?" His hands trembled with rage. "Derrick was a rebel and a traitor, and you were so blinded by your own grief that you decided to make my brother the villain instead of your own!"

Blinded by grief? "I'm not the one who is blind, Darren!" Why wouldn't he listen to me? What would it take? "Blayne isn't who you think he is. He killed your father. He staged an entire war! You are blind because you've always been his protector instead of seeing him for the monster he really is!"

"Where is your proof, Ryiah, *where*?"

"Darren—"

"Derrick was feeding you lies!" Disgust and despair tore apart his words. "You've had so much trouble coping with his death that you'd rather die for his cause than live for the truth."

"Darren..." There was a knot at the center of my chest. There was nothing I could say to make him believe me. I saw it in his face. He thought I was a liar, and I had broken his trust. There was *nothing* I could say.

Worst of all, I had no proof.

"Do I mean anything to you?" Darren punched the wall above my head so hard his knuckles bled. "Anything at all, Ryiah?"

"O-of course." Tears welled in my eyes.

"Then prove it." His voice lowered; he was no longer yelling. "Pick the Crown. Live." The next words were so desperate and broken. *"Pick everything we were."*

I shook my head; my whole body trembled; there was no way he could miss it. I couldn't meet his eyes.

The prince swore violently and released me with a shove.

For a moment, there was silence.

Then his voice cracked. "You asked me to run away

once.''

My eyes flew to his; Darren looked back at me. There was no hate, just regret. Something a thousand times worse than the first.

"So there was a time you would have picked us."

"I'm sorry." My whisper was hoarse. I couldn't pick him or my family now. There were others.

I'd been selfish then, but I needed to be better, *stronger* now. Wishing wouldn't change their fate. Picking the boy wouldn't save the rest.

The Black Mage rose and retreated to the corner of the cell, his hands stilling on the lock. "Not as sorry as me."

There was a sudden stiffness in my joints; I couldn't move.

"At dawn they are going to take your life."

Be brave, Ryiah.

"I won't be there." Darren's expression was the same as that day I found him on the bluffs. Something beyond grief. Something that called out to me even as I shattered. "I can't watch," he whispered. "Even after all that you've done. I *can't.*"

Tears streamed down my face, but I couldn't speak—not without breaking down into confession and selling my soul for the chance to take that pain away. I didn't trust myself with honor. I would have given *anything.*

I watched him go.

I let the boy I love turn and walk away, knowing he would never come back.

One more night.

So why did it already feel like the end?

* * *

The heavy thud of something splintering against the door was enough to drive me from my self-perpetuated misery. I had buried myself deep in nothing, ignoring every tormenting thought in an effort to escape the last few hours of my fate. It had almost worked, too.

Then there was a muffled shout and a second *bang,* and I couldn't ignore it again.

My eyelids fluttered open. I found a dank cell with rusting iron bars and the familiar stains of old blood on stone. I was surrounded by shadows and walls. There was no light now that the guards were away. There was no need.

There was the rotting stench of feces and urine nearby, something the guards had never bothered to collect. I breathed in unsteady gasps, and every part of me ached. The pain was coming back without remorse.

There was the agony of a body abused for days on end, the agony of what was to come, and the agony of Darren's last words, cutting deeper than any wound Mira could ever inflict.

Not as sorry as me.

There was the pressure of Darren's threat, closing in like a hand at my throat, squeezing until I lost all sense of control. Soldiers marching on Demsh'aa, and then the keep. My parents. Alex. Ella.

I had tried so hard to escape the fear, to hide from it in my little pit of despair.

The nightmare was back.

My village in flames. Black smoke crawling across the sky

as Derrick fell. Again.

Alex with a blade to his chest. Ella trapped and my parents falling to the soldiers' wrath.

And Darren. Standing next to his brother on the cold iron throne, a glistening crown of hematite stones as they laugh and laugh into the endless night.

I am trapped behind an invisible glass, pounding until my fists were purple and raw. Pounding until bones crack and my screams are muffled by the wind.

Who needed a hallucinogen when my dreams were the same as my fate?

"Ryiah!"

At first, I thought perhaps I was locked in another dream.

Paige appears, panting heavily with a sword clutched in hand; her chest rising and falling through the dim light of the stairs behind.

She blinks and tries to peer into the darkness, and then she utters a curse and begins to retreat, only to return with a torch.

"Well," she says, "he certainly could have given me an easier deadline."

There are bodies sprawled out just behind her, caked in blood.

"We don't have much time"—she races across the cell, her eyes darting back toward the hall—"before someone comes to relieve your guards." The knight digs into her pockets and produces a key from her vest, unlocking my cell.

I didn't think I would picture Paige in my final hours, but there she was. I stared up at the vision, grateful to have company, no matter her form.

"Ryiah?" She shakes me. "Ryiah!"

And a hard slap to the face sent the pain rearing back.

I blinked.

And she was still there. The pain had my whole head reeling and my cheek stung, but the guard was still there. "Paige?"

Her expression was incredulous. "Who else would it be? *Mira?*"

I blinked again. Still present.

The knight gave an impatient huff and unlocked the manacles keeping me in place. "I second-guessed myself for days after that rebel escaped." She was shaking her head as she pulled my bruised wrists out of the cuffs, one by one. "I knew there was something suspicious about the way you just gave up after your brother's death."

Somewhere just beyond, the bell tower gave twelve tolls for midnight. Six before the end.

"I know why you never trusted me." Paige wrapped one arm around my side, ducking under my shoulders with a groan. "It doesn't make it right." She let out a heaving groan. "But since you never told prince charming either, I've made my peace."

"Paige?" I was letting her pull me to my feet, trying to ignore the shaking in my limbs. There were parts of me that hadn't healed, and many that wouldn't, not without a healer to set things right. "A-are you r-rescuing me?"

"Mira has been watching me like a hawk ever since the news. I kept hoping your rebel friends would come save you like they did Derrick, but it appears the role of savior has fallen to me." Her lips pressed in a tight, thin line. "Trust your beloved to wait until the last possible minute to present the opportunity."

"Darren?" My mind raced and my head spun. Did he believe me after all? Had he helped Paige plot my escape?

The knight pulled a chain from the pocket of her tunic as the two of us crossed the room. "You two are the world's most complicated fools."

There was Darren's hematite necklace dangling from her hand. "Your beloved called a late meeting with Mira. The king is already in his bed. This should get us through the gates. No one but Blayne or the head mage would question the crown prince's orders."

There were so many questions spinning inside my head; I didn't know which to ask first.

"Here." The knight knelt down, and I started as I realized she was stripping one of the unconscious guards at the bottom of the stairs. "We need you to be wearing something besides a prisoner's rags. I don't want to give the others a reason to think something is wrong. We might need his sword too."

"H-how could you?" I paused. Both were mages Mira had employed during my interrogations. Any pity was immediately forgotten. They had enjoyed making a crown princess scream.

The knight caught my expression and gave me a toothy

grin. "They never expected a thing. I went after that one first. He couldn't pain cast like you. It was easy."

Trust Paige to be cocky during an escape. I rested my palm against the wall as I took in my bearings.

Seconds later, I was tearing off the remains of my dress, trying not to make a sound as Paige cut around crusted-over wounds. Then I was donning a gray uniform and the cloak Paige had been wearing over her clothes when she arrived.

Paige fisted a handful of my hair that was matted and sticky with blood. "I hope you don't have any attachment to your hair."

"Wh—"

Her knife whipped across the air and everything below my shoulders dropped to the floor. Paige wasted no time in gathering the strands, making a face as she did, and then stuffing them in the satchel at her waist. "Can't have them seeing the prisoner they expect," she explained, "and your hair is far too memorable as it is." The guard handed me a discerning amber vial. "Rub this in."

I didn't bother to argue; I already recognized the contents from my parents' shop. The scent was vile, but within seconds the sulfur had turned my hair a deep brown. The dried blood passed for dirt.

In my new garb and shorter locks, I passed for a male.

"Make sure you keep that hood down."

Paige started to climb the stairs, and I stumbled after her, catching her arm. I balanced a bit easier now, but I was still shaking. "Wait."

"Yes?" Her eyes flared in irritation.

"Why are you doing this? Why are you helping me? You

aren't a rebel—"

"We really don't have time for this." She huffed and helped me climb, slowing her pace. "All you need to know is I made a choice. Gods only know if it was the right one, but the moment the prince presented me with the opportunity, I took it. He promised me the necklace as payment for a life on the run, but..." She assisted me with the final step. "...my fealty hasn't been to the Crown, not since the moment they told me you turned traitor."

Something tugged at my lungs; I willed myself to blink away the tears fighting to break the surface.

"I don't know why you did it," she murmured, "and I don't know how, but I know *you*. If you took up with the rebels, there was a reason. Now, we have exactly thirty minutes to reach the stables before the next shift arrives. Darren assured me there is a mare already readied with supplies to last us as far as the coast." She paused and took a deep breath. "He wants you to take a ship to Borea as a fisherman's apprentice. He's had papers made, but I expect you want the rebels. We head north? To the keep?"

I nodded, unable to speak. She had answered my unspoken question. Darren didn't believe me. He wouldn't have ordered Paige to send me to the isles if he had.

He still cares, or he wouldn't have ordered this escape. He doesn't want your execution, even when he swore to hunt down your family next.

"I thought as much." Paige released my arm and made a motion for me to follow closely. "Now, don't look anyone in the eye and walk as fast as you can. Stop for no one. If they sound the bells, *run*."

Her laugh was bitter as we started down the dark corridor ahead. "Gods help me," she said, "there is no going back."

The two of us skirted the hall as quick as we dared, doing our best not to jump or flinch at every shadow and sound. Every muscle in my body ached. I had forgotten how many sets of stairs and winding corridors there were leading from the dungeon to the central level of the palace.

We were doing well, ten minutes in, before we came across our first pair of guards. Paige continued forward with her chin high. I shuffled at her side, trying to avoid notice.

"You there. Halt." A sharp bark made my hairs stand on end. "Names and purpose."

"Really, Pasha?" Paige faked a laugh and jerked her thumb at me. "You don't remember Gallaghen? He had dice with us that first week in the city."

I took a deep breath, holding my stance, and prayed they missed the purple bruising under my jaw. That the guards only saw a lanky boy with hunched shoulders and dark, coarse bangs. It was still dark and it was late, the time of day people were more prone to mistakes.

"Very well." The guard finished his cursory glance. "Purpose?"

"The two of us needed some time alone." Paige threw an arm around me with a cheeky wink at the men. "This is one persistent lad, finally won my heart after all these months."

The two guards guffawed. "You? A heart?"

"Oy, he looks a bit scrawny for your tastes."

My guard rolled her eyes and nudged me forward. "'Night boys."

The two of us continued past another set of guards; this

time they didn't question our presence. We made it past a third, and then I recognized a pair up ahead. Two mages from my interrogations. I reached for Paige's arm. "We can't go that way."

Her lips pursed as she considered our options. We had the main hall, with twenty guards near the palace entrance, an impossible feat, or we had the back doors to the gardens–taken up by the pair in question.

"We will just have to pray they don't recognize you."

Somewhere above, the warning bells tolled.

The two of us flattened against the wall.

"We were supposed to have more time!" Paige uttered a curse. "The next shift must have come early. We can't wait."

"No!" I pointed toward the kitchens. "There's a servants' passage inside. It will take us to the kennels."

"Fine," she gasped, "it's the best we've got."

"On my count... One, two, go!"

The two of us made a mad sprint across the corridor, our footfall and pace no different than the tens of guards scattering the halls. In another minute, I knew half the palace regiment would be at the front doors, the other half to check on the king.

We ducked into the kitchens just in time to find Benny clutching a butcher's knife, the surfaces of his dirty counters long forgotten as he made the sign against evil across his chest. "Sankt'ra Dien." *Gods protect us all* in the old tongue.

I dropped the hood as I inched closer. "Benny, it's me."

The man stared, eyes bulging. "Princess, but you are—"

"A rebel." My hand caught on the small catch that Darren had taught me to feel for during the apprenticeship. "Please, don't tell anyone we were here."

"How bad is it?" Benny's eyes darted to Paige who was clutching the hilt at her side, readying for a fight.

"I won't be coming back." I met the cook's wary gaze and prayed he wouldn't shout for the guards. I liked to think we were friends, but the man had no reason to trust a traitor.

He heaved a sigh and set down the knife. "You always were one of my favorites. Just promise me this isn't a mistake."

"Thank you."

A loud voice just outside the door hollered.

"One of you, check the kitchens!"

With one last look to Benny, I twisted the panel back and hopped inside with Paige at my heels. No sooner had we slammed the latch shut, then there were a pair of angry voices demanding if Benny had seen a fleeing prisoner.

I prayed Benny kept his word. If we had any luck, the guards would assume we were still hiding out in the palace. That we had never made it out.

It was time to run.

So, we ran. *Fast*.

We were stumbling around in the dark, sprinting over small bits of debris, coughing up dust, and dodging roots as we fled. More than once I lost traction from some throbbing muscle or loose bit of stone, and it was all I could do to hit the ground, breathe, and pick myself back up.

When we finally reached a small patch of light, it was long overdue.

The two of us caught our breath as we slid the second panel back and peered into the kennels beyond.

Everything was dark. But with the muffled shouts coming from the palace, we didn't have much choice.

No sooner had we shuffled into the room, something heavy collided with my legs, followed by a wet tongue.

"Hey there, old boy." I knelt down to pet Wolf as Paige groaned. She didn't hate dogs; she had stepped in something foul.

From the kennels, I heard more soldiers in the courtyard. It would only get worse.

We had to keep going.

I looked at the mutt with regret. I had spent too much of my youth fearing dogs when the real villains were part of my race. "I'll miss you." I wrapped my arms around the dog's scruffy neck and then stood, fighting the tightness in my chest. "Keep watch over your master for me."

A hand squeezed my shoulder. "You need a moment?"

I shook my head and started forward. If I started to think of what I was leaving behind, I would never stop.

When we reached the kennel exit, Paige turned to me and handed me her satchel, shoving me back inside the building.

"I'll get the horse. You wait here. If something seems wrong, make a run for the gates. No sense in both of us risking our necks. They are only looking for you right now, but who knows how long that will last."

The sky thundered and rolled up above; I watched Paige go, ducking along the castle grounds as rain sprayed the barracks and gardens below.

The next nineteen minutes were the longest of my life. The bell tower had just tolled an hour past midnight when she returned. I heard her footsteps just outside the door.

Only a second too late did I realize I was also waiting for two sets of hooves.

"And just when I thought you escaped."

The king stood, sopping wet, with a sword in hand and pointed at my chest.

Blayne.

I made a desperate attempt to slam the door, but he caught it just in time, yanking it back. I couldn't counter his weight, not after ten days of suffering in that cell.

I stumbled back, fumbling for the sheath at my waist.

The king strolled in at a leisurely pace, everything at ease except for the sword in hand.

I can do this. I kept my eyes on his blade as I backed away, withdrawing a blade of my own. *He's not a mage or even a knight.*

Then why was I afraid?

"I would ask you how you made it this far, but I suspect my dear, sweet brother has something to do with the circumstances of your escape." Blayne's eyes swept along our surroundings to the dark passage leading to the kennels, and his lips curled into a sneer. "The moment I heard he pulled Mira into some ludicrous meeting, I *knew*. I sent guards to check the dungeon." Paige had been right, the alarm sounded early. "And after that, it was simply a process of elimination."

The king took another step forward, and I inched back along the wall, the blade shaking in my hand. It was lighter, I realized, slender instead of thick, a rapier when I needed a broadsword.

"I thought I'd try the kennels," Blayne continued. "After

all, it was the place he and I used to hide when we were boys, and that passage, well, it was my first guess."

I bit down on the inside of my cheek, trying to hold my ground. "You don't have to be your father, Blayne. You don't have to do this."

The king cut me off with a laugh. "I'm not my father, Ryiah. I'm *better*."

I was back against the wooden fence. There was nowhere I could retreat, and to turn around and climb would be inviting a blade to my back.

Blayne didn't leave me a choice; he lunged.

I ducked left and parried right, clashing blades. The air shook with a resounding screech.

My blade was not the caliber of the king's own.

I withdrew and ducked, narrowly avoiding a swing that would have cut me from navel to chest.

Then I parried again at another slash aimed for my head.

Every muscle burned. I could not keep up the deflections forever, or even for long. I could call on my magic, whatever little I had recovered in two days alone in my cell without Mira's ministrations, but it wouldn't be enough for me to outlast Blayne.

Another twist and turn. Another deflection with only seconds to spare.

I caught his leg with a low sweep, but then I made a sloppy block. The impact rattled my bones.

I might have been the better swordswoman, but now? He had the better sword.

Blayne continued his advance with an onslaught of attacks. There was no chance to recover, no chance to think.

It was his sword against mine in a series of thrusts with every intention to kill.

With every counter I lost stamina. Sweat beaded my brow and I was hot—too hot. My heart beat like a drum against my ribs. I counted the minutes ticking by, trickling away the last moments of my life.

Slash and cut. Parry. Dance.

The next charge brought a deep cut to my arm. I switched grips as my teeth gritted against pain. I would have to fight left-handed. I couldn't afford my fingers to slip now.

I wasn't as good with my left.

Blayne pressed the advantage, his boots stirring up a swell of dust and straw as he advanced.

I was cornered between the wall and the fence.

Another slash, and this time, I had no choice—I drew too slowly with the sword.

My magic swarmed out like a whip. A phantom blade met the king's just in time. *Instinct.* A moment later, my real blade met its target, just as the magic fettered away.

Blayne pushed back.

My sword quivered; I didn't have much magic left to cast. My whole body shook under the pressure. It cost me just to hold, just to think.

Buckling under the king's weight, I felt Blayne digging down with his heels and the arching of his legs as he pressed forward.

He was trying to breach my defense.

No. I was not going to let this tyrant win. I'd worked too hard for it to end like this.

I shoved with everything I had, every fiber of my being.

Blayne stumbled back, and I charged.

Swing left and then up. Down. Right. Half-crescent spin. Another shallow cut at his waist. Parry and shuffle. Block again and strike. Cut.

Blood. Blood. And more blood.

I would cut the boy until he was a walking river of blood.

I pressed on, my eyes locked on the king as he fell back, one step at a time. Blayne ducked and staggered, and I was closing the distance, thriving in hate. How could this monster destroy everything I loved? How could I let his crimes go unpunished?

Someone had to be the hero, I wasn't sure that someone was me, but I was certainly going to try. I'd been holding back for Darren's sake, but what did it matter now?

Who cared if Blayne was a broken boy with monsters in his past? Blayne was a villain *now*.

Vaguely, I felt my energy depleting with each step I took, but I was no longer concerned. If I died alongside him, so be it. I wouldn't let Blayne walk out of this kennel alive.

Too late, my swing missed, a misstep from drilling too many days with the right arm instead of the left. A first-year's mistake, driven by adrenaline and emotion instead of the calm I needed to keep.

Blayne's counter caught my left shoulder on a downward sweep.

My sword clattered to the floor.

The king raised his blade to my throat.

My casting rose.

And something behind me let out a raging howl.

Wolf.

Blayne froze as a shadow leaped across the divide; the king couldn't hold off two attackers at once. His indecision cost him, and the dog sank its jaws into his leg.

Blayne swore as the dog evaded his kick and bristled, growling and snapping at my side.

I ducked low, scrambling to find my blade on the ground.

There was another bark just as my fingers closed on the hilt. I rose, ready to charge—just in time to watch the king of Jerar plunge his blade into Wolf's chest. "Should have killed that thing a long time ago," he drawled.

I roared and charged as the dog crumbled to the floor.

Wolf.

All I saw was red.

I swung with everything I had, again and again.

The dog whimpered at my feet; cold fury bound my lungs. Wolf was dying, and once again the villain lived.

I didn't even realize I was crying until my vision blurred to the point I couldn't see. I lifted an arm to wipe away the tears and the king lunged.

This time I didn't raise the rapier quick enough, or perhaps, fueled by a victory of his own, Blayne's swing was faster, *better*. Our blades collided, and a sickening crunch followed as my sword splintered and broke.

In the blink of an eye, my rapier was in half. My chest heaved as my magic rose to hold off the rest of Blayne's attack, but even that faltered under the king's weight.

There was a strange, tingling sensation in the back of my skull. That was all the warning I had before my casting gave way.

I dropped to the ground, ducking my head.

Blayne's sword cut the wall where my neck had been just seconds before.

Now I didn't have magic or a weapon. But the fight wasn't over.

My shoulder raged, and I could hardly see as I jabbed the jagged edge of my broken rapier into the center of my palm.

I bit down to keep from screaming out as the pain lit up my limbs, scorching every vein like hot water and ice. I twisted, *hard*.

The pain casting shot through me like an arrow.

The king hit the opposing wall with a thud.

His sword skidded across the dirt.

I sprinted forward and kicked the sword as far as it would go. Then I held the broken rapier against Blayne's throat, watching as the jagged end cut a light trickle of red across his pale skin.

Pale like a palace recluse, I had once thought. A boy who lived with shadows where there should have been light.

I faltered, the sharp metal biting into his neck. I heard the heavy thud of rain pounding the roof above our heads and the even heavier beat of his pulse. The king's chest rose and fell.

Do it. Do it now. There were so many reasons to end his life. Everything he had done. Derrick. Wolf. All the others, all the future lives that would be lost to a pointless war....

But in Blayne's face I saw the same haunted past as his brother. Blayne might have Lucius's eyes, but it was Darren's heart that would bleed.

And then I remembered that day Derrick escaped and the moment Darren found me in the hall. *Please.* The Black

Mage had chosen to spare my brother out of his love for me. Without ever knowing the truth, he had chosen me.

I needed to choose Darren.

I can't do this.

I started to withdraw the blade, and an unexpected blast hit my chest, sending me flying across the room. My shoulders slammed against the wall, and I struggled to rise.

My vision swam.

I barely had time to blink before my whole body was lifted and hung high in the air. My fingers shot to my neck, clawing desperately at an invisible noose. I sputtered and choked, trying to see who was in the shadows besides Blayne.

And that was when the king finished pushing himself up off the ground, brushing his dirty hands against his vest. No one else was in the room. He was watching me struggle with his lips curved up in a smirk.

Why had I never considered it? Because Blayne was born an heir?

The king had magic.

"Not as good as my brother." The king adjusted his sleeves. "But then again, becoming a mage was never my goal."

I choked as the knot grew tighter and tighter against my throat.

Blayne was good enough to kill me. As weak as the casting was, it wouldn't take much.

My magic wouldn't come, the pressure too much. I couldn't concentrate enough to cast. I was too busy struggling to breathe, my legs kicking up air.

"The red tunnels aren't the Crown's best kept secret." The young tyrant laughed. "You should feel privileged, sister dear. Very few know the truth, not even Darren. Only Father, and, well, he's dead." Another villainous laugh. "Of course, you *will* be joining him soon."

I couldn't see; all I could do was feel and wait for my neck to snap under the building pressure like a log split under an axe.

"It's a shame you chose the rebels. It really is." Even Blayne's voice faded. In another second, I would run out of air.

My eyelids fluttered shut.

Come on, Ryiah, fight.

I couldn't. Magic was struggling to break free, but the pain grew worse.

This isn't how my story ends.

And then the pressure stopped. The noose fell away as the king's scream hit the air.

I collapsed to the ground, unable to stand. I tried a hitching breath as I bit back a cry. I was in so much pain I could barely move.

"You!" Blayne's snarl jolted me enough to blink.

Through the shadows, I saw the king. Blayne was using one hand to staunch a flowing wound at his side as he glowered at a figure to his right. "You're supposed to fight for the Crown!"

The figure lunged, and the king swore, retreating a couple of steps back.

My breath hitched as Paige's voice rang out from the dark. "My loyalty is to Jerar."

The knight swung, twisting in and out of Blayne's defense as the king dove.

Paige countered just in time.

Two blades collided, again and again. Everything was on fire, but I didn't have time to rest. My legs quivered as I pushed up off the floor.

Paige advanced, backing the king into a corner of the room and knocking the blade right out of his fist. She was a better fighter, and he was weary from our duel.

Her sword pointed at his neck.

"Surrender," the knight ordered, "and I'll spare your life. I say this only once."

I saw the flare in his eyes the moment they turned to ice.

"Paige," I gasped as my knees wobbled in an effort to rise, "he has—"

But it was too late.

The blade he'd dropped shot up off the ground and caught her by surprise. The girl screamed as the sword spun and cut a crescent she didn't have time to defend against.

I couldn't run. I could barely even stand as Paige dropped to her knees, blood streaming from her chest.

Something inside of me snapped. Something angry and hot.

Magic bubbled and surged. It sang inside of my veins like a scream.

And then the king screamed as my magic lashed out and threw him against the wall. He cried out as I sent the second half of my rapier at his chest. I held my hand out in front of my face, casting the blade to twist.

The king slid from the wall to the floor, the second half of my rapier sticking out of his ribs.

Blayne clutched the shard in an effort not to move. His face was ashen and his lips kept closing and opening in a soundless cry.

I waited a moment, bracing for an attack with magic sparking along my fist... but if Blayne had the ability to pain cast, he hadn't mastered it. If he had any normal magic remaining, he didn't know how to control it. Not with the pain.

He wouldn't be stopping us now.

Darren.

Something tugged at my gut, and I swallowed, looking away. I couldn't think of the prince now.

And then I staggered forward, chest heaving as I reached Paige's side.

My throat was on fire, my pulse so loud I couldn't hear anything but the thudding of my heart.

Paige's face turned white and her teeth chattered as I knelt. "K-keep g-going, m-my lady."

"No!" I shook my head as tears blurred my eyes. This couldn't be happening. Not again. First Derrick, then Wolf, now Paige.

Paige wasn't even a rebel. Her only crime was believing me over the Crown.

She wasn't supposed to be a sacrifice.

"G-go..." Paige's face was strained and her lips were shiny and red as she coughed, choking on blood. Her skin grew paler by the second. "P-please, R-Ryiah..."

She never called me by my name.

"Y-you'll be f-fine." My voice was breaking. *I* was

breaking.

The knight shook her head and her face contorted with the effort. Her back was growing sticky and hot, and her pulse beat frantically under my hands...

Something smoldered in my chest. "I'm n-not l-leaving you."

Paige didn't reply; she couldn't. Her eyes were glassy as she raised a trembling hand to my cheek and a sad smile fluttered across her lips.

My fingers curled to fists and I clutched the girl to my chest, swallowing hard. Everything ached. The guards would arrive at any moment. Every second could cost my escape, but I couldn't leave her behind—even if that meant waiting out the last minutes of her life.

I would wait as long as it took.

The first tremors that rocked her body came too soon. Her whole body trembled against my arms, and the longer I held her, the more violent they got.

And then they grew less. Her head dipped as her fingers brushed my arm. At first I couldn't figure out what she was doing.

She kept repeating the same pattern over and over, tracing lighter each time.

She was trying to etch letters into my skin, to speak what she couldn't say aloud.

O-U-I-B-E-L-I-E-V-E-I-N-Y

A sob caught in my throat.

I believe in you.

Paige's tracing stopped and her finger rested on my skin. Her breaths turned shorter, and labored.

Behind us I could hear Blayne gasping for air. I clenched my jaw and blocked it out. He didn't deserve my pity. He deserved to die.

It would come quicker now that the king had nothing to plug his wound.

My hand covered Paige's, and I held onto my friend as the final breath left her lungs.

Her body went limp in my arms. It was that same moment footsteps sounded outside.

King's Regiment. I withdrew the half-rapier from Paige's back and blinked away tears as I gently laid her down. With two shaking fingers, I shut the lids of her eyes and then stood, crouching against the shadows and readying to run.

Her sacrifice wouldn't be in vain.

The steps drew closer as someone approached the kennel door.

"Paige?" Someone knocked. "I saw the horse. I know you're there."

I wanted to collapse in relief. *Darren*. It was Darren.

And then I remembered who else was in the kennels with me. I had already lived out this scenario once. I knew whom Darren would believe.

Blayne moaned from the other side of the room, but he was far past the point of shouting his brother's name.

My pulse thundered in my ears. I couldn't call out to Darren; I couldn't let him open the door and find me like this.

He'll know either way.

I bit down on my tongue. Blayne's muffled groans were growing softer. Maybe Darren wouldn't hear. Maybe he'd go away.

I drew a sharp breath as the door creaked. "Mira is only minutes behind me." Darren's outline was swathed with light. Storm clouds rolled behind his shadowy form. "I managed to lose her, but..."

He stopped talking.

I was standing in the center of the hall. My guard uniform was covered in blood, and my hair was plastered to my face and neck, short and brown. I looked nothing like my former self. Still, it took all of one second for recognition to cross his face.

"Ryiah?"

I didn't say anything. I stood there, watching his gaze slide to the floor.

To Paige.

A sharp intake of breath. "Why is s-she—"

His hand caught on the frame as he spotted Wolf. Darren let out a horrible choking noise as he rushed forward.

Then, he spotted his brother.

I stood frozen, unable to move.

The prince dropped to Blayne's side, hollering for a healer at the top of his lungs. His hands shook as he tore at his sleeve, desperately trying to plug the wound.

I knew I should run. I knew what it looked like. I knew what it was. I knew the guards would be here any second.

But I still couldn't run.

Darren's heart was breaking, and all I could do was watch him clutch his dying brother as Blayne sputtered, choking on his own blood.

"D-Darren..." My lips couldn't form the words; my throat

was dry and my tongue felt like sand.

Run, Ryiah.

But my feet were frozen in place. I had to explain; I couldn't.

"How could you?" Darren's voice was hoarse, and when I looked, there was only pain.

So much pain it was drowning me alive.

"It's n-not w-what you t-think." I stammered, seeing the betrayal in his eyes and the way his shoulders shook as he cradled his brother to his chest.

"Why run," he croaked, "when you can kill a king instead?"

I realized the broken rapier was still in my hand, dripping blood. It dropped to the floor. "I-I—"

"Paige tried to stop you." His fists clenched against his brother's shirt. "So you took her life as well."

"No!" My throat was raw. "Darren, y-your brother a-attacked m-me."

Darren wasn't listening. "And then Wolf." His voice caught as his eyes fell to his dog. The one happy memory from a dark childhood. "You took... *everything*."

I heard others running, but I couldn't bother to move. My eyes were locked on the prince as the kennel doors swung wide.

"Guards!" Mira's screech was all I needed to know that I'd been found. "It's the rebel! Stop her!"

The prince's gaze was still locked on mine. He made no move to correct the head mage's orders.

His expression was empty. Shattered.

Run.

I tore my eyes away. I didn't have time to think. I ducked as a spear flew over my head. My fingers dug into Paige's breeches, and I yanked the Crown necklace with a trembling hand and snatched the broken rapier with my other.

Something sharp whizzed past my shoulder as another knife narrowly missed my ribs.

I rolled, my shoulder roaring in offense. Then I thrust the jagged blade through my skin. I didn't stop until I scraped against bone. The pain almost made my legs give out.

Then the air gave a loud pop, an explosion of pressure and sound.

Anyone standing was thrown back against the wall with all the force of a tempest.

For a moment, there was only the heavy patter of rain and the dark sky from above.

I didn't look at him once. I couldn't. Not if I wanted to leave.

Then I was running. Through the doors, across the clearing, leaping onto the mare's saddle, and cutting the lead. I kicked my heels, leaning low as the horse took off across the palace yard.

There were shouts from just beyond. I jerked the mare to the right as an arrow soared just past my neck. I rode on and on while the storm muffled their shouts. Mira's men were forced to follow on foot.

I had only seconds to spare.

When we reached the iron gate, two soldiers were standing guard, polearms crossed.

I tossed the prince's chain at the nearest man's feet. It sloshed in the mud, but it's cut and color was unmistakable.

"Crown's orders!" My heart was halfway in my throat and the rain was washing away the brown dye with every second I sat there, panting. "Let me pass!"

The soldier looked up at me through sopping bangs, squinting through the rain. He wasn't supposed to question orders, and that necklace was as familiar as the throne. He couldn't argue with the stranger in front of him, lest he risk execution.

The man nodded to his comrade, and the two unlocked the bars.

The metal quivered and groaned, and I didn't bother to wait for them to clear more than a gap.

"Stop her!" Mira screamed at the top of her lungs, but it was too late.

I was just a shadow streaking across the cobblestone streets of Devon.

A shooting star, caught in the rain, cloaked in death and betrayal. Burning everything I touched with my crystalline shards.

I was breaking with every roll of thunder, every streak of lightning across the pitch-black expanse. But I kept on.

I was a traitor to the Crown.

And this time, there was no turning back.

FOURTEEN

THE FIRST TWO nights I didn't sleep. I rode as long and hard as I dared, taking what little shelter I could find in barns during the worst bits of the storm. It never ceased. The mare was exhausted, but at least she was able to rest during those brief stops.

I couldn't sleep. With every shift in the straw, every dance of hooves, and every branch that snapped outside in the winds, I was certain the Crown's Army soldiers were right outside the stable doors.

I survived on what provisions were stuffed into my pack; it was a week's supply for two. I tried not to remember why that was. If I started to reflect on my last night in the palace, I wouldn't be able to shut out the emotions that came with it. I couldn't escape the pain and loss forever, but if I caved to it now, the regiment would find me and then Paige's sacrifice would be for nothing.

My heart splintered with every mile I rode, but every so often the pain would fade. I still felt every broken rib and physical torment along my limbs, but the grief and regret were becoming a distant ache.

With every hour that passed, there was a scab growing

around my heart. A fire was burning out everything and leaving me with a hardened layer of coal.

After everything I had gone through in the last year, I had no more tears left to cry. I was stone, and everything Blayne and the others had done, everything *I* had done… It was all becoming ash.

War had a price, and this war hadn't even begun.

Two days of riding and I hadn't spotted a patrol once. I knew it was only a matter of time. Mira would have men scouring every inch of the land. As soon as Blayne recovered, he would have bounty hunters competing for my head. I didn't want to know Darren's role, and I refused to consider it.

There were too many concerns at hand.

I needed to get to Demsh'aa before regiment soldiers reached my parents. I needed to find my brother at the keep and make sure the Crown didn't take out my betrayal on those I loved. Once my family was safe, somewhere the king and his Black Mage could never find, then I could concentrate on the rest.

On the fourth morning, I had ridden the palfrey to her point of exhaustion. The little rest she received was not enough to make up for the miles and miles we'd covered in a short span of time.

I risked daylight to sneak into an inn's stable close to the King's Road. There, I switched out my mount for one of the occupants' instead. I could now add theft to my growing list of crimes, but I didn't have a choice. The mare was drawing too many eyes—not many traders had a thoroughbred that could fetch the price of a year's worth of rations—and I needed an energized mount, ideally a brown, nonsensical steed that wouldn't draw bandits and regiment mages to my trail.

The sixth day, I got lucky and came across a small hut off the road, with linens hanging out to dry above a bed bursting with root vegetables. I managed to steal two pairs of men's breeches and a fresh shirt before a tall, broad-shouldered man came to chase me away, hollering at the top of his lungs, but not before I snagged some carrots and parsnips.

Later that afternoon, I found a stream. It was so cold my teeth chattered, but I scrubbed until every last speck of blood was gone. Every part of me stung as I rubbed until I was raw.

Then I burned the old uniform, taking with it every memory of that night.

Like a phoenix born again, a red-haired boy emerged where a girl had once been.

The land had a familiar call the closer I got to home: crickets and the quiet rustling of clove trees alongside icy plain winds. I passed less and less farmland, and the terrain began to slope with more elevation and rocks. I recognized the boulders I used to climb as a child, just a speck in the distance but as familiar as rain.

I supposed it was only fitting that on my seventh day I came across a listing hammered onto a wooden post with a sketch of my face. There were more further west, lining the King's Road:

WANTED: RYIAH OF DEMSH'AA, FORMERLY A PRINCESS OF JERAR. HIGH TREASON. ATTEMPTED MURDER OF THE KING. HAS MAGIC AND VERY

DANGEROUS. NEW TITLES AND LAND FOR INFORMATION LEADING TO HER ARREST. BRING IN ALIVE.

My knuckles grew white against the reigns. The regiment had beaten me home.

My parents.

Common sense dictated I make a run for the keep. Alex and Ella. It might not be too late for them.

But even as the thought crossed my mind, I was kicking my horse into a gallop, urging him west. I couldn't leave without checking on my parents first. Maybe they had gotten out in time.

Or maybe the regiment had them, and if they did...

Just beyond the trees lining the main road was an old trail that circled back into the village. It wasn't used by most; there were too many dead ends and the unstable ground made it the last choice for a traveler on horseback, but I knew it like the back of my hands. My parents had sent Alex, Derrick, and I on countless supply runs for plants that grew along the trail.

I spent the next three hours climbing the hills and carefully edging my horse along a steep pass that wove around to the backside of my town.

I didn't come across a soldier or villager once. The road was as empty as could be. The ground was still frosted over, and it was growing dim; no one would be venturing to collect anything now when the land still had the last remnants of winter keeping the edibles deep underground.

When the trail finally came to a halt, I was standing outside the local tavern as the sun set, listening to the jumble of voices inside. That wasn't the sound of a village overwhelmed by the regiment awaiting a notorious criminal's return. It was the clink of glasses and celebratory day's end.

Still, just because I couldn't see or hear them didn't mean a patrol wasn't present. I wasn't taking any chances.

I tied my steed to a shaded fence and then ducked along the backside of the village, hiding under ledges and shadows as I made my way down the familiar alley. It was easy, really. Most of the villagers were already inside. Warm candlelight peaked through heavy curtains, and the familiar wafting scent of stew and rosemary hit me as I passed.

The only movement outside was the repetitive scratching of branches against the buildings' walls and the chickens scavenging for food. Occasionally I heard someone making their way across to the well, but that was in the town center, and I was skirting the back.

I had just turned the final corner when I lost my footing and stared.

The apothecary was still lit up from within. Even as far away as I was, I could hear the lilt of conversation over the wind. Shadows moved inside and someone was laughing—a light tinkle, like my mother's.

No one would be laughing if there were guards.

In all of two seconds, I was sprinting down the path, all semblance of stealth forgotten. My parents were inside, filling orders just as they always had, hours into the night.

And then as my hand hovered above the door, I started to back away. There was another female voice, too. A younger one. And now that I was here, the light tinkle of the first was a bit too high. It was the two apprentices that ran the shop with my parents. And I didn't hear a man's voice above the din.

What am I doing? But I couldn't bring myself to turn away. I had to know. I hadn't come this far just to run. I would face the truth, for Alex.

Refusing to spend any more time debating the chances of my parents' escape, I set to pounding on the door as loud and as fast as I could. The sooner I disappeared from the street, the better.

A moment later, the door swung open and I found myself facing Teegan. Her jaw dropped, and she stood there staring as the older girl shoved past, eyes bulging.

"Ryiah?" She didn't stare like the other; her hand was locked on the frame.

I didn't have time for niceties. I shoved my way past and slammed the door shut behind us, turning on both of them.

"Where are my parents?"

The first was still gaping, but the older, Cassidy, was clutching a knife. She must have grabbed it while my back was turned. I could see the distrust in her eyes.

"You tried to kill the king."

"I tried to do a lot of things." I advanced on both girls, brandishing a casted sword to remind them of who I really was and what I was capable of. I didn't have time to explain. "But that's not why I am here. Now tell me—"

"They ran," Teegan said. Her lip trembled as the blade pointed at her older sister's throat. "Two days ago. They just packed up and left us here to manage the shop in their stead."

"When did the patrols arrive?"

"Yester—"

"The knights put up those posters." Cassidy cut her sister off with a start. "They told us what you did, Ryiah. That you tried to kill the king." She was glaring at me, despite the blade. I had to give her credit; she was brave. "Is that why your parents ran? Are they rebels too?"

Both girls looked tense.

"They're blameless." I withdrew the sword. There was no point in sticking around now. My parents were safe, and who knew where the patrol was now. They could be in the tavern or watching the ridge.

"Why did you do it?"

I locked eyes with Cassidy. *Does she really want to know, or is she trying to stall me?*

"The Crown doesn't have its people at heart."

The girl studied my face, and I held her gaze with my own. No wonder my mother had chosen to apprentice her; she reminded me of myself—a younger version, if I had chosen to remain home instead of chasing my dreams at the Academy.

"You must be hungry." Cassidy motioned to the younger girl to go fetch a basket of bread. "Teegan will pack you enough to get to wherever you need to go. Would you like a bite to eat?"

For a moment, I considered her offer. I needed supplies—potions would help, and my stomach rumbled just at the mention of food—but this was all too convenient.

I was about to make my excuses when Cassidy's eye caught my own. A lump in her throat bobbed as her gaze darted toward the curtain, and then back to my face. "Stay," her words were light, but her expression was not, "I'll make some tea."

"Now that you've mentioned it..." My hand twisted the door's handle and the squeal of its hinges was all I needed to alert whoever was hiding behind the pair of curtains to my left. The girls darted right.

My casting shot off just as the mage emerged a second too late. My magic sent him sprawling against the wall.

I turned and fled.

Cassidy's screech followed me out the door. *"The rebel is here!"*

So much for loyalty. To be fair, she thought I was the enemy. I might have done the same, were our roles reversed.

I barely had time to cast before something hit my shield, sending a ripple of purple down my globe. I raced down the alley, this time not bothering to hide my presence, as shouts and more projections rained down on me like missiles from above.

In five minutes, I was severing the lead, sending my horse into a gallop as we tore up the rocky hillside, and fleeing north.

I didn't stop once. For the first hour, I heard distant shouts—sounds of the two or three regiment mages scouring the ground as fumbling soldiers tried to lead them through the dark. But in the end, it didn't matter.

I grew up in these woods; the mages hadn't. The soldiers might have taken up posts after their year in the Cavalry, but they hadn't spent summers climbing the trees and darting along the trails like the village children. They might have a vague idea of where I was, but in the time it would take to reach me, I would be long gone.

It was an uncomfortable trek without a full moon to guide my way; at parts I was forced to dismount and hike. The trail grew so steep and narrow that there was no other choice. But eventually, the sun rose and, with it, my relief.

My parents were safe. No bounty hunter would be searching for them when there was a rebel on the run with potential titles for her head.

Now I just had to get to my brother, because if the Crown had sent soldiers to Demsh'aa, the keep would be next.

* * *

I raced down the street as fast as my feet could fly.

There were shouts as three men came around the corner; I had about two minutes before they would pass and spot me in the baker's quarter.

Sweat stung my eyes. I swiped it away as I studied the streets.

"Stop that thief!"

Apparently they were faster than I thought.

I darted left and ducked into an alcove of stalls, desperately scanning the market for a place to hide. My horse was a mile outside of town, tethered to a tree near the mountain stream where I had camped, but I couldn't lead a parade of city guards through the forest now. I needed to lose the guards before they attracted a mob.

A shopkeeper that had yet to ascertain my role in the crowds was standing in front of me, oblivious.

"Excuse me, sir." I tried to push my way past, but he placed a large hand on my shoulder, halting me.

"You look familiar," he said, squinting.

"Must have one of those faces." I ducked my head even lower. The last thing I needed was for someone to recognize me now. It was midday, so the stalls were crowded, but it wouldn't take a lot to recall the wanted posters hanging off every post and shop. Eleven days of travel had washed out all trace of brown dye.

I broke free of the shopkeeper's grip before he could place my face and ducked left.

All for two mincemeat pies and a string of sausage left on an unsuspecting sill. I had run out of food three days ago. The whole situation could have been avoided if I had properly tied my saddlebags before running into a patrol mage and a bounty hunter in the forest. The mage's casting had spooked my horse, and I'd lost two days of scraps and a water skin on the run. It was the only reason I had risked my neck coming into town today.

I was too far away from the keep to last five days without supplies.

I squeezed past a large woman and three children and took to a side street less occupied than the rest. Maybe I could hide here until the men passed.

"Halt! Who goes there?"

I cursed under my breath as I spotted a pair of city guards closing in from the opposite end.

I had all of three seconds to make my decision before the closest guard's face lit up in recognition.

Thank the gods neither was a mage.

My feet took off before the soldier had even opened her mouth. I was scurrying up a tower of rusting crates, catching splinters in my palms as I scrabbled to the top. My balance was precarious.

I heard their pounding footfall as I lunged.

My hands caught hold of the nearest wooden beam, and I heaved myself up and over the building for all that I was worth.

There was a terrible jolt in the sockets of my arms and everything burned.

I staggered across the slatted roof, trying not to think about what would happen if I slipped, or, gods help me, stepped onto a piece of rotted wood. The beams shook and voices raised beneath—people wondering about the pounding feet over their heads.

Moments later a dagger whistled across the air. The soldiers had made it up faster than I expected. I didn't have time to cast a defense as all of my effort was in running across an unstable roof. The blade caught the back of my thigh.

I had all of one second to make a decision. I couldn't run with a blade embedded in my leg—it would damage the muscles with every leap—so I jerked the blade free as I cast out a globe. Then I ripped my sleeve and tied a makeshift wrap to my leg. My handwork was sloppy and rushed, but I didn't have a choice.

Just because I had a magic shield didn't mean they couldn't approach.

Everything throbbed, and blood pulsed heavily against my leg.

I stalled at the ledge of the building. There was another roof, but I didn't trust myself to make the leap with my injured leg. The drop was seven yards and there were no crates to climb, but it was in an empty alley, and no one would see. The fall would be agony on my leg, but it was doable. I just had to make the distance less than it was.

I ducked—the casting was still up as another throwing knife bounced harmlessly off its surface—and then I crouched, using my hands to clutch the beam as I hung off the side of the roof.

Then I let go, relaxing my arms and bending my knees as I braced myself for the ground.

I landed on the balls of my feet and fell to the right. The impact sent me back against the building's wall. I caught the worst of the impact in my arm. It saved me from a broken back, but from the pain in my lower body and the shooting pain in my wrist, I wasn't sure I hadn't fractured my arm in the fall.

But now I had to run.

The guards were calling to others over the noisy square. They weren't going to jump like I did; they were racing back to that first alley with the crates.

I limped my way to the front and scanned the crowd for the three angry men from before. I couldn't find them anywhere.

Good.

It was time to make my break for the woods.

I was barely three yards from the King's Road when someone's cry broke the crowd.

"The rebel!"

Someone had recognized me.

"It's her!"

And then one of the men from before yelled, "Catch that thief, boys!"

I had no choice. They knew who I was, so there was no point hiding my magic now. I cast a globe and started to run.

A terrible pain shot up my thigh as I lunged.

Behind me, the crowd was starting to break. Stones ricocheted against my shield.

Come on, Ryiah, run! But my limp was getting worse and the crowd was closing in.

"King killer!"

"Murderer."

I was running, but it wasn't enough. In seconds, I was surrounded.

A mob of angry villagers crowded around with the soldiers at the front.

Can I cast and buy myself enough time to run? That should have been the only question on my mind, but there was another, more pronounced: *king killer?*

Someone's blade jabbed at my globe. I flinched instinctively, and the bandage broke at my thigh. Hot blood slicked down the side of my leg.

The mob pressed in, their rage beating down on me like a drum. I was safe, my casting would hold. But for how long? Angry chants and more rocks hit the barrier, one by one.

Panic tugged at my gut. There were close to thirty angry villagers. I could cast, but what would it cost me? Could I go on knowing the price it would reap?

I couldn't take that many lives, not when the crowd's only crime was a misplaced faith in the Crown.

"Someone get me some shackles and send an envoy to

Devon. The reward will be enough to rebuild the entire village and feed our families for years."

I couldn't attack the crowd. They were only doing what was best.

The ground shifted and groaned. I barely had time to catch myself before I fell.

What...?

When I looked up, all I could see was smoke. The globe separated me from the fumes, but I couldn't see anything beyond it. All I heard were screams.

And that's when the first person slammed the side of my shield.

And then another.

I watched, horrified, as another slid down the side of my sphere, their hands and mouth trailing blood as they collapsed to the dirt.

I had no idea what was happening. All I knew was it was everywhere else—everywhere but me.

There were so many screams.

I should have reacted. I should have cast something to help, but I was numb. I didn't know who or what the person was casting, and all I could think was that *he* had finally caught up to me. Was it him? I wasn't sure I could fight.

I wasn't sure I should.

Then the screams stopped. A woman's hysterical laugh rose above the din. Smoke was still clearing, but from what I could see...

My casting faltered from the horror in my chest.

A ring of dead villagers surrounded my feet. The cobblestones ran red with their blood.

A hovering dagger appeared at my throat.

"There she is. Wanted *alive*." A familiar voice spat the last word with venom. *Mira.* Blayne's right hand. "The king sends fifty sniveling men and demotes *me* to a guard." She snorted. "And look which one of us finally caught up to his elusive little rebel after all."

I couldn't speak. Horror still flooded my chest—not for my sake, but the thirty others in the street.

"This," Mira added, "should change his mind."

"Did Blayne promote your brother instead?" My rebuttal was weak. I was stalling, trying to buy myself time to think. Darren wasn't here; it was just *her*. "Marius always was the better mage." The blade twitched, and I swallowed as it scraped against skin. "Blayne must have finally figured that out."

Everyone knew Marius had been King Lucius's favorite. It was a sore spot for the jealous sister. She'd had to team up with the king's heir to finally gain recognition.

The mage didn't react as I'd hoped. "You haven't heard." Her lips curved up in a merciless slant. "Well, this *is* a treat."

My pulse thundered in my ears.

"Blayne," she declared, watching my face, "is dead. The palace healers were incompetent. He was gone before sunrise the night you escaped."

But that means... My stomach dropped. I could be a *king killer* and there could still be a king.

Blayne had a successor.

The one person who was never supposed to wear the crown.

"The *new* king is the one who ordered the bounty on your

head." Mira continued on with a hint of glee. "You are to be his example to the rest."

I couldn't breathe. My heart thumped heavily and my lungs rose and fell, but nothing was coming. I was numb.

Darren was king.

I had never even *considered* a future in which his brother was gone. I'd been so convinced Blayne would survive.

And now.

I remembered his words that night: *"You took... everything."*

"After the war, he'll hunt the rest of the rebels down. Make no mistake."

I could barely process her words. "*After* the war? But—"

"What? You thought he wouldn't continue where his brother left off?" Mira sneered as she drew close. "Your beloved never believed a word you said. He sent the Crown's Army to march on Caltoth not two days after he was crowned."

But this couldn't be. Darren wasn't the enemy. The enemy was dead.

But he still believes in Blayne's cause.

"I'm sure they're almost to the border by now. They should reach Caltoth any day."

"But I..." I'd been hiding out in the forest for days, slowly making my way north, remaining miles off the main road except for today. It was possible.

No.

Darren wouldn't do this. "You are lying." She had to be; I couldn't believe the alternative.

"Am I?" Mira chortled. "Well, you will see soon enough."

The pressure of the blade was enough to draw blood. Little rivulets slid down my neck, slick and warm. The cut was a building sting, but it was nothing thanks to the panic in my lungs.

If Darren was almost to the border, had he passed the keep? Had he found Alex and Ella? Had he figured out who the rebels were?

There were a thousand questions, and the worst one was burning a hole in my chest. I couldn't even process its implications.

What have I done?

Mira's eyes narrowed to slits as she took a step forward, manacles in hand. "You try anything," she warned, "and I'll break both your legs. The king might want you alive, but he never said you had to be pristine."

One more step. Then another. I waited until the woman was six yards away.

She must have forgotten how long it took to bring me to my knees, to drain all of the stamina I had spent so many years building. She had grown too accustomed to winning with ten regiment mages at her side in the dungeon.

Only now it was just the two of us. And right now, I might have been beaten and bruised, but this was far from my worst, even with her blade at my neck.

And so my muscles relaxed.

I watched as a bit of tension fell from Mira's shoulders, her casting wavering just enough. She thought I wasn't going to put up a fight, and she had unconsciously allowed herself to mirror her opponent's stance.

You never were as good as your brother. Marius would

never make that mistake.

My right hand shot up to grasp the hilt of her dagger, and then I jerked it away. The cords of my muscles bunched under the strain, my arm was shaking just to keep the blade at a distance, but it was enough. My casting had strengthened my grip.

I overcame her hold. Her eyes flared in panic.

I'm second only to Darren. You never stood a chance.

My second casting took off. The projection struck against the core of my magic like flint against steel.

There was an explosion of light, so bright the entire square was nothing but white, and then a bolt of lightning shot out of the cloudless sky, striking the woman in the center of her chest.

The same casting she had used on my brother.

I watched the woman fall.

Mira's blade disintegrated into the air like ash. I ripped yet another scrap of cloth to serve as a bandage around my neck.

I should feel something.

The woman was just lying there, sputtering on her last shaky breath, coughing up blood.

Her ribs were rising and falling, but she couldn't even speak. She was *dying.*

She had killed Derrick. She had been Blayne's right hand. She was responsible for the deaths of hundreds, and thousands to come. I had dreamt about this moment for months, watching her in the palace, suffering in the dungeons, wanting to be the one to lock hands around her neck.

I wanted to feel elation or justice, something to make this moment *different*, something to make the act momentous.

Her eyelids fluttered shut as her chest stopped moving.

My brother's murderer was dead. I had killed for the first time with *intention,* and what did I have to show for it?

Shards like a vine of thorns closed in around my throat. It made no sense. I didn't understand why I was so numb, why I felt nothing when someone so vile was dead.

I wondered if I had lost too much to care, or if the glory of revenge belied the truth that nothing could take back what we had lost. This was but a small stitch in a wound that wouldn't heal.

And then my boot caught on one of the villagers' outstretched arms.

I had forgotten. Mira had stolen from them, too.

I knelt down, swallowing past bile and guilt as I pushed the limb to the side.

Heat rose in my chest and there was a roaring in my ears.

So you do feel something.

I could have stopped her. They had only been following the Crown's orders.

But you thought she was him.

I had been so overwhelmed with the possibility of Darren, that I had been too afraid to lift a finger in my defense. I had let the woman slaughter a small village because I thought Darren had come after me.

Thirty lives *gone* in the blink of an eye.

Thirty more to my conscience. A number I could never amend.

You can't hesitate again.

I bit down on the inside of my cheek, tasting warm, coppery blood. My fear had caught up to me, two weeks on the run. I needed to acknowledge the truth before it cost more unnecessary lives.

This wasn't my story anymore; it was theirs.

I made my way, limping past the bodies, using a fallen polearm to nudge their limbs aside. A part of me wanted to light a funeral pyre, but I didn't have the time, and it would draw attention I couldn't afford.

I'm sorry. I took a long breath and exhaled slowly, taking in their faces one last time. It wasn't the apology they deserved, but it was the only one I had.

I wouldn't make the same mistake twice.

* * *

The next two days were worse than before. My wrist wasn't fractured—just severely bruised, thank the gods—but between it, the festering wound on my leg without proper treatment, and the hunger pangs, I was making slower progress than I should.

The fifth morning, a raging fever broke out and I couldn't even make it astride my horse. That same day, I reached the bandit camp from my year before serving the Ferren's Keep regiment. For a moment, there was hope—*supplies, food, people.*

But the place was deserted. Not so much as a crumb remained behind. A part of me had hoped Nyx would deploy her men to the settlement. It was remote, and if the king had dispersed patrols and the Crown's Army to the borders, it would make sense.

But no one was there.

I tried not to think what that meant for the rebels.

I had been so sure they would be here. In our talks, Nyx had promised to keep my brother and Ella safe at all costs. I'd thought for sure she would have sent them away the moment their spy sent word of what had gone down in the capital. Or at least when they heard the news that Blayne was dead and the Crown's Army was still marching on Caltoth and hunting the rebels.

I would have taken the main road had I not been so sure I would find them here.

It had cost me two days to reach this place.

And now? I was upheaving what little I managed down, writhing on a straw mattress late into the night. All for nothing. And I was too weak to ride. I couldn't even walk.

I just had to cling to the hope they would return.

Two more days passed and I could feel every bone protruding from my ribs. I was delirious and couldn't hobble more than a few yards outside my cabin to relieve myself.

Trying to make the trek to the keep was impossible now.

I'd made it this far, and this was how it would end. I would never know what happened to everyone else. I'd die from starvation or fever, whatever won out first. I'd been fighting the former as best I could by boiling the rawhide straps of the horse's tether in a leftover pot until it was tender enough to chew, but it wasn't enough.

Eventually, I set the mare free, before the temptation became worse... I'd die either way, and I couldn't stomach the thought of slaughtering a horse. Foolish, perhaps, but it was one act I refused to commit.

Hours passed as the hunger grew. I fantasized about

conjuring a hearty venison stew, but the principles of magic wouldn't keep the casting forever. After my stamina dropped, the pangs would be back. Worse so, perhaps, because my stomach had adjusted to its fill.

It was better to hold onto magic to keep the stove warm during the course of the night, to boil the little well water I could manage. At least the effect of those two castings was true.

Another night and I couldn't distinguish the walls from the ceiling, let alone the floor. I was struck by tremor after tremor. Sweat drowned every one of my pores, drenching my clothes and sticking to my flesh like a second skin. The festering wound at my thigh was molten fire. It seared late into the night.

I couldn't stand. I couldn't sleep. It was like my time in the dungeons all over again, only this time infinitely worse.

Blayne was dead. Darren was king.

The villain marching on Caltoth was the broken boy from the cliffs.

Because of me. I had abandoned Darren when he needed me most. I'd assumed his brother would live... *And why wouldn't he?* The palace had the best healers in the land.

Surviving had been more important. I'd needed to save my family and warn the rebels. But now...

It wasn't Blayne's army at the border. It was Darren's.

The new king was committing acts he could never take back, and when the truth came to light—if it ever did—it would be *his* orders that tore the country apart. *His* words that sent innocent men and women to their death.

Darren had watched the only person he loved pass away,

alone. I'd left him to darkness and despair and a country on the brink of war.

"I'm afraid of what my love for you will make me."

Now we knew.

Would it have made a difference if I had stayed? Or would the Black Mage have been the first to condemn the king killer like the rest of them?

Why had Darren wanted me alive? To rot away in a cell? Or something worse?

The realization cut into my chest, twisting like a knife.

Someone had to stop him.

It couldn't be me. Not anymore.

It wouldn't be much longer until... the *end*.

But someone else needed to rise.

To save Jerar.

To save the boy from himself.

Before he destroyed the world.

FIFTEEN

WHEN I AWOKE, I was in the Realm of the Dead and the gods had taken me far away from my mortal toils. There was bliss that came from ethereal freedom and no physical corpse to remind me of hunger and thirst and pain.

And then I felt something cool pressed against my skin.

I wasn't supposed to *feel*.

But the sensation was so familiar that I had to open my eyes. I wanted to understand how I could still feel something akin to before.

I found myself peering into blue eyes as familiar as my own. I had been staring at them since the day I was born.

Alex fell back in his chair, swearing. *"Thank the gods!"*

He wiped a pale wrist against his clammy forehead, breathing deeply in and out of his nose. He did this for another minute or two while I swallowed, unable to think. Finally, he managed a shout: "She's awake! Ella!"

There was the sound of boots squeaking outside and then a door creaked open to reveal my best friend, her expression equally wild.

"Ryiah!"

I blinked up at both of them, but my throat was coarser

than sand. I could only manage to cough, hacking as I tried to push myself up off the straw.

My brother leaned forward to help as my friend charged forward with a flask she pressed to my lips. "Drink," Ella ordered. "It tastes like death, but it will help with your throat."

I took a sputtering sip, and then another. She wasn't wrong. The liquor tasted like rot, but after there was a slow-setting chill.

"H-how...?" I gasped. So much for the after realm. All my pain was coming back. The effort to speak produced something gravelly and rough. "H-how did y-you two... f-find m-me?"

The two people I'd been searching for. Not only were they safe and well, but they'd found *me*. And I was almost certain they'd saved me from the brink of certain death.

My twin ran a hand along his neck. His skin was almost translucent. I wondered how many hours he had been at work, casting out the fever and the infection in my leg. The skin was starting to tingle and itch—my least favorite part of the healing. "We had no idea you were alive, Ryiah," he said.

I took another burning sip of the flask, and then Alex handed me a water skin. I only managed a few swallows; the pit in my stomach had contracted from too many days of nothing. I was starting to feel sick.

"When our spy in the capital discovered you were caught, she sent an envoy." Ella cleared her throat. "But when the news reached the keep, it was already two weeks too late."

"We thought you were dead, Ry." Alex's voice was

steeped in emotion. "Nyx sent the rest of her men packing to Caltoth, but Ella and I... we couldn't, not without seeing for ourselves."

"I'm so sorry." I reached my hand out shakily, and he grabbed it, squeezing hard.

"You shouldn't be." Alex's grip tightened. "I shouldn't have let you return to the capital alone." His eyes flared. "What they must have done to you in that prison—"

"Nyx ran?" I broke off my twin's apology, unwilling to admit what had transpired in that cell. He didn't need that knowledge, and it would only remind him of Derrick. I could spare at least one of us that pain. "Everyone is in Caltoth?"

"All of the keep and several northern villages." Alex's gaze slipped to the floor. "Nyx knew that without you, we had no hopes of swaying Pythus. She sent the regiment to rally the villagers and transport what livestock and supplies they could. She knew the king would find out eventually, but by then it wouldn't matter."

His hand was still clutching my own as he swallowed. "Ella and I were halfway to Demsh'aa when we saw the posters. We didn't know until then that you had escaped."

Ella handed me a lukewarm bowl of broth that had bits of oily meat floating on the surface. "Try as best as you can to get some of this down," she said.

I nodded silently, taking a scoop as Ella continued where Alex had left off.

"There were rumors that the rebel girl had been spotted in Demsh'aa running north. We knew right away you were heading for the keep. We combed the forest for days but our real break was when that village got attacked and Mira's corpse was found in the square. It wasn't you that…?"

I shook my head. "Only Mira. The others… were h-her."

"The next day we ran into the others."

"Others?"

"The news had reached Nyx." Ella touched my shoulder. "As soon as she found out you were alive, she sent out a search party to help."

Alex looked me directly in the eyes. He already knew what I was thinking. "She wouldn't do it for anyone, Ry, but you are far too valuable to the cause. As a mage and…" His eyes flashed. "Your relation to the new king. The moment she heard, she was willing to dispatch ten of the best we had even though the Crown's Army was marching on Caltoth. We met up with them and Lief was the one to suggest this place. There were no sightings of you on the main road, and he thought you might have remembered it from before. Ella and I would never have known to look."

I forced down a big lump of stew, trying not to grimace at the taste. I felt both their eyes on me, and I didn't want the questions that came next. All I wanted to do was rest, even if I still smelled worse than any person ever should.

"How did you escape, Ry?"

"Alex." Ella nudged her husband's ribs. "She probably doesn't—"

"It's okay." I swallowed. "I'm sure you both are wondering. I-I want to tell you."

There was a moment where nobody spoke.

"The night before my execution, Darren sent Paige to help me escape."

"But the war, he—"

"He didn't believe a word I said. But how could he?" The air around me was getting too hot; I could feel it stifling my chest. "Would you have believed Ella if it had been the two of you instead?"

"I—"

"You wouldn't." I looked my twin in the eye. "He had a horse packed with supplies and papers for a ship to the east. He couldn't stand the idea of an execution. It was the only reason I escaped."

Silence.

"Where's Paige?" My brother ground his teeth. "Did she choose the Crown?"

My lips turned to ice. "She never made it out. We were halfway to the gates when Blayne caught up to us in the kennels."

The memories rolled off me like a wave. I'd fought so long to keep the emotion bottled up, but my hate returned; the room grew hazy with every word. "I spared his life for Darren." I gave a sharp intake of breath as my fingers balled into fists. "But he had magic—"

"What?" Ella's shock mirrored my brother's.

"Not like us, but he had enough. I just barely survived." *Breathe.* "And then he put a knife to Paige's back as she was helping me leave." The rage made my nails cut through flesh, and the tips grew wet with my own blood. "And I was so sure he would live. He was still breathing when Darren—"

"Darren saw you?"

My laugh was bitter as black spots danced before my eyes. It was the part that would drive me to madness. "He saw our horse. When he entered the kennels, he found me clutching a rapier with both of them on the ground, Blayne bleeding to death and Paige already gone." My voice took on an edge. "If Mira hadn't arrived, I could have explained..." My voice faltered and I bit down on my cheek. "But she was calling for the rest of the regiment and I knew." I still remembered the way Darren's expression had turned as he clutched his dying brother in his arms, betrayed by his wife. "Blayne would have executed me the moment he recovered. I'd have no chance to explain."

Whatever was in that flask was drugging me to sleep; Ella's arms wrapped around my shoulders to help lower me to the cot.

Then I shared the part that would haunt me for what little life I had left. "If I had known Blayne would die, I would have stayed." My voice was slurring as I shut my eyes. "I would have found a way to convince Darren of the truth." *This is all my fault.*

"You don't know that." Alex's voice was reassuring and soft. "Ryiah, Darren thought you killed his brother. You don't know what he would have done."

Ella's voice was so quiet, a flutter of wings against my ear. "At least with us, you can help stop the war."

Her answer was so simple. Perhaps, if I were someone else, I could have even started to believe it.

* * *

I awoke that evening a couple hours after the others' return. Alex and Ella explained that for the past three days the others had scouted the nearby roads while Alex and Ella remained behind, tending to me. Then, they introduced me to the best Combat mages of the rebels' force.

All of the faces held some degree of familiarity, but there were three my attention locked on almost immediately.

Lief.

Ray.

And Ian.

No one asked me about my escape. I suspected Alex or Ella had filled them in while I was at rest. But that didn't stop their stares. The unspoken questions festered just under the surface.

Lief's eyes were rimmed in red. All he did was clench and unclench his fists.

I wasn't the only one who had lost someone. Paige's absence hit him the worst. Whatever they'd had, it was gone. He had probably thought she was alive, fighting along the Crown's Army... An enemy, but still alive.

Now he knew better.

The former lead mage didn't say a word; he just stared at something along the wall as the others talked.

My guilt was deafening.

I forced myself to concentrate on my second bowlful of broth. I felt better than before, but it was nothing next to the thoughts dancing around inside.

"Ryiah is well on the way to recovery. Another four or five days and it will be like the fever never struck."

"But we don't have five days, Alex." An older woman with a scar across the side of her face folded her arms against her ribs. She was the oldest on our squad, thirty-five years old perhaps. Her stamina was better than most. "You can continue her treatments on the road."

My brother bristled. "Ry barely made it out of their dungeons alive and then two weeks on the run, she needs—"

"We can't waste any more time now that she's awake." Our leader, a burly mage named Quinn, took over, casting an apologetic glance my way. "We have to leave now."

Another young mage spoke up. "The Crown's Army arrived at the border two days back. Gods only know how many we've already lost."

"How many to the rest of us?"

"Almost four to one. We would have had more, but—"

"Half of Caltoth's force was disbanded to hold off the Pythian warships attacking their shores in the north. The border doesn't stand a chance. Horrace's regiment doesn't train like Jerar. Our worst soldiers outperform their knights, and their mages' stamina isn't even close."

"Believe me"—Quinn's voice was laced with regret as he spoke over the others—"if there were any other choice…"

"But every day you remain, hundreds die." It was a matter of fact.

He nodded. I could see why Nyx had appointed the giant our leader. He was calm and direct, seeming to weigh every decision in his head before he spoke.

"I've made it this far. I can manage the rest."

My twin made a disgruntled sound to my left, but aloud he said nothing.

The room's occupants started to disband. "We leave in two hours. Alex, since you are in charge of her recovery, Ryiah will share your mount."

"Is that it?"

All eyes, including mine, shot to the curly haired mage at

the back of the room. Ian's arms were folded across his chest as he glowered at our leader. "So," he spoke slowly, "are you going to tell her exactly why she doesn't need to be fully recovered, or am I?"

"I already told Ryiah. Alex can heal her on the road."

"That's not the only reason, and you know it."

"Ian?" My pulse hammered in my throat.

"You know what our mission is?" His green eyes locked on my own. "To stop him."

I nodded. This wasn't any surprise. It was the only reason Nyx would have risked her best men to hunt me down during the middle of a war. "You want me to negotiate, to reason with Darren." Because I was the only one he would listen to.

"No one thinks he will listen." Ian took a step closer, advancing. "No one cares, Ryiah."

"What are you—"

"You're bait, to lure the king away from his guards." The mage's irises flashed. "The posters called for you to be brought in alive. Darren feels *something,* whether he wants to kill you himself—"

My lips parted, but I couldn't bring myself to speak.

"—or lock you in a dungeon, it makes no difference. He wants you. He disbanded part of his regiment to hunt you and offered up a reward large enough to make any friend take part in the bounty. He slipped up, Ryiah. *Darren made a mistake.*"

Ian took another step forward until he was right in front of me. No one made a move to stop him. He took a long, shuddering breath, and my gaze slipped to Quinn and the others behind him. Not even Ray would look me in the eye.

Only Alex and Ella were watching me, seeming equally curious to what our friend would say next.

"We aren't here to negotiate with the king, Ryiah. We are here to kill him."

My heart stopped. "But Nyx promised—"

"She gave us the orders herself, Ryiah."

"No." A cold sweat broke out along my skin. The tremors were back. "That's not what she said. That's not what she—"

"The last time you spoke to the commander, Darren's brother was king."

"But that doesn't matter."

"It changes everything." Quinn dared to meet my gaze. "Ryiah, whatever she promised you, surely you can see the situation has changed. Before Darren was under his brother's orders, but now..."

"Now their deaths rest on him." Ian's voice was bitter. "I am sorry, Ryiah, but I thought you deserved to know the truth."

Ella put a hand on my wrist. Her skin was just as clammy as my own. "If he agreed to surrender, couldn't we just toss him in a cell? I'm not saying we forgive his actions, but surely—"

Quinn shook his head. "Darren is far too powerful. As long as his bloodline remains, Jerar will never be safe."

"But"—my hands were shaking—"if he surrendered and gave up all ties to the kingdom?"

"It's not enough. His blood is a threat to all future reign. So long as he is alive, there would always be dissenters calling for the old legacy, not to mention the riots for a man who has killed thousands—"

"But it's not his fault!"

The entire room went silent. Everybody stopped moving except for Alex who had come to stand beside Ella and wrap an arm around my trembling frame.

"Ryiah—"

"No! You are going to listen to *me*." I forced myself to stand on wobbling limbs, shoving aside my brother and friend to face our leader. "Darren believes the lies his brother gave him. He is *not* Blayne. Blayne knew the truth and planned to wage this war out of greed."

"The circumstances—"

"Darren might be king," I spat, "but it's his brother's war. Not his. *Those. Lives. Are. Not. His.* Do you intend to punish every single soldier in the Crown's Army? Because ten thousand men are following a lie?"

"It's not the same."

"It's *exactly* the same!" I swore at Quinn. "Don't you get it? Any one of us could be them! The only difference is Nyx found us and gave us the truth. Nyx cannot hold Darren accountable!"

"Ryiah." Quinn's tone was gentle, calming even. "A leader is held to a different standard than his men. And your brother already told us you tried to reason with Darren. The king refused to listen. He was given a chance, but he refused to take it."

My eyes shot to Alex, betrayed; my twin looked sick to his stomach.

"Quinn," Alex pleaded, "that wasn't what I—"

"I'm sorry." And our leader truly looked it. "I really am. But—"

"I don't care!" My scream broke whatever apology Quinn was attempting. Everyone's eyes were on me, the pressure making me see red.

"I have sacrificed everything for this cause." Ella attempted to place a hand on my shoulder, but I threw it off. My fingers balled into fists. *"Everything.* More than you. More than Nyx. More than the rest of you put together. I lost my brother. I betrayed my husband. I gave up the crown. I was willing to die in the gods' forsaken dungeons just to keep all of you alive! And the one thing, the *one* thing I asked was for Darren to be spared!"

"You don't have to come with us." A pair of green and gold-flecked irises met my own. Ian turned toward his leader. "We came here for Ryiah, but we can do it without her."

"Ian—"

"Give her a gods' blasted choice, Quinn."

The man went silent.

My friend looked me dead in the eyes. "You've given up more than any of us, Ry. Nyx gave us orders, and I agree with her reasoning, but you deserve the chance to walk away. I know what he was to you."

* * *

So that was my choice. Lure Darren to his death or walk away and sentence the others to their death.

It was never supposed to come to this. My fist found the wall, and there was a resounding crack as the wood splintered and broke. I pulled my hand away, dripping blood.

I didn't feel a thing. Not physically.

The others were gone. They had given me two hours to

make my decision—the time it would take for them to repack their supplies. Alex and Ella had remained inside.

"We didn't know, Ry." Ella's voice shook. "I swear, when they told us Nyx's orders, they didn't tell us that."

I said nothing. I had seen the look on their faces during Ian's announcement. Alex might not have been Darren's biggest fan, but even he had been surprised.

"What do I do?" My voice was hoarse.

"Whatever you choose—" Alex swallowed. "—we will stand by your decision, Ry. Ian is right. You've given up so much, you don't have to do this too."

"So I just sentence thousands to die?" I stared at my hand. I watched the crimson drops slide along my knuckles. "Because he will kill them, Alex. He's *already* killing them. Every day the war goes on."

My twin didn't answer.

"I… I'm not a fool." I sucked in a breath. "I knew it m-might come to him or us." Did I? *Or am I just lying to myself?* "I knew we might h-have to…" I couldn't say the words. I couldn't admit it existed. "But I just thought… I just thought that, if he surrendered, Nyx would spare him. I knew she wasn't happy when I asked, and I knew his brother was king when we struck the deal, but I…"

But a part of me had truly believed that, if Darren surrendered, she would uphold our pact.

My nails dug into the cuts in my palm. I was such a fool to pretend we were on the same battlefield. Things had changed. "He'll probably kill me first… He already heard what I have to say."

"Ryiah—"

"No." I shook my head, locks flying in front of my face. "Quinn's right. I already gave him a chance, Ella." A bolt of shame shot down my spine. "This isn't about what I want. It's what's best for the whole." Even if it wasn't fair to him.

"Ryiah." Alex grabbed my wrist and forced me to unclench my hand. "Did you believe Derrick the first time he came to you?"

"N-no—"

"Then why should you expect it of Darren? You didn't have any proof. It was his brother or his wife. Lucius and Blayne spent *years* making him believe a lie, and you only had a week and a half."

My palm tingled as Alex's casting commenced on my hand.

"Nyx is wrong." My twin's voice was barely a whisper as he leaned in close. "I'm not saying she doesn't have the people in mind, she does, but she is thinking like a leader and forgot what it's like to be a *person*." He and Ella exchanged a meaningful look. "Nyx's decision might be right for them. It might be the best decision a leader can make. I might even agree with her, but it doesn't mean you have to."

"I can't outrun them, not like this." I stared, unblinking, as the skin stitched together along my knuckles. It wasn't the most pleasant sensation. "What are you saying, Alex?"

"I'm saying there are three choices, not two. And Ella and I can help make the third one happen."

The third one?

"When the group locates Darren, we will make sure you have a head start. An hour, two at most." He was pacing. "If the plan works, and I'm not saying it will, you get Darren to call off his men and leave Jerar. But if you take too long, they'll catch up."

I swallowed, realizing what Alex meant.

"Lie to them." Ella locked her gaze on my own. "Tell them you'll cooperate, and we'll handle the rest."

Alex's hand found his wife's and a knot jumped in his throat as he spoke. "Do you understand why they wanted you as a lure, Ryiah?"

It should have hurt to say, but instead, I felt nothing. "They think that out of the entire regiment, I'm the one person Darren will seek to dispose of himself."

"Emotion is the one thing that will leave Darren open to mistakes." Ella looked to the ground. "His defense won't be what it should when he is facing you, but neither will yours..."

"There's a good chance he'll kill you, Ryiah. I know you want to believe..." My brother thrust his jaw out and ground the next words out like he was swallowing glass. "But if it were Ella and me, I'd make the same reckless choice. I'd want you to give me the same choice."

SIXTEEN

I DELIVERED AN ultimatum. It was a lie, of course.

"I'm the only way you are going to win this war." Alex was the one who had given me the idea. "I'm the best lure you have and the one chance to catch Darren off guard. Without me, the lot of you will never stand a chance. You want the bloodshed to stop? You want a chance to end this?"

Silence. I had their attention.

"Then you forget Nyx's orders and you listen to *me*. She may have the people's best interests at heart, but *I* am the one you need. If Darren surrenders and calls off his army, you are going to look the other way and let him escape. He'll never return to Jerar and make a play for the throne, but he will *live*."

Quinn frowned, but he didn't outright deny my request. They needed me to get close to Darren. The two of us knew it, and he didn't act the fool by denying it. He had probably thought I would accept the role outright, after all I had done for the cause.

"And what if he refuses to surrender? What then?"

"You carry out Nyx's order."

"You won't try to stop us?"

My laugh was bitter. "It wouldn't really matter, would it? We all know I'll be dead before anyone else."

For a moment, the leader said nothing, studying my face. Then he turned to the others. Out of the corner of my eye, I could see the dissent in their eyes.

"She's the best chance we've got."

"But to go against Nyx's orders!" The older woman from before spoke up. "To betray our commander, all for some lovesick girl?"

"Ryiah is not just some 'lovesick' girl." Ray shoved his way forward. "She's the best mage in the room, *in the kingdom second to him!*"

"Our goal is to end bloodshed." Lief still wouldn't look at me. "Whether or not we agree with her, too many have given up their lives for this cause. If we can end it, does it matter who we betray?"

"Klaus? Jeremiah?" Quinn cleared his throat. "Anyone else?" The group had stopped its collective arguments. "Ian, any final words?"

The mage shook his head, his eyes never leaving my face. There was a storm brewing beneath the surface, but whatever he was feeling, he was not about to admit it in front of the others.

"Very well. Ryiah, we accept your terms."

I nodded. Beside me, I felt Alex and Ella let out a long sigh of relief. They believed us.

Of course, they were probably lying right back. For all I knew, they were planning to go back on our promise. As far as they were concerned, they just needed my presence. The moment we arrived, I'd have no control over their actions.

It didn't matter, though.

Alex and Ella would find a way to drug them before they ever got their chance. I wouldn't warn Darren there were others. In the event I failed, the rest of our party would still have the distraction they needed.

* * *

"You shouldn't have done it..." Ian stepped out from the brush behind me. "Forcing Quinn's hand was a mistake."

I busied myself filling a skin in the running stream. We had stopped to make camp for the night, and the others had given me the easiest task since I was still recovering. "Nyx left me no choice."

"He's king." The mage shoved his hands in his pockets. "What else did you expect, Ryiah? Darren's men are waging a war on the border as we speak. You can't just look the other way and expect everyone to pardon his crimes."

I met Ian's glower with one of my own. "I thought you were on my side."

"I believe you have the right to walk away." His arms folded across his chest. "But you do not have the right to put the rest of our party at risk. This isn't your love story, Ryiah. This is about the crimes against a nation."

I cocked my head to the side. "And live on the run while the rest of you go off and get yourselves killed?"

"Nyx asked more from you than any of us." His jaw was set. "You've served the cause well. You don't need his death on your conscience. It would destroy you. Let someone else take that role."

I found myself growling. "What makes you so sure Darren won't listen?"

"He's too far gone." My friend had the decency to look away. "You've always been blind where Darren is concerned, Ryiah. He's not like us. And perhaps that's what drew you to him in the first place, but it's going to kill you if you continue on this path."

"You are wrong."

"If you were anyone else, I'd say go on ahead, but you are a liability, Ryiah."

"A liability?" My teeth gnashed together. "You think I'm not good enough? Second-rank doesn't stand a chance against the *Black Mage?* I'm the best you've got."

"I know you are good enough. That's never been the problem." Ian's jaw locked. "The problem is you won't fight back."

"I would. If I—"

"Liar. You still believe you can save him."

All I could hear was the quiet lull of the stream pooling against rocks.

"If he tries to kill *you*, Ryiah, are you going to fight back? If Darren leaves you no choice, would you kill him to save yourself? To save Jerar?"

"It won't come to that."

"It already has."

I couldn't stand there a moment longer. The strings of hysteria tugged at my lungs. I wanted to run away from Ian and Nyx, away from all of these choices I was never meant to make.

"Look me in the eyes and tell me you don't hold yourself responsible for what he's become. That you won't try to save him even if it means betraying everyone else."

My mind flashed to that day in the training room, to Darren and me and the darkness that followed. *"Run away with me."* I'd been willing to do it then.

No.

I was done listening to this two-faced traitor that I had once called a friend. He didn't know me, and he didn't know Darren.

"You are wrong."

Ian had never seen that broken prince on the cliffs. He didn't know about the little boy and his father, or the nights after Derrick died and the way my husband had held me to keep me from madness.

Ian only saw an entitled king who was following in his brother's footsteps.

"Darren will surrender," I hissed, "and I'll save everyone. *Every. Last. One. Of. Them.*"

The mage crossed his arms and glared at me. "You're not just lying to me, Ryiah. You are lying to yourself."

"What a shame it's Quinn's decision and not yours."

"I'll talk him around."

Go ahead and try.

"You are with me or against me, Ian." My words were cold. "But you will not stop me."

The mage marched off back to camp without looking back.

* * *

"Nyx gave the rest of the regiment a choice, even the ones that didn't know." Alex's voice boomed in my ears as his horse continued to climb the rocky expanse.

We had ridden for four days.

Narrow mountain trails in the heart of the Iron Range and the elevation were part of the trek. We couldn't rely on the King's Road if we were to catch the Crown's Army by surprise and the result was heavy tension among the party the further we climbed. None of us were immune to the dangers that lay ahead. The moment we reached the border, we would be in a race for our lives.

Only Alex—sweet, charming, somewhat oblivious Alex— seemed not to take note. My brother had spent most of the hours seeing to my treatment and answering my questions along the way as everyone else carried on in silence. Perhaps he was the wisest; anxiety only led to mistakes.

"The ones that didn't know were smart enough not to put up a fight." Ella pulled up beside us on her mare. We were passing through a narrow canyon and her voice echoed along the walls. "A few fled, but most took up the cause, and the ones that did... well, we knew it was only a matter of time before the Crown found out either way. Alex and I left that very same day."

Almost all the villagers northwest of the keep were gone. The few that we passed stood out like the straggled remains of a husk. The buildings and farms were empty. Even the livestock were missing. "They took what they could and joined our cause. Even the ones that didn't know about us, they had friends and family at the keep. Nyx sent a couple of envoys to warn the others and give them the same choice." Alex pointed to the road leading east. "The ones closer to Montfort are more loyal to the Crown. I'm sure they chose to remain."

"They did." Jeremiah spoke up quietly to our right. Unlike

Ian, the others were still willing to talk to me. "We lost a few of our men that delivered the message. The local command dispatched a couple of his knights to hunt them down on behalf of the Crown. Only half of ours made it back."

My stomach churned. I didn't want to talk about the villagers any longer.

Even into the beginning of spring, the north was rock encrusted in ice. Everything was sharp and slick. Barren twigs snapped under the horses' hooves the higher we climbed, and our voices got lost to the wind. The sixth day, I was closer to the border than I'd ever been during my patrols in the keep's regiment. It was *cold*.

Since the rebels hadn't been in immediate danger, they'd had time to pack supplies. But Alex and Ella had taken off right away for the capital. Their pack was much like my own, and none of us had brought gear for the climate ahead. Each night the three of us took turns casting heat to keep our tent warm, always choosing a protruding ridge to shield us from the worst of the northern winds. The others lent us what they could, some furs and durable wool, but it never seemed enough.

Toward the end of the week, I was ready to collapse. My fever was gone, but what ailments I'd lost had been replaced with a fear of black frost and survival ahead.

Hiking in snow wasn't like the mountains back home. I sweated constantly underneath my new layers of fur. I continuously stripped layers only to pile them back on as the next drift caught me unaware.

We also had to travel on foot: we couldn't risk the horses lacerating a leg and taking a rider over a slippery ledge.

That, and we didn't want to tire them out even more. Like us, the beasts had to work extra hard in snow. The drying process from cold sweat could take hours. The horses carried our supplies, and that had to be enough.

Eventually, we reached a flat expanse of white. Little bits of green dotted the edge. At its base was a thick, coursing river. The water was black. I cringed; the sound of the current alone was enough to assure me that whoever fell would live all of five minutes at best, going into shock after three seconds.

We had reached the border of Jerar. The river divided two kingdoms as it snaked along the northern divide.

Across the ravine was a range three times the size of our own, towering over the border like a giant among ants. It was covered in snow.

While we had four seasons, Caltoth only had one.

Ella took one look ahead and rolled her eyes. "Of course," she was muttering, "of course it would have to be somewhere cold."

"It's not that bad." Alex wore a rakish grin. Ella and Ray had been taking to the snow much worse than the rest of us. "We've been camping out in the snow for over a week. You knew Caltoth would be worse."

Ray's reply was instantaneous: "Worse is an understatement."

Ella shot her husband a look. "This is where the Shadow God sends the worst of us to live out an eternity of sin."

Alex and I hid a smile behind our hands. We didn't like the look of Caltoth either, but something about their dramatics was enough to liven the mood.

The three of us dismounted and approached the ledge with careful footing.

"Where is the army?" I started. "I only see mountains." It didn't help that the worst of them were right to our east. I couldn't see beyond them; a pit was beginning to form in the base of my stomach.

A moment later, Quinn confirmed the worst of my fears.

"That's because we are going to take the glacial pass. It's dangerous, but that will play to our advantage." Our leader took a spot next to the three of us, clutching a heavy, weathered scroll. "King Horrace gave us a layout of the land before we left. Nyx knew Darren would favor the main road since it's the easiest passage for a regiment the size of the Crown's Army. Once we ascend the pass"—his eyes flew at the intimidating wall to our east—"we will have the element of surprise. The Crown's Army would never expect an attack from the west, and there is an overlook just beyond it. The lookout isn't much of an asset, almost impossible to scale, but multiple sources suggested Commander Audric was going to station his command there to oversee the battle. If Darren is leading the mages, it's very likely he will be stationed somewhere nearby."

"What if he isn't?"

Quinn massaged his shoulder with a groan; the endless days were getting to everyone. "Even if he isn't, Commander Audric will be able to lead us to wherever they've hidden their king. We just need to find the neck of the beast, and the rest will follow."

Don't. I breathed out through my nose, crippling the sensation somewhere inside. I'd lasted this long without breaking apart, and now that I could see the final leg of our journey, nothing would change.

"Ryiah?" Ella leaned in, and I took a step back. I couldn't talk about it. I just needed to focus on *now*.

Alex took over for my silence.

"How are we getting the horses to the other side?"

"We aren't. We set them free and cast our way across. We'll spend the final leg of our journey on foot." The head mage pointed to our packs. "Divide up the final provisions and carry the saddlebags on your back. Bring nothing that is not absolutely necessary to our survival."

The group had already set to dispersing supplies. Weapons were passed around, flint and steel, thick wool, a couple of flasks, salve and bandages, a small metal pot that we could heat for cooking and drink, and a ration of dry ingredients like Borean rice and bits of bone for broth. A half hour later, we were ready to depart.

I shifted uncomfortably along the ledge. Even though the packs were light, we all had two steel picks and a pair of woven, rawhide rackets attached to our straps. Not to mention the trappings for our tent, weapons, rations for food, and the heavy sleeping rolls that we couldn't leave behind.

Everything weighed more when you were hiking in snow; I would have preferred to crawl among sand.

"As soon as we pass the tundra, it could be several yards before you touch granite. That, and the temperature plunges as soon as we enter the pass. You will have to use the rackets for the rest of the climb."

Ella and I exchanged panicked glances. We had used the contraptions during the last year of our apprenticeship; we had hoped and prayed we'd never use them again. Only trappers in the most uninhabitable parts of Jerar were forced to wear them; we'd never grown comfortable with their gait. It would take three times the effort and the time to get anywhere with them on. It was the worst sort of irony that we had been reunited with the devices in what could be the final week of our lives.

"What do you think, Ry?" My brother turned to me as the rest of our party stared down at the racing current in the ravine below. "Are we reliving the Combat course all over again?"

For a moment, I was back at the Academy. It was just Alex and me racing across the mountain trail. And then there was Darren, grinning wickedly as he cast a fissure to halt us in our tracks, forcing us to cast our way across.

A stab of feeling shot to my chest before I could blink.

How could we go from the non-heir and the lowborn to this?

I grabbed my arms and squeezed until the sensation was gone. Then I was staring into the wilds of Caltoth, contemplating the best way to cross.

Fifteen minutes later, our party crossed the divide. The ravine was steep, but it couldn't have been more than ten yards across, hardly a challenge for twelve Combat mages and one healer.

Ella and I levitated across the gap with my brother between us. We had been conserving all of our casting— save heat during the night—so it wasn't a terrible depletion of our stamina.

As soon as we crossed, the temperature plummeted.

There was also no marked trail. From here on, we had a compass and King Horrace's map.

Everywhere we looked, frosted pines climbed cresting peaks for miles on end. There was nothing but white and bits of pine green as far as the eye could see. Beautiful, but deadly.

The closer we got to the Glacial Pass, the darker it got. The red sun fell behind the shadowy ridge, and we were forced to make camp at the base of the Caltothian range. From where we stood, I could see a climb with no end in sight.

Quinn said it would take us four days to reach the summit. The overlook was somewhere just beyond it, nestled between glaciers. It looked over the eastern half. The armies were expected below.

Alex shivered as he joined me, clutching a steaming mug in the palms of his hands. "Gods help us scale this thing alive."

"Scared?" I grinned. He was afraid of heights; he had done well in the Iron Range, but Caltoth was something else entirely.

"Why do you think they gave us that pick?" His skin was sallow and green. "Do they expect us to climb ice?"

Ella was clutching her fur cloak and blowing air into her palms. She shook her head with a smile. "Oh, Alex."

"What if we fall?" His eyes bulged as he stared into the abyss. "We could die—"

"We could, but this won't be the place." Ella wove her fingers into his. "I won't let you fall, Alex."

The look they exchanged was enough for me to step away.

They deserved this brief moment to themselves; I was more than capable of turning as my brother took Ella's face in his callused hands, kissing her with a look that promised forever.

I helped the camp with the evening meal.

We boiled bits of bone and a pinch of dried herbs. We'd run through our supply of smoked meats the night before, we were down to a small ration of Borean rice and broth. I passed out the final portion and then set to keeping a fire and watch.

My hands were starting to crack and bleed from the cold, but it wasn't worth the casting to heal. We needed Alex's magic for the worse things to come.

Later, I took a post with a young woman I didn't know. I wanted to give Alex and Ella some time alone.

We kept the flames burning high with our casting, doing our best to heat the others in their rawhide tents. It was a necessary task, but I enjoyed watching the stars. Everything looked so much closer from this side of the border.

It was a gods' touched land.

As miserable as I was, I appreciated the cold beauty and, in it, its silence.

And then, right as the sky was starting to lighten, I saw them.

Dancing colors. Hues of violet and orange, verdant and a cobalt blue. It was every color shifting across the sky. A rainbow of light. The pattern lasted for ten, twenty minutes.

And then it was over.

When the colors ended, the sun was close to rising, and with it, a new day.

For the first time in weeks, I felt a flutter of hope.

SEVENTEEN

THE PASS MIGHT as well have been an army waiting in ambush. For three days we climbed, higher and higher until it was near impossible to breathe. The air was so thin. It felt like there was never enough.

Two of the men were sick. They did their best to carry on, but between their nausea and the rest of our headaches, it was becoming increasingly hard to ignore.

Ella and some of the others were getting dizzy. It was dangerous. We were on unstable ground, and all it would take was one slip of the boot...

More than once we had to retrace our steps.

Quinn claimed all of this was expected, but it still didn't take away the effects.

With the leather trappings attached to our boots, we were making miserable time. For every three steps, we needed to rest. My lungs worked twice as hard just to take in the same amount of air. We had enough water—thank the gods for the abundance of snow—but the broth was doing little to fill the pits of our stomachs. The Borean rice was gone by the end of the second night.

None of us would ever make it back the way we came; the

eastern pass was our only bet to make it down alive.

No one was talking by the third afternoon. That night, when we finally reached the first crest, the elation was as palpable as despair. There was a wall of ice, and it was time for the picks in our packs.

No one could muster the words to speak.

We shared another helping of broth, not even bothering to remove the scum that rose to the top; we were too exhausted to care.

The next morning when I awoke, it was just as bad as before. The one good thing, if you could classify it as such, was that we were leaving the rawhide contraptions behind. We couldn't scale a rise of ice with a racket attached to our boots.

Killian, a man with the arms of an ox who had grown up in the heart of the Iron Range, spent the first part of our morning demonstrating how to scale the mountain face.

"Feet parallel."

I exchanged a look with Ella as we spread out behind a line of others. We would be taking the face on two at a time. Alex, who was doing the very best he could to swallow his fear, was going before us. In the event he slipped, we wanted to be able to cast him to safety.

Everyone was relying on someone else.

"Hips in. Left shoulder back to get a good swing."

We mimed the movement with our picks in hand.

"Push hips out and then climb... Parallel." There was a pause between the instruction. "Make sure your body is center to the pick." He continued, "Swing again."

I'd scaled boulders during my youth and a cliff or two

during the apprenticeship—rock climbing was one of my strengths—but ice was a different sort of test. For one, our boots had little traction and we exerted a lot of magic just fighting to keep our hold.

Every so often, I put a bit too much weight into my swing. Then I was at the mercy of the pair spotting me below. They were all that came between me and an untimely death.

Killian was the last one up; his skill kept him from unfortunate mistakes. Still, I didn't release my breath until he was fully over the ledge.

It took us most of the day to reach the top. By the time the last of our party had recovered enough to continue, the sun had set and the air had dropped to an unbearable chill.

It was all we could do to make one final camp.

We didn't have to worry about a patrol spotting our fire late into the night; the summit's plateau was the highest peak in the Glacial Pass. That, and the Crown's Army sentries would never expect someone coming from the west.

"Get some rest because we set forth at dawn." Quinn chugged down the final bit of his broth, doing his best not to grimace like the rest of us. The marrow was long gone and the only flavor was from some rather tasteless herbs.

Little did he know those "herbs" were crushed valerian root treated with magic. Alex had found the flowers in Jerar not two days after we came up with our plan and saved them for our final night in Caltoth. The powder, he had promised, would buy us three hours before the others awoke.

My brother had wanted to administer the root at dawn, to give us time to recover, but I had insisted on tonight. Every hour that passed was another hour the war waged somewhere down below.

I didn't care if my stamina was somewhat drained. I didn't care if the cold stole my breath and left a skeleton of ice.

I needed to leave now.

A rational part of me knew I was being reckless.

But the sane part of me knew it was the only way.

A half-hour later, Alex, Ella, and I had finished dragging the bodies into tents and wrapping them up in the remains of our rolls. We couldn't keep a fire burning by magic, so the mages were paired together for warmth. We'd done our best to heat small chunks of granite and metal pots, tucking them in with their furs to help stimulate warmth.

The others would never survive the night without a fire, but they would for three hours thanks to the precautions we took.

"Was I wrong not to trust Quinn?" I stared out at the leader one final time, shouldering my pack. The wind howled behind us, and my fur-lined hood was just barely keeping my face from the worst of it.

I tucked the ends of my scarf into the neck of my cloak. I was sweating after heaving ten bodies across ice and snow, but I knew it wouldn't last long. I didn't want to think how much worse it would get.

"You had no choice, Ry."

My gaze fell to Ian sleeping soundly next to Ray.

I had no choice.

My friends would never forgive me. If we survived.

I'm not picking Darren over Jerar. My fingers curled around the stolen map. It would never come to that. This was about giving the king a chance.

Ella finished adjusting her scabbard, and then we were off.

The stars lit the way.

* * *

Two miles in the dead of the night and all around us the granite glittered with ice, sharp and translucent. It was almost ethereal to be someplace so deadly and enchanting in the same breath.

We took the ridge slowly as we began our descent. The pass had been aptly named. Snow compacted into ice, frozen solid by years of neglect in a land with only one season. The summit sloped down and led to a cavernous passage littered with glaciers.

Everywhere we turned, there were beds of black ice and snow-dusted rock. It would have been so easy to fall and slip, impaling oneself on a jagged rock or, worse, over the ledge. We couldn't spot anything from the top of the pass; the mountain descended steeply into a second, lower peak where the overlook was kept. It was there we would finally be able to see the war waging below.

By the end of the second hour, we were numb from the waist up. Even with the constant movement and the heavy furs lining the inside of our cloaks, it wasn't enough. The temperature had continued to plunge, and we needed a moment to reheat our limbs or risk losing them to black frost.

Ella and I took turns casting heat—there was no wood nearby for a fire as the top of the mountain and its passage were treeless—as Alex set to work treating our skin. My twin did the best he could with the supplies he had in his pack—birch leaf and the remains of valerian—but he was holding off magic. For now.

We were sore, hungry, and tired.

The one thing I wasn't? Thirsty. Thanks to the abundance of snow.

Once again, we shared a meal of boiled water, only, this time, there wasn't even an old bone to give it the semblance of broth.

My stomach felt like a ravenous pack of dogs. Every step took twice the energy as that morning. A part of me wondered what it would have been like if I had succumbed to a night of rest.

"How much further?" Ella cupped the steam from her mug so that it heated her face.

I squinted at the map. The wind was blocked from where we stood; jagged walls of granite and ice kept the worst of it at bay.

"If this boulder is the one indicated here"—I pointed to a little dot on the scroll—"then we are close. A half-mile from the overlook. We'll have to keep a lookout for—"

The sound of ice splintering behind me was all the warning I needed.

I spun. Two balls of flame hovered above my palms as I faced the sentry head on. Alex had a broadsword, and Ella provided a glowing sphere to shield the three of us. I thanked the gods we had taken the time to talk through an attack earlier on.

Then I saw who it was.

"Ian?" My casting vanished immediately.

Our friend was pale as a ghost. His lips cracked as he

strode forward, and his arms wrapped around his cloak.

"Y-you can't d-do this." His teeth chattered as he spoke, but his eyes were livid.

Alex put his weapon back in its sheath and Ella lowered her casting.

"It's my choice." I was fighting hard to remain calm. Now that Ian was here, we were in trouble. How much, I wasn't sure. Were there others? "You told me that the day you arrived, remember?"

"That was when I thought you would be smart enough to walk away." His eyes flashed. "You have the right to not play a part in Darren's death, Ryiah, but you don't have a right to save him. That stopped being your choice the moment he took the throne. You can't put the others at risk."

Alex studied our friend's face. "How did you know? The broth—"

"I've been watching Ryiah all week." Ian's words were steeped in resentment. "By the time she tossed her portion, it was too late. I was the only one who had waited for her to eat." His brows knit together. "I tried to warn Quinn that day at the border, but he seemed to think we could handle her."

"So he *wasn't* going to uphold his promise!"

"Neither were you." Ian glowered at me. "Both of you were just saying what the other wanted to hear. I, at least, was honest that day he recruited you to our mission."

"I'm sorry." And I was—to a point. "But it was the only way, Ian."

"They'll freeze to death overnight. Did you ever think about that?"

"They will only sleep for three hours." I bristled. "And we

made sure they were warm, but you already know that. You were there."

"Am I supposed to thank you?" Ian's expression was incredulous. "Ryiah, please. Think about everyone else. Think about what will happen if you fail."

"Then the rest of you can finish the job." I refused to consider the implication. "I just need to try it my way first."

"Ryiah—"

"No." My voice rose. "You don't understand what you are asking me, Ian. I've given everything to this damned cause. *Give me a gods' forsaken chance to save him!*"

His voice was so quiet. "And if you can't?"

"He was your friend once." My voice was as hard as steel. "Are you so willing to condemn the boy you once knew? Tell me, *Ian,* if Darren was willing to call off his men and rescind his claim to the throne, if he left Jerar to spend the rest of his life repenting his crimes, would you call his murder justice?"

Ian stared at me, his jaw clenched, but he didn't respond.

"All I want is a chance." I met his hard gaze with my own. "Alex and Ella will hold you off here, or you can come with us. But I'd rather have my friend's support."

"Ryiah won't tell Darren there are others." Alex came forward to press a hand on Ian's shoulder. "The three of us can keep guard at the front of the cave... We will still have the element of surprise. Darren won't know we are there, and he won't know the rebels are coming."

"If she fails..." Ian locked eyes with my brother. "...you know what that means, Alex."

"I do." My twin was doing his best not to look at me, so

was Ella. They supported me, but that didn't make them unafraid. "But it's still Ryiah's choice."

"Three hours." Ian looked to the sky. "I promise you three hours, Ryiah, and not a second more. If you still haven't convinced him by the time the rebels arrive..."

We all knew the answer.

* * *

For a moment, I could pretend this was the apprenticeship and we had never actually left. Ian, Alex, Ella, and I were scaling the side of a mountain as we prepared for a mock battle ahead.

Only this time, the adversary was the boy I'd been competing with all along. The non-heir was playing the part of the villain, and it was up to us to capture the leader.

Darren had used me to get to Ian that first year in the desert. Now the rebels were using me to get to Darren. Our strategy hadn't changed at all. And once again, I was leading the fight.

A frozen stream wove around a pile of towering granite covered in snow and ice.

"That's the trail." I pointed to the map. We were minutes away. The cavern was just beyond it—and with it, the overlook.

And just like any mock battle, we ran into a cluster of sentries before we could reach the final base. We didn't know the guards were there until the path took a sudden dip. They caught us by surprise.

The eight Combat mages took one look at the four of us, and it took all of us a second to react.

Ian, Ella, and I threw up our casting just in time.

Our magicks melded together at once.

My whole body shook with the effort to hold. Our barrier hummed and groaned, but none of us buckled under the weight. Alex drew his blade, guarding our backs.

The other mages advanced, shooting a second round of castings at our defense.

"We can't keep this up forever." I addressed the others loudly as the others' attacks drowned out my voice. "We have to fight."

"No." Ella shifted against my arm. "*We* fight. You go on ahead, Ry. You are losing time."

I was losing time, but I couldn't bear to leave them alone. Two Combat mages and one healer against eight of the King's Regiment. I didn't like those odds.

"We can take them." Alex's voice was muffled as our wall shook and held. The assault was relentless. "You asked us to trust you, and we do. Now trust in us."

"But..." I hesitated. *My three hours are slipping away.*

"Take them from the left?" Ella jerked her chin toward a mage much older than the rest. "His castings are barely making a dent. Ian, you cast Ry's shield, and I'll blast them out of the way."

Ian's nod was barely perceptible from the corner of my eye. "Sounds like a plan."

"On the count of three, Ryiah," Ella said. "Then you run." *Go save Darren.*

It was the apprenticeship all over again every step of the way.

"One. Two..."

On "three" I took off, sprinting as fast as my legs could

lunge. Ian's defense kept off most of their attacks, but it did not keep my boots from skidding along the ice.

I swerved right just as Ella's powerful gust sent half the men sprawling against granite and snow.

A second later, a blade came at my head. I swung with all my might. The impact with my speed sent the man stumbling back. Then I blocked another before it caught me in the ribs. Two more mages sent castings and Ella sent out another gust of wind.

Only kill if there is no other choice. My friends were upholding their vow.

The mages fell to more shouts, and Ian's casting paved my defense. A part of me begged to help, but then their sacrifice would be for nothing.

Now trust in us.

I continued to run, slip-sliding along the ice until I reached a second narrow ledge. It led straight to a thick, towering structure of granite and compacted snow.

The cave towered. Layers and layers of thick ice and black rock stood out like a palace of crystalline shards. It was so large I couldn't see where it ended, only the beginning. The frozen stream ran along its entrance.

Darren might not be here. But a part of me knew he would. If the overlook was as impressive as Quinn claimed, the king would be nowhere else. Were our roles reversed, it was the place I would pick.

Bits of broken granite and ice littered the ground. My footsteps echoed along the tunnel as bits of wind whistled through sculptures of ice.

Everywhere I looked, all I saw was blue, shades of the

most brilliant hue. Icicles hung down from the granite and snow, drops of frozen rain paralyzing in their effect.

An ocean of indigo water, suspended and hung, glistened like translucent oil under a fallen sky. All of it was so fragile and haunting. In all my life, I had never seen anything so achingly beautiful.

Small bolts of the night sky peaked through little holes in the ceiling. Bits of moonlight and twinkling stars. Other parts of the cave were dark; I had to trace my hand along the icy walls.

Eventually, I came across three twisting passages. Each time I let my compass lead the way. The overlook was east. It was the only reassurance I had.

And, finally, I found my way to the brightest part of the cave.

My heart caught in my chest.

He was standing there, dressed in the black ceremonial robe and a crown, staring out at something beyond the ledge, his shoulders lit up by stars.

He didn't turn around.

A fire crackled to his right, heating the outer ledge.

The icicles near the entrance of the cave's overlook dripped.

Drip. *Drip*. Tiny raindrops of water hit the ground and the sound traveled back to me.

I took a step forward, cringing as my leather boots scraped against stone.

He still didn't turn.

But there was a sudden intake of breath. I wasn't sure how I heard it. My pulse was now strangling my lungs.

"I would have given you the world." Darren's back was still to me as he spoke. "And instead you took mine and destroyed it."

His words echoed along the walls, sending splinters of ice right into my chest.

"So tell me, love…"

The mage king turned around and his garnet eyes flashed as he took me in. They were burning with hate.

"Tell me, *my wife*," he said, "why I shouldn't destroy yours?"

EIGHTEEN

I COULDN'T SPEAK. I couldn't breathe. All I could do was stand there and stare.

Darren had been waiting for me all along, and I had walked right into his trap.

"You've always wanted to save the world." The king laughed darkly and motioned for me to come forward with the casual flick of his hand. The black hematite crown gleamed as he turned toward the valley below. "Why don't you come and see what you've wrought."

I knew what he was about to show me.

And, for some reason, I still walked. My footsteps echoed along the cave as I approached the lookout and peered out over its ledge.

Down below were hundreds of flickering flames. Torches and little bits of shadow raced in patterns, no bigger than ants. Thousands of men and women dressed in uniforms, battling late into the night. There were large catapults filled with fire and the clash of shields. The wind carried the sound of each cry to the precipice.

And their screams as each one fell to the blade of a Crown's Army knight.

"Commander Nyx is dead." I didn't even have a chance to react before Darren continued. "She was one of the first when I dispatched my army." He laughed. "Didn't take much to figure out who your leader was after we found the keep empty."

All of the emotions I'd worked so hard to hide surged to the surface; my fingernails cut into flesh.

"I told them your brother should be next." He was still watching the crowd below. "They haven't located Alex yet, but it's only a matter of time."

"D-don't." The word came out a broken whisper.

"Why?" He turned, and there was an inferno in his eyes. "You killed mine."

Darren took a step forward, and I instinctively took a step back. "Even after I spared Derrick."

"Darren—"

"You could have run away and never looked back." Disbelief and hatred were etched into every line of his face. "You could have spared Blayne—for *me*, Ryiah. For all that we were, all that you claimed to feel, you could have given me that. Even if you believed in their rebel lies."

I tried. I opened my mouth, but Darren wasn't listening. The wind howled on the ledge and his rage built with every word.

"I betrayed the one person I swore my whole life to protect for the one person that betrayed me." He took another step and the flames lit half his face, the other shrouded in shadow.

"I never t-told you because I... I didn't want you to choose between us." My voice was hoarse, and I could hear the desperation in my words. "I was trying to protect you."

"Protect me?" Darren's sneer was cold. "The only one I needed protection from was *you*."

Inadvertently, I had let him lead me to the ledge. My back was to the drop. I swallowed, doing my best to hold still.

Darren's final step placed him mere inches from my face. The heels of my boots dug into the slippery granite and ice.

"Still no weapon?" His eyes flared in the dark. "You don't need to pretend to be the hero, love. We both know the villain is the traitor who called herself my wife."

"Darren, please, just listen—"

His reprimand was sharp: *"I heard enough of your lies the first time."*

I took a step back. "I'm not going to fight you."

"Perhaps this will change your mind." He raised his hand and produced a knife. In all of a second, he had dragged it across his wrist. Blood spilled freely onto the snow at our feet.

Somewhere miles below, the ground exploded in light.

I spun around to look, gasping, only to have the king grab me by the arm and send me hurtling back toward the cave with a jerk of his wrist.

My shoulders hit the wall with a terrible thwack.

"Time to find out who the best mage really is." Two axes appeared in his hands. The iron heads whistled as he spun them by the haft. "You always wanted my title."

"D-Darren." I was choking on air. "P-please don't d-do this!"

"The only way to truly know," he continued, and I edged back along the granite, my fingers trailing the frozen edge, "is a fight to the death."

My teeth clenched. "I won't."

The king laughed, and it made my stomach go hollow. "If that's your decision."

And then he attacked.

A part of me refused to accept the hurtling blade flying across the cavern—not Darren, never the boy I loved—but another part of me, the part that had spent years honing an instinct to survive, knew better.

My defense was a translucent sphere, something so intrinsic I didn't even stop to think. The casting rose just as our eyes met across the way.

And then I ran as my sphere shattered from his axe.

Darren yelled as my boots skidded along ice.

"You can't run forever, Ryiah." His voice reverberated through the passage as I pitched forward and ducked to the right. *"Sooner or later, you will have to fight."*

A moment later, another axe found the corner, a whisper's width from my head.

Chunks of ice clunked to the floor.

I spun, casting a metal shield as the Black Mage sent out a bolt of ice. *How fitting.* I sucked in a breath and my defense shifted to a wall of fire before the ice could find a way to my hands.

There was a pool of water at my feet.

"Please..." My words were stuck in my throat, and my hysteria was rising. This wasn't supposed to be us. "Darren, this isn't you!"

"You don't know anything about me." He spat the words as a hoard of knives rose above his head. "You never did.

You only saw someone you could use."

I threw up my hands and a wall of stone caught his attack. The force of his blow, however, was enough to send a wave of pain down my wrists. Darren wasn't holding anything back.

Panic flared in the pit of my chest.

"Just listen to me!" I shouted the words as I ran. I would not return his attacks; I *couldn't*. "I never lied about the rebels!" I ducked around a formation of ice as a ball of fire hit not two inches from my neck. The flames hissed and sparked as a trickle of water wound down the column of ice.

"Blayne wasn't who you thought he was! You were always blind to his cruelty—"

The entire barrier shattered like glass, like it was nothing. Little shards of wall crumbled into crystalline studs.

I dove, my heels digging for traction along the ice.

But this time, I wasn't fast enough.

Darren's casting caught me in the ribs and slammed me against another column of ice. The impact rattled my bones, hitting along every point in my spine, so hard and so fast that I lost control of my defense. My magic ceased. I choked on my own blood, fighting the upsurge in my stomach, as I dropped to the floor on my knees.

Darren made no motion to follow up his attack; instead, he stood there watching me, two yards away, toying with a bit of cloth he had tied around the slim cut at his wrist.

"I was going to run away with you. Did you know that?"

His confession was so abrupt that every muscle in my body halted in place.

"I didn't believe a word you said, but I had made up my

mind. Paige would get you to the docks, and I was going to come find you after the war. I knew it was wrong... but a part of me just couldn't let you go."

"Darren." My voice cracked. I'd had no idea.

"I was prepared to turn my back on Jerar. My family. The Crown. This robe. *Everything I had ever known.* For exile with you." His eyes shot to mine, and I saw twin pools of fire. "I would have died before I let my brother take your life. I would have done everything in my power to save you even after all you had done..." His words shook as his hands fisted at his sides. "And then you took his life instead."

My whisper was hoarse. "I d-didn't mean to—"

"You think I enjoy this war, Ryiah?" Darren's voice rose as he cut me off, echoing along the walls; I felt it right down to my bones. "That I take pleasure in wearing my dead brother's crown?" He sent off another blast of magic that shook the cavern behind us as he shouted: *"You think this was supposed to be me?"*

"Then call your army off." I pulled myself up slowly, wincing, taking an inch at a time. I could see something in his eyes; it was there, that panic, that desperate boy on the cliffs. I just needed to reach him. "You can stop this, Darren." *Please, listen to me. I know you are still there.* "Even if you don't believe in the rebels, we can still end the war." My next words came out in a tumbling rush. "You don't have to be king. You never wanted this. You can walk away and let someone else take up the throne."

Rage contorted his face, and whatever I'd glimpsed was gone. "I will die before a pack of traitors take up the crown."

"They aren't traitors." A plea was seeping into my throat.

"Darren, please, they aren't who you think they are. They sent me to—"

"To distract the king while they play 'take out the leader?'" His snarl cut the air like a whip. "I know there are others outside, Ryiah. Who do you think taught you that tactic in the first place?"

"That's not why I—"

"Let me guess." His lips twisted in a smirk. "You are here for *me*." He closed the distance between us; I let him. Darren's eyes gleamed as he placed himself in front of me, his fingers reaching out to capture a strand of my hair, twirling it in his hand. "They voted to kill the king, but you wanted to reason with him. *Surely* he would understand if you could just explain."

"This isn't a trick!" Why was this so hard? I could see the disbelief in his garnet irises, and it had my pulse thundering in my ears. "Maybe they don't believe you can be trusted, Darren, but I know they're wrong. I won't let anything happen—"

"And you won't let anything happen after I recall my army."

My eyes searched his, pleading. "Yes!"

Darren's grip tightened on my hair until it hurt. "Such a beautiful liar."

"Darren, *p-please…*" I knew it was wrong, but I lifted my hand to touch his face. His other hand caught it, slamming my wrist high against the wall.

"Don't *ever* touch me again." His chest rose and fell heavily as he hissed, "I am done playing games, Ryiah. You aren't some cowering victim; you never were."

"This isn't a game!"

"I know your friends are out there." The scorn was etched into every line of his face. "And I know exactly why you are here."

"I'm not—"

My protest turned to a cry as Darren released my neck and used his free hand to produce a dagger.

"Fool me once," he said, "shame on you. There won't be a second time."

Then he plunged the blade into the center of my raised palm.

For a moment, I just stared with disbelieving eyes. There was a faltering in my chest, a hitched intake of breath, and something as precious as hope shattered with the piercing sensation of iron.

And *then*.

Everything.

Was.

On.

Fire.

There was nothing to describe the way the steel cut through muscle and scraped against bone. The incalculable sting of a puncture and the betrayal in my chest.

"I wonder how much more it will take for you to break." Darren pressed close as I fought back a sob. The pressure was doing terrible things to my insides, and it was all I could do to keep my magic at bay. "You can choose to drop the charade now, and fight..."

I took a shuddering breath. "It's n-not a—"

His grip shifted on the knife, and I couldn't breathe. All I could taste was hot metallic blood as I bit down my cheek to keep from crying out loud.

"Or I can continue until your screams bring the others out of hiding." Darren's lips curled in a sneer. "One way or another, I'm going to get my fight, Ryiah."

A part of my hand was numb, plastered against the ice, and the rest was writhing in a gulf of fire and agony. It was hard just to think.

Fight him.

No.

Fight, or die.

I blinked against a wave of ever-mounting pain. I wouldn't fight back, any defense would trigger something I couldn't take back. My control was slipping, and I was afraid just how hard he would push.

He believes you are here to betray him. Fight, and you lose any chance of bringing him back.

"No." The word tumbled from my lips, and it was nothing next to the scream that followed.

Darren twisted the knife.

Pain tore a molten trail up every part of my arm, and my screams singed the air as I fought the magic threatening to break.

"Fight me!" Darren slammed me against the wall. The back of my head hit rock, and I choked, struggling to breathe. "Stop pretending and fight me, Ryiah!"

His shout echoed my cry, but I could feel the shaking in his limbs.

Whatever he felt, he wasn't immune. There was still a part of the boy I knew.

I just had to hold on, even if the pain was eating me from the inside.

"Y-you want me to f-fight…" I gasped; the overwhelming pressure was making it hard to speak. "B-because if I d-don't… it m-might m-mean B-Blayne was wrong."

"Liar." Darren's chest was rising and falling, but his fingers were trembling against my skin.

The pain was building, and there was a terrible pounding in the back of my head. Every instinct urged a defense, but something screamed at me not to move. Not yet.

"No."

Darren still held the dagger trapping my hand; his other fist dug into my shoulder blade as he pinned me against the wall. But I could feel the erratic beating of his pulse against my own. He was slipping. "You are just a-afraid of the truth."

"I already know exactly who you are."

"I know *y-you*." My voice cracked and I felt him flinch. "Whatever you t-think you b-believe, you d-don't want this."

I saw a flicker of something, and I pushed. "You want to s-save Jerar," I whispered, "and you still c-can."

I had him. For just a second, I could see the indecision in his eyes.

And then the pounding of footsteps and voices reached us.

Darren's shoulders went rigid as his eyes shot to black.

"Ever my *distraction*." Darren withdrew the blade and a cry escaped my lips. "And here they are, just in time."

"Ryiah, *Ryiah!*" I could hear all three of their shouts echoing throughout the walls. They must have heard my screams.

Gods, no. Darren thought…

The king cocked his head to the side. "Looks like I won't have to look for your brother after all. And is that Ella and Ian I hear?"

"Get out of here!" I screamed the words as Darren released me, stepping back to face my friends head on.

But of course, my panicked scream only made them come running.

I had less than a second to decide as magic crackled in his palm.

Fight, or watch the most powerful mage in Jerar take on my brother and two best friends. He had used my screams to draw them out, just like he promised.

Fight Darren. Or watch them die.

I launched myself from the wall and ripped the sleeve off my cloak, wrapping it as tightly as I could around my hand. The blood seeped through, but I didn't have time to fix it now.

The Black Mage kept his gaze on the passage as the footsteps grew louder. "A bit too late, my love. We have a score to settle first."

"Ryiah!" My brother was first to turn the corner.

And I raced forward, palms outstretched as I screamed, "Alex, run!"

Darren's magic took off like a storm. Miniscule shards of ice collected in a whirlwind that would shred its victim to bits. Some of the older mages in our apprenticeship had once demonstrated something similar in the desert with small granules of sand.

My brother skidded to a halt as I threw myself in front of

his path.

My casting roared to life, and I threw my hands over my ears, praying the others would copy the defense.

The vibrations rose like the toll of a heavy bell; I felt the rattle in every part of my chest. The screech was ear shattering and set every nerve on edge.

My magic turned Darren's casting to dust.

For a moment, the air was thick with a crystalline powder, and the only thing I could hear was an endless ringing in my skull.

I released my ears just as the first icicle crashed to the floor.

An icicle the size of a small house.

Another followed. Ice was dropping from the ceiling and bits were cracking along the walls.

I couldn't see where Darren was across the passage. Things kept falling.

The cavern… was breaking. In my haste to counter his magic, I had forgotten where we were. The effect of so many vibrations in a prism of ice.

Boom.

I leaped back just as another splintered in my path.

Pop. Swissh. Craaaack.

"Run!" I turned and shoved the three of my rescuers back; Darren would be on us in seconds.

Ella hesitated, but Alex's eyes were locked on my bandage, his outrage rising. "Ryiah, you're—"

"Ella, get my brother out of here!" My screech was frantic. I didn't have time to argue as a flare of light lit up the room, and I spun, magic rising.

The barrier rose just as the passage exploded in a torrent of arrows. The fireheads hissed and sparked as they smacked against my casting and crumbled to ash.

I braced for the next onslaught, but Ian had already taken off, sprinting toward the king, twisting and diving around heavy mounds of ice.

"Ian, no!"

Darren had two axes in hand.

Ian launched a javelin.

And I tore off after them as fast as my legs could manage.

Darren deflected the older boy's casting with an axe that spun, sending both of their blades skittering off to the side. Then he lunged forward, his second weapon in hand.

Ian circled, his chest rising and falling, his eyes darting everywhere as he searched for an opening.

I reached Ian, joining my magic with his just as Darren launched the second axe and an onslaught of knives.

"Isn't this a surprise," Darren snarled as the weapons collided with our globe, "the two of you, together again."

"Go." I tried to push Ian back, but he was too busy fiddling with a scabbard at his waist. "Ian," I tried again, my panic rising, "leave him to me."

"I'm not going anywhere." The sword was in his hand.

"But—"

A blast shook our shield, and for a moment, all I could see was a whirlwind of red. It was only a matter of minutes before Darren breached our defense. The throbbing ache was building in my head with every second. The sheer effort to hold a casting of this magnitude was depleting my stamina too fast.

I could barely blink from the pain, much less think.

"He's trying to kill us, Ryiah." Ian's breaths were ragged. He wasn't faring any better. "Even you." He took a step back so that his shoulders were parallel to my own with the weapon drawn. "All bets are off."

Darren's voice thundered behind our shield. "You two must have enjoyed playing me for the fool all these years."

Thud. Crasssh. Our shield was splintering, and my grip was slipping down threads of control like a web.

There was another ear-splitting screech, and then the magical bond Ian and I shared snapped.

I ducked and dove, skinning my knees and palms—the bandage included—along the ice and rock. Ian collapsed; he hadn't been so quick and had received the blunt force of Darren's attack.

"Ian!"

I heard rather than saw my friend fall as a blur rushed us by.

Another jarring echo and whatever Darren cast next hit something solid, blocking it from the obvious path.

I blinked and the shadows registered, the ache subsiding in my head just long enough to focus.

Ella.

She and Alex had never left, and she had thrown herself in our path while my brother clutched a blade.

Alex was kneeling at Ian's side, green magic flickering along his fingers as he saw to his wounds.

I struggled to rise, but my arms, especially the one with the bad hand, refused to hold still long enough to push. The pain was making me see stars.

Outside of my vision, there was another clash, and then a loud *clap* as steel hit something across the way.

"You don't have to do this." I could hear Ella shouting. "For Ryiah's sake, Darren—"

Bright light flared across the cavern, and I pushed harder, biting down to keep from screaming as I rose to my knees.

"—But if you do—" Ella gasped as something slammed against her defense, again and again. "—then I have no c-choice."

I was pushing to my feet as the sound of splintering glass crowded my ears.

I recovered my vision just as my best friend ducked low, narrowly avoiding a dagger to the ribs. She had a set of arrows hovering above her hands. They soared through the air the same moment fire appeared in the Black Mage's palms.

No.

Hysteria exploded in my chest, and I couldn't think. I just moved.

Twin streaks of magic shot out of each of my hands.

And the two hit the wall. Ella slumped to her knees at my left. There was the crunch of bone to my right. My vision locked on a staggering king with a thin trail of blood trickling down the corner of his mouth.

"Your fight isn't with them." My fists were shaking as I screamed. Fury made it hard to focus on anything other than Ella. *Ella.* I couldn't watch my best friend go down fighting a battle I was too afraid to fight. "It's with me!"

For a moment, Darren didn't move; he just stared.

And then he threw back his head and laughed. *"Finally."*

"Ryiah, no—"

I twisted my neck and shared one last look with my brother and friends. Ian was struggling against my brother's hold. Alex refused to budge, his gaze locked on mine. I could see the resolution in his jaw and the agony in his eyes. He would honor his promise, even if it cost me my life.

Ella just watched me, hot resignation staining her cheeks. She knew why I had stopped their duel. She knew what I wanted.

She knew I could never forgive them if it was someone else.

She looked away.

My words were barely a whisper. *"I'm sorry."*

I couldn't let them die at the hands of the boy I loved. My fate was sealed the moment I betrayed a king.

Ian fought my brother's grip. *"Ryiah, don't you dare—"*

I shut my eyes and sent a bolt of power at the ceiling. I didn't wait for the torrent to land as my feet hit the air.

I just ran.

I ran and ran as fast as my legs could fly. I could hear Ian's bellow as I increased my pace. My lungs burned like fire as I crossed the threshold just in time.

"Ryiah!"

The mage's words were cut off by the thunder of ice and snow. An avalanche of rock followed as the cave's ceiling came crumbling down.

Shards of ice cut away at my clothes as I continued to run. A misting of white cloaked the air, and I was choking on dust. The walls quaked as I ran.

And then it was over.

I ducked just as Darren did the same, and the two of us ended up in a wide passage much brighter than the rest. A frozen pool of water was at our feet, lit up by the gaps of starlight above.

There was a mountain of rubble behind us, and I could hear Ian's muffled shouts as he tried to cast a way through. He wouldn't reach us. Nobody would.

The overlook was our only way out. That, or an army of mages paving a way through debris. Rebels or Crown's Army soldiers, it didn't matter. By the time they reached us, only one would be leaving the cave alive.

Darren cleared his throat. "You could have killed us both."

I withdrew a broadsword from the scabbard at my waist. "If that's what it takes."

The two of us circled, and for a moment, I was back in the Academy armory. It was the two of us and a winter solstice as a boy taught a girl how to fight.

I swallowed and shoved the memory back. That Darren was gone. This was a cruel stranger in his place. He might not be his brother, but he believed in Blayne's lies. He would kill for them.

He had already shown me *exactly* what he was capable of.

I couldn't keep clinging to the past.

Everything we had...

Say it, my brain screamed. *Admit everything you have is gone.*

The king was the first to lunge. I caught the glint of *bagh naka* in each of his fists. The brass blades were attached to his knuckles by a leather thong. He swiped in and then crested right, ducking back out before I could place a hit. His footwork was fluid like a jungle cat in shadows, his blades like claws.

But I wasn't second best for nothing.

I spun and twisted, cutting and lunging in return. Everything I did, my magic mirrored his assault. My muscles knew the patterns without recall. So many years of practice, my body recognized Darren's next choice before it caught up to my thoughts.

And he, mine.

It was just the two of us, pulses beating out the frenzied dance as we twisted and turned in the fight of our lives.

…But every chance I could land a blow, I was still holding back. I knew it. He knew it. My heart was caught up in a deadly game, and it was blocking my mind when I needed it most.

Come on, Ryiah, fight.

Darren's gaze locked on my own; something twisted in the crevice of my lungs.

Fight.

My grip faltered and a ripple of agony shot down my arm as one of Darren's blades caught on my sword, forcing it to the side as the other swiped at my casted shield, the screech of metal grating in my ears.

My knees buckled under the weight; my mind cried out at the mounting pressure of his magic against mine.

Fight.

Gods blast it, he could have killed my friends!

He was waging a war.

How much more would it take?

Fight him.

Steel took up a reservoir around my heart and the projection lunged. My casting became a chain. I dropped the sword and ducked, twisting right. I used the end of my chain to catch on one set of blades as I coiled it around the second. In the blink of an eye, I had his *bahj naga* in chains.

Before Darren could react, I contracted my arm, pulling the king in until the two of us were just a hair-width apart. Then I sent him soaring across the ice as far as I could throw.

I clenched my eyes shut as he landed flat on his back; his head hit the ice with a hard thud.

It's not him, it's not him, it's not him. The lies weren't working; I could feel myself starting to break.

Craccckkkk.

My eyelids fluttered open in time to catch Darren's hand against ice.

I lunged to the right as a fissure ripped across the floor like a legion of teeth. I landed with my thigh just narrowly avoiding a large skewer of ice.

There was a crackle of bright yellow and gold as Darren pushed himself to his knees.

I knew what was coming next.

My casting caught the blunt force of Darren's lightning at an angle, the energy crackling in a ball above my head. The effort to keep Darren's magic at bay was like pulling my limbs from their sockets. The agony that tore up my spine and into my mind was like a molten trail of metal burning me from the inside out, incinerating the air in my lungs as it turned my senses to ash.

My vision faded to black, and it was all I could do to

stand there and hold, the projection a bubble ready to burst.

It was boiling over, and my lungs expanded as I clung to my casting for all that I was worth.

Hold.

My heels dug into rock as every ounce of my will battled his.

Hold.

Spots of red mixed in with black, and I wasn't sure if I would die from the casting or the flames writhing inside my head.

And then, like a bit of flint against steel, my magic caught. The casting ignited. A wave of cool relief washed over my bones as the weight disappeared.

My vision returned as I collapsed, keeled over with my face between my legs. The lightning was gone.

I spewed saliva and blood as I gulped in great gasps of air.

"You've gotten better."

I glanced up through sweaty bangs. Darren was leaning heavily against a column of ice, one hand propped up to keep him from falling, his other on his knee as he swallowed, his crown askew.

The rapid depletion of stamina had taken its toll on both of us.

"My tolerance for pain got better," I choked, "after a week in your brother's dungeon."

For just a moment, a frown graced his mouth, but it was gone as quickly as it had come. "Nothing more than you deserved."

I forced myself to rise. "You didn't think so then."

The Black Mage approached, one step at a time as the

hem of his black robe dragged along ice.

"Back then I thought you were someone else." His eyes met mine, and what I saw was bitter and cold. A wasteland of desolation and hate. "My mistake."

A trickle of heat slunk down the back of my neck as the two of us returned to our fighting stance, a bit worse for wear than before.

My mind raced as I tried to decide which casting to turn to next. From the throbbing ache in my head, I knew my stamina was dangerously close to its end. I had depleted close to a third of my stores on the trek up the mountain and Darren was no ordinary mage. He held nothing back; each attack was like a battering ram against my head.

I bit down on my cheek as I caught sight of gleaming metal across the away. I had dropped my sword before the lightning, and now I was too far to reach it. I had two arm sheaths with daggers, but they meant close combat if I didn't cast. Darren would deflect any attack from a distance; my only hope was to press the advantage up close.

But that meant exposing myself.

I wasn't sure I was strong enough to stand that close and do what needed to be done. All those years of training had never prepared me for the enemy being someone I knew. Someone I loved.

Someone I still—

Don't finish that thought. I fished the first dagger from its holds and made my approach.

"Run out of magic already, love?" Darren's smile was cold.

"You fought three mages and I've only had you." I gave

him my best smirk; it was too strained, and I knew he wouldn't believe it for a second. "I think the odds are in my favor now."

"You must have forgotten our duel in Langli." Darren discarded the belt and scabbard at his waist. Then he reached into his robe. Attached to his upper arms were daggers identical to my own. "I don't need magic to beat you, Ryiah. I don't even need two blades."

Darren pulled the first dagger to his palm, flipping the hilt up and then down with the flick of his fingers. I watched it spin outside his wrist.

Could this really be it? That our final battle would come to this?

The two of us circled closely now, our eyes locked on the other's form. I could feel my pulse against my throat. It beat louder and louder as I took a daring step forward, the blade drawn back against my side.

Darren crooked the blade from his shoulder. He was going to counter my attack with the traditional grip. I might have speed with the reverse, but his stance had reach. He didn't need agility when he knew every lunge would outdistance my own.

But we both had to play to our strengths. Dexterity for the reckless lowborn and brute strength for the boy who had it all.

It was anyone's guess, but I was determined to win.

I was the first to lunge. Something about the wait, about wanting to end this before my emotions played a part, had me foregoing my regular approach.

I swept in low and slashed to the left as Darren stepped

just out of reach.

"You'll have to do better than that."

Our boots scratched against the slippery ground.

Again, I lunged, this time with a feint high and a jab toward the ribs.

But Darren wasn't fooled. He caught my arm and twisted, bearing down on my blade arm as he swung his dagger down from above.

I ducked and rolled, but not before the hot bite of metal caught my shoulder in passing.

I narrowly avoided a curse as I fell back, dripping red. The wound was shallow, but Darren had drawn first blood, and it didn't bode well this early in the fight.

Darren lunged forward, and I sidestepped his attack. I sent a cross-punch, slashing out diagonally with my blade.

The Black Mage blocked the attack with his fist, but the defense wasn't without its cost. The serrated edge of my dagger pressed down against his skin. A bit of steam rose when his blood hit the floor.

The two of us continued to circle and lunge.

I tried not to think about how this moment would end, but with every passing second, it was becoming harder to pretend.

Our chests rose and fell heavily to match the beat of our pulses. A couple of minutes and then one of us would land a cut. A moment later, the other would follow.

Back and forth. In and out.

And blood.

Cutting, slashing. Gods, it was getting harder just to breathe. Sweat stung my eyes, and I grew dizzier with every lunge.

I wondered who would be first to collapse.

Stop worrying about the end, just focus on now.

I swung wildly as my boots slipped on ice.

Darren's arm came up and out.

For just a moment, our wrists caught in one solitary blow. My breath came out hard and fast. I swallowed, feeling the dance of magic just below my skin.

Cast. End this now. *Fight.*

I had never agreed to "no magic," and who would honor a deal with the villain? I could cast now. It would be so easy.

The second dagger withdrew from its sheath at my arm.

Darren's gaze flit to the blade hovering in the air.

"Do it." His eyes were twin pits of black; his taunt daring and cold. "Kill me."

The second dagger dipped low against his chest. One swift push was all it would take.

Do it.

My casting trembled in the air as the magic pulsed along my skin.

Kill me.

There were a thousand and one reasons to take the Black Mage's life. My friends. The rebels. Jerar.

My stomach clenched as my eyes locked on his. He was a monster, but I wasn't any better. And if I did this…

Ian had been the one to say it: *"Look me in the eyes and tell me you don't hold yourself responsible for what he's become."*

My friend was right. I did. And if I cheated our magicless duel, I was no better than the traitor Darren believed me to be.

I couldn't do this.

Gods, I knew everything Darren had done, everything he would do, but I still...

No.

Not like this.

"One blade." My mouth was dry as I croaked the words. "No magic."

The second dagger returned to its sheath.

Darren would kill me. His eyes locked on mine and I could see it. There was hate. So much hate. It was drowning me, and it was everything I had ever done. I could see it right there in his eyes.

Fight.

It was the two of us, our arms crossed and weapons drawn.

My fingers trembled against the blade, and my wrist burned where his skin pressed down against my own. I could feel his pulse hammering against his veins.

Do it.

An ear-shattering roar cut the air, and for a moment, for a moment I thought I'd made a mistake.

But then it happened again.

My eyes were still on Darren as the ceiling creaked and groaned up above. They remained on Darren as the walls began to quake, as the pool splintered and the two of us staggered back, the ice shattering like a web.

His eyes were on the passage behind us. "Yours or mine?"

I heard my friends screaming at the top of their lungs: *"No!" "Stop, Quinn!"*

"Mine."

The rebels didn't need to kill the king; they just needed to bury him alive. And if I was a casualty? Well, sacrifices had to be made.

There was another *boom* and my pulse caught in my throat.

This was the part that I was supposed to accept, the part where I proclaimed my unrelenting devotion to Jerar. The hero didn't fear death, and up until that moment, neither had I.

But, gods, here and now? Like this? Under a mountain of rubble instead of a quick blade to the neck?

I had blocked our only reasonable escape; my reserve wasn't large enough to cast a way out the way we had come.

It isn't "our" escape. It's yours. Take advantage of the confusion and slit his throat.

The dagger was right there in my palm. Darren was distracted, staring out at his crown as it sunk into the dark waters below; it must have fallen during the first attack.

This is it. If I did it now, the rebels might even find a way to get to me in time. I might still live.

Another loud thud and I jumped. The first shard of ice hit the ground two yards to my left. It exploded apart, spraying my arms and legs.

Seconds later another followed.

My gaze shot to the ceiling just as a large chunk broke away. Right above our heads.

I couldn't move.

Something hard clipped my side—Darren. It was all the warning I needed.

I started to run. Darren was already sprinting toward the western tunnel. The dark passage led to gods only knew—a dead end or escape.

It didn't matter either way.

My mission was to kill the king. Wherever he went, I followed.

* * *

We were still running as thunder rained down from above.

Large spirals of ice plummeted like daggers to the ground, tearing their way into the earth. Snow and rock followed, splintering the walls.

We skidded along the passage as fast as we dared. Bleeding knees and crippled hands made every leap harder than the last. We ducked and dove in a maze of ice with a palm of light to guide the way.

The pain in my head was almost blinding. Again and again, I had to cast enough force to blast the parts of the ceiling that were seconds from crushing my limbs. And from the labored gasps up ahead, I could tell Darren wasn't faring much better, if at all.

My legs ached. Every muscle was on fire, and I could barely feel my lungs save for the flames eating my chest from the inside.

The rebels had set an avalanche in motion, and it was only a matter of time.

Parts of the passage were colder, darker, impossibly narrow with jagged bits that reached out like jaws. My shoulder caught against something sharp, but I didn't dare stop. I kept running with my arms tucked close to my sides, dripping blood.

And then, *finally,* just as I was ready to collapse, we reached a wide berth. A frozen riverbed scattered with bits of rock and ice that had already started to drop in the catalyst that set about the glacier's descent.

Unlike the frozen pond from before, it wasn't skylight that showed me the way.

There was a crevice in the wall across the pond. It was real.

We could live.

Darren sprinted across the stream, and I wasn't far behind.

The whole place was crumbling down. The walls shuddered and groaned. Bits of ceiling crashed to the floor as the wind howled against my ears. And still I ran.

So close.

No more than two hundred yards...

My bootstrap caught on a rock.

I lost my footing.

And then I went down, crying out as my palms hit the ice. I landed on my bandaged hand and the world went red.

The ceiling above gave a terrible moan.

Get up. Move. Run. My nails dug into the ice, but I couldn't get enough traction to stand. Panic and pain were making it impossible to project.

And as the shard came plummeting down, I shut out the world. My senses screamed, but, gods, if I were going to die, it wouldn't be because I failed to cast.

The world spun as I reached down *deep*—to the girl who'd spent countless library nights in meditation and binding magic to her will. The girl who had almost won a Candidacy and beat Darren's lightning head on. *She* had control. *She* wouldn't fail me in this moment. *She* would control the pain.

And then that boulder-sized glacier exploded right above my head; I'd won.

Seconds later I was on my knees, coughing up blood.

A second explosion sounded just behind my back.

I spun, righting myself as I stood.

Darren was hunched over, his fist still in the air. And there was another bit of fallen ceiling, easily twice the mass from the first, yards from where I had fallen on the ground.

My gaze flew to the king and something twisted in my lungs. *Did he just save me?*

Darren turned on his heel and started to run. I limped after him. The cavern was still well on its way to collapse.

The king was only ten yards ahead of me when the closest pillar fell. I didn't see at it first because my eyes were glued to the ceiling straight ahead.

The Black Mage must have missed it too.

By the time the noise drew our attention, the structure had ripped free of its foundation and was starting to fall.

Darren threw out his hands and a spark of violet flared out across his palms.

But then it flickered and stopped.

Why...?

My heart stopped in its tracks. He had used up his magic.

I stopped breathing as my feet took off and my casting went hurtling out.

"Nooooooo!" I couldn't even hear my scream.

The column rammed Darren's side and chunks of ice and rock exploded the second my casting hit the edge. But it wasn't enough.

I was too late.

Darren went down.

His black robe flapped out like wings as his body hit the floor. He didn't even try to rise.

My pulse beat so loud I could no longer hear the room's collapse.

All I saw was the boy and the wall's crevice fifty yards away.

This was it. The Black Mage had fallen. And I would live.

I wouldn't even need to use a blade to take his life.

Run.

Run, Ryiah, run. My mind was screaming at the top of its lungs. The walls were quaking all around. *Run.*

Tears streamed down my cheeks as I stood, caught between the boy and freedom, between my life and everything else.

He's a monster.

He's not yours to save.

He's dying.

He'll never make it out.

Run.

My lips moved, but there was no sound. I was doing things with my hands, and then I was stumbling forward but not toward the wall.

There was a flash of light.

A violet hue as an amethyst globe appeared above us both. My casting quivered but held.

I sank to my knees by the king sprawled out across the floor. My vision blurred and my hands shook as I kneeled.

"You got w-what you w-wanted." Darren's chest rose and fell as he sputtered; his lips were stained with blood. "Your v-villain is dead."

"But—"

"You fool." Darren choked as he tried to sit up and swore, his face white as snow. Red seeped through the tunic covering his chest, bits of scarlet pooling underneath. "G-get out of h-here."

"You saved me." There was a blinding ache in my head. I could feel each time the casting trembled and shook. My projection was growing weaker with every second that passed, every time a bit of roof collapsed. "Why?"

How long would my magic last?

"D-didn't save y-you." He was struggling to breathe, and his words rattled in his chest.

Something inside of me snapped. Darren had never been in that second glacier's path when we'd heard the explosion—he'd had no reason to cast.

Unless he'd been attempting to save me.

"Liar!"

Darren's laugh was weak as he looked up at me. "S-so w-what if I a-am?"

It was like a blow to the ribs. I couldn't breathe.

He swallowed.

"You h-have your a-answer." The words were pained. "N-now g-go."

The projection was splintering inside my head; I could feel it as every last strand snapped across space. So much of my world was awash in pain. So much of it was black.

You have your answer.

I did.

But I couldn't leave.

I reached for the second strap at my arm. I felt the sting of cold metal as I slipped the blade from its sheath and plunged it into my bandaged hand.

Then I screamed.

I screamed as pain enveloped me whole. Needles stabbed along my spine and my mind roared out in shock. I screamed until my voice was hoarse.

Then the magic washed over me like a cloud of shadow, filling in the spaces traditional casting couldn't hold. It kept the roof from caving in.

I kept the dagger centered as I opened my eyes. My whole body trembled, but I was already on the ground. Had I been standing, I most certainly would have collapsed.

I sucked in a sharp lungful of air, wondering how long my pain casting would hold.

"G-get out of h-here... *p-please*." Darren's voice was hoarse. My eyes flew to his, and in Darren's... in Darren's I saw grief.

My fingers shook violently as they brushed his wrist. "I-I can't."

His eyelids fluttered shut, and for a moment no one spoke.

"Y-you are g-going to die." His face was more ashen than before.

My laugh was hollow. "I always was too reckless."

The pain was mounting in my skull, like a bank gathering snow.

"P-perhaps they w-will... f-find y-you in t-time."

His breaths were raspy and loud.

My fingers burrowed into his sleeve. I wanted the king to look at me. I was kneeling here on the ground, spilling blood as the last of my magic gave way to the last few minutes of our lives. I needed him to see.

Gods, if we are going to die together, I need him to see me.

I needed him to understand.

"They won't."

Garnet met my blurry eyes, and he swallowed.

"You've a-always l-loved me... d-didn't you?"

I nodded, and something burned in the back of my throat.

"It w-was Blayne? A-all along?"

I didn't have to ask what he meant.

"He loved you, but..." I swallowed as another wave of pain cut off the rest of my words. "...but he wasn't the man you thought he was. Y-your father got to him too young."

Darren turned away from me; his shoulders shook violently as he choked. He was seeing our past for what it really was.

Realizing what his actions had cost.

"Darren—"

"A-all t-that I-I've done..." He couldn't look at me. "Y-you should... just l-leave m-me here to d-die."

I shook my head violently until I realized he couldn't see it. Tears poured down my face. "No." My hand grasped at his wrist. "D-Darren... I..." Hysteria was mounting and making it hard to speak.

"Please l-look at me," I begged.

His jaw twisted, and I could see the pain in every line of his face. It was worse than the pain inside my head. I saw a broken king.

"I should have t-trusted you," I whispered. "I-if I had…" If I had, this wouldn't have been us.

His hand trembled as he placed it on top of my own; it was icy cold.

"C-couldn't have k-known."

My heart was fighting its way right out of my chest. After everything, this couldn't be it. This couldn't be us. Anger, sorrow, guilt, and regret were rising and rising, and there was nowhere left to go.

"It's not fair!" This wasn't supposed to be how our story went. In fairy tales, the prince saved the girl. In mine, the princess destroyed him.

My shoulders shuddered uncontrollably, and I couldn't stop from repeating the words. *"It's. Not. Fair."*

"N-nothing about us h-has ever been f-fair."

He said it and I swear to the gods a part of me shattered. I felt cheated. I'd fought so hard for us, and now our story would be over. Before it could even begin.

"I…" Darren's voice cracked and he shut his eyes, his lips thin with pain. "I-I w-wish…"

I stifled a sob in my throat, but it did no good. There were too many things unsaid.

We didn't have enough time; we never would.

He was dying and my pain magic was fettering to an end.

The ground was covered in red.

Somewhere just beyond us, the cave gave a shuddering groan.

And then the final part collapsed.

An avalanche of ice and snow.

I fell back, releasing Darren's hand as my magic screamed inside my mind. I could feel *everything*.

I was holding the sky in my hands, and it was all crashing down.

"...l-love y-you..." His voice seemed so far away.

I couldn't even look at him; all I saw was white. My fingers were numb as they clung to the dagger in an effort to keep the world from falling in. But the pain, as terrible as it was, was not enough.

My magic wouldn't last forever.

But then...

Then my fingers tightened against the hilt.

Darren struggled to breathe with ragged gasps and his chest convulsing.

This isn't the end.

I inhaled as hard as I could, letting every bit of air fill my lungs as the sphere above me collapsed.

And then I plunged the dagger into my chest. Right into my beating heart.

I gave up everything I was.

I felt the kind of pain you can't describe. The kind that takes your soul.

I made my *last stand*.

It was the kind of magic you died for.

I released my blood and my body and my magic to the gods as I gave the final casting of my life.

I gave my all... for *him*.

I only hoped it was enough.

I wasn't a hero, but at that moment, I could be the girl I wanted to be.

I could save the boy.

And so I did. And as that last gasping breath took in an intoxication of violet and ice, I lost myself to the end.

And then?

I was free.

NINETEEN

Last Stand (noun): a selfless act. The act of pain casting (see "Categories of Magic") in its rawest form. To invoke so much pain it takes one's life. This form of magic is reserved to only those with the ability to pain cast.

The power behind a mage's last stand is only as good as its caster. The level of potency depends on one's established stamina prior to the act. The magic invoked in one's last stand isn't inherently logical; however, if the person casting has developed a high level of control over pain in the past, they stand a better chance at invoking the casting they want.

Most recorded acts were performed by mages under the instruction of commanders during war, a sacrifice for the rest. Because the act is fleeting and final, our scholars are still attempting to study the full extent of this casting. It is possible there are some effects and/or facts yet missing from our account.

So this was death.

It felt different than expected. To be fair, I had never expected to feel anything. From the stories of the Shadow God and his realm of lonely souls, I had never expected to experience thought. So the idea that I was conscious and could feel... It was both a blessing and a curse.

Perhaps it was more of a curse.

The things I felt... they weren't pleasant.

Whoever said pain left you after death, well, clearly they had never died. Because I felt everything.

There was an inferno in my chest. I was on fire. My lungs burned up from the inside, and jolts of hot, piercing agony ran up and down my spine. My mouth tasted of ash.

And then came the memories.

I hadn't known the dead retained them.

I wished we couldn't.

More than the pain, it was the memories I wanted to stop.

Why would one wish to live out an eternity remembering everything they lost?

I hadn't lived out the happily ever after my parents promised. Not even close.

Here? Forced to *feel*? I was bitter and angry.

I was going to spend the rest of eternity regretting the life I never got.

I took a ragged breath, cursing the hot air that burned down every inch of my lungs.

Wait.

I can breathe?

What else could I do?

My eyelids fluttered open and a blur of color overloaded my sight. Flashes of color and faces. So many faces.

It was right then I started to hear. Voices. Familiar and excited. Some of them were shouting my name.

They were so far away, but they were here.

Were they real?

My heart thundered in my ears and spots danced before my eyes. It was all too much. I couldn't handle all of my senses overloading me at once.

Time ceased to be.

* * *

The next time I regained consciousness, the room was quiet and there were no faces to see.

I was able to adjust to the darkness and silence much easier than the noise.

It took close to an hour just to accept this was real.

A room. Not a shadow-filled realm. Familiar and cold. Rough, gray stone and a single window lined with bars.

I lay on a bunk made of pine. To my right was a small dresser lined with vials of all different colors and sizes. Some of the labels I could read; from what I gathered, they were for healing.

Was I truly alive?

I flexed my fingers and toes, and immediately regretted it as a fresh, biting pain swept over the subsiding ache from before. I definitely hurt. And from the bandages wrapped around my chest and hand, I suspected I wasn't dead.

How?

Something was wrong.

I had cast my last stand. My life had ended there in that cavern made of ice. If I was alive...

Had I made a mistake?

Gods.

Was—*No.*

No.

I would not accept that.

I'd died for him. If the rebels had found a way to save me, if my casting hadn't worked, then they would have saved him too. Alex and Ella would've made sure he was alive. For me.

So why was I so afraid?

Even though I felt like I was ripping every muscle under my skin, I pushed myself off the cot and went to the window instead.

Just as my suspicion led, I recognized the familiar landscape below. Flickering torches and fortified walls. The remains of a recovering forest just beyond.

I was back in Ferren's Keep. And from the number of tents and men milling on the ground, the Crown's Army and rebel force had returned to Jerar.

Was the war over?

Is Darren—

I staggered out of the room with my hand sliding along the rough granite for support. I needed to find him. I needed to find someone.

I didn't have to travel that far.

There were two guards posted a couple yards down the hall from my door. I thanked the gods I didn't have to travel that far; already there were shooting pains in my stomach, and my legs were seconds from collapse. I wouldn't last much longer.

"Please…" My tongue was as dry as sand. "Tell me where I can…" Another shuddering breath. "…find the k-king."

"The king?" The older guard exchanged looks with his comrade. "You mean our *queen*?"

"She means the prisoner," the second said. "She just awoke. No one has told her."

"Prisoner?" Blood rushed to my head and spots flooded my eyes. Darren was a prisoner? *But he's alive!* Who was the queen?

I started to totter and a pair of burly arms caught me before I fell.

"Get her back to the chambers," the second murmured. "I'll send word for a healer."

"My..." My lips were so heavy. "My... brother..."

"That's right." The soldier's voice was fading. "I remember now. We'll get you Alex too. He's one of them."

And then I drifted away. Again.

* * *

"—Not going to wake her. She needs rest!"

"Quinn won't be happy."

"I don't care whose orders they are, Jace! If that man wants answers, he'll have to come down here himself. When I say he can!"

There was an angry grumble and then the slamming of wood.

A second later, I opened my eyes. I was in the same room as before, only this time Ella was on my bed, brushing hair from my forehead.

I blinked, and her fingers froze upon my face.

"I'm going to kill that man." Alex was somewhere near the wall, swearing, "After what he—"

"Alex." Ella cleared her throat. The two of us were staring, and I couldn't speak. My heart was a pulsing tangle of emotions, and I wasn't even sure this was real. "She's awake."

"Ry!" Alex spun around and gasped.

I thought I'd never see him again. Something crumbled in my lungs.

I mouthed his name.

My twin dove forward with a cry. His arms locked around my shoulders, too tight, but I couldn't bring myself to push him away. He was sobbing into my hair.

"I thought I lost you."

I swallowed back the lump in my throat. I thought I'd lost everyone.

I was never supposed to wake up.

Ella tugged on my brother's sleeve. "Alex, you are hurting her."

My brother pulled away, shame-faced. "I'm sorry, I just..."

I took a shaky breath and smiled, shaking my head. But I still couldn't speak.

Ella adjusted some pillows so that I could sit up. Her fingers trembled as she brushed my wrist. She was fighting hard to keep herself in check.

All three of us were struggling to hold back.

Ella was the first to speak. Her eyes were glassy. "You should be dead, Ry."

"Quinn gave the orders to collapse the cave..." My brother's hand sought my own, squeezing. "We tried to stop the others. Even Ian."

I remembered their screams and the moment I realized what they meant just before the ceiling came crashing down.

"They outnumbered us," Ella rasped.

"And then we found you—"

"You were buried under glaciers the size of a house."

"You should have died, Ry."

Why am I not dead?

"The rebels"—my voice was hoarse as I forced the words aloud—"didn't s-save me?"

My brother's face was pale. "We got there too late. I did what I could after, but… you shouldn't have survived that."

Ella hesitated. "There was a dagger in your chest, and Darren had another in his. Between your wounds and the cave—"

I didn't hear the rest of her words. Something she had said was wrong. "There was a d-dagger in his c-chest?"

"You don't remember?"

How could I? "Ella, I-I didn't…. The d-dagger wasn't mine." I tried again. "Did o-one of the r-rebels…?"

"It was there when we got there." Alex's brow was furrowed. "Wish it had been me. The scum stabbed his own wife." My twin rattled on angrily, but something was still wrong.

How did the dagger get there?

Did Darren try to end his life when he saw the cave crumbling down? But then, how did he survive?

How are either of us alive?

I lurched forward as sudden panic swarmed my chest. "Alex," I choked, "h-he's alive, isn't he? The guards said—"

Alex and Ella exchanged looks. "Yes, but—"

I didn't hear the rest. Yes was all I needed. My pulse pounded in my ears; I could breathe again.

"Ryiah." My brother stared hard at my face. "He stabbed

you in the heart."

"It's not what you—"

"Darren tried to kill you!" Alex's face was scarlet as he started to yell. "Tell me how you can possibly defend that!"

"Alex." It hurt to raise my voice. "I stabbed myself."

Ella grabbed my brother before he could lunge. "Why in the name of the gods would you do something like that?"

Deep breath. And again.

"It was my last stand, Alex."

My brother fell back in Ella's arms, sputtering. "What?"

I waited for the truth to sink in.

"You were trying to save him?" My brother looked so betrayed. "Why? *How could you, Ryiah?*"

Ella's eyes hadn't left my face. "Darren finally believed you, didn't he?"

My brother froze, his face going as white as a sheet.

I couldn't speak; I just nodded.

Ella was still trying to piece together the events. "While the two of you were alone... you finally got through to him."

Alex's hand squeezed my wrist so hard I was surprised it didn't break. I forced myself to use words. "N-not at first. I'm not sure w-what I did to convince him... But he saved my life near t-the end."

My brother's grip lessened, but only slightly.

"And that's when you cast your last stand... to save him?"

I nodded; Ella took a shaky breath.

"Ryiah, if you didn't do it and the rebels didn't... that means it was him."

"H-him?"

"We were wondering how you both lived." She looked me

in the eye. "You cast a last stand... That might explain why Darren is alive, but not you..." She sucked in a sharp breath. "There is only one explanation that makes any sense."

The realization hit me like a rock.

Why hadn't I thought of it before? The dagger in his chest.

"He cast a last stand."

Darren tried to save me too.

"It's how both of you survived." Ella's eyes were as wide as moons.

"Each casting... canceled the other's price." Alex's voice was hoarse. He was struggling to process Darren's benevolence with the violent villain of the past. "It's never been done. Why nobody knew, not even the healers..."

It shouldn't have worked.

But it did.

A last stand was a selfless magic. Perhaps it didn't have to make sense.

Ella cleared her throat, and I caught her guarded look with my brother. "We need to tell her."

I stared at the two of them, trying to decipher their glance. Then I remembered the guards from before. The prisoner.

"Darren's in the dungeon, isn't he?"

Ella flinched, and Alex wouldn't meet my eyes.

"There's more." My friend swallowed. "Ry, when we found the two of you and you were still alive... The healers immediately saw to you, but Darren... We didn't know he'd turned. He was alive, but barely."

Alex lifted his chin. "The rest of our band helped carry him down to call off the Crown's Army command... But when we were done, and Darren had somehow miraculously survived, which we know now was the effect of your casting, there was too much confusion. The people needed time to adjust."

Fear cinched my throat. "W-what are you saying?"

"His execution is set a week from today. A day after the new ruler is crowned."

For a moment, I couldn't hear anything. Every part of me was ringing as I tried to calm down.

This isn't the end. The new ruler doesn't know. We can change this. I can explain.

"The declaration has already been made. Announcements were sent by envoy to every city in Jerar. The other kingdoms are already involved."

"Who is it?" Whoever it was, I would see them at once, even if I had to have Alex and Ella carry me every step of the way.

"Priscilla."

My jaw dropped. *Her?* Of all the potential rulers in Jerar?

"But she's a mage!"

"So was Darren, and she has already renounced her robe for the Crown."

Alex couldn't look at me as he picked up where Ella left off. "The advisors needed someone to satisfy the rebel leaders and the influential families of court. She was the best choice."

Priscilla belonged to the house with the greatest wealth. The most power. It was why Darren's father had arranged a betrothal so many years before.

"But she served the Crown's Army, why wouldn't the

rebels object?"

"Baron Langli passed away the week before Jerar went to war. Priscilla never got to fight." Ella looked bitter. "Her hands are clean. She never took rebel lives. We have no other suitable candidates except you..."

And they would never agree to it. I may have fought for the rebels, but I'd betrayed their plans in the end. I was the wife of a traitor king.

And there it was. My nemesis, the girl who had always wanted the crown, was going to end up a queen.

I had never seen it coming.

"I need to talk to her now." My jaw was hard. As soon as Priscilla heard my case, she would pardon Darren for his crimes. I'd make sure of it.

"You think she'll listen to you?" Ella bit her lip. "Ryiah, she hates you. Perhaps we should—"

"She's not who we thought." I met my friend's gaze confidently with my own. "Trust me, Priscilla will listen."

The girl wasn't a tyrant like Blayne. There were parts of her I admired.

"If that's what you really want..."

I nodded and braced my palms against the bed, trying hard not to wince as pain shot up my arms like knives.

Alex made a sound in the back of his throat. "You're not ready."

"I don't care."

"We've got a week—"

"Alex." Ella cut my brother off with a disapproving scowl. "Would you wait a week for me?"

My brother's face fell. I knew he wanted me to rest, but

he couldn't argue with that.

And so we began our walk.

* * *

We found Priscilla at the highest turret overlooking the keep.

She looked different somehow. Or perhaps this was who she was always intended to be.

Her spine was erect, shoulders straight. Dressed in a blood red gown and lace with her hair pinned up, long ebony locks curled slightly against the back of her neck, Priscilla looked every bit a highborn queen.

A queen with Darren's fate in her hands.

She was deep in conversation with Quinn and two Crown advisors I vaguely recognized from my life at the palace in Devon.

As soon as we arrived, the others' attention flitted to the stairs where my brother and friend supported me between their arms.

Quinn choked at the sight. "Ryiah—"

"Don't." My brother took a step forward, snarling. "Don't you dare address my sister after what you did."

"Quinn is here on my orders." Priscilla's curt voice cut off my twin's reply. "He is not yours to command."

Alex started to grumble, and my nails dug into his arm. I needed the girl to listen, and I wasn't sure where we stood.

The future queen fixated on my face. "I had no idea you were awake."

"Please." My voice was strained—it had taken a great deal of effort to climb those steps, and I was dangerously close to collapse. "Can we have an audience... alone?"

Priscilla didn't even hesitate. Apparently I had risen in her esteem after my latest trip to the infirmary. "Quinn, you, Fletcher, and Claudius are dismissed."

It was the first time Priscilla had ever treated me with something I would almost deem as respect.

The mage and two elderly men scowled in passing, but I kept my gaze locked on the queen. I wasn't sure I could acknowledge the former knowing he gave the orders to bury me alive. It might have been the best decision for Jerar, but it was also the reason Darren and I had nearly died.

I waited until they were gone. "Thank you."

"It's nothing." Priscilla made a flippant gesture with her hand and smirked. "Now why are you three here? I trust it was not to congratulate me on my upcoming coronation."

"It wasn't."

Priscilla raised a brow at Ella. "And I see you haven't changed one bit."

"You made my best friend miserable for years."

"She was a threat. She understands. Don't you, Ryiah?"

I nudged Ella who was busy spitting back a reply. "Let her be."

My best friend ground her teeth but didn't speak again.

"You are to be queen."

Priscilla lifted her chin. "You aren't getting my crown."

"I don't want it. I need you to pardon Darren for his crimes."

Ten seconds went by and nobody spoke. I watched as her expression went from disbelieving to incredulous.

"You are joking."

"It's not what—"

"You were a rebel," Priscilla sputtered. "You know what he and his family did. Quinn told me everything... Gods, Darren had patrols hunting you, Ryiah. I know you always were a little slack-jawed where that boy was concerned, but I should think the moment he tried to kill you, you'd finally grow some sense."

"No!" My voice rose and Priscilla paused, momentarily stunned. "I mean, yes, Darren did most of those things, but there's more."

I proceeded to explain everything.

To her credit, the queen-to-be didn't interrupt once.

Alex and Ella took turns retelling parts I had missed, or whenever I ran out of breath. It was a complicated tale.

When we finally finished, the three of us waited expectantly.

"I don't know what to say." Priscilla's face was pale. "It's too late."

My fingers dug into Alex and Ella's arms. "What do you mean 'too late'?"

"I have to restore the peace." Priscilla looked skyward. "I gave Horrace my word."

"What about Darren?"

"Ryiah, you don't understand."

"I have done everything for Jerar!" Fury had me tasting ash. "Doesn't that mean anything?"

"It does." She cringed. "But it's not my choice."

"You are going to be queen!" Ella rolled her eyes. "Don't tell us you can't do it, Priscilla."

"You, a *highborn*, should know better," the girl snapped. "The other kingdoms are ready to cut Jerar off at its head!

No one wants to sign a new treaty with a country that has already betrayed their compromise once. King Horrace is willing to pardon the rebels, but he is not willing to forgive the rest."

"Horrace is not our king. He's not even a part of Jerar! We helped *him*. Without the rebels, his country would be a wasteland right now!"

Priscilla didn't look away. "You have no idea what it means to be queen, Ryiah. I have to consider our peace before everything else. We don't need the greedy Pythians picking off our remains now that Borea and Caltoth have turned their backs." Her arms folded across her chest. "We need to give Horrace whatever it takes to bridge that alliance. His one request, which is far better than the slaughter of our army and all those who unwittingly partook in the wrong side, mind you, is the life of the king that took his kingdom to war."

"But Darren was b-barely even king!" My voice cracked and it hurt to speak. "Priscilla, please—"

"Ryiah." The future queen placed her hand on my shoulder, and I flinched.

"I know we haven't been the best of friends." Her tone was somber. "You could even say we were enemies... But despite everything we were, everything we are, I would help you if I could. I swear it."

"Then do something!" Alex lunged forward, taking half of me with him. "Sentence Darren to exile. It doesn't have to be execution!"

Priscilla drew a sharp intake of breath. "You think I wouldn't consider that if I could? Darren has the blood of the old family running through his veins. So long as he breathes, he is a threat to King Horrace. Even if Darren never contested my rule, and I don't believe after what Ryiah told me he would, his children's children could come back and try to reclaim it. One man's life for a lifetime of peace is a reasonable price. I can't reject an alliance to uncertainty, no matter how I wish I could."

"So that is your stance?" I was shaking so hard my teeth gnashed together. *"You are just going to let an innocent man die? You two were friends. You were willing to marry him—"*

Her eyes held my own. "Darren's not innocent, Ryiah. He might regret his crimes, but he still committed them."

"Only because of his brother!" My heart slammed my ribs, again and again. "You know that!"

The girl looked to my brother and Ella. "I know she'll want to see him. You can take Ryiah, but the guards will have to remain for the visit."

"I didn't give my life just to watch him die again!"

"I'm sorry," Priscilla's sharp apology cut through my screams, "but that is the best I can do." Somewhere behind us there was the rustle of chainmail as her guard approached. "Alex, Ella, please escort her out. My men will send word to the dungeon that you are expected."

"Priscilla!"

"So long as she doesn't cause a disturbance or any sort of attempt on his guards, Ryiah will be welcome at all hours leading up to his execution."

"You are no better than Blayne if you do this!"

She finally looked at me. "I am, but you've put me in an

impossible position."

"But… it's *Darren*." Tears slipped down my face.

"I know. And for that, I am sorry, Ryiah. I truly am."

* * *

When we entered the prison's hall, there were ten scowling mage guards awaiting our arrival—all of them from our former mission in Caltoth.

The rebels were definitely displeased to see me again.

"Weapons!" barked the one nearest. "All of 'em."

I gave them a challenging stare. I was leaning heavily on my brother, dressed in a flimsy white gown for sleeping with a giant bandage that constricted my ribs. I couldn't carry a weapon if I tried.

Alex tossed his scabbard to the ground; his eyes remained locked on the knight from earlier. He still hadn't forgiven the rebels for trying to bury his sister alive.

Ella dropped her scabbard next, and two concealed knives that were tucked around her ankles. She then disposed of another pair strapped to her upper arms; she did so with a smirk, waggling her fingers. "What a shame you can't take my magic, boys."

"You try anything—"

"Simmer down." She rolled her eyes. "It was a joke."

Their expressions were humorless as stone.

It wasn't a surprise that Priscilla and the others only trusted rebels to guard a former king… I wondered if they wished I were dead. Then I could be their fallen hero instead of a troublemaker to the Crown.

Ian wasn't among them, but the rebels probably didn't trust him that much either.

Kenan, an older man with close-cropped hair and squinty eyes, cleared his throat. "The queen has already given you a warning for conduct. We won't hesitate to enforce it."

Alex opened his mouth to snarl a retort and Ella kicked his leg. "Shall we?"

My eyes were locked on the door as two of the mages removed a heavy steel bar and turned their key.

I couldn't see anything inside.

It was so dark.

My muscles went lax as I recognized the stench within. Old urine and blood.

It brought me back to the dungeons in Devon.

A whimper escaped my lips. Darren.

Ella and Alex didn't bother to wait for their eyes to adjust. They marched me through the threshold as all but one of the guards followed us inside.

We made it halfway when one of the guards lit a sconce.

Then I saw him.

The king was lying in a pool of crimson, his skin as pale as snow. Cuts and bruises mottled his skin. His hair was matted with sweat and dirt.

One of his arms stuck out at a strange angle. There was a gaping wound in his leg, oozing blood and yellowing pus. His vest was in tatters and his boots were missing. His breeches were ripped and stained red.

His eyes were clenched shut as we entered.

I didn't realize I was screaming until Darren's eyes flew open and the guards started to yell.

"Who did this?"

No one answered.

"Which one of you did this?" I couldn't breathe; hot blood boiled in my veins and all I could see was red. *"Was it all of you? Was it?"*

"He deserves far worse—"

I struggled and lunged, breaking free of my brother and Ella's grip. I caught the smug rebel with my fist, and the two of us went down with my hands locked around his neck.

"Ryiah!" Alex and Ella tried to pull me away.

But I wouldn't budge. I couldn't. Every part of me was in flames.

The mage's dirty fingernails cut into my wrists, drawing blood, but I just squeezed harder. All I could think about was hurting this man like he hurt Darren.

And then his magic hit.

I slammed against the wall with a thud. Every part of my body roared with hot, blistering pain. There was a snap in my chest and I was choking, spewing blood.

My hand shot out in front of my face.

I would make him pay. I would make him experience every cut and blow.

…But nothing came.

Something was wrong. I tried again.

I couldn't feel it.

It was usually there, bubbling just underneath the surface, waiting… But this time, it wasn't.

This time, my magic was gone.

My brother's face appeared in my line of vision, his mouth opening and closing rapidly as his fingers brushed my head.

There was a flash of green, and then everything stopped. I

was dizzy and numb; I couldn't feel my own arms. A warm rush of relief slipped down through my skin, and then my eyelids fluttered shut.

The rest of my body followed.

* * *

The next time I awoke, I was back in the chamber from before. Alex slouched on a trunk at the side of my bed, his head nodding off as he slept, fingers still locked tight around my wrist.

There was a splitting ache in my head and my whole body trembled so violently I wanted to fall straight back to sleep. But I was too busy remembering everything from before. My heart started to beat heavily against my chest.

"Darren!" I choked out his name and lurched forward, only to fall back in pain.

Alex jerked awake. Almost immediately, green sparks danced along my wrist.

"Ryiah—" my brother's voice was stern, "—you can't do that again."

He wasn't talking about now.

My hands trembled under the pulse of his magic. "Darren wasn't just their prisoner, Alex. They were beating him. He looked—"

"I know." A lump rose and fell against my twin's throat. "But if you do it again, Priscilla won't let you back." He swallowed. "You attacked a guard, Ry."

"I lost control."

"Ella spent hours convincing Priscilla you deserved a second chance. If you hadn't pulled back on that casting—"

I gulped, suddenly remembering that moment before he

cast me to sleep. "I didn't pull back, Alex."

He frowned. "What do you mean?"

"My magic... it wouldn't come."

"But you've had over two weeks of rest." My twin's eyes were wide. "You might not have your stamina from before, but you should be able to cast *something*."

I lifted my palm from the blankets and concentrated, throwing every sense into the projection I was trying to cast. A minuscule flame. Something a novice could accomplish with ease.

Nothing happened.

Alex said nothing. His eyes locked to my palm as I squinted and tried again. A bead of sweat dripped down my forehead, but nothing else came.

After a couple minutes, I dropped my hand. My head hurt, but there was no blinding ache the way it usually felt after trying a casting when my stamina was too low.

No ache. No magic.

Whatever I'd once had, it was gone.

"Do you think it's because of your last stand?"

"Maybe." I didn't know. A knot twisted in my gut. "Did it happen to Darren?"

"With the condition they've kept him in, no one would know." Alex's voice lowered to a whisper. "If he can't, Ry, do you know what this means?"

My fingers twisted in my lap.

Alex scooted closer. "When the two of you each cast your last stand, you canceled out death, so the casting took something else."

"Our magic." I knew it was true as soon as I said it aloud.

It was the only reason we were alive. It was the reason I felt nothing when I tried to cast, not even an ache.

"There is no record in the books, so there would be no way to know for certain." His brows furrowed. "You might just take longer to recover your stamina."

"It's been two weeks. There's nothing there. If there was, I would feel it."

For a moment, there was only silence. Neither of us knew what to say, but I was too busy remembering that dungeon to mourn the loss of my magic.

"What do we do?"

"The rebels won't hurt Darren again. Priscilla gave Ella her word I could treat the worst of his wounds so long as he keeps the rest to please Horrace."

"It's not enough."

"You can see him." Alex's eyes were somber. "You can see Darren and be with him now. And every day we will plead his case to Priscilla. It's all we can do."

It isn't enough.

TWENTY

WHEN WE ENTERED the Keep's dungeon, I didn't scream. I wanted to, but I didn't.

The guards were still there, watching me. I refused to acknowledge them. The only one I bothered to share contact with was the one I'd attacked. Kiefer was sporting a bloody lip. For a second, I felt a sliver of something other than despair, but then it was gone.

I was standing in front of Darren's cell. The guards weren't concerned with a potential escape. Darren's wrists and ankles were attached to manacles on chains.

They unlocked the bars.

I tried not to stare at the prisoner's blistered skin, rubbed raw from every time he shifted in place. There was a bucket in the far corner—empty. Priscilla must have ordered it changed after my first visit, but the stench was still enough to water my eyes.

Darren's eyes were half-closed, his chest rising and falling as he slumped against the bars. This time, he was sitting up—barely—and I could see blood seeping through his rags.

A cry rose up deep inside. *Darren.*

I knelt down beside the fallen king and my chemise

puddled at my feet. Alex and Ella helped me adjust. It didn't matter, not when this boy was in front of me, slowly fading away in his cell.

I placed a trembling hand to his wrist, doing my best to fight the knot in my lungs.

"Ry...iah." Darren's voice was rough and unused. I could hear how much it pained him to speak.

"I'm here." I didn't want him to see me cry; I needed to be strong.

Ella placed a calming hand on my back. "We brought Alex here to help, Darren. He's going to treat some of your wounds."

My brother knelt. "What hurts the most?"

Darren's lips were white as he bit out the words. "No... need."

Alex looked to me, and my nails dug into my thigh until it burned. "Darren," I croaked, *"please."*

For a moment, the king didn't speak. Then he drew a sharp breath and shut his eyes. "My... chest."

Alex splayed five fingers across Darren's ribs, and the king's face went ashen and pale. Something burned in my lungs. Whatever the guards had done, it hurt a great deal, much more than he let on.

"I'm going to do my best," Alex murmured, "but Priscilla only wants me to see to the worst of it. If I do too much—"

"I... understand." Darren's face contorted as the first spark of green seeped in under his skin, but still, he held strong.

I didn't realize I was shaking until I felt the pad of a callused thumb against my wrist. I started, and the king smiled, his lips cracked and red.

"You're... still alive."

My heart stammered in my chest. "I was your l-last stand?"

Darren's eyes held my own, and I saw a thousand different emotions at once. His answer bespoke everything I had wondered those last few minutes in the cave. All those things left unsaid.

My fingers locked on his wrist. "You were mine."

The king's smile fell away. "Shouldn't... have."

"In a week..." My voice caught as I read the set of his jaw. Darren already knew. "I'm g-going to stop it." My voice was hoarse and desperate. "Priscilla is queen. I'll f-find a way to convince h-her."

Darren didn't say anything, just stared out at the wall.

"You d-don't believe me."

"I'm not..." The king's jaw worked as he tried again. "I'm... not... a hero... love."

Don't save me, I could read it in his eyes.

Something stabbed at my lungs, twisting until they bled.

I opened my mouth just as Darren's hand fell away, his shoulders convulsing violently against the bars of his cell.

Ella helped me shift as Alex took over my spot. Not all healings were painless. Sometimes they got worse before they got better.

My fingers scratched across stone, inches from Darren's own. I wanted to touch him so badly it hurt.

When it finally stopped minutes later, the king slumped against the wall; he couldn't even lift his head.

I leaned in closer, but Darren's eyes remained shut,

clenched tightly against the pain. "Darren?" I'd never seen him like this, not even in the cave.

"He has to rest." My brother gripped my arm. "And so do you. Ella can get you a healer upstairs."

"No." I shook my head. "I'm not leaving."

"Ryiah—"

"I said no, Alex!"

My brother dropped his hand. Then he looked to his wife.

"Ella," he said, "can you get a second healer?"

The girl nodded and left.

It was a half hour later when she returned.

There was a knock at the door, and one of the guards went to open it, peering out at the people on the other side. There was a low murmur as the three exchanged words and then the guard stepped aside.

Ella appeared with two others, not one. A healer in her Red Restoration robes and Ian.

The latter had a bundle in his arms. He took a hitching breath as his gaze fell on Darren.

Seconds later, there was a pile of blankets in my lap. Ian's eyes were bloodshot.

"All this time," he croaked, "I thought he'd... but he didn't?"

"No." It was the only word I could manage.

"When Ella told me... I knew you wouldn't want to leave, so I thought..." He nudged the blankets in my arm.

There was a burning in the back of my throat.

"Thank you, Ian," I whispered.

"It's nothing."

The mage cast another glance at Darren and then back at

me. He noticed my stare and gave the slightest nod with his chin.

Then he turned and left, without looking back.

I spread the blanket across Darren's legs and my own. The second healer knelt to my side and saw to my wounds.

I hardly noticed the pain.

It was only as I was drifting to sleep that my fingers brushed a bit of parchment tucked tightly into the folds of my blanket.

The last thing I remembered was Ian's nod, and then I closed my fist around the paper and drifted to sleep.

* * *

I know you are planning something. Whatever it is, I want to help.

-Ian

I read the words over and over again. It was late into the night, and the guards had grown lax, content to chatter amongst themselves instead of watching the rest of us for hours on end. They had our weapons, and there was only one exit to the dungeon; they weren't concerned.

Planning something... Want to help.

Darren tossed and turned at my side. A fever had broken out within hours of Alex's casting. My brother was still seeing to Darren's healing—constantly assuring me that the fever was a good sign, that he could now fight off infection on his own—but most of Alex's treatment had changed to that of a court physician.

We had to let the fever run its course.

Darren's side of the blanket was soaked with sweat. He

alternated between shivers and burning skin. He cried out in his sleep. Every time he did, it was like a dagger to the chest.

Only this time I couldn't save him.

No magic.

My fingers dug into the blanket. I'd never felt so helpless in my life.

I took a shuddering breath as I repeated the lines, again.

Planning something... Want to help.

Was it a test for Priscilla and the rebels? Or did Ian truly want to help?

Did it even matter?

My pulse pounded in my throat.

I knew what I had to do.

* * *

Seven hours later, I was ready. I hated leaving Darren, but I didn't have a choice. Plotting and gathering support would do more than pining away while he slept.

Alex and Ella helped me back to my chamber in silence. I knew they were worried about me. I had refused to eat or drink anything since I awoke, but there were more pressing things on my mind.

What I was about to say next, I couldn't risk being overheard. But first...

"Alex." I addressed my twin as soon as he shut the door. "Can you find Ian?"

"I knew it," he muttered. "You are planning something, aren't you?"

"Please."

"You trust him?"

I didn't have a choice; I needed all the help we could get.

What I was planning… it would be a miracle in itself. And Ian had shown true regret. He had also fought for me against the rebels. That would have to be enough. "Yes."

Twenty minutes later, my brother was back, Ian in tow.

"You got my note?"

There was a knot in my stomach, and it wouldn't go away. I nodded.

Ian took a spot next to Alex against the door. His fingers flickered momentarily, bright as he cast a barrier for sound just in case anyone was listening on the other side.

"What I want to ask you all"—my fingers twisted in my lap—"I have no right to ask. It's treason and I can't promise we won't get caught."

No one spoke.

"I want to help Darren escape. I want to get him out of Jerar, and I'm going with him." I met each one of their eyes. "If you want to walk away, I'll understand. I just ask that you keep this plan between us. Give me a chance to do it myself."

"Are you really ready to exile yourself and live in hiding the rest of your life?" Alex fought to keep a neutral expression, and failed. "Priscilla and Horrace will send men to find you. It's dangerous and"—his hands fisted at his sides—"if you are caught… Ry, I don't want to lose you again. I-I already thought I lost you once. And after Derrick…"

The knot in my chest expanded and I bit down on my cheek, hard. I knew what I was doing was selfish. Gods, I'd nearly lost myself when Derrick died. How could I subject Alex to my own death, twice?

And how could I not—for Darren?

"But what about Jerar?" Ella's words were quiet. "What will happen if King Horrace finds out Darren escaped? Emperor Liang and King Joren might not care, but Horrace will. And the treaty would be void."

I exhaled. The truth was she was right. I didn't want Caltoth to turn its back on a potential alliance with Jerar... but Horrace had been a peacemaker for decades. Perhaps nothing would come of it.

"Horrace will be at the execution." Ian cleared his throat. "Are you planning the break out then?"

"It's the only chance I'll get."

Ella paled. "Horrace will know Darren's alive, Ry. He'll know Jerar didn't fulfill his terms."

"I think—" Ian paused. "—I think if Horrace sees Priscilla making every effort to uphold the execution, he'll still sign the treaty." His eyes locked on my own. "My father met with him for years representing the rebels' cause. Horrace is a reasonable man. The Caltothians owe us a debt for fighting their war. That's not to say he won't be upset."

Alex guffawed. "Horrace might sign the treaty, but he will make it his mission to hunt the two of them to the end of his days."

"That will be my problem, not yours."

"But neither of you have magic!" My brother was furious. "Horrace will send his best mages, and the two of you won't be able to fight!"

"We can still fight." My eyes flashed. "Darren and I didn't just train in magic, Alex."

My brother folded his arms, and Ian looked between the

two of us, mouth gaping. *"Why won't they be able to fight?"*

"I lost my magic. We think Darren did too… I didn't want to ask him around the guards."

"It was how they both survived." Ella shifted uncomfortably on the bed. "It wasn't luck, Ian. They both cast a mage's last stand. The casting couldn't kill them since they were saving each other, so it took their magic instead."

His eyes were wide. "Does anyone else know?"

"No." My response was firm. "And you can't tell them. We need every advantage we can get."

"How would you propose the escape? There are going to be thousands of people and guards as far as the eye can see."

"I don't know, but it's going to be our only chance to get Darren outside. If we try now, we'd have to fight our way through an entire fortress with an army of soldiers inside." I swallowed. "We need the other rulers to see it so they know the Crown wasn't involved, so Horrace sees Priscilla making her best effort to honor his terms."

Ian cracked a smile. "Five days to plan the riskiest escape in the history of Jerar. Why doesn't it surprise me the three of you are involved?"

"I'll understand if any of you choose to pass."

"Ryiah—" Ella's fingers twined with my own, "—you don't even have to ask."

"It's selfish." I stared down at our hands. "I could be making things worse for Jerar."

"We'll ensure that doesn't happen."

I clung to that promise like it was air.

Ian cleared his throat. "I'll help. Darren… I'm not sure what he deserves, but it isn't an execution like this."

"Alex?" I looked to my brother.

My twin ducked his head. "I just pray the gods are on our side."

* * *

In the days that passed, I was a walking shade. The first two were restless and emotional. I spent all of my time in the prison seeing to Darren and letting the others act, but as the third drew to a close, I was tired of waiting for answers. We had only two more days to plan, and one of those would be largely impossible; the queen's ascension was expected to last most of the sixth.

All communication was done by mouth.

It was too risky to meet again. Now that we had a plan, it was up to Ian and Ella to gather what information they could and pass it along. Alex served as communication to me, and I maintained my guise of despair.

I knew the rebels were watching me. But if my hands were clean, what could they claim?

Our first stroke of luck came the fifth morning. Until that point, we'd had no solid leads on the execution. The soldiers had started building a gallows and Ian was one of the sentries guarding its construction.

They were going to hang the king.

For a moment, I couldn't speak.

I forgot all of our planning.

All I could hear was the thump-thump of my pulse.

How did you think they were going to kill a king? A casting of mercy? The people want a spectacle.

You should thank the gods it wasn't the guillotine.

You can work with a noose. It will be easier to save him.

You want to save him, don't you?

Yes?

Then pull yourself together and ask the questions that matter. You only have two more days.

I turned to my brother, my breaths shallow and fast. "What else did Ian say?"

"He's going to get an idea of the count. He said one of the men is finalizing their numbers for Quinn. Ian's going to try and sneak a look tonight."

"If he fails?"

"He'll keep talking to the others. The guards are going to need an outline for the final formation. We'll get their positions soon. And once we know the layout, we can stash some weapons for the day."

I nodded, heart racing. "Anything else?"

"There was another summons while you were away. Priscilla wants you to meet with her in Commander Nyx's old chamber before dinner. The messenger specifically noted that this was not a request."

"How am I supposed to face her?"

Alex's hand found my shoulder. "You will find a way. And no one will suspect a thing."

Hours later, I was put to the test.

* * *

"You're late." Quinn greeted me with a scowl as I entered the room.

Nyx's old chamber looked exactly the same as when she'd been alive—barren save the thick rug and a seating area to the left.

I was the last to arrive.

I took my place at a long rectangular slab that served as the table. Priscilla was already seated with Marius at her left and Commander Audric to her right. Further down were Quinn and several of the rebels' former command. And then there was Merrick, Priscilla's cousin and quite possibly my least favorite mage until quite recently.

A scribe was near the back, his quill scratching away.

"Ryiah." Priscilla smiled up at me, and for a moment I froze. She'd been kind the last time we met, but it was just as jarring to see her smiling now, when I was used to a smirk or a sneer.

Where had the girl from the Academy gone?

"I called this meeting because I wanted to discuss some upcoming changes for the Crown. I plan on making the announcements during the feast."

She didn't wait for us to react, but, then again, she was about to be queen. "In a show of good will to Horrace, I will be altering some key positions among my staff."

Priscilla's eyes found the gruff commander at her right. "Audric, you were the one to lead the Crown's Army into Caltoth. No one here, and certainly not me, faults you for obeying your king's orders, but that doesn't take away your role in the war. And for that reason, I need you to step down."

The man's hands fisted at his sides. "I've served the Crown loyally for decades."

"And I will repay you in kind." Priscilla nodded to the scribe. "You will be given the title and lands of my father."

"What?" Merrick jumped up, sputtering. "That's mine!"

Priscilla gave her cousin a belittling smile. "You are

disinherited from the family title."

"You can't do this!" The boy's face was purple with rage. "I'm your own blood!"

"And I'm the queen." The girl turned to a guard at the door. "Remove this one immediately."

The mage went kicking and screaming.

A part of me, a small part, smiled.

Priscilla returned to Audric. "You'll also be commanding the Langli regiment. It's not the Crown's Army, but it's the best I can do."

Audric didn't speak. The young queen-to-be had just freely admitted he deserved better. Unheard of for the Crown.

The commander finally spoke. "I accept your terms, but I won't take part in the execution." I finally noticed the shadows under his eyes. "Darren... he was like a son to me."

"Very well, I relieve you of any obligation to attend." Priscilla's eyes fell to the former Black Mage. "Marius, I would like you to be one of my advisors. You served Jerar well, and Horrace won't contest your presence. You were still in the desert when the Crown's Army marched on Caltoth."

The mage nodded, his gold hoop dangling in the flickering light. For a second, his eyes flitted to me, and I saw quiet defeat. Someone must have told him about his sister's role in the war—and mine in her death. There was no hate, but he looked older than before. The truth had aged him.

I bit back the silent regret that followed. War had stolen from us all.

"Quinn, you are now head mage of the King's Regiment. I need someone I can trust, but more so, I need a lowborn guard the people will respect."

"Ray, Klaus, Jeremiah, Tianna, Cade, Baxter, Silas, Ailith, you will be given lead positions over key regiments in the Crown's Army. The former command will step down and be displaced to city regiments. And last..." Priscilla turned to me. "I want you to be my Black Mage, Ryiah."

I stared, disbelieving and numb. *Does she honestly think this is what I want? Now? After everything that had passed?*

"You are the best. And you fought for the rebels to the end."

She was really asking me to take Darren's place.

"You wouldn't make a good queen." Priscilla had the decency to avert her gaze. "The people need someone who understands the intrigues of court, Ryiah, especially in the delicate state we are in... but I would be willing to grant you a dukedom, the highest rank in nobility save my own."

I waited for her to finish. She was trying, but she wasn't offering the one thing I wanted. And she knew it.

"I don't accept."

The room went silent.

Priscilla's tone was clipped. "I'm giving you everything I can."

"You can't buy me off with fancy titles." My teeth gnashed together as I spoke. "You want my allegiance? Call off Darren's execution instead."

Everyone's eyes were on me. I had just disrespected our future queen and the robe I had always claimed to want.

Funny, it took losing everything to understand what truly

mattered in the end.

"You know I can't."

I snarled. "The only reason you are holding Darren accountable is because he's a martyr!"

"He was a king and the Black Mage." Priscilla's voice had taken on a discernable edge. "Whether you like it or not, his actions have consequences. That's what being a sovereign means."

"And yours?" I slammed my fist on the table. *Might as well make this a show.* Priscilla would never expect me to take to Darren's execution easily. "You're willing to persecute a man you once meant to marry? A man you admired enough to call your friend?"

"I do what I have to for the people, Ryiah." She glared at me. "You've always been too reckless. You couldn't possibly understand."

"I understand perfectly." I rose and shoved my chair to the side.

"I'm not finished—"

"You want my advice?" I turned from the door. "End the Candidacy and take away the factions. Let people train for whatever magic they want. *Is it any wonder Darren chose war when our legacy had us preparing for it our entire lives?*"

When I finally reached the hall, I half expected a guard to come after me. But no one did. For a second time, I had disrespected the queen-to-be and she had let me walk away.

She's not Lucius or Blayne. She'll make a better queen.

I just wanted her to save him.

Not every story has a happy ending.

No, but I would make sure Darren's did.

* * *

After dinner, I found my way up the winding stairs and looming walls to the dungeon just beyond. The two guards on duty heaved a heavy sigh, and then I was in.

Darren was leaning against the furthest wall of his cell, the back of his head slumped against the wall. There was a wooden barrel of water for washing and a pile of discarded blankets at his feet.

Darren's bruises still hadn't faded. His eyes were open when I arrived.

"You shouldn't have come."

"I told you I would."

"I wish you'd reconsider." His voice was empty of all emotion and remorse.

Darren didn't want me here. I'd discovered this the day the fever had finally passed.

Now there was only a cold stranger in his place.

"You can hope." I waited as the nearest guard unlocked the bars to Darren's cell. "But that won't keep me away."

Darren didn't reply; he just shut his eyes and exhaled.

I took the moment to study him. I knew every cut and bruise along his arms. I could see the dent of his ribs and the gaunt lines of his face. Even the sharp curve of his jaw—a determined slant since I'd arrived.

My brother could only heal so much. He'd seen to Darren's chest, and then Priscilla had sent him away.

It wasn't enough. It wasn't even close.

"I know why you came."

Darren's rasp tugged at my heart.

"You don't know anything."

The prisoner opened his eyes and smiled; it was cloaked with regret. "You want to save me... but you can't."

"I will."

"Love." His words were bleak. "I don't want to be saved."

I knew what he believed. I could read it in his eyes. But it wasn't his choice.

Darren didn't get to give up after everything.

I wouldn't let the darkness win.

He had fought for me those weeks after Derrick's death, and it was my turn to fight for him.

"Priscilla will listen."

Darren shook his head. "She won't. And neither would I." His tone wasn't bitter; if anything, it was calm. "A queen has... more pressing concerns than the life of a traitor. And in case you've forgotten—" His laugh was hoarse. "—she hates us."

"Darren." It was killing me to hold everything inside. Why couldn't the guards just disappear? I needed to tell him. I was afraid of what would happen while I was away.

"Ryiah." The fallen king lifted his chin to meet my gaze head on. His jaw worked as he spoke. "Let me go."

I was on my knees in front of him. "You don't mean that!"

Darren continued on as if I hadn't spoken. "You have a good life here. You could be... happy."

He was wrong. My nails dug into my palms to keep from screaming out in vain. He couldn't just give up. I wouldn't let him.

"I'm not the only one." Darren cracked a smile, but his

eyes were empty and colorless. "I know you think this is the end, Ryiah... but it isn't. I'm not worth it. Don't throw..." His fists balled at his sides, and I could hear the sharp exhale that followed. "Don't throw your life away on the villain."

Tears blurred my sight, and my heart beat away in my chest. "Darren, you're *not*."

"Please," his voice cracked, and a part of me shattered. "Please," he whispered again, "just go."

I didn't want to leave.

But ever since he'd awoke...

What choice did I have?

The former king of Jerar, the Black Mage, the most arrogant, confident, prideful man I knew... he had given up.

He wanted to die. And worse, he believed he deserved it.

The second-born son had finally stopped fighting.

I pulled myself up off the ground and blinked away the tears stinging my eyes. "I'll be back tomorrow."

"I wish... you wouldn't."

There was a knot in the back of my throat. It was growing bigger with every second, and I was afraid it would swallow me whole.

The guard swung open the cell bars, and I didn't look back.

I couldn't. Right now I needed to be strong for both of us.

My legs shook as I walked.

Darren might have given up on himself, but I hadn't.

TWENTY-ONE

THE FINAL DAY before the execution came and went. Priscilla was crowned Queen of Jerar. All of the great rulers of the Western Realm—King Horrace, King Joren, and Emperor Liang—as well as their guards, were present and watched the ceremony with discerning eyes.

For my part, I did my best not to scream.

Duke Cassius tried to approach me after the ceremony, but he stopped after he read the expression on my face. I was tired of scheming rulers and pacts made behind closed doors. Pythus was not my friend. What had our alliance even bought? Certainly not peace, and I wasn't going to offer him Jerar.

Priscilla was the right choice for the throne. I could see it as she went around the room. Darren and I had trained our entire lives for war, but the raven-haired beauty? Her father had prepared her to serve alongside a prince. She was calculating and shrewd, but she also knew the court like the back of her hand.

The queen couldn't save the boy I loved, but she would find a way to appease the Caltothians after we were gone. The declaration that Jerar was cutting down its infantry, and that the study of magic would no longer be restricted to the best, was met with apprehension, but also respect. Priscilla, with the help of Marius, her chief advisor, renounced the individual factions and the Candidacy. Magic was now opened up to the study of *all* pursuits.

War would no longer be the focus of Jerar.

I hadn't expected Priscilla to embrace my idea, but perhaps she had been listening after all.

Jerar would be a new land, one that I would never get to know.

Did you ever imagine that despicable girl from the Academy would become a respectable queen? That the boy you loved would bring a country to its knees? That you and your friends would commit treason against the Crown?

I hadn't. If I'd known...

I found myself at the dungeon doors for the second time that day.

Darren looked up at me as I approached, but he didn't push me away.

To him, this was our last night, and I had failed.

I wanted to tell him I hadn't. That I wouldn't. That Ian had hidden weapons, and all of our plans were set for the morning. That we knew the guards' positions and we were going to succeed.

But there were guards listening, and for the first time, Darren wasn't looking away.

He took my hand as I sat down next to him in the corner of his cell.

For awhile, I just listened to the steady beat of his heart. It was so loud. Or maybe it was my own. I couldn't tell.

"Darren—"

"Please…" His fingers tightened against my own. "No… words."

He had already accepted his fate.

Minutes slipped past and the shadows pressed in. Those minutes turned into hours and the sun was pushing past stars. I watched it all from the corner of our cell.

My hand never left his.

I was drifting to sleep, the back of my head against the cold stone wall, when his lips brushed my hair.

Darren must have thought I was dreaming.

"Gods." Darren's voice was hoarse. "I'm going to miss you so much."

No. I jerked out of my trance and snapped awake. "Darren—"

And then there was the creaking of the cell bars as heavy boots approached from the outside.

Darren's eyes were locked on me as the guard slipped a key inside his manacles' lock.

"I love you," he whispered.

And then the guards dragged him away.

* * *

I hadn't seen the gallows until that morning. Somehow, in all of our plans for the week, I had avoided stepping foot outside of the keep. Perhaps it had been a conscious decision.

Standing here now, taking it all in, I could see why I'd been unable to make the approach.

The sky was too lovely for such a terrible day. Spring air—a mixture of pollen and pine—wafted across the field as a crowd gathered fifty yards from the fortress's entrance, lured in by the promise of blood and a looming gallows just beyond.

There were so many faces. Young and old, highborn and lowborn, all gathered around the square. The queen's court dressed in an array of colors, vibrant gold, and their finest Borean silks, instead of the mourning black.

A king was to die today, and I was faced with a rainbow instead.

People were shouting, mouths open and wide, but all I could hear was my pulse. I pushed through the crowd, my eyes taking in every inch of my surroundings. It killed me to be so far away from the front, but a strict sense of control kept me back. Every rebel guard was watching the grounds.

I couldn't afford any more risks.

My back was hunched, and I wore a tattered gray cloak. The guards had been given orders to look for a girl dressed like a soldier. No one looked twice at a pock-marked woman with a cane and a limp.

Itchy red hives covered my arms and face. I'd had a hearty serving of mutton just before my approach. It was the first time I'd been grateful for a childhood reaction to sheep.

My transformation hadn't been hard.

I'd traded clothes with Ian's mother in the stables that morning. Each of us had donned a wig to match the other's appearance.

Then there had been a loud proclamation that I was leaving Jerar as Ian's mother rode away pretending to be me.

An old woman had hobbled out of the stables while the guards spread the word that I was gone.

Now I was searching the grounds for the mark Ian promised. It was hard with the crowd. He had buried a knife during the gallows' construction. It wasn't a sword, but it was better than my fists.

Five paces from the perimeter to the west. Look for the guard with the red beard; he will be stationed near its right. Two small stones and a slight indent in the ground.

When I finally located the mound, I made a show of dropping my cane. Then, I ducked my head and crouched, clawing at the dirt just underneath my cloak.

My nails scraped against steel just as a hand caught the pit of my arm.

I froze as my eyes leveled with a guard.

"You dropped this." He had my cane in his fist.

Oh. My heartbeat returned. I thrust the knife into my boot's heel and then clasped the cane in gratitude.

"W-what a kind s-soul."

The guard gave me a toothy smile and released me with a reminder to watch my step.

I nodded and continued on my way.

Weapon: check.

Now to stand and wait for the guards to bring Darren out.

I felt oddly calm.

Watching him leave the prison at dawn... it was the hardest thing I'd ever had to do. But I hadn't let myself break. There'd been too much at stake. I'd returned to my chamber and waited for the hour to pass. And then I'd followed the rest of the morning as planned.

And now, while the sun was high in the sky and the herald called for attention, I was ready.

To lose or to win. Whatever the gods had in store, I'd give everything I could for the latter.

To the right of the stage was a sectioned off dais with chairs and a pergola roof. Instead of vines, it was dripping curtains to provide the visiting monarchs respite from the late afternoon sun. There were a couple of attendants serving refreshments and a pack of former rebel mages, including Ian, guarding its entrance.

To the front and center, close to the noose, was Ella. Both she and Alex were dressed in peasants' garb, their faces streaked with dirt. It wasn't the best disguise in the world, but with no weapons and the other "me" leading Priscilla's guard on a wild chase through the Iron Mountains, no one would be looking for my brother and his wife.

Just a couple of yards away, Alex waited with a flask. It smelled like spilt ale, but it carried an alchemist's potion inside, capable of creating enough smoke to obscure the entire square. Ella had snuck it from the rebels' private stores. The potion would cost a small fortune in the capital.

A hush fell over the crowd; my eyes flew to the stage.

A pair of guards carried two ends of a chain as they led a prisoner up a set of steps at the side.

Darren.

A cry caught in the back of my throat.

He looked different from this morning. One of his brows was split and he walked with a limp.

His hands were bound and bleeding. I could see fresh cuts where the cuffs scraped against his wrists. Perspiration pooled below his bangs as he struggled to match the men's heavy pace. There were fresh bruises lining his jaw—red, where the blood had just collected beneath the skin.

She promised the guards wouldn't hurt him again. My fist gripped the cane so hard it throbbed. Priscilla must have only meant the days leading up to his execution.

After all, this was all in the name of the Caltothian king.

My eyes flew to the shaded pergola and the hidden rulers inside. I wondered what they thought as they watched the fallen king of Jerar limp across the stage.

Why was the cost of peace always death? Why did there have to be a cost?

One of the priests strode forward as a guard yanked Darren to the center of the stage.

"People of Jerar," the elder proclaimed, "I give you, on behalf of our new queen, the former king of Jerar." One of the guards jerked the chain back so that Darren stumbled across the dais. "Today marks the first day of Queen Priscilla's reign and the burgeoning peace between two enemy nations, Jerar and Caltoth."

The crowd erupted in cheers; the priest waited for it to die away. "The death of a criminal, the young man before us now, will be the first of many steps in reestablishing our old alliance and fostering peace, instead of war, between nations."

"Kill the traitor!"

"Make him suffer!"

Shouts rose up as the people surged forward, calling for blood, but the priest held up a stiff hand, shaking his long gray locks in disgust.

"Our gods punish those in time, but we, as a race, are not one without compassion. We shall let the young man speak."

The crowd was silent.

"Speak, boy." The elder turned to Darren. "If you have anything to say to your gods and the people you've wronged, say it now or forever hold your tongue."

My jaw clenched as I scanned the crowd again for Alex. This was it. This was the time.

Where is he?

"Good c-citizens of Jerar…" Darren's voice brought me back to the stands. "I have failed you."

A cry rose in the square and someone else's jeer echoed the first.

"I called on a war that was not n-needed." A lump rose and fell in Darren's throat as one of his guards reached for the rope at his left. "I was not the king you deserve, and as… as such, I shall…" His eyes were scanning the crowd as he searched for someone below.

My heart slammed my ribs.

He was looking for me, but I was missing. Darren's gaze passed right over my face.

"…Suffer this crime without your forgiveness… I only p-pray—"

Another angry shout cut the prisoner off, and then another. An elbow found my ribs as the crowd surged.

My gaze broke off as I desperately sought my brother below. Alex should have used the flask by now. Something was wrong.

"—That you never make my mistake… T-that you cherish… the ones t-that you l-love—"

Darren's gasp brought my eyes to the stage. Blood was trickling down the side of his face.

Someone had lobbed a rock at the prisoner in chains.

Someone else threw the next.

And then all restraint released. I shoved my way forward just as the guard jerked Darren back to his feet.

Darren was still choking the words as they lifted the noose above his head.

"A-and that... you see beyond y-your hate... To truth—"

I couldn't hear him anymore as I clawed my way forward with everyone else. There were too many. So many bodies.

Everyone else was running forward too. I'd never make it in time.

My fist found someone to my left. I thrust the cane into someone's ribs.

The crowd was bellowing for blood.

A large man's boot found my heel as my fingers grasped another woman's braid.

"Kill the pig!"

"Peace for Jerar!"

"Death to the traitor king!"

And I screamed Darren's name at the top of my lungs, but my voice was lost to the rest.

I was running.

I was calling on magic that wouldn't come.

I was fighting my way forward as a third guard pulled the lever at Darren's right.

The trap door swung.

The panels dropped.

And Darren was in the air, his feet dangling five yards above the ground below.

His neck swung from the rope.

"Noooooo!"

Everything was red. I was screaming and the dagger was in my hand. I extended my arm at the stage, taking aim just above his head.

And the grounds exploded in smoke.

Thick, wafting gas surrounded us, black and heavy, tasting like ash.

Alex.

The crowd broke out into chaos with cries and shrieks of alarm. Instead of forward, the bodies turned toward me. They were now a stampede of shadows, and I was the one shoving back.

Coughing, I ran with the hand holding the dagger covering my face. I couldn't make out the guards from the crowd, but any time a hand caught my wrist, I swung.

My cane was long forgotten in the chaos that ensued. I used one hand to pummel as I shoved my way past the fleeing crowd.

Darren.

My heart was beating itself out of my chest; I couldn't feel anything but the heavy slam against my ribs as the world roared in my ears.

My eyes locked on the dim outline of the gallows ahead. Five more seconds passed and the smoke cleared enough to take in the rope.

It was swinging without an anchor.

My legs were searing as I lunged.

The noose had been cut. Darren was missing.

…Our plan.

Did Ella make it in time?

And then I noticed two shadows near the edge of the crowd, not five yards from the gallows' base. One figure dragging another through the smoke.

Quinn's voice rose above the din. *"Get the traitors!"*

And I knew.

I knew it was them.

There was a cluster of villagers blocking my way; I raised my knife and screamed at them to move. My fist sent the slowest to the ground, my muscles straining against my skin.

I was almost there.

There was more shouting and flares of color as magic shot back and forth across the crowd. Ella needed help; she couldn't hold off an infantry by herself.

I dove and caught the nearest soldier unawares. He dropped his sword as my blade pressed against the back of his neck.

Sucking in a sharp breath, I slipped around to the front and sent a fist to the soldier's nose. His neck snapped back as he tumbled unconscious to the ground.

I might be a traitor, but I wouldn't kill a man fighting for Jerar.

Instead, I gathered the soldier's weapons and cut my way through the rest of the pack.

I didn't need magic to win this fight.

Everything in me was a raging storm, and today I wouldn't fail.

There was one word. One name. It kept me fighting all the way to the end.

I reached the edge of the crowd and found them.

Ella was struggling to drag Darren behind a pile of crates.

There was a hazy amethyst barrier keeping them safe from the guards' flying assault, but her magic wouldn't last forever.

I reached them in an instant. And then I stopped breathing.

Ella was holding Darren up by the pits of his arms; she was all that kept the fallen king from crumbling to the ground. His eyes were shut, and I couldn't tell if he was breathing; all I could fixate on was the red bruising around his neck.

Was he—

A whimper escaped my lips, and Ella's hand shot out to grip my wrist.

"His neck—" her lips were tight as she continued to cast; the magic was taking everything she had, "—Didn't break... G-got to him in time."

All at once, I could feel everything and nothing; I was rising on air.

There was a crunch of rock and sand.

I swung, sword ready.

And found Alex instead. He was sporting a fresh bruise on his cheek and his lips were stained red with blood. His face was white as he spotted Darren in Ella's arms.

"Someone knocked the flask from my h-hand," he choked. "I c-couldn't g-get to it in t-time."

"H-he's alive."

My brother slumped in relief.

"I don't have much more stamina." Ella's strained voice broke through our reunion. "Can you two carry him the rest of the way?"

Alex and I jumped in to wrap a slumped arm around each of our necks; Ella ran a wrist across her forehead, wiping away beads of perspiration and dirt.

"L-let's get... out of here."

And then the three of us were running.

Ella cast our defense, fending off the keep's regiment while the smoke continued to clear. We headed west toward a cluster of trees just past the square.

My shoulder collided with a highborn at my right. The young man spun, outraged, screeching profanities.

Merrick. Priscilla's younger cousin.

Recognition dawned as he raised his hand to cast.

And I sent a flying fist to his face.

The boy went down with one even crack.

"Always wanted t-to do t-that," I gasped.

And then we were running again.

The further we ran, the less Ella had to cast. With Darren's rags and our disguises, we were hard to discern among the hundreds in the crowd. Every lowborn was dressed the same: a patchwork of brown and tattered gray.

The highborns were like colorful birds, fluttering around in expensive gowns, confusing the guards with their screams.

And then, ten minutes later, we were there, huddled within a small collection of pine, bordering the keep's edge.

Ian had yet to arrive.

Ella set up guard near the trees, and Alex and I lowered Darren to the ground. The king hadn't stirred once when we carried him through the crowds.

My heart raced as Alex knelt, his fingers feeling for a pulse.

I dug my heels in the ground, biting my cheek to keep from voicing my fears aloud.

Why is Darren still not awake?

"It's a coma." My twin looked up from the king's side. "He had… a heavy blow with that rope… But he'll… He should wake."

But not everyone does. My nails cut into my palm. I was drawing blood, but I couldn't seem to stop. I'd heard too many stories from the palace infirmary.

Alex gripped my arms as he stood. His mouth was opening and closing, but I couldn't make out his words.

Then he shook me, hard.

My lungs retracted as the breath left my chest.

"Darren will live, Ry." Alex's fingers tightened around my wrists. "You've fought this hard, just give him time to wake."

I willed myself to breathe. Darren would wake. I just needed to be strong.

"Ian's almost here." Ella broke the silence as she returned from her patrol. "Are you ready?"

Would I ever be? I was leaving behind everything I had ever known.

But Alex and Ella had a mission too, a critical role to play in the aftermath of today.

"Are you ready—" I took a deep breath. "—to help Priscilla pick up the pieces of Jerar?"

Ella gave a twisted smile. "Was I ever?"

"We'll find a way." Alex stepped in to press a kiss to his wife's forehead, his hand lingering across her stomach just a moment too long.

I sucked in air, stammering, "A-are you...?"

My brother blanched as he realized what he had done. "We didn't want to stop you from leaving, Ry."

"How l-long have you known?" Chains squeezed at my chest and they wouldn't let go.

"Only a couple of days..." Ella's cheeks were flushed. "Alex thinks it's going to be a boy."

"A boy?" My best friend and brother were going to have a child. It was the best news... and it hurt me in ways I'd forgotten to feel.

"We are going to name him Derrick."

There was something hot in the back of my throat; my brother pulled me in, and I pressed my face to his chest. Alex's grip was the only thing that kept me from breaking as a horse and rider appeared through the brush.

Ian hopped out of the saddle, looking flustered and red. "It was harder to slip away than I thought." He froze, his gaze catching on my brother's and my embrace. "Is Darren...?"

"Alive." Ella took over since my brother and I were still struggling to speak. "The guards didn't notice?"

"They will, eventually, but by the time they do, I'll have returned."

"Someday..." My brother's eyes were glassy as he focused on my face. "Someday you'll be able to return, Ry. Or we'll come to you."

"W-what if we never c-can?"

Alex's arms locked me in tighter like steel. "I refuse to believe in a future where we don't."

The final phase of our plan was complete.

I could feel it in my bones. It was time to say good-bye.

Whether I was ready or not, this was it.

"Take care of our p-parents and Ella… and D-Derrick." My voice caught on the last part of his name.

"I will." Alex's voice was hoarse. "And you… and Darren."

"I-I will." My face was covered in tears.

I held onto Alex a moment longer. And then I let my brother go.

Ella was next.

Neither of us spoke. She and I were both leaving those girls from the Academy behind; we were embarking on new parts of our lives we could never take back. My heart was breaking, just breathing her in. She was my best friend, and there was a part of her that was wholly mine. Just as a part of me was wholly hers.

She deserved all the happiness in the world.

My friend—the rebel who had every reason in the world to betray me—was the last to come forward.

Ian wrapped his arms around my waist. "I'll…" He couldn't say it; he just swallowed, again and again.

I gripped him tighter in return. "Me t-too." That feeling would never fall away. Friends like him were… undeserved.

I wondered what life he would lead now that the rebels were done and the war was over. Would Ian serve the Crown's Army and meet a beautiful girl who loved him the way he deserved? Or would he find peace in solitude? Would he grow old with that same crooked grin?

I stepped away and told myself this wasn't the end.

All three of them helped Darren into the saddle after me. One of my arms circled around my husband's waist as the other clutched the reins. I stared out into the distance, at the smoke-covered fields and the forest beyond—at my future, where everything would change.

And then a figure emerged from the trees. Its dress was indiscernible, peasant's garb like our own. Ian and Ella drew their swords as Alex took a step toward me.

"Who goes there?"

The stranger raised her chin and the tattered hood fell away.

Violet eyes and spiraling curls as sleek and dark as a raven in flight.

"Priscilla?"

The queen tossed a package, and I caught it as something gold and black slipped out of its casing.

A hematite necklace. There were only two in Jerar.

"It's one of the Crown necklaces," she affirmed. "Take it. It will buy you passage in Langli. There is a trader who will accept you and Darren onboard, no questions asked."

"How did you—"

"I followed Ian." Priscilla's lips curved up in a smirk. "You were always so predictable."

"Why are you helping us?" My fingers trembled around the necklace; I wanted to accept her gift, but I was wary and afraid. Was this a trap? Were her guards lying in wait?

"Because I believe in a better ending than gallows and blood."

No one spoke, and the queen continued, "I'm not as heartless as the four of you would choose to believe. My men have been feeding the guards information to pass along to Ian this entire week."

My friend reddened. "I didn't…"

"I couldn't stay the execution, but I secured your passage east. There was more than one reason to make Audric the baron of my family's estate."

She'd been helping us all along.

"Thank you." The words were so small in contrast to what she had done.

"I regret very little." Priscilla met my eyes. "But I regret that first year at the Academy, Ryiah. In another life, I think we could have been friends."

I would never doubt her again. I thrust the necklace into my saddlebags and then pulled away, blinking rapidly.

All four of them were staring up at me.

It was time. I couldn't put the others at risk any longer. They had already risked so much.

I pressed my palm to my chest. I held their gaze for a single moment as I took one last, retching breath. A thousand words were conveyed into that gesture. I felt every single one of them beating at my lungs.

It was a good-bye to friends. To family. To Jerar and the kingdom it would become. I said it all in silence with my hand and my heart.

And then I dug my heels into the stirrups and leaned forward in the saddle.

The mare took off on command.

And then the lowborn and the non-heir were gone. Hooves hit the ground, again and again.

We were soaring.

Out and toward the sun.

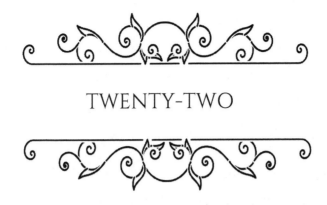

TWENTY-TWO

IN THE TWO weeks that followed, there were parts that were hard.

Impossible days and sleepless nights. Parts where I never stopped looking over my shoulder for patrols. Parts where I grew restless and plagued with doubt.

There were even parts I lost. Every second I closed my eyes and saw everyone and everything I was leaving behind.

But there was also Darren. And he was all the reason I needed to keep pushing on.

On the fifteenth night, we reached Port Langli. I had ridden our horse to exhaustion, but somehow we managed.

As promised, there was no city regiment on alert. Audric had come and gone, arranging for an unsuspecting trade ship near the docks.

I handed an elderly captain the Crown's necklace, and the man helped us on board his ship, no questions asked. The crew, a group of straggly sailors, did not so much as look at their two passengers twice.

We were given the captain's room, the only one not shared with the crew, and then we were off.

I was leaving Jerar. We were headed to the Borea Isles,

and I would never return.

The captain assured me there would be another ship waiting when we docked, one headed further east. The man didn't know anything about the countries past our western divide, but it was freedom, and that would have to be enough.

* * *

Later that night, I had one of the crew bring me a list of supplies. They brought out two meals as well, but mine went untouched.

I spooned broth and a flask of drinking water into Darren's mouth. I waited patiently for each sip to pass, and then I spooned the next, easing his head up to help the liquid go down.

I tried not to think about how much weight Darren had lost in the course of two weeks. His ribs were all too prominent along his chest and his cheekbones too sharp. Honey and hot broth weren't enough, but anything thicker might make him choke.

I dipped my rag into the soapy bucket at my feet. I was on my knees next to our cot. The bed was hardly more than a packed mattress of straw and woolen blankets, but it was more than we had seen in days.

The crewman had also deposited an armful of old shirts and pants. I was grateful. The ones I'd brought for us were too soiled from the road.

I peeled away Darren's clothes and sponged him from head to toe. I washed away all the dirt and the grime from our travels. I washed away everything else without blinking an eye. We had been through so much; I couldn't find the effort to grimace.

I spent extra time tracing the lines along his jaw, combing Darren's damp hair back with my nails.

I stared down at the man I loved and told myself this wasn't it. Darren would wake. If I willed it hard enough, he would return.

My brother had seen worse. Healers talked about miraculous recoveries all the time.

He will wake. You just need to hold on.

I was so lost in thought that I drifted to sleep on my knees.

In my dreams, I could lie.

There, the prince was confessing his feelings in the Academy's tower. Surprising me with a dance in the ballroom. Challenging me to a duel with an arrogant smirk. Kissing me breathless as he pulled me into bed.

There, he was Darren.

It was only in waking I lived out despair.

* * *

The next few days trickled by, and with every passing second, I was more restless than the last.

On the road, most of my energy had been diverted to scouting the roads and planning the quickest escape should patrols show up along the trail.

Here, I had nothing but fear.

Doubt was pressing in and there was nowhere to run.

I never left his side. My day was an endless routine of one-sided conversation and darkening thoughts.

I wasn't sure how much longer I could hope.

I told myself to be strong, that I wasn't allowed to be weak.

But another day passed and it was harder than the last.

Two more followed, and my resolve was leaving me behind.

Another.

And then a restless night with heavy winds as the crew saw to the sails.

My will finally snapped.

Darren hadn't so much as stirred. And it had been three weeks.

If he kept losing weight... he would die. *After everything.* To die of starvation, unconscious in his sleep.

I'd fought too hard for this boy. Too many times.

"Dying is the easy way out!" I screamed, shaking his shoulders over and over again. "You hear me, Darren? *You told me you were the best, now, gods blast it, prove it!*"

There was no response, not a flutter of the eyelid or a twitch of his hand. It was probably a good thing I didn't have magic, because I was certain I would have lit the boy on fire again.

Five minutes passed, and I could feel the hysteria flooding my lungs. I was ready to implode, but I was fighting so hard to stay whole.

He was alive. *Why couldn't that be enough?*

My fingers dug into Darren's shirt, and I told myself to breathe.

Then I inhaled and exhaled, gradually, one breath at a time.

After a while, my pulse slowed, but the beat didn't fade. If anything, it was faster.

My palm splayed against Darren's chest. It wasn't me.

His pulse was beating faster than before.

He must have reacted to my voice or the pressure of my hand.

He was starting to respond.

I gasped for air, fighting back tears.

Darren had decided to fight.

* * *

More days passed, and with each one, I caught little signs that meant everything. It didn't matter how long it took for Darren to respond. Now that I knew he was waking, it was enough.

I talked and I talked, and even when my voice was hoarse, I filled in all the bits and pieces he had missed.

I told him how much it hurt. The day of our wedding and the truth that broke my heart. My regret over his brother and the night I lost Paige.

I told him of life on my own. Mira slaughtering an innocent village. Nearly dying in the forest alone. How Quinn and the others had found me, and the deal that we struck.

I told him what it had been like to find him in that cave. And after, the price of our last stand. I told him of my friends and brother and Priscilla's unexpected help.

I told him everything.

And the day that Darren finally opened his eyes—it was only for a moment—but it was the best moment of my life.

And then the next day, and the next. And then when he finally whispered my name, stars burst inside of me.

There was nothing but light.

But it wasn't the end.

* * *

"You should have left me to die."

I sat there on the wooden planks, watching every dream rip right out of my chest.

"No." This was the prisoner in the keep's dungeon, not the boy I had saved. This wasn't the happy ending to our story. It wasn't an ending I would accept.

My hands were shaking, so I shoved them into my lap. "You d-don't mean it."

Darren shut his eyes, and I hurried on. "That boy and girl we talked about, we can still be them. We are g-going to Borea. We can start a new life—"

"Ryiah"—Darren's voice was hoarse—"I don't want a new life."

I could feel myself falling. Down. Into a pit with no holds.

"I started a war that cost hundreds of lives." The words were pained. "You need to take me back."

Tears stung my eyes. "I can't."

"You could…" He opened his eyes, and I saw twin pits of despair. "But you won't."

"You thought I'd betrayed you!" Hysteria was taking hold and making it hard to breathe. It was all I could do to keep from shaking Darren and screaming into his face. "You can't hold yourself responsible for believing your brother's lies!"

His lips twisted. "That night I helped you escape the truth no longer mattered to me, Ryiah. I didn't *want* to know which one of you was a liar."

My hands twisted in my lap.

"A good man would have sought the truth." His laugh was hoarse. "But me? I was selfish. All I wanted was the both of you to live."

"You were trying to save the people you loved—"

"Love shouldn't have played a part." Darren couldn't even look at me. "And after I only cared about revenge."

"You never had time to grieve." Desperation was seeping into my voice. "You were all alone in a role you were never meant to have."

"You can't make excuses for a king, Ryiah. That's not how it works."

Silence followed. I was desperately running through a trail of words to make him believe, searching for something I could do to show him he was wrong, that he deserved to be here.

He made a mistake.

A terrible choice. One that would haunt him forever.

But so many good ones too.

I knew who Darren was. He was the little boy who fought monsters in the dark. The arrogant non-heir who saw a first-year struggle and chose to help despite all of his training to walk away. The person who believed in me before I believed in myself.

He was the second-year who fought off enemies in the desert without a second thought to himself. The apprentice who risked his life for a few soldiers in Ferren's Keep. The young man who loved a girl, but was strong enough to push her away until he secured a treaty first.

He was a prince who fought for his brother in a darkness too deep to be saved, and then, in a moment of weakness, a young king who gave into the madness, the kind only brought on by grief.

Darren did a terrible thing.

But so did I. I ran.

Blayne... I would have stayed if I'd known. But I didn't and I hadn't.

Was it too late for both of us? Was Darren right?

But what about regret, did it mean nothing?

What about all of the good things we'd done?

What about the people we wanted to be? The amends we desired to make?

Did our actions make us the hero or the villain in the end?

"Please." Darren's whisper was broken. "Take me back."

I knew what he wanted. I knew he believed it would bring him peace.

But, gods, I couldn't give him up.

* * *

The gods had the cruelest intentions of all.

They'd allowed me to bring Darren back from the brink, twice, only to subject us to this. They were toying with me, dangling the boy I loved on a string. How hard would I fight? How many times before I stopped trying? Would it ever end? Was this what it meant to live?

I spent that night on the deck, pacing, staring up at the indigo sky and telling myself a thousand different ways I would convince Darren to live.

But each one ended the same.

"It's my choice." Darren's fists clenched at his sides. He was still too weak to reach the cabin door or he would have found the captain himself. "Take me back to Jerar and let me pay for my crimes."

"Priscilla wanted you to live."

His eyes flashed crimson. "She made a mistake."

"You can't just decide to give up!" I slammed my palm against the door. The sting brought with it an odd sense of relief. "You want to make amends for your past? Execution won't solve anything." I slammed my palm again for the sake of feeling a different kind of pain. It was numbing. "You could help people. You are just too afraid to try!"

"Let me go, Ryiah."

"I can't." There was a hole in the center of my chest. It was growing into an abyss and my heart was breaking with every plea.

"You can."

I collapsed to my knees in front of him. "Please." I didn't even try to fight the tears; I was too blind to read his face. *"I need you to fight."*

His voice was so quiet I almost missed his reply. "I wish you didn't."

* * *

Two days later, I went to collect the evening meal for Darren and myself, but when I arrived, I was informed the other passenger had already come and gone.

For a moment, I was relieved. Darren barely had enough strength to walk, but if he was hungry and had found his way to the galley on his own, that meant he was no longer refusing to eat…

But then I noticed the rations spread out on the table were next to a set of knives. "The salted pork was tough to cut." The man followed my line of sight. "I offered to do it before he left, seeing how he could barely stand, but he insisted he would do just fine on his own."

The pit of my stomach dropped. And I knew.

That morning, when I'd told him there was no way we'd ever return to Jerar, he'd been so furious.

I should have known.

My feet took off against the floor.

I raced across the deck, staggering into the hatch and into the passage below.

I ripped the door off its hinges.

And I stopped.

Darren was on his knees, shaking violently, his hands across his face.

His whole body convulsed with sobs.

The knife was on the ground. Unblemished. No blood.

He didn't... He wasn't...

I collapsed to the floor next to him without saying a word. My arms went around Darren's neck, and I held on as tightly as I could. I felt every single beat of his pulse.

It matched my own.

I held onto him the entire night.

And hours later, he held onto me too.

* * *

The next morning, I helped transfer Darren to the bed. He had stopped shaking, but his eyes were bloodshot and his skin as cold as ice.

I settled the blankets around him and forced myself to wait.

I wasn't sure what he wanted. I wasn't sure who I needed to be.

The knife was still on the floor.

I stared at it, hating the object the way I had never hated

anything before.

More than anything, I wanted to take it and every sharp object and throw them all out to sea.

But this had to be Darren's decision. After last night, no matter how much I wanted him to live, he had to choose for himself.

I finally found the courage to speak.

"Do you... want it?"

Darren swallowed and a lump rose and fell several times in his throat. "No, I..." He forced himself to look away from the blade. "I... want to fight."

Warmth exploded across my chest, seeping into every inch of my skin.

"I-I can't promise... that it will be..."

My fingers shot to his, and I clenched them as hard as I could. It didn't matter how hard it got. If he was willing to fight, I was willing to wait.

To stand by his side and take on whatever darkness awaited. Forever.

"We'll do it together."

* * *

It was two more weeks before we finally approached Borean shore.

The days were still hard. The nights were worse. Sometimes all I could hear were his screams... Sometimes all he saw were my tears. But we had something worth fighting for.

And nothing would take that away.

I knew it could be months, years, for the old Darren to emerge.

Perhaps when he did, he would be someone new. Perhaps I would be, too.

The sea here was green. I leaned across the rail, taking in the unfamiliar breeze. The air was musky and cloyingly sweet. From where I stood, I could see small specks of traders carrying loads along the sandy shore, crates of spice and bottles of rum. Trees towered just beyond the beach, and there were huts as far as the eye could see.

I had always wondered what the islands looked like. The descriptions in the Academy's scrolls had hardly done them justice.

The one before me was breathtaking.

There was the soft creak of wood as someone took his place next to me at the rail. And even though it made no sense, even though we were miles from Jerar, he still smelled like cinnamon and pine and cloves.

Darren was still my home.

His garnet eyes were on the tree line ahead. "The Borea Isles."

"Our second ship departs in two days." I sucked in an unsteady breath. "Somewhere east."

This was it, a chance for us to amend the wrongs of our past. A chance to find out the people we could be, past the magic and pride that had cost us so much.

"Our… new start."

I turned.

He was smiling. It wasn't a big smile. It barely raised the corners of his mouth, but it was still real.

It had been so long since I saw something other than pain. For a moment I forgot to breathe.

Then my hand found his and I squeezed.

"Our new start," I whispered.

Outside, I was shaking.

But inside, I was soaring. And despite everything, in that moment, I knew we would finally be okay.

The boy and the girl could still have their happily ever after.

It wasn't too late.

EIGHT YEARS LATER:

DARREN

HE STOOD SILENTLY in place, his limbs locked with his breath caught in his lungs. Blood pulsed underneath his skin, thundering violently as fear drilled deep inside his chest. Darren heard the murmur of voices just beyond the door.

His eyes clenched shut. It was an involuntary reaction, even eight years after the event.

Almost a decade had passed, but their screams still plagued his dreams. He still felt the bite of those shackles on his wrists and the terrible jolt as the guards let him fall. His neck should have snapped. It was only fool's luck that it hadn't.

For just a moment, he was numb, paralyzed with indecision and regret. Was this a mistake? He'd spent so much time away that he'd almost, but not quite, forgotten that broken boy on the ship, the one who'd been willing to forsake everyone and everything—even *her*—to make the pain stop.

And now he was here, and it was a fresh blade to his throat. His strength was ebbing away, hope fraying under the cut of a serrated edge.

Everything was wrong.

Darren didn't belong here. The walls were too constricting. Even after all these years, he still felt that faint ache in his palm. It was a call to magic that would never return. Especially here, in this place. Magic and his fists had kept the darkness at bay as a child, but what happened when the shadows remained?

What happened when the monster you were running from was yourself?

No. He clenched his fists. He would enter that room, no matter the cost.

Darren had broken once, shattered to bits of rubble, and that should've been the end. But it wasn't. She'd urged him to fight. It'd taken that final moment—when the choice was solely his and the knife was pressing down on his wrists—to finally understand.

Amends.

It was her plea and a promise that had brought him back from the brink: *amends.* He hadn't just owed amends to the world, he'd owed it to her, and it was there at that moment he'd finally laid down his blade.

When a second ship had deposited Darren and Ryiah in Kuador, that vow never left...

Kuador was an island overflowing with trees. Miles and miles of green canopy spread as far as the eye could see. The sun was sweltering as the Borean ship docked.

Darren and Ryiah disembarked and set forth into a damp jungle teeming with creatures that slipped in and out of the brush like the sea's tide. There were great cats that hunted like wolves, snakes as long as a man, and flowers and plants without a name.

A week later, they discovered a small village following a beaten trail. The people didn't speak the same tongue, but they were kind. Darren and Ryiah traded labor for shelter until they were able to fend for themselves.

On quiet nights, Darren sat among the tribe, watching the elders tend to maladies that came and went. No one ever suffered long. Aches and pains, even illnesses, were gone in a matter of days.

The people didn't have magic, but they didn't need it. From what Darren had gathered, the eastern gods embedded it in their land. The jungle reaped more bounty for the people than any market back home.

Darren took to recording those plants and the ways they were used. At first it was nothing more than a distraction, a way to ease the restless roving of his mind. But months later, a band of the men departed with half of the village stores and returned bearing Borean wares.

Darren and Ryiah finally discovered the Kuadian term for "ship," and they came up with a plan: he'd send his work back to her parents in Jerar.

Having spent a lifetime around the healers in his father's infirmary, Darren had almost forgotten not everyone could afford magic. Darren wasn't a healer, but to imagine that a lowborn might suffer less from his account…

Amends.

That was the first night bloodied faces and a village square didn't haunt his dreams. It was also the first night Darren took Ryiah into his arms, the first night he allowed himself to feel something other than broken. He was able to give his wife the parts he locked away and lose himself in something other than grief.

Afterward, it'd only been a matter of communication. He and Ryiah spent weeks conferring with the village council, learning all there was to know of Kuador. From what the elders indicated, certain plants were native to different territories and there were twelve villages bordering the island's rim to specialize in certain treatments and salves.

They set out on foot the next month, walking for weeks. They studied a village for months at a time. Darren took notes as Ryiah traded labor for necessities and a small sachet of seeds to send back home to Jerar.

For three years, they were almost content. And then, visiting the sixth village, Ryiah took ill.

Any dreams Darren entertained had vanished.

It took the midwife five tries before she was able to calm him enough to explain.

Pregnant.

For a second, Darren was too stunned to move.

Then he dropped to his knees, cradling Ryiah's face in his hands as he kissed her and choked out her name.

That moment had been everything.

She'd been everything; she always was.

Ryiah refused to quit their work; she was far too stubborn. She labored alongside the tribe until the day she finally collapsed.

That night, her hand never left his, squeezing until both of their palms were ready to crack. She squeezed as the midwife came and she cried as she brought their beautiful child into the early island dawn.

Until that moment, Darren had never understood his loss. The king had always been a monster, a merciless tyrant with an even colder heart. But at that moment, clutching a little girl to his chest... Darren felt it. An unconditional bond that would grip him to the ends of time. With it came the knowledge that he'd give up everything for that woman and the child. He was a father.

They named her Eve.

Even now, that moment brought fire to the back of his throat.

Two more years came and went. Darren and Ryiah visited villages and finished archiving the island's plants. Their little girl grew into an unstoppable force, stubborn like her parents, challenging their limits and getting into trouble whenever they looked away. And then, a Borean trader brought word...

After years of slow-building peace, a new treaty had been signed in Jerar. The alliance between Jerar and Caltoth was forever sealed.

Their seventh year came to a close when a ship arrived, bearing an envelope with a waxen seal. The captain claimed a Crown envoy had paid him well to carry it to the bearer of the Kuadian letters. They'd opened it with trembling hands:

"Queen Priscilla of Jerar and King Horrace of Caltoth

grant fugitives Ryiah of Demsh'aa and former Prince Darren pardon from their previous crimes. In accordance with our two nations' treatise. The two may return with a formal renunciation of the throne."

Darren wasn't ready to return. But one look to his wife and he knew he couldn't refuse.

Not after she'd sacrificed everything for him. Not when she still had people waiting for her in Jerar.

Ryiah deserved to return home.

And so now they stood outside the great doors of the palace throne room, waiting for the guards to summon them forward.

Ryiah cleared her throat, her face pale as she took a shaky breath. Darren had been so lost in his thoughts, he'd almost forgotten she was present.

"I know you think you don't belong"—she stepped away from the wall and twined her fingers with his—"but you do."

Ryiah wasn't a fool. She knew what his silence meant.

There were phantoms roaming these halls; Darren felt their glares on the back of his neck.

Traitor. Villain. The pressure mounted in his lungs.

Ryiah thrust her chin forward as her grip tightened on his hand. She regretted parts of her past too, but Darren could see the challenge in her stance.

Whatever the Crown proclaimed, she would fight for them both.

A guard summoned them forward.

Darren swallowed hard as they entered the room.

There was no turning back.

When the herald declared their names, Darren and Ryiah knelt before the queen of Jerar. They renounced their claim to the throne and that of their heirs. They swore to spend the rest of their lives atoning for their past.

They would always be in the people's debt.

Priscilla cleared her throat. "You've already begun."

She proceeded to explain everything she'd learned in the past couple of years.

It'd started with Jerar's trade. A booming surge of product along the King's Road. New treatments and salves had spread across the nation's merchants like wildfire, even into Caltoth, Pythus, and the Borea Isles.

After years, Crown advisors had finally traced the treatments' origin to a small apothecary in Demsh'aa and a plot overflowing with unfamiliar plants. And then they'd found the letters. "I should have known." Priscilla snorted. "You two never could leave well enough alone."

She continued, "There's been a steady decline of fever since we received those Kuadian records. It's not something any of the rulers can overlook. Even Horrace."

Hesitation made Darren stiff. "What do you require of us?"

He couldn't fight in a regiment. Even for peace. If Priscilla had called them back to serve Jerar's army, he would be forced to walk away.

Freedom wasn't worth the price of his soul. Not again.

Ryiah cleared her throat and added, "We've seen enough blood."

"If you must know." The young queen regarded them with an amused curve of her lips. "Enrollment at the Academy has tripled now that study has broadened to factions outside of war. The staff is overwhelmed."

Ryiah's quick intake of breath mirrored his own. "But we don't have our magic—"

"That won't be a problem, will it, Master Barclae?"

An intimidating man took a step forward in his gilded cloak. His salt-and-pepper beard was now fully gray—the only testament to age. "Most of our instructors are well past the age of their potential's limits. You don't need magic, just experience to instruct. And discipline."

Another man came forward, white teeth gleaming against his dark skin. Darren recognized him as Sir Piers, the knight who'd always pushed them to their limits in physical drills. "You two were prodigies." His smirk was devious. "It'd be a shame to waste that reputation."

The words were out of Ryiah's mouth in a second: "We accept." A moment later, she shot Darren an apologetic look. But there was no need. He wanted this too.

It was more than he deserved, but he couldn't bring himself to refuse.

"Good." Master Barclae looked pleased. "Between the two of you and the Academy's new headmaster, those first-years will finally be put in their place."

New headmaster?

Darren followed the man's gaze. And then he stifled a groan.

Ian was grinning shamelessly in a robe like the one Barclae had worn at the Academy. The sandy-haired mage caught Darren's eye and winked. "The old trio, together again."

I celebrated too soon.

"Those first-years have grown too comfortable now that they aren't competing for an apprenticeship." Master Barclae gave Darren and Ryiah a stern nod. "Do your best to make them competent."

It was as if they'd never left.

* * *

Later, Darren found himself standing at the ballroom's balcony, staring out at the northern valley of Jerar. The sun was setting, casting a hazy orange glow on the forest down below. People still gave him a wide berth; for most of the night, they'd left him alone. He'd been reduced to a passing concern; Priscilla's revelation about his work in Kuador had taken away most of the court's hate. That, and eight years of peace.

The Black Mage's war was a thing of the past. So was its king.

Darren had always wondered what it would be like to be free from the chains of his family's reign. What it would be like to be a boy instead of a prince. To marry that impossible girl and start a family of his own...

Now he knew.

And he would never give it up.

He'd seen the way Duke Audric's eyes had gone bright when he introduced his daughter earlier that night. That moment had gone a long way toward warming the ice flooding his veins.

The former commander was more of a father than Lucius had ever been.

That last realization came as a blow; Darren hadn't

thought he'd left anything behind.

Ryiah appeared soundlessly at his side, smiling as her brother spun Eve around the floor.

Amends. That word was a pulsing beat in Darren's chest. It roared as their daughter spun and twirled around the room, her little legs wobbling under the weight of her dress.

Ryiah sighed against the railing. "Eve's happy here."

So was she. There was a glow Ryiah had never had in Kuador. He'd seen it in the reunion with her parents, and Ella and Alex and their four little boys.

Darren looked away from the room to study his wife.

After all these years, she was still as beautiful as the day they'd met. A girl burning so bright he'd been drawn in against his will, even if it'd taken a while to recognize the signs.

Ryiah was still the same maddening girl he'd fallen in love with so many years before. She was still the same girl he didn't deserve, the same girl who'd challenged him time and time again.

He'd been a Black Mage and a king, but she was the strongest person he knew. People would never sing ballads about the lowborn who'd chosen exile with a traitor over a hero's title back home, but Darren knew who Ryiah really was. He knew what she'd really done.

She was reckless.

She was brave.

She was incredible.

And she'd saved him from himself.

Darren would never deserve Ryiah; he never had.

"That day we met," he muttered, "I should have asked

your name."

"My name?" She scrunched her face as she laughed. "I believe your glare was enough."

"When we get to the Academy, I'm going to try again." One hand found her waist as Darren tilted her chin and pulled her close. "I'm going to get it right."

Ryiah grinned. "Well, if we are going back to the start, I'm going to knee you in the groin for that day that you—"

He cut her off with a kiss.

As soon as his mouth found hers, he was back.

Darren was a prince teaching a pretty first-year how to fight, a boy in the desert apologizing to a girl, a jealous apprentice lashing out any way that he could...

And then he was following her up the stairs, kissing her because he couldn't get her out of his head. Because he couldn't breathe. Because he'd fallen in love and he hadn't even known.

Then he was choosing Jerar, telling himself to walk away. Losing the girl and pretending not to care.

He was screaming her name in a burning forest, running as fast as he could.

And then he was opening a letter, reading Emperor Liang's promise, and storming a feast.

He was watching her stroll through an arena, ready to duel.

Holding her the day she fell apart, refusing to leave her side.

He was marrying that girl, dancing with her in the forest, and then, after everything that followed, saving her life.

Saving her because that reckless, beautiful girl was trying to save him, because he loved her, because he knew only one of them deserved to live.

He was swimming in darkness, and she was pleading for him to fight.

He was dropping the knife... he was choosing to live. Choosing amends.

And now he was kissing his wife, here, as their daughter danced in the crowd.

Ryiah had become everything, and she hadn't even tried.

Darren gripped her waist harder, kissing her as flames fanned his heart and his lungs and his mind.

He would spend the rest of his life fighting to be the man she deserved. As a father and a husband, as a boy to the girl.

He'd love her endlessly.

"I'll love you endlessly," he whispered.

And then he'd do it again.

AUTHOR'S NOTE

Want to read Prince Darren's backstory before he met Ryiah at the Academy of Magic?

Sign up for Rachel's newsletter on her website so you can receive the exclusive e-novella and be notified of new releases, special updates, freebies, & giveaways!

ACKNOWLEDGEMENTS

READERS. The final book is here because you guys made it happen. Thank you for sticking with Ryiah and Darren all this time, and I hope their story made you half as emotional as it made me. I've wanted to tell this saga since seventh grade and YOU are the reason I was able to write it. Thank you for every one of your kind messages, reviews, and support along the way—they meant the world to me!!! This is the end of my first series, and I hope to give you many more.

SAKINA MADRAS. This book benefited from your selfless act to beta read for me on tight deadlines and give it to me straight. Thank you for being such an epic critic and telling me when a scene needed to up its game. Also for making me write that epilogue, because you were totally right; I feel more closure now. Pretty sure all the fans thank you too, because I swore up and down I'd never do one. Ha.

FRIENDS. You guys have been my rock since day one: ROTNA PENHEIRO, SHELLY BLALOCK, COURTNEY MORALES, and SHANTEL KELLOGG. I'm not sure I can ever articulate what it means to feel so loved and supported when I took on such a risky career! I have the best friends in the world.

FAMILY. Your support means the world—especially the HUSBAND who dealt with the worst of it and held me up every time I wanted to break. Side note: *Babe, I love you, but please stop telling me that every plot I've ever thought of has been done in anime first (I refuse to accept this!!!).*

AUTHOR COMMUNITY—for helping me with all things publishing. RACHEL VAN DYKEN, ALEX LIDELL, ELISE KOVA, SCARLETT DAWN, and LAURA THALASSA. There are plenty of authors I owe favors to, but you five played a large part in my sanity in some form or another.

EDITORS (Hot Tree Editing) and COVER ARTIST (Milo). Again, for dealing with all my pickiness and crazy deadlines for four books all at once.

My PA (TIANA GRIFFIN) who volunteered to help me with my launch. You truly are a generous person (and did I mention you did this while you were preggers?).

Lastly, *huge* thank you to my PROOFERS who not only go out of their way to meet my crazy deadlines and hold my hand, but also send me constant updates ("how dare you"/"you killed…"/"I hate…") as well as those beautiful e-mails when they finish. I also feel the need to mention that the map in this edition is new, but ASHLEY CHEESMAN made me the most awesome, epic map when I was starting out and framed it. Way to make my cry at a book convention (and with every e-mail)! My lovely team of proofers: ASHLEY (aforementioned), MIRANDA STEED (who catches more errors than humanly possible, you're a machine!!!), SARAH KATHRINA SONG (your sweet emails, meticulous notes, and then our chat of Darren fanfic!) MEGAN MCGORRY (not just proofing, from our very first Tammy talk to our obsession with fantasy and daily writing struggles! I can't wait to read *your* books!), EMILY-ANN WALSH (in addition to reviewer extraordinaire), & SANDRA DEEB (yet another reviewer-bookish friend who fangirls with me over the same books... cough, cough, Kelly Oram)!

ABOUT THE AUTHOR

RACHEL E. CARTER is a young adult and new adult author who hoards coffee and books. She has a weakness for villains and Mr. Darcy love interests. Her first series is the bestselling YA fantasy, *The Black Mage*, and she has plenty more books to come.

Official Site:

www.RachelECarter.com

Facebook Fan Group:

facebook.com/groups/RachelsYAReaders

Twitter: @RECarterAuthor

Email:

RachelCarterAuthor@gmail.com

ALSO BY RACHEL E. CARTER

The Black Mage Series

Non-Heir (e-novella only)

First Year

Apprentice

Candidate

Last Stand

61843045R00271

Made in the USA
Lexington, KY
22 March 2017